GIFTED

Louisa Amy Law

Copyright © 2020 Louisa Amy Law

All rights reserved.

The characters and events portrayed in this book are fictitious. Any similarity to real persons, living or dead, is coincidental and not intended by the author.

No part of this book may be reproduced, or stored in a retrieval system, or transmitted in any form or by any means, electronic, mechanical, photocopying, recording, or otherwise, without express written permission of the publisher.

ISBN-13: 9798307864593

Cover design by: Jamie Peak

For my family and my friends.
Your support made the dream a reality.

This book contains scenes of violence and sexual assault.

Introduction

Smith

He slammed his fist down on the table with such force that the wood cracked and splintered straight down the middle.

"We cannot allow this to happen! If this child survives, it will be strong enough to put us all in danger."

He turned to face his newest employee, the replacement. Her replacement. Sure, she was just as good as the numerous women who had come before her. She did what he asked when he asked it. She obeyed his rules and knew when to keep her mouth shut. But she would never compare to the one he really wanted. The one who had left him eighteen years ago. No woman would ever compare to her.

"Smith, the girl is too powerful. If you try to stop this, if you try to take the child, there will be consequences. There's no way of—"

Smith stormed towards her and grabbed her face in one of his strong hands. She could feel his stagnant breath against her face, cutting her words off mid-sentence.

"What? There is no way of what? If this child is born, it will have more power than we have ever seen in a Gifted. It cannot be allowed! Its mother should not have been allowed!" He screamed the words at her, like it was her fault, like she had created the child herself.

"But there's no way of telling how she will react. Who or what she will destroy to protect it. She could destroy full cities within seconds if she wished it. I have seen what she can do. We would all be dead before there was even a chance of seeing the child," she paused for a moment to consider her next words. "We both know the real reason you despise these people."

Smith could see the sadness in her eyes. He could see she had spent too much time watching the girl, trying to fit into her life undetected and understand how her family behaved. He knew that the girl's charm would pull her closer and closer until she forgot why she was there in the first place. How could he blame her? Power and beauty, just two of the many gifts the girl possessed. The most irresistible qualities there were. Just like her mother. Had he not succumbed to that same beauty once too? Twenty-four years ago. She had haunted him ever since. His newest assistant was no different from him. Temptation had made her lose her way. But there were ways of dealing with the ones who lost their way. Tragic accidents and such. He had been stupid enough to hope that this one would be different, that she would be able to resist her charm and prove to Smith that she was more fitting for the role than those before her. He liked her well enough; he could picture her wearing less than the tight-fitting, low-cut dress she wore to their meetings. She was certainly easy on the eyes. After all, that was one of the reasons he had hired her for the job. She was a good-looking woman. But she wasn't his woman. Which meant that she was disposable, just like the rest of them. He just needed to remind her of how disposable she was in the hope that she might find the strength to do what was required of her.

He took a few deep breaths to calm himself and steady his voice before he spoke again.

"Oh, my dear. You worry me. You are growing a soft spot for that girl. She is pulling you in like she pulled in others before you. Let's not remind ourselves of their unfortunate endings. Or, would you like me to remind you?" He said it with the smallest of smirks pulling at the corners of his mouth, but it was just enough for her to feel the threat behind it.

She took a step closer to him and rolled her shoulders back a little, arching her back and pushing her chest out slightly as she took a deep breath in.

"I feel no emotion for her, Smith. Her parents understood the decision they took, and it is they who have failed her. Just tell me what you require of me, and I will provide."

She was more intelligent than Smith would ever give her credit for; she knew better than most how to press his buttons. Although it wouldn't take a genius to figure him out. She wondered, not for the first time, how so many women had managed to fail him in the past. She inched closer again until there were only millimetres between them, teasing him with the heat radiating from her body. She looked up at him through her long eyelashes and watched as he took another deep breath in, inhaling her scent.

"Then let us prepare," he said, fighting his urge to allow her to distract him. "We only have eight weeks left, at best."

It would be much less than eight weeks, she thought to herself as she closed the gap between them, moulding her body into his. She wrapped her hand around the back of his neck, her nails gently pressing against his clammy skin, and pulled his head closer still, allowing her lips to brush over his earlobe.

"Tell me what you need, Smith."

"Do what you want with the girl, she'll be no threat to us when we have her child. Oh, and bring me the girl's parents too. They have been away from home for long enough."

She felt a shiver of longing run through his body with the anticipation of having the girl's parents back where it all began, back to their own personal hell. She locked eyes with him and nodded her head in understanding. As she turned to leave, Smith grabbed the top of her arms tightly, digging his fingers painfully into her soft skin. He smirked as a combination of shock and fear momentarily flashed in her eyes. Then he pulled her back to him and kissed her hard, his hands traveling greedily all over her body. She froze and fought her instincts to shudder in disgust. When he was finished with her, he loosened his grip, and his arms dropped to his sides as he took a step away from her. Smith's eyes travelled down to her arms, where small bruises had begun to appear, then back up to her mouth, admiring his work. She licked her lips nervously, and her mouth filled with the familiar metallic taste of blood. He had bitten her.

"Go and see to that, Anya," he said, with revulsion clear in his tone. "She was never as weak as you."

1

Rainey

"This place looks worse every time I come. How hard is it to paint a wall?" Rainey said as she picked at a flake of dull grey paint peeling from the wall.

She looked around the room, at how run down the place was becoming. A bit of paint peeling from the wall was the least of their problems. The whole place was filthy and looked a lot like it might fall to the ground if anyone so much as sneezed. Her eyes fell on to Lexi, who, as usual, was the only person in the room smiling.

"If you don't like coming here Ray Ray, nobody's forcing you, but you know you won't last two days without seeing this beautiful face." Lexi replied as she framed her face with her hands and pouted like a trout. Rainey leaned towards her with the same pout mirrored across her lips.

"Yeah, no thanks." Lexi grinned, and she pulled away from her. "Maybe it's you who should be in here instead of me. You're crazier than I am."

"You know... we could break you out without them even knowing you were gone. You could come stay with us. It's not like we can do much there that we can't already do here, but it would still be fun. Only five weeks to go and then you can help me change dirty nappies all day." Rainey raised her eyebrows in question as she rested her hands on her round and swollen stomach.

She came to see Lexi every day, without fail, and asked her the same question almost every time she came - Why was Lexi still living in this shit hole, when they both knew she could leave whenever she wanted? Not necessarily with the permission of the staff, but it's not like she needed a key to break out.

Lexi was just like Rainey, she was a Gifted, which meant she had been 'gifted' with powers that most people did not possess. Neither one of the girls thought that Gifted was a suitable term for what they were; cursed, doomed, even damned might have been more appropriate.

The only reason Lexi was in this dump was because her powers had led to the death of her parents, and the only reason she wouldn't break out was because she refused to use her powers again out of fear of hurting somebody.

"It's just easier this way, Ray." Lexi's ultimate statement which told Rainey that it was the end of the conversation. That's the only answer she would give anymore.

Rainey rolled her eyes and turned her attention to the room around her. She noticed one of the nurses watching them from across the room. She stood with her arms folded over her chest, giving both girls a disapproving look. Her hair was tied back in a tight bun on the top of her head and the bags under her eyes made her look tired and probably a lot older than she actually was. When she noticed Rainey's glance, she began to walk towards them, manoeuvring her way around the other patients scattered around the large sitting room and narrowly avoiding Mrs. Noland's knitting pile. Mrs. Noland was a tiny, frail-looking woman who had been in the hospital for so long that she had become a part of the furniture. She chose the same seat every day, next to a boy no older than Rainey and Lexi, who would talk happily to himself for hours while rocking forwards and backwards in his chair. Rainey had never seen Mrs. Noland with any visitors, but she would try to strike up a conversation with anyone visiting the ward and on the rare occasion that she stopped smiling it was usually because someone had disturbed her knitting. She began to gather up her wool, looking flustered and glaring at the nurse who had upset her.

Rainey pulled her coat on to her shoulders and squeezed the buttons shut around her huge belly.

"Alexa, visiting hours finished fifteen minutes ago. It's time for your friend to leave I'm afraid." She smiled sweetly at Lexi as she spoke, before directing her attention to Rainey.

Her eyes drifted down to look at her pregnant bulge and her overly sweet smile changed into a look of disgust. She set off back across the room muttering to herself about 'teenagers these days'.

Rainey rolled her eyes and Lexi bit her lip in an attempt to stop herself from laughing. Yet another name that Rainey could add to her list of people who think she is too young to have a baby. She had gotten so bored of telling people that she was in fact eighteen, and therefore had legally been able to have children for over two years now. What did it matter what they thought anyway? The people who mattered to her knew why she was having a baby and any strangers who walked past her pulling faces or voicing their unwanted opinions, didn't make the least bit of difference to how happy she was.

Rainey pushed herself up and hugged Lexi tightly.

"See you tomorrow, then. Let's hope nurse *'I've got a stick up my ass'* is on her day off."

Rainey flashed a smile at the nurse who was now sitting back at the opposite end of the room. She didn't return the smile but stared at Rainey as she pretended to shoot herself in the temple with her fingers and giggle her way out of the room, leaving Lexi to snort loudly with laughter.

"Goodbye, Rainey, love," called Mrs. Noland, smiling happily again with a tangle of yellow wool matted into her hair.

"Bye, Mrs. Noland." Rainey called back.

Rainey waddled her way down the long corridor leading to the stairwell. A bored woman leaning against the wall looked up as she approached. She pressed a code into the keypad to open the doors, giving Rainey a quick nod as the buzzer sounded, alerting the empty corridor to the unlocked doors. It wasn't often there were enough staff actually working all at the same time to have every one of the doors manned. Most of the time Rainey typed in the code herself.

The stairwell was wide and steep and not something Rainey was looking forward to walking down with all the extra weight she was carrying, but even the four floors of steep steps was better than taking your chances in the dimly lit lift, which seemed to jump up and down entire levels rather than glide smoothly.

Jerry, the security guard, gave her a wave as she reached his desk at the front doors, and he unlocked one of the doors with the button under his desk.

"Until tomorrow, Rainey," he said, with a nod of his head.

Rainey smiled and pulled open the heavy oak door leading to the car park. Rainey liked Jerry. He was one of the few people who knew, or at least suspected, what she and Lexi were capable of, and he didn't judge them for it. He saw Rainey as just another visitor, one who he could chat to when he was bored from sitting behind his desk all day or night.

Rainey rummaged around in her bag for her car keys, which she found easily because they were attached to no less than eighteen key rings, all of different shapes and sizes. One keyring from each and every family holiday she had ever taken and most of which had involved Italy.

It was cold outside, with dark grey clouds lying thick and low in the sky. But this was Yorkshire – 'God's country', and if you expected to have more than a week's worth of sunshine throughout the year then you were either an idiot or a tourist.

Rainey took one last look back at the sitting room window on the fourth floor to wave goodbye to Lexi, but she wasn't there.

To any unsuspecting hiker who may just happen across the hospital on their travels, the building might have looked like an abandoned nineteen-hundred's gothic mansion, filled with mysterious history. In reality, it was a rundown glorified house filled with crazy people and abandoned kids. Rainey hated every facet of its design. To her, it represented misery and loneliness. If it hadn't been for Lexi, Rainey would have refused to enter such a building for fear of it being haunted. A cold shiver ran down the length of her spine.

She rushed over to her car to get out of the cold. Rainey loved her car. Her parents had given it to her on her eighteenth birthday, just after she had learned how to drive. It had been a step down from the car she had begged them to give her; the bright white, enormous Range Rover that her mother had refused to part with. Instead, the car she had been given was a little sporty hatchback. Although she had wanted it in a loud red or a brilliant white, her parents had told her that she already stood out from the crowd enough as it was, and that she would have to make do with it in black instead. She had to admit, it did look pretty cool, especially with the blacked-out windows. It definitely wasn't bad for a girl who had never worked a day in her life. Not that she didn't want to, she had nagged her parents for weeks to let her get a job. Working in a shop maybe, or cleaning. Anything at all that might allow her to have a bit of normality in her life. But they had more than enough money to support the family and they didn't like Rainey to be away from home for long periods of time. They worried about her a lot and Rainey had grown to expect their paranoia. Her parents might have seemed a little odd to anyone else.

She flopped into the driver's seat and started the engine, turning the heater on as she strapped on her seat belt. Then she plugged in her phone and started to scroll through her music collection. Rainey loved music. Any music. Something she had inherited from her mother who would walk around the house singing all day while her dad was hard at work in the office. She chose an alternative rock album from a band she hadn't heard of before, but Lexi had persuaded her to download it earlier in the week. It was only a thirty-minute drive from the hospital to her parents' house, twenty-five if she put her foot down and the traffic was light. There would be just enough time to listen to four, maybe five songs.

Rainey lived in the very centre of Yorkshire, in a small village where she had grown up. Her parents' house was separated from the rest of the village by a large meadow, dotted with cherry trees. It wouldn't be long until they were covered with pink and white blossoms. The meadow had always been one of Rainey's favourite places to go if she was ever in need of some quiet time, or as quiet as it could be with music blaring through her headphones.

She drove home in autopilot, thinking of nothing in particular, while odd little hand and foot shapes stuck out of her belly from the inside. It was 6:00pm when she drove up the long drive leading to her house, and almost completely dark outside. Rainey couldn't think of anyone who was looking forward to the end of the cold February weather more than she was. She hated the dull days and dark nights. Winter seemed to last most of the year when you lived close to the moors. Between November and March everywhere had a constant covering of damp and the sky was an almost permanent shade of grey. The few rays of sunshine that did manage to break through the gloom would brighten up the hillsides in a glorious show of light. Rainey supposed that was why it was known as 'God's country'.

As she pulled up to the house Rainey could just make out the outline of a figure sitting on the white Victorian-style iron bench in the middle of the garden. She knew it was Joe before she was close enough to really see him because he was playing with what looked like a perfect ball of light in his hands.

Joseph John Denyer was Rainey's boyfriend, although they both thought that boyfriend and girlfriend didn't sound like a strong enough term for what they were. They had been close since they first met when Rainey was just thirteen, and it hadn't taken long for them to fall for each other. Joe had eventually moved into the family home with Rainey and her parents.

Just like Rainey and Lexi, Joe was a Gifted. He could control the light and dark. He could make a glowing ball appear from his hands which could light up a football pitch or form a dim glow to help him find something in a dark cupboard. Joe could also form shadows, at least, they looked like shadows. The light would disappear from any area that he willed, it made it pretty difficult to see him if he wanted to hide. He could also help people to heal. Rapidly. But this gift came at a cost. Rainey didn't doubt that he would be able to bring someone back from the dead, that is, if he wouldn't mind trading his own life to pay for theirs. He could quite literally take his own energy and force it into another being.

Right now, Joe was fashioning a ball of light about the size of a tennis ball. It looked almost like a dim glow of yellow-white light floating directly between his open palms. He looked up from his hands at the sound of the car's tires drawing closer. Joe raised from his seat and headed towards the garage, the ball of light still firmly in place between his hands. As he walked through the dark garden scattered with shadows, he gently threw the ball of light on to the pond, where it hovered above the water for a moment, its glow reflecting on the gentle ripples and lighting up the reeds and water lilies, before it sank beneath the water and disappeared.

Leaving the car parked outside the garage, Rainey heaved herself out and waddled towards him. Even now, after five years of knowing him, Rainey still liked to take a step back and appreciate Joe for what he was. Tall, muscular, athletic and beautiful. His dark brown eyes, the colour of melted chocolate, matched his hair perfectly. The type of boy to turn heads in the street.

Gently, he placed his hands on either side of Rainey's bump and leaned forward to give her a long but soft kiss. When he pulled away, he knotted his hand in hers and led her up to the house. She leaned into his side as they walked, and he switched their hands so that he could rub her lower back. He looked down at her protruding stomach from the corner of his eye.

"Just say it." Rainey said, bluntly.

"Say what?" Joe replied.

"I realise how disgustingly hideous I am right now," she said, using her spare hand to indicate exactly what she was talking about. "And I swear, if this baby gets one more kick on my bladder, I am going to pop!"

Joe sighed in a rather over exaggerated way.

"You look gorgeous, as always. It won't be long now. Your mum thinks it could be in the next few days. Apparently, a Gifted baby doesn't need the full nine months, he'll already be strong enough. He just wants a little more time to relax." As he spoke Joe mimicked the voice of Aimee, Rainey's mother, and Rainey cringed at how poor his impression was.

"You know, there's a good chance that she'll tear your face right off if she ever hears that terrible impression."

Joe laughed and bumped hips with her playfully. He seemed perfectly happy, talking about the upcoming birth of their child and joking about how over the top Aimee could be at times. But Rainey knew just how terrified he really was of what would happen when the baby stopped wanting to 'relax'.

"And what makes you so sure it's a he, Mr. Denyer?" She nudged him gently in the ribs with her elbow.

He stopped abruptly and pulled her into his chest, folding his arms around her torso as she wrapped hers around the back of his neck. Smiling mischievously, he looked down into Rainey's ever-changing eyes. Today they looked almost electric, a bright grey with minute speckles of sky-blue running through them.

"Rainey Rose White, should you really be throwing those elbows around in your condition?" He teased.

"I could still take you," she pouted, transforming Joe's smile into a grin.

He tucked a strand of loose hair behind her ear and then trailed his fingers down her cheek, finally settling them under her chin so that he could tilt her head slightly. He looked deep into her eyes, searching them for any hint of the fear that he knew she could see in his.

"You have no idea how much I love you" he whispered.

"And I, you." Rainey wrapped her fingers into the hair at the back of his head and pulled him to her.

She bit his bottom lip lightly before brushing her lips against his. He felt hot and soft under her touch. Rainey's heart started to race, and her breathing accelerated as she edged closer, wrapped herself around him. Her hands ran down over his strong shoulders and gripped the muscles at the tops of his arms. Every moment spent this way felt absolute for Rainey. Stood in the safe shadows of their garden, lit up by the moonlight and wrapped in Joe's protective arms while she carried his unborn baby. She would never be able to get enough of this feeling, no matter how long she spent moulded to him, breathing in his scent mixed with the fresh spring aromas which had begun to fill the garden. This was as close to perfect as Rainey could ever imagine. This precise moment. And she could have lived in it forever - if it wasn't for her parents.

"Rainey, would you untangle yourself from that boy for five minutes and get in this house! I've been working all day in the nursery, and I think it's done. I just need to know if you both like it."

Rainey's mother was more than obsessed with making everything perfect for the arrival of her grandchild, she had list, after list, after list of things she needed to buy, things she had already bought, arrangements for the birth, plans for the nursery and the longest and most in depth birthing plan anyone had ever seen. And everything else that could possibly be needed when expecting a new arrival. Even a list of things that Joe would need to do before and after the baby had arrived, just in case Aimee stopped talking about it for more than five minutes and Joe somehow managed to forget everything she had drilled into him for the past few months. Of course, having a gifted baby was very different from having a human baby, which had made Aimee even more obsessed than usual with her preparations and organising. Rainey and Joe couldn't argue, she knew what she was doing when it came to Gifted births, from a part of her past which she refused to discuss with either of them.

Rainey followed her mum into the house with Joe trailing along behind them. The house was Aimee's pride and joy. It had been little more than a crumbling wreck when Rainey's parents had first moved into it. They had had it knocked down, and in its place, they built the home Aimee had always dreamed of. Rainey didn't know a great deal of her mother's upbringing, but she did know that it had not been an easy one. What Aimee had lacked in her younger years, she had made up for in her own home.

The grey stone colonial mansion towered over the other houses in the village. With large, panelled windows framed in brilliant white and surrounded by charcoal grey window shutters, and sturdy white pillars supporting the decorated porch. The pillars had been mounted at the top of the wide stone steps which led to the front door. Rivets of green ivy snaked up the walls and clung to the windowsills. Every inch of the building, both inside and out, had been declared perfect by Aimee, from its wide towering chimneys to its ornate wooden beams.

Hidden along the side of the house stood the wide double garage which housed Aimee's and Rainey's cars. A gravel driveway curved from the garage to the front of the house, before it wove its way through the garden and its many flowers and plants of all different shapes and sizes. There were small walkways through different parts of the garden which led to unseen and hidden places. A white iron bench overlooked a small pond, and in one corner an old willow tree stood tall and proud, its leaves and branches creating a curtain between the garden and a small peaceful area which Rainey's mother considered to be the best part of the garden. Rose bushes and lilies in all different colours had been scattered everywhere, because those were Aimee's favourites. In the summer, when they had bloomed, Aimee would sit admiring them for hours. All around the garden stood tall hedges and trees which had been expertly placed to cut off the garden from the meadow and the outside world. In the summer, it was the pride of the village, right now it looked a little depressing. Just a few green shoots had begun to rise from the ground and the bushes and trees were showing the first signs of spring. But it wouldn't be long until Aimee could busy herself with the gardening again.

The inside of the house, however, was the complete opposite of the traditional grandeur display on the outside. The attic had been converted into a large additional bathroom and an office for Rainey's father, who spent most of his time hidden away up there. The entire ground floor of the house was open, with one room leading straight into the next. The furniture all oddly shaped and basic, with bright and bold colours splashed skilfully around the rooms. The only room in the house that did not have a completely modern theme, was the newly decorated nursery.

Not knowing if the baby would be a girl or a boy had not made the slightest bit of difference to Aimee's decorating plans. Aimee had transformed an old unused bedroom into something light and refreshing but delicate and cosy all at the same time. There was no doubt about it, Aimee was a genius when it came to her house. The white papered walls had tiny delicate flowers engraved into them which could only be observed when the light caught them just right. A dark wooden floor supported the off-white vintage furniture which had been expertly placed around the room. A cot lay in the very centre of the nursery with a white gossamer veil hanging from the ceiling and flowing down either side. Positioned around the room were a collection of pastel-coloured soft toys, and a full collection of Beatrix Potter books sat on the bookshelf. Floor-length curtains hung on either side of the window in the centre of the back wall, looking down on to the garden below.

Aimee looked from Joe's shocked expression to Rainey's.

"Well? Don't leave me hanging. What do you think?"

Her eyebrows were so high up on her forehead Rainey thought they might disappear into her hairline if she held the suspense any longer.

"It's beautiful," Rainey said, simply.

She had wanted to say something a little more appreciative, but her words escaped her. Judging by Aimee's reaction, Rainey's face must have said everything her voice could not. Aimee beamed and danced her way out of the room, leaving Rainey and Joe to stand open mouthed, staring at the most breathtakingly beautiful nursery either of them could have imagined.

2

Rainey

Rainey woke with her head resting on Joe's chest. Her eyes battled to stay closed as she searched for the bedroom window. The open curtains fluttered gently in the light breeze and the sun shone in beams through the panes of glass. Rainey sighed contentedly. She didn't want to disturb Joe just yet, so she enjoyed the sensation of his warm skin against her cheek while his chest steadily rose and fell with each breath.

Absentmindedly, she began to control the air around her, gently pushing and pulling it in little waves and swirls around the room, watching it gather up dust motes the size of pin heads as they floated through the beams of sunlight.

Controlling the air around her was just one of the many talents Rainey had learned since she was a child. She was one of the few Gifted in the world who could learn to use any of the powers she was introduced to, if she worked hard enough that was, Rainey had always been a lousy student.

One of her learned talents was to change her appearance. She couldn't completely transform the way she looked or stumble across a new face in the street and decide to borrow it for a day, but she could alter the individual qualities of her body. Sometimes she enjoyed to play around with her laugh lines or her skin tone. She could change her eye and hair colour, add a beauty spot here or there. But she couldn't change the shape of her natural features. She had enjoyed experimenting with the colour of her hair as a teenager, she could be blonde one day, dark brown the next, black with a pink streak down either side. It wasn't something that interested her after she had grown out of her vain teenager stage. And while she had never really found a useful purpose for that particular talent, she had enjoyed freaking her parents out on more than a few occasions as a child. She had always regretted not working harder to learn the full potential of the skill, just in case she ever decided to become an undercover detective or rob a bank.

Rainey's parents had introduced her to many unique and interesting Gifted throughout her childhood, but they never stayed long enough to really challenge her abilities. Another of her parents' friends had taught her to sketch colours and shapes into her flesh, and the flesh of others too if their bodies were connected, giving the impression of permanent tattoos on her skin. Her parents hadn't been especially happy with the Gifted who had helped her with that particular trick. It had taken some serious convincing to stop one of Rainey's primary school teachers from contacting social services when she discovered that she couldn't clean away the butterfly Rainey had decided to sketch on to her cheek. She had been so sure it was a bright pink tattoo on the child's face, until Rainey saw the panicked look in her mother's eyes and the butterfly disappeared. She had been forbidden from using the talent out of the house after that day.

One of her more impressive talents had been taught to her by her mother; Rainey could generate electricity from the earth or the air, and although it hadn't always been easy to find opportunities to practice, her parents believed Rainey's skills had surpassed that of her mother's. She could easily create bolts of static energy as she wished. Rainey had never experienced Aimee's power to its full extent, but her father spoke freely of how it was both terrifying and beautiful to witness.

Rainey's personal favourite however, was her ability to control the elements. The gift which had been the most difficult to learn, had taken a great deal of effort and caused endless disappointments from both the teacher and the student.

When her Uncle Jason died on her fourteenth birthday, Rainey had stopped learning new gifts. It had become a painful memory of their time together; one she couldn't bring herself to face. Her mother continued to push for her to learn new levels of protection. Just what required such a level of protection Rainey had no idea. There was nothing in the world she had ever experienced that could threaten her strength.

As she watched the dust motes make tiny waves in the air above Joe's stomach, a small sphere of brilliant gold appeared directly above his belly button. A smile pulled at Rainey's lips, and she turned her head to kiss the skin on his chest.

"I didn't mean to wake you. I was just admiring the view." She grinned.

"Then why do you look so sad?"

Joe placed his hand under her chin and gently tilted her head back, drawing her eyes to his.

"I'm fine. Just thinking," she replied with a shrug.

Rainey had always been the type of person to suffer in silence, he wasn't about to push her for an answer. He could read her like a book anyway, and the only time Rainey was ever really upset was when her mind strayed to one of three things: Lexi in her hospital; her Uncle Jason, or the worry of the immense strain giving birth would take on her Gifted body.

In an attempt to distract him, Rainey started to doodle little hearts along her fingers and the palms of her hands in deep grey lines. Joe smiled to himself and leant down to kiss the top of her head. Rainey pulled his hand into hers and watched as the hearts travelled down the tips of her fingers and crawled on to his.

"You should leave one on there," Joe said after a little while.

"A heart?" She replied.

"Why not? Just a small one. We could be matching. I always wanted a tattoo anyway."

Rainey studied the tiny hearts already sketched across Joe's skin. She erased all but one, sitting on the fleshy patch of skin between Joe's thumb and index finger on his right hand. She made a matching heart on her own hand.

"That is just about the most disgustingly romantic thing I've ever done." She said, admiring her handiwork.

Joe laughed and kissed her again.

They spent the rest of the morning lounging in bed in a comfortable silence as Rainey made patterns and whirls in the air and Joe trying to distract her mind from darker places, until the morning sunlight became trapped behind the clouds.

Realising that it was almost time for lunch and that they had spent nearly the full morning daydreaming in bed, Rainey heaved herself up with the help of Joe. She waddled through to the small en-suite attached to her bedroom, small but completely essential, as she had spent the first few weeks of her pregnancy violently throwing-up in there. She quickly showered and brushed her teeth before drying her hair in the bathroom mirror. She stared at the reflection of her naked body for a moment, examining the stretched skin over her extended stomach. Gentle-violet stretch marks had begun to appear, leaving small tears across her otherwise smooth skin.

Shrugging her shoulders, she made her way back to the bedroom and pulled on a pair of comfy jogging bottoms and a t-shirt. Then she returned to the mirror to watch herself as her grey eyes transformed into an illuminating blue glow, a trait said to be inherited in a Gifted, to show when their gift was about to be demonstrated, like a little warning signal. Rainey didn't know where she had inherited her eyes from. While her eyes were usually an exact replica of her mother's, bright grey with a blue tint and a dark grey ring surrounding the irises, neither of her parents displayed the same blue glow, like electricity was surging through them. Her father said it was a warning of her strength.

Spending half the day in bed had not complimented her skin, little pink blotches covered her cheeks, and her eyes betrayed her by showed her exhaustion. She evened out her tone and brightened the dark circles surrounding her eyes, before pulling her hair back into a rough knot on the top of her head. She took one last look at herself in the mirror before turning to leave the bathroom and join Joe and her parents for some brunch. Her stomach growled as she took the stairs one at a time towards the best smell in the whole world, the smell of sizzling bacon.

"Well, good morning." Aimee said from the stove, and the source of the bacon smell.

Joe was sitting at the table with Rainey's father, William, deep in conversation while they waited patiently for their sandwiches. Aimee looked up at the clock hanging on the kitchen wall. 12:01pm.

"Make that good afternoon," she said as she raised an eyebrow in Rainey's direction.

"Sorry. I've been sleeping a lot more this week. I guess because it's almost time."

Rainey looked down at her bump as she spoke, but she didn't miss the anxious glances the three of them exchanged. Anxious wasn't the right word, terrified was a better fit.

They didn't try to bring up how dangerous it was going to be when the time came for Rainey to give birth. Rainey understood the risk she was taking. Aimee had not held back when she shared the gruesome details of the Gifted she had helped to bring into the world. She had tried to educate her daughter from a young age in the hope that Rainey might choose another path for herself. But her efforts had failed.

Creating life for the Gifted was tricky, to say the least. Even with Aimee's midwifery background and the hundreds of Gifted babies she had helped to deliver in her youth, not one would compare to the baby her own daughter would deliver.

Each child born to a Gifted would usually be stronger than its parents, often so strong that the mother would not survive the birth. Aimee had explained it as nature's way of ensuring that there were never too many Gifted in the world. One must die to make way for another. Aimee had been lucky. She had survived due to Rainey's lack of power. It wasn't until Rainey was almost three years old when they discovered that what Rainey could do was learn. Joe's mother had not been so lucky.

"So, what are you two planning for the day?" Aimee said as she placed a plate of bacon, fried eggs and hash browns in front of Rainey and squeezed her shoulder before taking her own seat next to Rainey's father.

"We thought we would go see Lexi," Joe said, as he examined his glass of fresh orange. "Rainey thought it might be a good idea to visit as much as we can before she can't waddle up the stairs anymore."

Rainey scowled at him from across the table as she shovelled half an egg into her mouth.

"Well then, Mrs. White," Rainey's father said with a hint of a smile creeping on to his lips. "Does that mean I have you *and* the house all to myself? I wonder what we could do with our time."

"Really?" Rainey cringed, through a mouthful of food.

"Well, I can think of one thing," Aimee smirked, brushing William's blonde hair back with her hand.

"Do you not see us both here?" Rainey pointed a finger from Joe to herself before pushing her empty plate away.

"Did you chew any of your food or just inhale it?" William said with an eyebrow raised.

Joe laughed as he collected the used plates from the table and loaded them into the dishwasher.

"Don't judge me. I'm eating for two. Joe, I really think you should go get dressed now so that we can leave. Before we're sick."

Joe closed the dishwasher door and headed for the stairs, laughing as he left the room.

"I actually have a little work to be getting on with this afternoon,"

William said, before gulping down the last of his coffee.

Rainey's father ran his own chain of small, family-oriented restaurants, six in total. The closest one stationed only a few miles from their home and the others scattered around the country, with the exception of Rainey's favourite restaurant, in the heart of Turin, Italy. Joe had never had the opportunity to experience Rainey's favourite of the restaurants. When she was a child, they had visited every few months, but after Jason died Aimee had decided against all travel. William was forced to place an old family friend in his place until he could return. Her name was Maria and Rainey adored everything about her. The fact that the restaurant had been built inside a prestigious hotel had been an added bonus. If they could ever convince Aimee to go back, they would be able to stay for as long as they liked. Rainey looked forward to reliving her childhood summers and creating new memories with a child of her own. If she made it far enough to have a child of her own.

William worked from home most of the time now, running his business from his office in the attic and training Joe to one day step into his shoes. William owned a second business, which involved investing in old, rundown buildings, buying them through auctions and handing them over to Aimee, along with a budget, to arrange the remodel, redesign and the decoration of each, before selling them on for a profit. It was more of a hobby to keep Aimee busy than it was a business model. William had hoped that by decorating and designing other houses, Aimee might stop trying to make amendments to their own home quite so much. Unfortunately for all of them, it had not worked.

Aimee loved to work, and she would find new projects for herself if she ever had spare time on her hands. She couldn't bear to spend more than a few days without a plan or project to be working towards.

Aimee had once been a midwife for the Gifted, but beyond the horror stories her mother had shared, Rainey knew little about Aimee's life before she had come along. Aimee refused to talk about that part of her life with anybody. Rainey had always assumed that her mother's stories must have been the worst part of her younger years, but the way Aimee shied away from her former life had Rainey questioning what other horrors her mother had experienced. Rainey did know that her mother's role as a midwife to the Gifted had led to her meeting William. But when she asked her parents too many questions, they would both shoot her down with a look that told her to be quiet.

William was also a Gifted, he could sense the powers of another Gifted and enhance or weaken them. Over time, William had grown reluctant to use his gift. He had once used it as a way of making a living in the Gifted world, but his power had become temperamental and at times uncontrollable. William was as secretive as his wife when it came to his former life, but Rainey knew something bad must have happened to make him stop using his gift.

Rainey gave her father a kiss on the cheek before she wrapped her arms around her mother's waist and squeezing her tightly.

"See you both later," she smiled, and she made her way to the front door.

"Be careful," they called after her simultaneously.

She pulled a cosy looking, light-pink hoody from the coat rack by the door and barely managed to squeeze her stomach into it before pulling on some comfortable suede boots and yanking the door open.

The morning sun had disappeared, leaving a thick blanket of cloud across the sky. But it was dry out and the temperature was mild, so Rainey wandered over to the Victorian cast iron bench and took a seat. She watched the fish glide around the bottom of the pond in front of her as she waited for Joe to appear.

After a few moments, her eyes drifted on to the gentle ripples of the water and an image surfaced in her mind. A memory. One she normally would have tried to suppress to save herself from the agony of having to relive it. But today she wanted to relive it. So, she closed her eyes and allowed the memory to play from behind her eyelids.

"Ok. So, you can feel the water? Feel the pressure building behind it? Now try to push that pressure away from you."

Rainey used every bit of her concentration as she tried to push the water away from her using only her mind. She watched as it began to roll back on itself, creating little waves in the pond. Though she was sitting on the bench and well away from the water's edge, she felt cold as she tried to manipulate how the water moved, the same way she felt warm when she tried to manipulate fire. She was getting better at it. Every minute of spare time was spent learning new tricks with her Uncle Jason.

He wasn't really her uncle, but he was the closest thing she would ever have to one. Jason was Aimee's best friend. They had been best friends since they were ten years old. They had grown up together and supported each other through difficult childhoods, and they had followed each other everywhere ever since. Jason could control the elements, and he was trying to teach Rainey to do the same. She had been practicing for months now and she was finally starting to get the hang of it. She could manipulate the air, the earth and fire, but water was her final hurdle, and she was finding it difficult.

They had had some fun playing with the weather over the past few months, but they had to be careful not to raise too much suspicion with the locals. Although the humans knew the Gifted existed, they did not take kindly to them as neighbours.

Rainey felt frustrated a lot of the time. She longed to use the full force of her gifts, to experiment with how powerful she could become, but Aimee would not allow them to stray too far from the safety of the house during training sessions. Rainey was getting stronger and stronger by the day, something that her parents had insisted she train daily to achieve. But Aimee had taken every possible precaution over the years to make sure that their powers remained a secret. Rainey wouldn't be entering into any local talent contests anytime soon.

"If your mum can teach you how to generate electricity then this should be as easy as breathing." Jason sighed, showing his irritation.

"I'm trying my hardest! What else do you want me to do?"

"Yeah? Well, you're not trying hard enough."

"When was the last time you tried to learn a new power?"

She was starting to feel pretty pissed at Jason for being so pushy. But he knew exactly what he was doing, she was always stronger when she was angry.

"Lose the attitude Rainey, it doesn't suit you." He teased.

She tried again to lift the water and force it back over itself. She was concentrating so much she had risen from her seat. A single bead of sweat ran from her forehead and trickled down over her temple. She stood a few inches from the pond, leaning over the reflective water and blocking the sun from her workspace. Finally, the water rolled back over itself and Jason continued to look unimpressed.

"Is that it?" He laughed.

Rainey span on the spot, snapping her head around to glare at Jason. A flash of rage momentarily moulded her face into one that was not hers. Her eyes lit up with an electric blue and Jason smiled in anticipation. Behind Rainey, the murky water was rising from the pond. It pulled forward into a wave which continued to grow in height until it cast a dark shadow over the pair. Twigs and moss discoloured the ripples, and a panicked frog tried to *paddle its way back down to a safe height. Rainey thrust her hands forward and the wall of water warped around her body and surged toward Jason, hitting him with enough force to knock his feet out from underneath him, he held on to the bench for support as the water fell around him. It sloshed on to the ground before it settled and ran back into the pond in small streams through the now soggy grass. Jason was dripping wet from head to toe, but not a drop of water had touched Rainey. They stared at each other for a moment, her anger matching his shock, until Jason's shoulders began to shake with laughter. Rainey couldn't help but join in.*

"Well done, Rainey Rose. I knew you were just being lazy."

"I hate it when you piss me off like that!"

"Hey! Watch your mouth! If your mum hears you cussing, then one of your angry tidal waves will be the least of my problems."

He squeezed her into a crushing hug, her clothes soaking up the pond water.

"Seriously?" She said, looking down at her damp clothes.

Jason laughed again and ruffled her hair playfully.

Rainey snapped open her eyes and stared at the spot where Jason had been standing in her memory. A single tear rolled over her eyelashes and down her cheek. She brushed it away with the back of her hand. She would never see Jason again. Only in her memories. No matter how painful they were, she didn't want to block them out forever. She wiped away another tear and turned her eyes back to the still water while she waited for Joe. She wondered if her mother had allowed herself to think of Jason yet. She knew that the pain she felt when she thought of him was nothing compared with what her mother would experience.

A few short moments later, Joe appeared next to her on the bench, shaking Aimee's car keys in the air. Joe loved Aimee's car and would drive it at any given opportunity. He took one look at Rainey and the grin evaporated from his face.

"Hey, what's going on?" He said, pulling her chin up with his free hand and forcing her to look up at him.

Rainey smiled gently and took in a deep breath. She blew it back out again, like she was trying to blow all of the sadness out of her heart.

"I'm fine. Honestly," she added, seeing the sceptical look on his face. "I was just thinking about Uncle Jason. I miss him, you know?"

"I know, Rainey." He kissed her on the tip of her nose and then pulled her in to him and held her tightly for a moment.

"Come on," Rainey said as she grabbed his hand and pulled him along with her. "You take forever to get ready. And if we wait any longer then we'll miss visiting hours and we'll have to wait until tonight to go."

"Yeah, like that's ever stopped you."

As soon as Rainey had adjusted the seat belt to accompany her stomach, she leant over and turned on the radio. An upbeat and energetic pop song blared through the speakers, and she bopped her head along to the beat.

"You are such a turn on when you dance like poultry," Joe smiled.

"I am sort of limited in my choice of dance moves at the moment," she said, drawing an invisible circle around her belly with her hand.

Joe rolled his eyes before putting his foot down on the accelerator. The car sped down the long driveway and out on to the main road. Rainey sang along to every song that played through the radio as they cruised down the winding back roads that led to Lexi's hospital. Even the songs she didn't know the words to, Rainey would sing along anyway, making random noises as she tried and failed to guess each word. She didn't care in the slightest that she sounded ridiculous.

"I spoke to your dad last night," Joe interrupted.

"That's not difficult to believe, as we live in his house." She replied, sarcastically.

Joe gave her a serious look.

"He told me he misses you."

"He sees me every day, how can he miss me?"

"You know what I mean, Ray," He raised his eyebrows at her.

Rainey sighed, heavily.

"I keep trying to talk to him about it, but it just feels sort of awkward now."

Rainey and her father had always been close, right up until she had told him she was pregnant. It wasn't that he had an issue with her having a baby, even if she had been totally irresponsible. It was the risk she was putting herself in that he had an issue with. He had voiced his concerns to Rainey about the dangers of a Gifted having a child, and they had argued and argued until eventually he had had to accept that Rainey would be having this baby, no matter what the consequences were.

William loved Rainey more than anything, but he couldn't forgive her for risking her own life. After the arguments, they had found it increasingly difficult to talk to one another. Rainey was upset with him for not being able to see past the bad and focus on the good. And William refused to accept that his daughter would not take her own life into consideration. He loved her too much to see her die, just as many of the Gifted had before her when it came to childbirth. For William and Aimee, life without their daughter would be an unbearable existence.

Rainey stared out of the window as they rolled to a stop at a junction.

"Rainey, there are only five weeks left, if that. If something happens to you…" Joe closed his eyes for a second with a pained look on his face and took a deep breath. "Do you really want it to end it like this with him?"

Rainey continued to stare out of the window. She started to sing again. It wasn't the first time Joe or Aimee had tried to have this conversation with her, and it wasn't like she hadn't tried to set her relationship right with her father. But something had changed between them, and she was no longer the daddy's little girl she had always been.

Lost in their own thoughts, they didn't speak for the remainder of their journey.

When they arrived at the hospital, Lexi was waiting for them in the sitting room. Rainey realised instantly that it wasn't going to be an enjoyable visit. Lexi was having an 'off day'. She found things to fiddle with just to keep her hands busy, not joining in with any of their conversations, jumping when anyone said her name. She seemed nervous. Lexi had days like this every now and then. The doctors had put it down to post traumatic stress disorder, caused from what they thought had been the terrible accident which led to the death of both Lexi's parents. But Lexi's parents hadn't been in a terrible accident. At least, not the kind of accident that the doctors thought they had.

A nurse lingered close to them at the next table along, keeping an eye on Lexi. She was one of the few nurses Rainey actually liked. Usually, she would bring out a cup of tea for Rainey and sit down with the girls for a good catch up. But today she didn't so much as smile at her.

After many attempts at awkward conversations, Rainey and Joe being the only ones to really speak, Rainey headed off towards the toilets. The nurse followed Rainey's every step with her unreadable gaze. Rainey wondered what her problem was today. She locked eyes with her before closing the bathroom door and locking it behind her. She felt a little lightheaded as she leant over the sink to look at her tired reflection in the mirror. She ran a hand over her forehead and blinked a few times to try and clear her head. She felt a small but reassuring kick from inside her and she smiled to herself.

"I'm here, jellybean. We'll be ok. We will be just fine."

Rainey couldn't look at herself in the mirror as she said it. She didn't want to watch herself lie.

3

Joe

Lexi listened for the lock clicking into place on the bathroom door before shooting an urgent glance in Joe's direction.

"We need a minute," she called over her shoulder to the nurse.

The nurse promptly stood from her chair and made her way to the office, but her eyes remained fixed on them through the lattice patterns in the glass.

"How long does she have left?" Lexi blurted out.

"You know how long. Five weeks until she's full term."

"If I wanted to hear how long she *should* have left then I would have asked her myself. How long does she have left, Joe?" Lexi repeated, impatiently.

Joe hesitated for a moment before answering. He rubbed his eyes with his thumb and index finger and let out a shaky sigh. When he looked back at Lexi, he could almost see her heart break all over again through the sadness in her eyes.

"A week, tops. Aimee has everything ready at home for her. The plan is to keep her at home as much as possible after today, but you know what she's like. I can't keep her from coming here."

"Don't worry about that. We'll tell her I'm being transferred for a while, just like Aimee planned. Here, this is the number you can contact me on when it happens."

She handed Joe a scrap of crumpled paper with a mobile number scribbled on to it in scrawly writing.

"It belongs to Jerry at the front desk. He never leaves this dump, so he's the best chance you'll have of reaching me."

"And you think you'll be able to get out?"

"It's fine, I'll handle it. Is she doing ok? She avoids talking about this stuff and you haven't been in weeks." Lexi said.

Joe closed his eyes and rested his head in his hands. He rubbed his eye lids with the heels of his hands and Lexi thought he looked as though he was about to have a breakdown. The bags under his eyes where unmistakable and his hands shook.

"She won't talk about what could happen. She seems happy most of the time, but then I catch her crying when she thinks she's alone, or I walk into the room and she's just staring into space. Sometimes, I don't think she even realises when someone walks in."

He opened his eyes to study Lexi's face but regretted it instantly when he saw that her expression mirrored his anxiety.

"She's talking about Jason again."

Joe watched as Lexi chewed on what remained of her nails. He startled at the sound of rattling china behind him.

"I've brought you all some tea," the nurse said quietly, placing a tray with three teacups and matching saucers on to the table.

Lexi looped her fingers through one of the handles while Joe eyed the nurse suspiciously, wondering just how long she had been standing so close and unnoticed. She smiled warmly at him, but Joe could not return the gesture. Lexi took a sip of her tea and sighed warmly.

"You make the best tea. Thanks, Anya."

4

Rainey

Rainey stood outside the bathroom door and stared at Joe and Lexi from across the room as they discussed her. She watched as they both tried to control their emotions—breathing deeply, rubbing their eyes, clenching their fists to stop themselves from crying or screaming or throwing a table across the room. She felt a familiar pain flash through her chest, like a fiery hand squeezing her heart, forcing all the air from her lungs. She was breaking their hearts by putting them through this. Nobody understood that better than she did. But what choice did she have? There was nothing she would ever want more than a child. She had been told that as a Gifted, it would be damn near impossible for her to ever fall pregnant. Just knowing that had almost destroyed her. It wasn't common for Gifted women to bear children, and when it did happen, they would almost certainly die at some point throughout the process.

Her parents had tried to scare her with horror stories, but from the first moment she knew there was a tiny person growing inside her—a miniature version of herself and Joe all mixed into one—no horror story could distract her from the possibility of having a baby of her own. The only thing that mattered anymore was her child, and she would pay any price, however big, to make sure that that child made it into the world. Even if that meant Rainey couldn't be in it anymore.

She thought of all the people she would hurt: Joe, Lexi, Aimee, William. Uncle Jason. But Jason wasn't here anymore, and now she would be doing to them what Jason had done to her when he died.

Rainey didn't know if Aimee would be able to handle that level of pain. When Jason died, Aimee locked herself away for weeks. After almost three weeks of not seeing her mother, Rainey had crept into her bedroom, just to make sure she was still in there. She wished she had never gone in. Aimee had been a mess. She looked skinny and pale, like she had been locked away for months, not weeks. The worst part was the way her eyes never really seemed to focus on anything. She would stare straight through people. She didn't talk. She didn't eat. She didn't even cry after a while. She was empty. She was broken.

Things had started to get better after a few months. But would Aimee be capable of making it through the death of her own daughter?

Rainey had been staring straight through Joe and Lexi as her mind displayed images from a darker time. She didn't even notice when they stood from their table and moved away. She searched the room for Joe and spotted him leaning on a table close to the exit with his eyes fixed on the empty corridor connecting the sitting room to the patients' dormitories. Rainey scanned the room quickly, looking for Lexi, but she was no longer there. Only one face stared back at her from the depressing space. Anya's eyebrows were pinched together, her eyes sad. Rainey recognised her expression as pity. Anya pitied her.

A hand closed gently around Rainey's elbow, causing her to startle and break her gaze with the nurse.

"It's just me." Joe said irritably.

Rainey gave him a reassuring smile, but Joe turned and led her silently out of the sitting room.

"Wait, I need to say bye to Lexi." Rainey said, tugging on his grip.

Joe didn't look back at her as he answered.

"She didn't want to say goodbye."

Rainey couldn't be sure, but she thought she heard his voice break.

5

Rainey

It was summer, and the garden was bursting with bright colours and the scent of Aimee's lilies. The sun shone down, warming Rainey's skin where it filtered through the willow tree's branches.

Rainey, Jason, Joe, Aimee, and William were enjoying a picnic under the tree's shade, their own little secret garden. Rainey's fourteenth birthday was just two days away, and patience wasn't a skill she possessed—a trait inherited from her mother.

They had finished eating the sandwiches and sponge cake Aimee had prepared for them and now, with full stomachs, they relaxed as they digested their feast, watching as Jason taught Rainey more about the elements.

Rainey and Jason had already received warnings for turning the beautiful blue sky into dark clouds, so they began experimenting with other elements, comparing their abilities. Aimee had taught Rainey how to control and generate electricity from a young age, and Rainey was now trying to outshine her Uncle Jason with tiny bolts of electric energy shooting from her fingertips, weaving them together in the air just centimetres from her nose.

Jason tried disrupting her focus by tossing objects into the bolts—leftover bread crusts, small rocks, even his shoe. When he playfully attempted to pull off Aimee's sandal, Rainey lost her concentration and burst into laughter.

"Alright, see if you can top this." Jason challenged, conjuring a small flame in his palm.

Rainey laughed and summoned a gust of wind, extinguishing the flame. Jason grinned at the challenge and a crack began to form in the ground at Rainey's feet, creating a circle around her. Rainey concentrated on the crack, coaxing drops of water from the surrounding soil until it filled with water, like a moat around a castle.

"Would you two please stop ruining my garden!" Aimee scolded.

Jason clicked his fingers and the moat disappeared, leaving a puddle of water to slowly sink its way back into the earth.

"I may have taught you too well, Rainey Rose," Jason chuckled, rubbing his head as he tried to come up with a new challenge.

A smile slowly stretched across his face. He held his hand out flat in front of him with his palm to the sky. Kneeling down, he gathered some dry dirt in his other hand and sprinkled it onto his palm. Rainey watched as the dirt swirled into a miniature tornado, growing taller and wider as it spun. At its base, the dirt gradually transformed into water, swirling around the tornado in Jason's palm until it resembled an upright whirlpool.

Rainey stared, in awe of what Jason could do. She glanced up at his triumphant

expression and giggled. He thought that he had beaten her. But Rainey hadn't told Jason about the training she had been doing on her own. She took a step closer, holding his glare as she placed her hand above the rush of water hovering above his palm. She bit down on her lip in concentration, then smiled a wicked grin as the water froze into a solid whirlpool-shaped ice sculpture. Rainey couldn't stifle her laugh when she saw the shocked expressions of her family around her. She had outdone Jason. Beaten him at his own game. And she had never seen him look so proud.

Joe sprang up from the grass and seized the icy block from Jason. As he examined it in amazement, Rainey couldn't help but smile mischievously. The ice reverted to water, losing its shape and splashing all over Joe's t-shirt.

Rainey woke with a start, as though the cool water from the whirlpool in her dream had splashed all over her. She looked around frantically, trying to figure out what had startled her. Then she felt a wriggle inside her stomach and realised that it was some*one* who had woken her, not some*thing*. She smiled to herself.

"Little monkey." She murmured at her ballooned stomach.

"I've been watching him wriggle around all night. I'm surprised he didn't wake you sooner." Joe said, making her jump.

She hadn't realised he was awake. She glanced at the alarm clock on the bedside table. 3:02am.

"What are you still doing awake?" She asked as she stretched out her limbs.

"Couldn't sleep," he shrugged. "Somebody kept kicking me."

Joe nodded toward Rainey's stomach and smiled. Rainey returned the smile. She nestled into him, and they held each other tightly. He traced the tip of his nose down her forehead, over her nose, lips, chin, and then down her neck. He kissed her gently at the hollow of her throat, trailing kisses along her collarbone, stopping at her shoulder. He placed his hands under each of her arms and lifted her gently, until she was leaning against the headboard, half sitting, half lying. Then he positioned himself over her, with his strong arms on either side of her body, being careful to not rest any of his weight on her. Rainey wrapped her legs around his waist. He kissed the hollow of her throat again before placing small, lingering kisses down her chest. He lifted the shirt she had borrowed from him over her head and continued to trail kisses over her bare chest and stomach. Their skin tingled as they brushed against one another, absorbing each other's heat. Rainey gently clung to Joe's skin, not wanting to let him go. She didn't want it to end. She didn't ever want to leave him. But she had made her choice, and Joe would have to live with the consequences, even if Rainey didn't.

When Rainey woke later that morning, the sun shone brightly through the window, warming her body where the sheets failed to cover her naked skin. Trying her best not to wake Joe, she crept into the bathroom and took a long, hot shower.

By the time she had dressed herself, Joe was using the shower in the main bathroom down the hall. She quickly made the bed and tidied around the room before making her way down to the kitchen to prepare breakfast.

Aimee and William had left the house early and everywhere was quiet. Rainey cracked three eggs into a pan and sliced some bread, ready to be toasted. As she plated up two servings of scrambled eggs on toast, Joe joined her in the kitchen. He kissed her on the lips between mouthfuls of toast, and they chatted over fresh orange juice, finishing their breakfasts together. Rainey glanced at the calendar hanging from the side of the fridge, it told her it was February. It was actually the third of March, but nobody had bothered to turn the calendar to the next page. Joe noticed her looking at it and jumped up to change the page himself when the click of the lock turning in the front door sounded, announcing the return of Rainey's parents. They walked into the kitchen and Aimee took a seat beside Rainey. Rainey watched as William passed something to Joe before joining them at the table. She looked away as Joe attempted to hide the small white box in his back pocket.

"Well, I'm glad you two are up. It's beautiful outside today, far too nice to waste the day indoors," William remarked as he settled into his seat. "Looks like it'll be another March heatwave this year. It was freezing just a few days ago. No telling what the weather will do next."

Rainey chuckled to herself at her father's rambling and Aimee's dramatic eye rolling.

"Rainey, do you want to take some blankets out to the meadow later? Maybe have a picnic or something?" Joe asked.

"Well, I did have a full day of sitting on my backside planned, but sure, why not," she replied. "What time should we go see Lexi today?"

"We can figure that out later," Joe replied, glancing away and catching Aimee's eye.

Yesterday's visit to see Lexi hadn't gone exactly as planned. Lexi hadn't managed to give Rainey her excuse to hopefully keep Rainey away for the next few days, and Joe had forgotten to update Aimee on the situation.

Rainey started to clear up after breakfast while the others lounged around the table and chatted about a conversation William had had earlier that morning with one of the restaurant managers. Rainey had just finished rinsing the plates when Joe and William suddenly stood and left the room. Aimee joined Rainey by the sink, wrapping her arms around her shoulders and giving her a gentle squeeze.

"How are we feeling today, baby?" Aimee asked.

Even at eighteen years old and carrying her own child, Rainey was still Aimee's baby. Rainey smiled at her mother.

"I'm feeling like I could eat another breakfast. How fat am I getting? Be honest with me."

Rainey leaned back, giving her stomach the illusion of being even larger than it already was, and they laughed together.

"Hey, you look a damn sight better than I did when I carried you."

"Give me your hand," Rainey said, grabbing one of Aimee's hands and placing it on the top of her stomach.

They grinned when a kick from inside made Aimee jump. They stood for a moment, feeling the movements under Rainey's skin, trying to guess where the next kick would be.

"Lexi's hospital called this morning," Aimee said, watching Rainey's face carefully. "They told me that Lexi had to be moved to a different hospital for a few days while they have some renovations done."

"Well, about time. That place is a dump! Which hospital is she at now? I hope it's not too far; I don't think I can sit still for more than half an hour now without wetting myself," Rainey joked.

She snorted at her own joke.

"It's Saint Andrews, in Scotland. I'm sorry, Rainey, but you're just going to have to make do without her for a few days."

Rainey looked at her mum, expecting a punchline, but when one didn't come, her face dropped.

"What? Why would they move her so far away?"

Panicked thoughts ran through Rainey's head. If Lexi went to Scotland, then there would be no chance of seeing her again until she came back. What if she didn't come back until after the baby was born? What if everything went wrong with the birth and Rainey never saw Lexi again?

"They said it was the only other hospital in their chain that had enough room to house everyone. It might only be for a few days..." Aimee trailed off.

"But?" Rainey pushed.

"They said it could be up to a few weeks."

Rainey looked at her mother with her mouth hanging open as she continued to speak, but Aimee didn't look back at her. Instead, she looked at the floor, the worktop, a thread on her jumper, anything but Rainey. It didn't take a genius to see that Aimee was avoiding her daughter's eyes. Rainey frowned. She didn't think her mother would lie to her, and what could she possibly have to gain from lying about Lexi's hospital? Her eyebrows pulled together as the thought momentarily distracted her.

"Look, honey. I know that you're worried you won't see her again but I don't want you to put yourself under any extra strain. You have enough to worry about as it is. Lexi will be fine for a few days and so will you."

"But what if she isn't back before the baby?"

"She will be, we'll make sure of it."

Aimee kissed her forehead.

"Now, go and get some blankets ready for when you head over to the meadow."

Rainey didn't argue. She headed up the stairs to find some blankets, moaning about the hospital under her breath as she searched.

When lunchtime arrived and it was warm enough outside to wear just a cardigan over her dress, Rainey and Joe grabbed the blankets and took some juice and sandwiches with them to the meadow. They found a nice spot under a cherry tree filled with pink and white blossoms.

Each time the breeze picked up, a handful of blossoms would float down to the ground, like pastel-coloured snowflakes. They laid out on the blankets and talked while they ate their picnic, and when they had finished, they enjoyed the sun in each other's company, and brushed blossoms from their hair every now and then.

"I bought something for you the other day. Your dad picked it up for me this morning."

Joe held out his hand, and in it lay a small box coated in white silk. Rainey took the box and opened it slowly. Resting inside was a tiny, delicate silver bangle. Gently, Rainey pulled it out of the box to get a closer look. Engraved around the edge were the words: 'If I knew what perfect was, you would be it.' It was something Rainey and Joe had always said to one another. A smile spread across Rainey's lips.

"You had this made for the baby?" She asked.

Joe nodded and Rainey leapt forward into Joe's arms, almost knocking him over. She squeezed him tightly.

"Thank you," she whispered. "It's beautiful. I love it."

He eased her back into her seat before standing.

"I have something for you, too."

He held out his hands and she placed hers into them. He gently tugged on them to help her stand and when she found her balance, he let go of her and took something from his back pocket. Joe watched her expression as he opened the small box wrapped in his hands.

"Don't get your hopes up," he laughed when he saw the look of horror wash over Rainey's face. "It's not a proposal."

She let out a sigh of relief. Inside the box was a silver bracelet. It had a single charm hanging from it on a thin silver chain. Rainey ran her index finger over the bracelet and then carefully scooped up the charm, lifting it to her eyes. A single diamond shone from the side of the charm, it caught the sun as she turned it in her fingers, making tiny rainbows dance in the air. The charm itself was in the shape of a pram.

"Now you can stop collecting those stupid key rings and start collecting charms instead." Joe joked.

She nudged him playfully with her elbow.

"I had no idea you hated the key rings so much."

"Rainey, if you get any more damn key rings there won't be any room for your keys." He said.

Rainey laughed and Joe took the bracelet from her fingers and began to wrap it around her left wrist.

They admired the bracelet as it trailed over the top of her hand.

"What's the occasion?" She asked, suspicious.

Joe laughed.

"Do I need an excuse to spoil you?"

"Well, no. But you don't normally just go off and buy me expensive looking charm bracelets."

Joe shrugged his shoulders innocently. Rainey studied his face carefully for a moment before coming to the conclusion that he did just want to treat her, and she hadn't forgotten an important date. Then she twisted her fingers into his hair and pulled him closer.

"Thank you," she whispered against his lips. "For the bracelet. And for not proposing."

Joe smiled against her kiss.

They spent the remainder of the afternoon sitting in the shade of the tree in the meadow, blowing blossoms from each other as they fell from above their heads and watching the occasional cloud go by in the almost clear sky.

When the sun began to set, changing the sky from a light blue into an assortment of pinks and oranges, Rainey headed back into the house, dragging Joe along behind her.

Rainey sat on the sand covered blanket with Joe and her parents. She had picked a quiet beach-like patch next to the river to spend her birthday with her family. It was hidden away behind a deserted field where the grass was now overgrown and filled with wildflowers.

It was a place they could be themselves without having to worry about anyone seeing them. Not that the locals didn't know that the Gifted existed, because they did know. But it wasn't something that was talked about openly. To be Gifted was to be feared, and that was not what Rainey's family wanted for themselves.

They had been waiting almost an hour for Jason to show up. It wasn't like him to be late, especially to an event as important as Rainey's birthday, which was why Aimee was beginning to worry. Rainey counted the candles which had been pressed into her chocolate birthday cake, there were fourteen in all. The cake was now melted on the top from the heat of the day, the candles leaning dangerously in different directions, and sand had been sprinkled down one side of the cake because William had shaken the blanket to get rid of a bug.

Rainey and Joe sprawled out with their toes submerged in the cold water as they waited.

"I think we might have to buy a new cake on the way home," William said, giving the cake a prod with a twig he had picked up from the ground.

"Maybe we should just head back. What if Jason forgot we were meeting out here and he's waiting at your place?" Joe raised his eyebrows at William who looked to Rainey for an answer.

"Yeah, I suppose. Well, this sucked."

Rainey pulled her feet out of the water and dried them on the blanket while William and Aimee gathered their things together.

They had started their walk back to the car across the field, weaving their way through the tall grass, when Aimee's phone rang from inside her bag.

She placed the ruined cake down on the ground and rummaged through her bag to find it.

"Unknown number." She said, looking at the screen before she answered.

Rainey and Joe continued to walk slowly through the grass hand in hand. They had only taken a few steps when they heard Aimee gasp from behind them. Rainey spun around, letting go of Joe, just in time to see Aimee's hand drop from her ear, her mobile hitting the floor with a dull thud. Aimee's knees buckled beneath her and a sickening scream erupted from her throat.

For Rainey, everything seemed to happen in slow motion. William leapt for the phone and began shouting to the person on the other end, trying to grasp what had happened. But Rainey couldn't concentrate on what he was saying, she couldn't take her eyes off her mother, screaming on the ground. Her hands gripped her chest like she was trying to stop her heart from beating. Her nails dug into her skin and left smudges of blood where they punctured her. Rainey's head snapped up at the sound of her father's voice. He wasn't shouting anymore. He looked directly into Rainey's eyes.

"Jason's dead."

Rainey inhaled deeply but she couldn't blow the air back out again. She looked from her father's pale face, to her mother screaming on the ground, to Joe, who was frozen, his eyes wide and staring back at her. She shook her head from side to side.

"No," she whispered. "You're wrong. Where? How?" Her voice was rising in hysteria.

"A fire, at his house. They want your mum to go to the hospital to speak with someone-"

He hadn't finished talking before Rainey took off, sprinting across the field.

Joe tried to grab hold of her, but she was too fast for him, and she slipped through his fingers. He tried to chase her, but he couldn't catch up. Rainey ran and ran while hot tears began to spill from her eyes and fall down her face, making it difficult for her to see. She tripped on a rock and collided with the ground hard, winding herself and causing the skin on her hands and knees to graze. She picked herself up and set off running again. She would not stop until she got there. She would not believe it until she saw it for herself. Jason would be fine. He had to be. She didn't know what she would do without him in her life. She didn't know what Aimee would do.

By the time she reached Jason's house, her muscles were screaming in protest, and she was covered in dirt and blood from her grazes. Jason's house was in the middle of a secluded area, cut off from the road by tall Leylandii bushes, but Rainey could smell the smoke before she stepped around them.

The house was no longer there. It had been replaced with a hole in the ground where the foundations lie, filled with black, smoking soot and ash. The odd shapes of Jason's burned belongings stuck out of the rubble in different directions, like the candles on Rainey's melted birthday cake. Everything was gone.

Jason was gone.

Clouds began to roll into the clear blue sky above Rainey as though they had appeared from the heavens. A tortured scream rose up her throat and escaped through her lips as lightening streaked the sky.

Rainey gasped for air as she sprang into a sitting position in her bed. Sweat coated her skin and she fought to control her rushed breathing.

It was just a nightmare, she told herself.

Except it wasn't just a nightmare, it was a memory. One that she had not dreamt about in a long time.

Joe sat up beside her and wrapped her in his arms as she shook with the effort to control her sobs.

"You were screaming in your sleep. You haven't done that for a long time," he spoke softly to her while he stroked her hair, letting her cry into his chest.

She didn't talk until she had calmed herself down enough to breathe steadily again.

"I'm sorry I woke you," she whispered to Joe between hiccups.

"Don't be ridiculous. I'm glad you woke me. I'll go get you some tissues."

"It's ok, I'll go," Rainey replied, pecking Joe on the cheek.

She pulled back the duvet to climb out of bed and they both froze as they looked down at the sheets. Rainey was surrounded by a puddle of deep red blood.

6

Rainey

"Aimee!" Joe's panicked scream filled the silence of the house.

Rainey remained frozen in place, staring at the blood seeping through the bed sheets.

"Aimee! Will!" Joe yelled again.

The sheer panic in his voice haunted Rainey. She had never heard him sound truly terrified before. Rainey heard a loud bang down the hall as her parents' bedroom door flew open and swung back, colliding with the wall. She could hear the heavy footfalls of them sprinting towards her room. She lowered her hands into the puddle, testing to see if it really was there or if this was all a part of her dream. She raised her hands to find them covered in thick, dark blood and a helpless sob slipped through her lips.

She looked up to see both of her parents standing in the doorway.

Aimee took a step into the room before her eyes landed on the red-stained bed sheets and it took her a moment to comprehend what had happened. A rush of both panic and devastation flashed across her face before she had time to control it.

"It's strong," she said to herself, confirming their fears.

William's knees wobbled beneath him, and he held on to the doorframe to stop himself from falling to the floor. Rainey looked at him and saw on his face what Aimee had now managed to compose on her own.

Wasting no more time, Aimee bolted from the room screaming instructions at William and Joe as she ran between rooms, collecting everything she had prepared.

"Get her upstairs, now!" Was her final instruction, before she disappeared into the attic.

William and Joe helped Rainey to slowly stand at the side of the bed. As she shifted her weight on to her feet a sharp flash of pain stabbed through the bottom of her stomach and down her legs, making her yelp and bite down hard, grinding her teeth together.

"What's wrong? What is it?" Joe asked helplessly, trying and failing to make himself sound calm.

"I'm fine. We need to hurry."

Rainey pulled on Joe's and William's arms to heave herself back on to her feet.

They helped her to shuffle her body forwards. She took small steps, careful not to rush and risk another bolt of pain, but it came anyway. This time it was more intense, not just a quick flash. Instinctively, she let go of her father's arm to hold her stomach where the pain was making it feel like her insides were being torn apart. But she lost her balance and William had to grab her shoulder to stop her from falling.

"This isn't right. Where are the contractions? There was no build up, no warning. It shouldn't be like this."

Rainey looked to Joe for an answer, but he had his head turned away from her, looking back at the room behind them. Rainey followed his gaze and felt her heart drop into her stomach. Blood trailed across the floor, from the bed to the doorway. Not just a few drops, but puddles, deep red puddles. Rainey looked down at her feet to find the insides of her legs coated in fresh, warm blood. She could feel the panic taking over her body before she had time to register what she was seeing. Her chest began to tighten, and her legs felt like jelly. She swayed dangerously. Her mind filled itself with the inevitability that this would be her end. She had been preparing for it since the day she had discovered she was pregnant. But she wasn't ready. How could she ever be? Tonight, she would die.

Joe placed a hand under her chin and pulled her face up to his. But while her head moved, her eyes remained fixed on the scene behind her.

"Rainey, look at me."

He had managed to take back control of his voice and it was firm and demanding again. It soothed her a little.

Rainey dragged her gaze away from the blood and looked into his deep brown eyes.

"Rainey listen to me. You are going to be fine. Do you hear me? I love you too much to let anything take you from me. Right now, you need to concentrate on what I want you to do. Ok?" Joe ordered.

Rainey nodded numbly with a tiny jerk of her head.

"We need to get you upstairs, right now. And I don't think you can move quickly enough, so I'm just going to carry you. You need to stay focussed, Rainey."

Joe placed one arm behind Rainey's knees and the other behind her shoulders. She leaned back into him, and he took her weight easily as he cradled her against his bare chest. He headed towards the stairs, with William hovering close by his side, hands at the ready in case Joe's arms gave way.

When they reached the top of the stairs, they headed straight for the bathroom. Aimee was sitting on the floor, surrounded by fresh white towels and various tools and equipment. She continued to lay them out around her, a determined spark glinting in her eyes. She paused as Joe staggered into the room, Rainey lying limply in his arms.

"I need her over here," Aimee said, fluffing up a couple of pillows she had placed in the centre of the tiled floor.

Joe sank to his knees as slowly as he could and placed Rainey down on the floor with her head resting on one of the pillows. Aimee took one look at Rainey's blood dripping from Joe's arm, and the stream of blood that had followed them into the bathroom, before she leapt to her feet and sprinted from the room.

When she returned a moment later with a mobile phone held between her ear and her shoulder, Joe knew it must be Lexi she was trying to contact. She unwrapped a chilling metal object from its wrapper as the phone rang and rang.

"There shouldn't be this much blood." She told Joe and William as she knelt beside Rainey.

"So, does that mean…?" William whispered.

Aimee didn't answer. She continued to unwrap different tools from their sterile packaging.

"What?" Rainey screamed. "What does that mean?"

Aimee locked eyes with Joe and gave one firm nod of her head.

"It means this is going to be difficult, Rainey. It means that this baby is probably going to be very strong and definitely Gifted. I need you to be brave and say goodbye to Joe." She turned her attention back to Joe. "You need to go and get her, there's no answer on the number she gave you."

"Go and get who?" Rainey sobbed. "Joe, you can't leave me. Please."

"He has to go and get Lexi. We need her help." Aimee replied.

"But she's not here anymore."

"Rainey, I lied to you. I had to get you to stay in the house and the only way I could do that was to tell you she had gone. If this had happened when you were at her hospital, we might not have been able to get to you in time." Aimee tried her best to explain but there was no time. "Joe, you need to go. Now!"

Joe leant forward and took Rainey's face in his hands. He looked into her grey-blue eyes and tried to blink away the tears threatening to spill over his eyelashes.

"I love you." His voice shook as he spoke. "I swear that I will be back with Lexi as soon as I can. I want you to hold on for me, Ray Ray. Ok? You're going to be fine. You are. And in a few hours, we will be back in our bed, with our baby asleep between us."

He was trying to convince himself as much as he was Rainey. A single tear broke free of his eyelashes and fell on to Rainey's chest. She placed her hand on the back of his neck and pulled him to her. Their kiss burnt with the determination that it would not be their last.

"I love you." Rainey whispered to Joe.

Rainey released her grip and he stood and walked to the door.

"What if they come?" Joe said to William.

"What if who come?" Rainey interrupted.

"They won't. Not yet." William replied.

William looked defeated and lost. His eyes were red and sore from holding back his tears. Joe took one last look at Rainey lying on the floor, blood pooling around her legs. Then he turned and ran for the stairs.

"What if who come?" Rainey repeated, pushing for an answer.

But before she could push any further, she threw her head back and let out a piercing scream. The pain was so strong she could not focus her eyes, her vision clouded as her eyes darted around the room trying to make sense of the blurred shapes surrounding her. William filled Joe's place beside Rainey and took her hand in his, he looked at her and gave her a teary smile.

"It's ok sweetheart. We're here."

Aimee leant over Rainey and ripped her long shirt in half straight down the front so that she could feel Rainey's stomach. She moved her hands around expertly, feeling for the baby, putting all of her skills she had learned as a midwife into action.

"We just need to keep calm until Joe gets back with Lexi," Aimee said when she had located the baby inside Rainey. "Head down and low, he's in a perfect position. We just need you to be strong for us,

Rainey."

"Why do we need Lexi?" Rainey croaked, her voice had strained with her last scream, and it felt rough in her throat as she spoke.

"Since the moment we found out you were pregnant, all three of us started working on a plan. We knew that if this baby was to be a strong Gifted, like you, then we would need to have something in place for the birth. We all knew the dangers, including you. Lexi is the only one who can knock you out without risking any permanent damage. There isn't an anaesthetic strong enough that could do the job before your system burns off the effects. We arranged for Lexi to get out when the time came. Jerry agreed to help us." Aimee explained.

"When Lexi gets here, she's going to drain your energy, just enough for you to pass out but not enough to leave any lasting damage." William added. "It's dangerous, but it's better than the alternative. If you're unconscious, then you won't be able to do any damage to yourself while your mother works to get the baby out safely."

Rainey was silent for a moment while she let the information sink in. There were so many questions she wanted to ask about everything they had been keeping from her, but there wasn't time. A fresh wave of pain gripped her stomach. Her whole body tensed. She felt like someone was stabbing at her insides with a white-hot poker. Her vision blurred as she battled to stay conscious and then the screams began again.

7

Joe

Joe froze at the front door as Rainey's scream tore through his body. Listening to her scream and walking away from her felt as though someone had taken a hold of either side of his heart and brutally ripped it in two. Half of it would stay with Rainey, and the other half would beat painfully in his chest until he could return it to her. But as much as it pained him to leave her, he knew he had to be the one to do it. Aimee and William could do more for her now than he could. His part came after the birth. Not to mention how he was the only one capable of driving fast enough down the pitch black and deserted roads, in the early hours of the morning to get Lexi and help her break out of the hospital unnoticed. He stepped out into the cool air and pulled the door shut behind him. He raced over to Aimee's car parked in front of the garage and unlocked it with the key fob. He yanked open the door and climbed in, starting the engine with one hand and fumbling for his seat belt with the other. The engine roared to life and Joe slammed his foot down on the accelerator, sending gravel flying up from under the wheels and crashing into the garage doors. The clock on the dashboard read 2:13am. If he could get to Lexi and have her out of the hospital and into the car by 3:00am then maybe he could make it back within an hour. Could Rainey hold on for that long? Would her heart still be beating for him the way his did for her? His hands began to tremble against the steering wheel as he tried to shake the thought of the alternative from his head. But the possibility of Rainey not lasting that long was too high, and he gripped the wheel tighter to steady his hands, the skin on his knuckles growing white under the pressure. He pushed the accelerator down to the floor and the engine surged the car forward.

The deserted roads worked to Joe's advantage, but the darkness made driving difficult. Joe knew if he crashed into anyone at the speed he was travelling, neither one of them would survive. He waited until he was hidden from view on the country roads, away from any houses or late-night dog walkers, before he tried to make the road ahead of him brighter. Small orbs of brilliant white light appeared ahead of the car, amplifying the effects of the car's headlights, but it was too difficult to maintain, he couldn't concentrate on forming and holding the orbs in place while focussing on not wrapping himself around a tree. Giving up on the idea, he returned his efforts to making sure he didn't crash on one of the winding bends and end up killing himself in his effort to keep Rainey alive. He risked a glance in the direction of the speedometer. Eighty miles per hour. His foot edged further down on the pedal, but his mind was racing in too many other directions to risk going any faster. He dropped back down to eighty. He was terrified that he would not make it back in time, that the worst possible outcome would happen to Rainey and the baby. And he needed to figure out how he was going to get Lexi out of the hospital unnoticed. If Jerry, the security guard, wasn't on the night shift then it was probably going to be very difficult for the pair of them to sneak out. If Jerry was working, then surely he would have answered his phone when they called him. He didn't know the precise reason Lexi had asked for his mobile phone number, but he understood the urgency. Where the hell was Jerry, damn it! Joe punched the centre of the steering wheel with his fist, making the horn sound loudly into the deserted countryside.

A startled deer bounded out of the tree line and into the road. Joe yanked on the wheel just in time to swerve dangerously around the creature, the car's tyres screeching in protest.

"Shit!" He yelled, as he fought for control of the vehicle.

He needed to calm himself down before he arrived at the hospital. Looking at his reflexion in the rear-view mirror he could see that his eyes were bulging and red, the purple bags underneath them continued to show through the sheen of sweat that was beading across his skin. His hair stuck out in odd places where a mixture of his sweat and Rainey's blood had matted it together, and he was wearing only his jogging bottoms with a pair of ratty once-white trainers he had slipped his feet into as he ran from the house. And to top it all off, his chest and arms were smeared with blood from carrying Rainey up to the bathroom. If he wasn't so desperately anxious, then he might have seen the humour in turning up to a psychiatric hospital to break out a patient, whilst looking like he had just murdered half the population of a small village. There was nothing he could do to fix his appearance now; he could only hope that he wasn't spotted by one of the nurses and reported to the police. He didn't have time for delays. Rainey didn't have time for delays.

When he finally arrived at the hospital the car skidded to an abrupt stop. He didn't bother to use any of the empty spaces in the car park. Instead, he left the car right outside the front doors and locked it as he sprinted towards the front doors. He peered in through a small window next to the securely locked doors. He could see Jerry asleep in his desk chair with his feet resting on the worktop in front of him and he shook his head impatiently. Joe tapped on the window as loudly as he dared, trying to wake Jerry without drawing any unwanted attention to himself. The plump middle-aged man didn't so much as stir in his sleep. Joe knocked on the window again, a little louder this time, and glanced over his shoulder nervously. But still there was no movement from inside. He scanned the room through the glass, double checking that there was nobody else in sight, before he focussed on the dim light bulb hanging from the ceiling. Beneath the bulb, Joe formed a perfect sphere of bright light, illuminating every spot in the room until it was difficult to look at without squinting his eyes into narrow slits, but still, Jerry did not react.

"Oh, for crying out loud!" Joe whispered under his breath.

He concentrated on Jerry's hands knitted tightly together on top of his round stomach, lifting slightly with every snore. The sphere began to drift down through the air until it was sitting millimetres from his skin. It must have been bright enough to create a red glow behind Jerry's eyelids because finally he began to stir, attempting to block out the unexpected light by turning his head away and swatting at the air with his hands. The instant he opened his eyes, the light disappeared, leaving Jerry in the dim light of the office, squinting around the room for the source of what had woken him from his nap. Joe tapped on the glass again and Jerry jumped so dramatically that his feet pushed against the desk, throwing him backwards and out of his chair. Joe sighed irritably. Jerry had to be the worst person Joe had ever met to ever work as a night guard. A flashlight shone through the glass, shortly followed by the buzzer for the door, indicating Joe's signal to enter through the now unlocked doors. As soon as he was through and the doors were closed behind him, he turned to Jerry with a furious gaze.

"Where's your phone, Jerry?" He whispered angrily as Jerry positioned himself back in his chair with a sigh.

"The wife took it. Thinks I'm having an affair. Stupid woman. Doesn't know what she's got…" he trailed off into a mumble as he examined Joe's expression.

"Are you kidding me?"

During any normal day, Joe would have taken great pleasure in winding Jerry up about something so ridiculous. How anyone could accuse Jerry of having an affair was beyond laughable, but of all the times for Jerry to have his phone confiscated, it was just their luck that it had been on the one day they had ever really needed Jerry for anything.

"Jerry. Rainey's in trouble. I need to get Lexi out."

At his words, Jerry seemed to notice the state of Joe's appearance. His eyes zoned in on the now dried blood covering the skin across Joe's bare torso and he leapt to his feet from his chair. He rushed around to Joe's side of the counter, where he grabbed a hold of Joe's hand. He pulled a blue pen from his pocket and began scribbling a series of numbers on to the only clean patch of Joe's skin he could find. He explained each number as he wrote it.

"This one is for the first door up the corridor, then this one will get you into the fire escape. Take the stairs from there up to Lexi's floor. This code is for the door there. All of them will be locked at this time but the nurses shouldn't be about. The only place you might bump into one of them is on the floor, but they should all be in the office. Don't let them see you Joe, make things *dark* if you have to. Her room is number…" he paused while he scanned through the different rooms in his head. "Seventy-four, yes, that's it, it's definitely room seventy-four. I can't leave the desk, Joe, but I'll wait here for you to get back so I can let you out."

"Thanks, Jerry. We owe you." Joe clapped his hand down on Jerry's shoulder.

"Damn right you do, kid." He replied, eyeing the dried coat of blood smeared across the hand resting on his shoulder.

Joe took off, sprinting down the corridor, stopping only to frantically jab at the buttons on the code pads at each of the locked doors. He made it into the fire escape in under a minute, and bound his way up the concrete stairs, taking them three at a time. When he arrived on Lexi's floor, the door had been propped open with a doorstop. The lights were all on, but he couldn't hear anybody moving about on the floor. It was completely silent. Joe closed his eyes and began to drain the light from the entire floor of the building. He could feel it creeping towards him, leaving shadows in its wake, building up a resistance to him as the area around him grew darker. Joe felt it like he was pulling on an enormous elastic band, the darker the room grew, the more the resistance grew, until it became difficult to drag the last few embers of light from the room, causing him to strain against the pressure. By the time he was finished, darkness had engulfed him. The only light remaining came through the windows, where the silver-white glare of the moonlight helped to cast eerie shapes into the shadows.

Silently, he crept through the open door and began searching for the walkway leading to Lexi's room. Through the large sitting room, he could see the office where the nurses would normally be stationed as they watched their patients with their visitors. Even in the dark he could see the room was empty, which meant that if there were any nurses on the floor, they were on the move, probably trying to figure out what had caused the power cut.

At either end of the sitting room, two corridors led off in opposite directions. Joe continued across the room, heading for the bigger of the two corridors, when he heard a clatter behind him. He dropped into a crouch on the floor and spun around, searching through the darkness for the source of the noise. He couldn't see anyone in the shadows, nor could he hear them. Still, he crouched, frozen in place and listening into the still air. He reminded himself of where he was. William had promised him that they wouldn't come yet. The noise had to have been caused by a nurse or a patient. There was no chance of him allowing either one to stand in his way of taking Lexi to help Rainey. He didn't want to make anything difficult for Lexi by alerting the nurses she would be leaving the building, with or without their consent. But he was running out of time. And the thought of not making it back made his palms begin to sweat again and his heart pound faster in his chest. He crouched still for as long as he dared but he couldn't waste another second on the floor of the sitting room. He crawled under the tables, getting closer and closer to the corridor. If there was somebody in the room with him, they wouldn't be able to see him, it was too dark, and he moved silently, drawing the shadows into him for extra cover. He reached the final table and made a dash for the entrance of the corridor. Then he jogged for a few seconds until he found the first door with a shiny plastic number stuck to it. Forty. He pulled himself closer to the wall as he continued down the wide corridor, leaning into the doorways as he passed to stay as far away from the moonlit windows as possible. He reached the end of the corridor and turned left. He read the numbers to himself in his head as he moved. Sixty-eight, sixty-nine, seventy. Joe sprinted past the last few doors as the last of his patience abandoned him. He had no idea what time it was or how long ago he had left Rainey, what could have been minutes felt like hours, and he hoped he was not getting close to the target he had set himself.

Finally, he could see room seventy-four. He stopped outside the door and placed his hand on the handle but stopped when he heard a shuffle of feet in the darkness behind him. Joe turned slowly and carefully released the elastic band. Light began seeping back into the corridor, just enough for him to see a figure standing in front of him. Out of the darkness, the outline of a body emerged, slim and tall, but still a little shorter than Joe, with shoulder length dark hair and a navy-blue nurse's uniform. He recognised her as Lexi's favourite nurse. He remembered seeing her yesterday when he and Rainey had visited the hospital. She had brought him a cup of tea and given Rainey all sorts of strange glances. Almost as though she knew what was waiting for her just around the corner.

"W...what on earth do you think you're doing?" She stammered.

"I need to see Lexi," he said, simply.

He had come this far, and already wasted enough time. He needed to get back to Rainey, and he would not be leaving without the girl he came here to get.

"At this hour? What could possibly be so important that you need to come sneaking around here at this time of night?"

She stepped forward to see him a little better in the shadows and her eyes fell on to his half naked torso. She couldn't help but gasp and stumble back a step.

"What did you do?" She pointed to the blood on Joe's chest with one hand, the other covering her mouth and her horrified expression.

"I didn't *do* anything. I just need to speak to Lexi. It's important." He turned back to the door and began to push the handle down.

"It's started, hasn't it?"

"Excuse me?" He replied, his hand poised on the door handle.

"The baby. The labour. It's started."

Joe let out a long sigh and his head dropped, defeated. He could not answer her, but his reaction was all the answer she needed. She stepped forward and placed her hand on Joe's shoulder.

"I'm so sorry," she said, empathy leaking from her every pore. "Good luck."

"I don't need your luck," he snapped, shrugging her hand away.

Joe had never been rude to any of the nurses at Lexi's hospital, he had never so much as made fun of them behind their backs, like Rainey and Lexi did regularly, but he did not like the way she had said those last words. Like they were already too late. Like there was nothing that could be done to save Rainey. What did she know about Rainey? They had spoken a few times when Rainey visited, but since when was Rainey best friends with any of the nurses at the hospital? Had Lexi shared a little too much information about what they were? Had Rainey?

Pushing the handle all the way down, he stepped into the room, slamming the door behind him. As the noise of the door filled the silence, Joe let the full extent of the elastic band loose and bright yellow light hit every crevice of the room. He blinked as his eyes adjusted to the brightness. Lexi was on her bed in the corner of the room, curled into a ball with her arms wrapped tightly around her legs. She peeked her eyes over her arms and a wave of relief washed over her face. Her whole body seemed to relax as she recognised Joe standing before her.

"You scared the crap out of me! What the hell happened to you?" She gasped.

Joe looked from Lexi's wide eyes to her shaking hands still wrapped around her knees. He was about to ask her who she had been expecting to walk through her door? Who could stir up such fear in a girl who tried so hard to portray that she was fearless? But the moment his eyes landed on the walls; the thought flew from his mind. He had never seen Lexi's room before now. Glancing around, he could see that there was no doubt this place belonged to Lexi. It was a small space, with a single bed in the far corner. A dressing table stood against the wall opposite, but it didn't have a mirror, mirrors were not allowed, at least, not the glass ones. A small pile of Teddies littered the end of the bed. The bed covers, curtains and various blankets that had been scattered around the room were all in different shades of pinks and yellows, bright and summery, just like Lexi. And a tall chest of draws stood against one wall next to a locked window. Every inch of the walls had been covered with photos and drawings. Bits and pieces she had collected over the years, which were all of some importance to her, were pinned to the pictures scattered around the room. Most of the pictures were Rainey and Lexi together. A few were Rainey with her parents, and Joe too. There were even a few of Jason mixed in with the others. But the ones that caught Joe's attention most were the pictures of Lexi with her parents. Her mum looked just like an older version of Lexi, beautiful pale skin with the same short and messy blonde hair, and deep blue eyes the colour of the ocean. Her dad was a tall man with sandy blonde hair and brown eyes. In every picture they were smiling and looking at one another with nothing but affection in their eyes. Even now, with Rainey at home in labour, risking her life while Joe was trying to break Lexi out of a psychiatric hospital, he felt sad as he looked at these pictures. It hurt him to know that even though Lexi's mother had lived through the birth of her only daughter, a daughter who had grown up knowing and loving both of her parents, she would never see them again. They had been taken from her by the burden that was her life. Her life as a Gifted. Joe knew the reason for his distraction was because of his own mother. The pain of knowing she had died for him during his birth was so real, even after eighteen years he still felt a wave of guilt wash through him at the thought of how she had given her life for his. Joe had never known his mother. He had never even seen a picture of her. All he knew of her was her name. Attempting to imagine how Lexi must feel was unbearable. Not only did she have to live with the fact that both of her parents had died in a terrible accident, but knowing that she had been the cause of that accident. Knowing that she had killed the two people she loved unconditionally, just as they loved her. Joe had never known his father either. He had been brought up in orphanages, passed from one to the next, like an unwanted pet. If it was painful for him to think of his parents, then he couldn't imagine how Lexi must have felt carrying the guilt of what had happened on her shoulders.

Joe pulled his eyes away from the photos on the walls and turned his attention back to Lexi. She watched him carefully with her head cocked to one side.

"Rainey needs you. We have to leave, now."

Getting out had been easy with Jerry there to help. They didn't run into any more nurses and the one nurse who did know what they intended to do hadn't alerted anyone else to their plans. Lexi told him her name was Anya and that she knew all about her, Rainey and Joe.

She tried to explain how Anya had told her that she was also a Gifted, but she had very limited power. Lexi shrugged her shoulders when Joe asked what Anya could do. She continued to share pieces of information she had learned about her Gifted nurse, but Joe couldn't focus on her words and the road at the speed he was driving. The way Lexi's words came tumbling out of her mouth, Joe wondered if she was trying to distract herself from what they were about to face. He turned his full attention to the road ahead of him, blocking out anything else she had to say.

The race home didn't take long with the roads just as deserted as they had been on the way there, and by the time they reached the driveway it was 3:25am.

"I'm surprised we actually made it here and you didn't crash us into a ditch on the way back!" Lexi shouted at Joe.

"Do you want to help or not?" Joe snapped back.

Lexi had made it clear that she was less than impressed with Joe's driving technique through her occasional gasp and tut from the seat next to him, but she knew why it had been necessary and had refrained from scalded him until they arrived safely in the village. If he had driven any slower, she probably would have complained that he wasn't going fast enough.

They sped along the driveway and Joe slammed on the breaks, forcing the car to skid to a halt, dragging the tyres across the gravel. They opened the doors, ready to jump out, and were greeted with the sounds of Rainey's screams. Lexi turned to Joe with a look of horror that was equally mirrored on his own. They didn't wait to hear another scream. They didn't even bother to close the car's doors behind them. Bursting through the front door of the house and heading straight for the stairs, Joe and Lexi hurled themselves towards the top floor bathroom. On the second set of stairs Lexi slipped and banged her shin on the step.

"Oh, my God," she whispered, as she realised what it was that had made her lose her footing.

The trail of blood was still wet on the floor where Joe had carried Rainey to the bathroom. Lexi forced her eyes away from the blood and pushed herself further up the steps. She followed Joe into the bathroom, where he had left Rainey with Aimee and William.

Rainey hadn't moved from her spot on the floor. There was no colour remaining in her skin. Her breathing was shallow as she clung on to both of her parents' hands, her nails digging into their skin, creating small, crescent shaped cuts. The blood was everywhere, but what scared Joe the most was the look on Aimee's face. She no longer showed her determination like she had before he had left. Just like everything else in the room, Aimee was now covered in blood. It was smeared across her forehead where she had tried to wipe away her sweat with the back of her hand. It was streaked up her arms in smudged lines, soaked into her clothes, tangled in her hair. Her eyes looked swollen and red and there were tear stains clearly visible on her cheeks. She looked defeated and desperate and exhausted.

William stared silently at his daughter with watery eyes, his hands shook so much that Joe wasn't sure if Rainey was holding his hand for support or if it was the other way around. William looked up at Joe with pleading eyes. Joe dropped to his knees beside Rainey and leant forward to kiss her on her forehead.

"I am so sorry," he told her, his throat tightening around his words.

Rainey opened her eyes to search for him and the corners of her mouth pulled into a weak smile.

"You're here." She whispered, in a hoarse voice.

"She keeps trying to push, but it's just making things worse. She won't stop. She won't listen to us," William said, the panic clear in his voice.

"Oh, Rainey." Lexi sobbed from the doorway.

Aimee's head snapped towards her. She stretched out her hand and wrapped her fingers around Lexi's wrist, yanking her to the ground beside her.

"You need to do it now!" Aimee demanded frantically. "We can't wait any longer. She's dying!"

Lexi looked at Rainey's face as tears began to pour down her own. She took two long, deep breaths to prepare herself.

"I love you." She mouthed to Rainey, and she closed her eyes.

The air in the room seemed to become tighter around them, making it uncomfortable and difficult to breath. Aimee and William watched as the colour of Lexi's skin began to change, grow fuller somehow, her cheeks flushing pink. As Joe observed Lexi drain the little remaining life from Rainey, he saw her grip loosen around her parents' hands and watched as the last hint of colour drained from her skin. Her breathing became rhythmic for a few short moments, then slowed. Joe looked down at his hand, resting on Rainey's stomach. What should have been a solid grey heart between his thumb and index finger was fading to a barely visible line. He watched in horror as it disappeared altogether. Aimee followed Joe's gaze to the perfectly untouched skin on his hand. She ran her thumb over it and let out a small sob. She gripped his hand in her own and they watched in silence.

They watched as Rainey died.

8

Rainey

"I love you, too" Rainey had tried to say back, but it had barely been a whisper.

She wanted to reassure Lexi, let her know that everything would be ok. If it didn't work and Lexi took Rainey's life in the process, then she had to know that Rainey would never have blamed her. Rainey didn't want to die, but if that was the price that had to be paid for her baby to live, then she would pay it. She needed Lexi to understand that that was what she wanted. She needed her to know that she was doing the right thing.

She watched as Lexi closed her eyes, then she turned her head towards Joe. She held both of her parents' hands in her own and gave them a squeeze with the little strength she had left in her fingers. She had no energy left to talk, she could not form the words in her head, force her lips to move. Instead, she looked into Joe's warm brown eyes with her grey-blue gaze and told him everything that she needed to through them. That she loved him, more than anything she had ever thought possible. That every moment she had spent with him would stay with them both forever. That she would never forget the times when he had saved her from herself. That he had perfected every part of her life. And that if she ever knew what perfect was, then Joe would be it.

Everything around her started to feel tight, as though the air was squeezing her, preventing her lungs from filling, and a wave of panic jolted through her. She could no longer hold the heaviness of her eyelids as they slowly closed, blocking out the brightness of the room around her. She listened to the panic surrounding her, listened to the voices of the people she loved as they began to sound muffled, as though her head had been submerged in water, until they grew quieter, and eventually stopped. And when they stopped, so did the pain.

She was floating in a great stretch of nothingness. That was how she felt. No sound. No sight. No senses at all. She couldn't feel the pain anymore and she was so relieved, so grateful that it had stopped. Her entire body felt light, as though there was no gravity to pull her down to the ground. Or maybe she had no body to pull her down. She knew that this was it, she knew that she was dying, but she couldn't find the part of her that knew that it was wrong. The part of her that would fight. The part of her that knew everything she loved and everything she had ever wanted was waiting for her to just open her eyes. The only part of her she could find was the part that felt at peace. At peace with what she had had before she came to this strange place. Yes, she was dying. But she was dying knowing that she had loved and been loved. This was the part of her that said, *this is easier than the pain.*

> She was floating.
> Floating away.

9

Rainey

Rainey's eyelids fluttered. It was bright in this place. Too bright for her to open her eyes right away. She lay very still, trying to grasp her surroundings. There was no noise, it was silent except for the sound of her even breaths, in and out, in and out. She could feel that she was lying on something soft and comfortable, she clenched and unclenched her fists around the thick, cushioned cover that lay over her legs and waist. Slowly, she stretched out each limb and listened as her joints popped and complained.

She could see pictures behind her eyelids, memories maybe, but she couldn't piece them together. A bathroom floor, towels, blood, tears. And screaming, lots and lots of screaming. Her head ached with the pressure of gluing the memories together and she felt her stomach lurch uncomfortably as she went dizzy.

Everything ached, every single part of her body ached. She lay there for a while longer listening to the silence ringing in her ears and watching new pieces of the memory flicker behind her eyelids, until the silence was abruptly broken. By a small cry.

Rainey's eyes snapped open, and her hands automatically clutched at her stomach, but there was nothing there. Her round, swollen tummy had been replaced by a much flatter, softer stretch of flesh. She yanked her body upright, ignoring the stabs of pain puncturing through her insides, and looked frantically around the room. It was her room, exactly the same as it had always been. It was too bright where the sun shone through the window and reflected from the white furniture and bedding, causing her eyes to sting. Rainey looked down at the bed she was sitting in and gasped, as more memories flooded back to her of the last time she had been in this bed. She ripped back the covers and grabbed at the sheets with her hand where her blood had gathered in a pool before... before... before what? How long had she been in this bed?

Every flicker of memory began to fit into place. The blood she had woken up in, the pain that had followed and should have led to a birth. Instinctively her hands clung to her stomach again and she looked down. An empty, hollow feeling tore through her body, gripping at her heart. She struggled to breathe as fear threatened to take control of her. What had happened to her baby?

Rainey's feet touched the floor, and she leaned forward slowly, resting her weight on to them. With a final push from the bed, she wobbled on to her feet. The pain made her squeeze her eyes shut tightly, and she tried to breathe through it as she clung to the edge of the bed for support. Her insides felt as though they were trying to push their way out through the bottom of her body, and she clutched at her stomach in an attempt to relieve some of the pressure.

Taking small and careful steps, Rainey made her way to the bedroom door, but soon realised she would not make it any further without first relieving her bladder, so she turned and headed to the bathroom as quickly as she could.

She yelped when she realised using the toilet intensified the pain. She washed her hands and left the bathroom, not bothering to look at herself in the mirror. As quickly as her fragile body would allow, she headed for the bedroom door.

The cream carpet which usually covered the landing outside Rainey's bedroom had disappeared and been replaced with a brilliant white one which felt soft and warm under Rainey's bare feet. She guessed that it must have been replaced when Aimee couldn't get the blood out, but how had the carpet been removed and replaced so quickly? How long had she slept for?

She had to take the steps one at a time and hobble down them, using the banister to support her weight. The pressure that continued to push down from inside her was so intense, every shuffle was agony. Aimee waited at the bottom of the stairs with a huge, beaming smile on her face.

"Hey, baby," she said, as she helped Rainey down the last few steps.

Aimee gently wrapped her arms around Rainey and stroked the back of her head with one hand. "How are you feeling?"

"Uncomfortable?" Rainey offered.

"We were so worried. You were so close to, well, you know. But there was nothing we could..." Aimee trailed off, hugging Rainey again, just as softly as the first time.

"Mum, where's Joe?"

"He's just through there," she smiled, as she let go of Rainey and took a step back to look at her properly. "With the baby," she added with an excited smile.

Rainey's breath caught in her throat. Joe was just a few feet away. With the baby. With her baby.

She set off walking, holding on to her mother for support, irritated by how slowly her body insisted on moving. She rounded the corner into the living room and stopped when her eyes landed on Joe, standing in the middle of the large plush rug, with a tiny bundle of white wrapped in his arms. Joe stepped closer to her, his smile bright and affectionate and his eyes showing his relief at seeing Rainey awake and on her feet. Rainey looked from Joe to the tiny bundle in his arms and she reached out without so much as thinking. She could feel a deep longing to hold her child push her body forward, and she took the final few steps, closing the distance between them. Joe placed the bundle in Rainey's arms, and she felt the warmth and weight through the soft blanket. Balancing the baby in one arm against her chest, she delicately brushed the fingers of her free hand against the baby's cheek. She looked down at the perfectly round cheeks, the tiny dimple in the chin, the full head of dark brown hair, the long eyelashes and the tiny nose with its perfectly round tiny nostrils which flared slightly with every breath. Rainey was speechless.

There were no words to describe the sensation spreading outwards from her heart to the rest of her body. A warm and intense feeling that told her there would never be anything else in the world that mattered as much as this tiny baby she held in her arms. There was nothing she wouldn't do, no length she wouldn't go to, to protect and care for this child. The rush of complete and unconditional love she felt was overwhelming, almost unbearable.

"He's beautiful," she whispered.

"Actually, *she's* beautiful." Joe grinned back.

"She's beautiful." Rainey corrected herself, a smile spreading across her face.

As she examined every curve and line of her daughter's tiny face, the baby stirred and stretched her arms out above her head, opening her mouth into a yawn. Then her eyes fluttered open and Rainey caught a glimpse of her breathtakingly bright blue eyes. Rainey looked up at Joe's proud face and grinned.

"Now I know what perfect is," she said.

"So, do we have a name then?" Aimee called from the back of the room where she had been observing with William.

"Lily," Rainey looked at Joe as she said it. "Lily Rose Emily Denyer."

Joe was silent for a moment, and Rainey started to think that maybe he didn't like it.

"Thank you," he said.

Rainey had not told him she had been planning to use his mother's name as part of their child's name, had she been a girl. She knew he had a deep love and respect for his mother that he would never truly understand. Maybe, now that he could see his own child, after a birth which had almost cost Rainey her life, he would understand that his mother's death had not been his fault.

"It suits her." William said, stepping forward and placing a hand on his daughter's shoulder. "Well done, Rainey, she really is absolutely perfect. She has barely cried at all since she was born. The complete opposite of what you were like."

Rainey smiled in return.

"How long have I been asleep?" She asked, lifting her eyebrows in Aimee's direction.

"Almost four full days. I'm just thankful Lexi and Joe made it to us when they did. You almost gave me a heart attack, Rainey." She tried her best to put her serious face on, but she couldn't hold it there for long. "I have never been so terrified in all my life, I thought we were going to lose you."

"I don't really remember everything. Is Lexi ok? I know how hard it must have been for her."

"She's fine. She told us she hadn't used her powers since the death of her parents. She struggled at first, but she did what we needed her to do." Aimee replied.

She went on to explain that Lexi had taken what little life Rainey had left so that her body would stop trying to naturally force the baby out. With her muscles dead and lifeless it had been easier for Aimee to work and get Lily out safely with the use of a few tools she had managed to collect during her preparations for the birth. They had had to work quickly to get Lily out before she had grown too weak to survive after Rainey's heart had stopped beating, they knew that Joe would not have been able to bring them both back from the dead.

Lily had been strong, as all newborn Gifted usually were, with the odd exception of course, and so she had survived when her mother had not, with the help of Aimee. But Lily's strength also meant that Rainey's body had been badly damaged. After Lily had been born as naturally as possible, Joe had then used his gift to help his new daughter to regain some of her energy while Aimee and William had started working on bringing Rainey back to life. Once her heart had started beating again, Joe healed Rainey as best as he could, stopping the bleeding just enough for her body to begin the long job of repairing itself. Healing her in this way had taken its toll on him, leaving him exhausted for two full days while he regained his own strength.

While William and Joe told Rainey their own sides of the story, and Rainey struggled to tear her eyes away from her perfect baby girl, Aimee cooked everyone dinner, and an hour later they were sitting around the dining table, ready to eat stuffed chicken breasts with green vegetables and potatoes. The only food Rainey had digested in the past four days had been in liquid form and fed to her through a plastic tube. She was famished by the time dinner was ready, although she only managed to eat a few small mouthfuls.

Lily lay silently in a white Moses basket close to Rainey. When she began to stir, Aimee rushed off to the kitchen and reappeared a few moments later with a freshly made bottle.

Rainey and Joe took Lily upstairs and into their bedroom to feed her and to find some quiet time to be alone together. Rainey couldn't take her eyes away from Lily. She watched her as she drank her bottle, exploring all the different features of her face, stroking her tiny hands and fiddling with strands of her dark hair.

"I am so proud of you," Joe said quietly to Rainey.

"And I am so proud of you. I'm sorry for what I put you through."

Joe sat down on the bed next to Rainey and leaned back against the headboard. He pulled Rainey against his chest with Lily still in her arms, drinking the last of her bottle.

"What was it like?" Joe said with a pained look.

"What was what like?" She said, absentmindedly.

"You know what, Rainey."

Rainey thought for a moment before she could answer.

"Painful. I don't really remember much. I just remember screaming a lot, seeing you one minute and then the next you were gone. More screaming. My parents were really upset, and then you and Lexi arrived. And everything went dark. I felt very light, almost like I was floating. I couldn't hear of feel anything anymore."

Joe swallowed the lump in his throat.

"I'm sorry I couldn't heal you better. I used everything I had just to get the bleeding to stop. It was awful, Rainey. We all thought you'd gone. I thought I'd lost you." His voice was just a whisper by the end.

Rainey stretched up and placed a hand on the side of Joe's face, pulling his lips down to meet hers. They kissed softly and then Joe held Rainey as they watched Lily spit out her bottle in her sleep. They didn't know how long they lay there, silently watching their daughter's chest rise and fall. But eventually, the sun began to disappear over the horizon, and they drifted off to sleep in each other's arms.

10

Rainey

The days and nights all seemed to blur into one long, never ending day for Rainey and Joe. Wake up. Feed Lily. Change Lily. Feed selves. Try to sleep. Wake up. Feed Lily. Change Lily. Feed selves. Play with Lily. Watch Lily sleep. Feed Lily. Change Lily. Every spare moment they somehow managed to find was spent taking speedy showers, squeezing in a few extra minutes of sleep or searching for clean clothes that miraculously hadn't been covered in baby sick. Rainey still had a lot of healing left to do, since she had decided not to allow Joe to do any more of her healing for her. She couldn't stand to see Joe so drained of life as he recovered. It wasn't easy for him to heal others, and from what Aimee had told her, Joe had looked pretty close to death himself after his efforts to keep Rainey alive. But despite the dull ache Rainey felt with every step her body took, despite all of the crying and sleepless nights, they had never been happier. Aimee had returned to her normal self, singing songs around the house that nobody had ever heard of while she cooked and cleaned and fussed over everybody. William had returned to work, which meant he was hidden away in his office almost all of the time, only appearing to share meals with his family or go for the occasional walk through the garden with Aimee.

Rainey hadn't seen Lexi since the day Lily was born, and she hadn't properly introduced the two yet either. It had been decided for her that she should not leave the house until she was healed, or at least a little more healed. Her efforts to talk with Lexi on the phone had been largely unsuccessful on account of Lily and her impressive ability to scream. Joe had had to visit Lexi alone while Rainey stayed inside the house, much to her annoyance.

Gradually, everything settled into a routine which became their new normal, and after almost three full weeks of being cooped up inside, Rainey finally decided enough was enough. She felt strong enough to take Lily for a walk through the garden and into the meadow, although Aimee had taken some convincing.

Though it was only the end of March, the garden was warm with the early afternoon sun. The spring air felt refreshing on her skin as Rainey stepped outside the house for the first time in weeks. Rainey had been looking forward to the day when she could finally introduce Lily to Aimee's pièce de résistance.

Joe wiped away the last of the morning dew from the old iron bench with his sleeve before Rainey slowly lowered herself on to the cool metal. Lily rested peacefully in Rainey's arms, wrapped in her cosiest cotton blanket. A cool breeze brushed playfully at the loose strands of hair from Rainey's ponytail, and she closed her eyes, enjoying the sounds and smells of Spring in Aimee's garden. When she opened her eyes again, she saw Joe smiling was beside her.

"What are you smiling at?" She asked as she nudged him playfully with her shoulder.

"Am I not allowed to smile while I watch my two favourite girls enjoying their first trip outside together?"

Rainey grinned and rested her head on his shoulder.

"What are you thinking about?" He asked her after a few minutes.

"I'm thinking about all of the memories we will create for her, here in this garden. I want her to love it here as much as we have."

"She will love it here. Just as long as she doesn't try to pick any of your mum's flowers."

Rainey laughed at the thought of how her mother might struggle to cope once Lily was old enough to terrorise her way around the garden. Aimee had grown very protective of her landscaping since Rainey had been young enough to enjoy picking flowers and jumping in muddy puddles on the lawn.

"She seemed to cope just fine when I destroyed half of the house with blood stains." Rainey smiled.

"You were unconscious. Believe me, she did not cope well."

Rainey lifted her head from Joe's shoulder and smirked in his direction. As much as she wished she had been present during the first ninety-six hours of her daughter's existence, she did not regret missing out on what she was sure would have been a mentally exhausting few days of listening to Aimee fret about carpet colours and bleaching blood stains from the woodwork.

They fell into a comfortable silence as the sun slowly moved across the crisp March sky.

"Joe," Rainey said after a few moments. "I don't want her to grow up not knowing who he was."

Joe took her hand in his and gave it a light squeeze.

"She won't have to. We'll tell her everything there was to know about him." He replied, leaning closer to kiss her on the cheek.

They stayed on the bench until Lily woke from her sleep. And then Rainey told her daughter all about her Uncle Jason. They walked under the curtains of the willow tree and Rainey showed Lily where all of the lilies and roses would soon begin to return, the very same flowers for which she had been named. They walked through the meadow, under the cherry blossoms in their full bloom. And all the while, Rainey told Lily stories of all of their adventures. She told her of the Christmases they had spent together, her father and Jason wearing matching pyjamas. She told her about their walks through the countryside and the times Jason had taken her to the park and gotten stuck in the swings. The books they enjoyed to share and the games they had played. Rainey knew that Lily couldn't possibly understand anything she told her, but she told her all the same. And she would continue to tell her of the memories they had created together, in the hope that they would live on, and a little piece of Jason would live on too.

By the time Rainey's body ached too much to stay on her feet any longer, the fresh air had worked its magic on Lily, and she fell into a deep sleep against Rainey's chest.

"Do you think you might be ready to go and see Lexi today?" Joe asked Rainey, as she dressed a still sleeping Lily in a frilly white dress with tiny white socks to match. "If we set off soon, we should be able to make it in time for the evening visit."

"I don't know, Joe." She replied, busying herself with gently squeezing one of Lily's feet into the fiddly garments.

"Are you not feeling up to it yet?"

"No, it's not that. I feel almost fine now. It's just that... well..."

"What is it?" Joe asked.

"I've spoken to her on the phone plenty of times since that night, but I haven't seen her face to face yet. I just feel so guilty about what we made her do. She hasn't used her powers since her parents... you know. It must have been really hard for her."

"Yeah, it was hard for her. But she did it because she wanted to help you, not because we made her. She loves you, Rainey. And she would sooner use every power known to the world than let anything happen to you. You have nothing to feel guilty about."

"I feel horrible that she *had* to do it though, you know?" Rainey took in a deep breath and exhaled loudly, trying her best to blow away the disappointment she felt for herself.

"I saw her room when I picked her up that night from the hospital."

"Really?" Rainey replied, curious.

"It made me feel bad, that we have all of this," Joe raised his hands, gesturing to their house and the family they shared it with. "While she sits in there, every night, on her own, looking at the same four walls. Which, by the way, are covered in pictures of her parents and you and me. And your parents."

"I've never seen her room. She's never let me in there."

"I didn't think you two had any secrets."

Rainey shrugged her shoulders.

"I have asked her so many times to move in here. There's more than enough room for her and mum would love to be able to spoil her. She complains that she hates it in that place but then she refuses to leave it. And when I ask her why, she just says, *'it's easier this way'*, whatever that's supposed to mean."

"But she tells you that she hates it?" Joe asked. "That's strange," he added as Rainey nodded her head.

"Well, you can be my guest if you want to ask her for yourself."

Rainey thought she had succeeded in ending the conversation but after a moment of silence Joe shuffled uncomfortably on his feet.

"When I walked into her room that night, she was scared of me."

"You probably just made her jump, bursting into her room when she wasn't expecting you."

"No, Rainey. She knew I was there. She must have. I had taken all of the light from the entire floor. And then I was talking to the nurse right outside her door, plenty loud enough for her to hear me. I wasn't exactly quiet when I walked into her room either. But when I first saw her, she was curled up on her bed in the corner of her room. She looked terrified." Joe recalled to Rainey.

"But why would she be scared of you?"

"I have no idea."

Lily let out a small cry, interrupting their conversation.

"Come on, if you go and feed Lily now then I can make some bottles up and get her bag ready. We should make it in time." Rainey said as she lifted Lily on to her chest and carefully stood up.

They headed down to the kitchen where they could prepare Lily's bottles. While Joe settled into a chair with Lily in his arms, guzzling down her milk as though she hadn't been fed in days, Rainey packed a bag full of nappies, wipes, spare clothes, bottles of milk and water, and spares of anything else they were likely to need during their first official outing. She was trying to be as organised as her mother would no doubt be, but she knew that the moment they left the driveway, she would suddenly remember something crucial she had forgotten. While she packed, she thought about Lexi and pictured the scene Joe had walked in to. She couldn't imagine why Lexi would feel the need to be afraid of anyone, especially anyone in the hospital. As much as Lexi hated to use any real power, Rainey was pretty confident she would be able to do it if she was threatened. And God help the person who would choose to pick a fight with Lexi. Rainey's pondering was cut short by a huge belch from behind her, signalling that Lily had finished her bottle. Rainey smiled to herself at the sound.

"Well, aren't we a greedy girl today?" She cooed at Lily. "Are you ready?" She added to Joe.

"I'll go get the car seat."

Rainey took Lily in her arms while Joe disappeared from the room to collect the seat. When he returned, Rainey secured Lily into it and covered her legs with a cotton blanket. They collected their supplies, which probably could have sustained an entire nursery of babies for the day, and headed for the front door.

"Oh, wait." Rainey said, putting Lily's bag on the floor. "I forgot something."

She rushed up the stairs as quickly as she dared, she still had the feeling that all of her insides might drop out of her for every second she stood upright. On her bedside table stood a silver picture frame. She snatched it up and carefully removed the photo, before heading back down the stairs to where Joe and Lily waited for her at the front door.

"What's that?" Joe asked, spotting the photo in Rainey's hand.

"A photo," she grinned.

"Well, thank you, captain obvious," he rolled his eyes. "What's *on* the photo?"

Rainey held it up so he could see the picture clearly. It was a photo William had taken of Rainey, Joe and Lily and had printed and framed for them. Rainey and Joe beamed out of the picture and Lily's bright blue eyes seemed to dance with electricity as they reflected the flash from the camera.

"She can add it to her collection," Rainey shrugged.

They left the house and headed for the garage but as they opened the garage doors, they soon realised the car Rainey and Joe usually shared was nowhere to be seen. Instead, Aimee's car waited for them, dazzling white and mean looking, in the middle of the garage with a note stuffed under the windshield wiper. Joe pulled it out and read it aloud:

> I borrowed your car because you both drive like idiots!
> My car is safer, especially when Lily is with you.
> You know where the keys are.
> Mum xx

Joe raised his eyebrows at Rainey.

"Does she take our car every time she leaves the house just incase we decide to go out one day?"

"Probably," Rainey said, rolling her eyes.

Joe carefully placed the car seat, with Lily in it, on to the ground next to Rainey's feet, where it rocked gently back and forth.

"Guess I'll go find the keys then." Joe said as he walked back out of the garage.

He returned a moment later with the keys and he unlocked the doors and waited while Rainey strapped Lily's seat into the back. Then he opened the door for Rainey to climb in before getting in himself.

The drive to Lexi's hospital didn't take long, but Joe had to bite his tongue for the majority of the journey while Rainey nagged him about the speed he was driving, the way he took the corners, how he wasn't looking long enough for other traffic before he pulled on to roads and how he used his mirrors.

"Is this how it's going to be every time we take Lily out in the car? Because if it is, then you can drive," Joe called over the noise of the car doors slamming once they had climbed out.

"Oh, shut up. It's not my fault you drive like a maniac."

Rainey stuck her tongue out at Joe as she unstrapped Lily from her car seat.

"My driving is one hell of a lot better than your driving," Joe said under his breath.

"I'm sorry, I didn't quite catch that?" Rainey said with a sweet smile.

"Nothing, beautiful." He grinned back.

With Lily wrapped safely in Rainey's arms, Joe closed the car door for her, and they headed across the car park and to the large oak doors. Joe pressed the buzzer as Rainey scanned the windows with her eyes and shuffled uncomfortably on her feet.

"Are you ready to meet your Auntie Lexi, baby girl?"

"I called ahead to let her know we were coming." Joe said, resting his hand reassuringly in the arch of Rainey's back.

Rainey chewed on her lip nervously and silently prayed that Lexi would be as happy to see her and she knew she would be to see Lexi.

11

Rainey

Lexi's beaming smile could be seen from across the sitting room. She leapt from her seat the moment she spotted Rainey with a now wide-awake Lily clung to her chest.

"It's about time you got here! What took you so long?" She yelled excitedly, above the noise of the other patients.

Rainey laughed as she made her way through the tables and chairs, her mind instantly at ease. She had missed Lexi a lot in the last few weeks, but she hadn't realised just how much she had missed her until she laid eyes on her cheery face. As she passed, Rainey smiled at a curious Mrs. Noland who had paused her knitting to see what Rainey had hidden between the blanket and her chest. As soon as Rainey was close enough, Lexi could not contain her excitement and she wrapped her arms around Rainey, careful not to upset Lily.

"It took us a while to get past Jerry. I never knew he liked babies so much." Rainey said.

"And there's my gorgeous little niece. Hello. I'm your Aunty Lexi. Yes, I am. Lesson number one, I am the coolest person you'll ever meet." Lexi rambled on in baby talk.

"Lex, what have I told you about talking to my girlfriend's chest like that?" Joe joked.

Lexi scowled at him.

"I see it didn't take long for the dad jokes to kick in."

Joe winked at Lexi playfully and took Lily from Rainey so that she could have a long overdue catch up over a hot cup of tea. They talked about everything that had happened in the last few weeks, but most of the talk came from Rainey, because, as it turned out, the hospital had been just as dull as it always had been. Rainey was thoroughly enjoying the horrified look on Lexi's face as she described in detail the consistency of a dirty nappy. After a little while, their conversation was interrupted by a quiet cough behind them. They turned to see Anya standing there with a heartfelt smile warming the features of her face. As Joe turned in his chair to face her, Anya's eyes fell on to Lily, asleep in his arms, and her face changed. At first, her eyes began to melt in what Rainey would expect as a totally normal reaction to seeing a new-born baby. But then her smile dropped suddenly, and her mouth became a sharp line, transforming her face into a hard mask.

"I just came over to see if you would like another drink?" She asked, her voice cold.

She carefully avoided Rainey's eyes as she spoke, looking only at Lexi. Rainey glanced quickly at Joe from the corner of her eye to find that his face mirrored the same bewildered look as she was sure hers displayed.

"No thanks, Anya. We're fine," Lexi paused, before adding, "Hey, are you ok? You look strange."

"I... I'm fine. I just... I... I must get back. To the office." Anya stuttered.

She looked down at Lily once more before turning and striding quickly across the room and back into the office.

"That was weird," Joe said, looking to Lexi for an answer, who shrugged her shoulders back at him. "I'm going to change Lily before we leave, I won't be long."

He picked up the bag full of Lily's things, throwing it over his shoulder, and headed for the toilets.

"Um, Joe?" Lexi shouted after him.

"Yeah?"

"Those toilets don't exactly have the best baby changing facilities. You could use my room instead? Just don't leave me any hidden gifts! This place stinks enough as it is."

Joe laughed and manoeuvred his way around the tables, heading for the corridor and Lexi's room. When Joe was safely out of earshot, Rainey made a grab for Lexi's hand and pulled her closer.

"Joe told me about what happened when he came to get you that night."

"And...?" Lexi pressed, creases appearing on her forehead as she raised one eyebrow in question.

"He told me that you seemed really worried about something when he got here."

"Well, yeah. You could have died that night."

"That's not what I'm talking about."

"Oh. Then, I don't know what you mean."

She looked down at her knees before curling them up into her chest and wrapping her arms around them.

"Lexi, if you are worried about something, or maybe someone, you would tell me? I mean, you know that I can help if there is ever anything wrong, right?"

"Wrong, right? That kind of contradicts itself, Ray Ray." Lexi laughed, but her smile never reached her eyes.

"Stop trying to change the subject. Joe said that you looked really scared when he walked into your room that night. And don't tell me it was him who scared you, because I know that's a lie. If you don't feel safe here then you need to tell me, so that I can do something. You can still come and live with us, there's loads of room. You would have your own room and the guest bathroom upstairs would pretty much be yours for the taking."

"Yeah, right. I would rather face anything this nut house has to throw at me than fight Aimee for that bathroom. Besides, I don't think I'll ever set foot in there again after what happened the last time I was in there. I'm fine here, Rainey. Honestly."

Rainey didn't like the way Lexi could not look away from her knees as she spoke. She opened her mouth to argue but stopped abruptly when she spotted Joe making his way back to them from across the room.

He passed the office where Anya now stood, leaning against the doorframe. Rainey watched her closely as her face changed again at the sight of Lily. Only this time, she looked pained. Like something was deeply upsetting her. Joe risked a quick glance at her from the corner of his eye as he passed.

"What the hell is wrong with her today?" Rainey asked Lexi.

"I have no idea. She's been acting strange for a couple of weeks now. Maybe she's hormonal or something," Lexi shrugged and stood from her seat.

Rainey looked back at Anya just in time to catch her dabbing at the corners of her eyes with her sleeve. When her gaze met Rainey's, she quickly looked away again and walked back into the office, closing the door behind her. Rainey had never seen her act so oddly before, but then, she had never brought a baby into the hospital with her before either. Maybe Anya couldn't have a baby. Maybe she wanted one to call her own but didn't want to take the risk Rainey had as a Gifted. Or maybe she was already pregnant and worried about what was to come. Rainey had known for some time that Anya was a Gifted. She had been quite open in telling them how disappointed she had once been with her underwhelming power while they indulged in one of her famous cups of tea. Although she had never actually shared what that power might be. Rainey had assumed she was embarrassed to share her abilities and she had not pushed for her to tell the girls. In fact, she had completely forgotten about it until now. She shook her head and turned her attention back to Joe as he joined them again, but she could not clear the feeling from her mind that something wasn't right about Anya today.

As they gathered their things together and prepared to leave the hospital, Rainey pulled the photo from Lily's bag where she had been keeping it safe. She passed it over to Lexi and watched as a soft smile pulled at her lips.

"I thought you could add it to your collection," Rainey said.

Lexi took hold of the photo in one hand and offered her other to Rainey.

"Come on. I'll show you."

She led Rainey to her room, leaving Joe and Lily to wait in the sitting room. They walked along the wide corridor hand in hand, and Rainey looked at the picture frames hanging on the walls between each doorway. Every picture had either a flower or a rainbow on it, some were paintings and others photos. They were all warm, cheerful pictures, but they seemed out of place, hanging on a wall with dirty, cream coloured paint peeling around them. When they reached room seventy-four, they stopped.

"I didn't let you in here before because this feels like the only part of my life I have any control over. I just wanted something that I could keep to myself and not have to share with anyone. But I guess I've wanted to show you this for a while now, I just never really found the right time." She nodded towards the door, signalling for Rainey to go ahead.

Rainey stepped through the door and looked around at the almost completely covered walls. Photos, posters, pictures and doodles on scraps of paper were pinned everywhere. There were odd bits and bobs which had been attached with coloured tacks, and scraps of paper with scribbles or bits of writing on. Rainey walked to the closest wall and saw herself looking back at her from the photos. Some of them were just her on her own, others were her and Lexi together. Rainey could see a few from their school days when they were younger, with their old school friends surrounding them, before Aimee had pulled Rainey out to home-school her after the other kids had grown suspicious of how different she was. She looked at a pair of cinema tickets pinned to the wall; they had been saved from the first time they had been allowed to visit on their own without their parents. There was a drawing of an animal they had created on a very rainy and dull day back when they were thirteen, a poem someone had scribbled down on to a creased scrap of lined paper, the lyrics to a song on another shred of paper. A gold locket hung down across a picture of Lexi's mother, Rainey carefully opened the clasp to see Lexi's mother in one side and her father in the other.

Rainey moved slowly along the walls, tracing her fingers gently across them until her eyes landed on a photo she had not expected to see, making her legs freeze in place. A lump formed in her throat, and she swallowed to try and clear it. She brushed her index finger carefully across the photo, where her Uncle Jason stared back at her. He wasn't smiling in the photo, but he was happy. It must have been taken shortly before his death, because he looked just as Rainey remembered him the last time she had seen him. His dark brown hair was messy and sticking out in different directions, his chin covered in stubble and his piercing blue eyes shone in the photo just as they in real life.

She took a step back and looked more intently at the pictures. Jason was everywhere. Smiling, laughing, pulling faces. In one picture he and Aimee were covered in custard and cream, after chasing each other through the kitchen. Rainey remembered that day, she had been just eight years old. Jason had really wanted to eat some trifle, so Aimee had made one, which they had then had a food fight with when Jason realised that he didn't really like trifle. Aimee had later told her that the exact same thing had happened when they were teenagers and that he hadn't liked trifle then either.

Rainey didn't realise that she was smiling straight away. This was the first time since his death that Rainey had seen any pictures of her Uncle Jason. In the weeks after his death, when Aimee had locked herself away from the world, William had gathered everything up from the house that could possibly remind her of him and locked them away in his office. The house had seemed empty for such a long time after that. Aimee still couldn't look at any of it without risking a breakdown, so they had stayed hidden away in boxes. Or so Rainey had thought. But apparently, Lexi had gotten her hands on some of them.

Rainey wiped a stray tear from her face. Lexi appeared behind her and wrapped her arms around her middle. They stood that way for a few minutes, silently comforting each other. Rainey wasn't the only person to have lost someone that she had loved, Lexi had lost twice as much as she had. But loss was loss, and no matter who it was that had been taken from their lives, they both grieved and longed for what was gone.

Lexi stepped away from Rainey and pulled open one of her drawers. She rummaged around for a moment before fishing out a small plastic tub filled with drawing pins.

"We're not actually allowed these, but it's not like I've ever broken any other rules. Recently." She grinned as she unscrewed the lid of the tub and pulled out a bright pink coloured pin.

After hiding the tub back in her drawer, Lexi looked for a perfect place to pin the new photo Rainey had given her. She held it up in a few places first to evaluate how it looked, and eventually settled on a spot between a photo of her parents and a drawing of Lexi's old home, next to her bed. She pushed the pin into the wall with her thumb and stepped back to admire it, just as Joe appeared in the doorway with Lily, her chin covered in the milk she had just spit up. Rainey rolled her eyes lovingly.

"Sorry to interrupt but are you ready to leave yet? That nurse is really creeping me out. She's been staring at me for the last ten minutes."

Joe passed Lily to Rainey, and she pulled a wet wipe from the front pocket of the changing bag to clean Lily's chin. Taking one last look around the room, Rainey smiled at the happy faces staring back at her from the photos.

"Thank you. For showing me this." She said to Lexi as she left the room.

Rainey turned back to Lexi from the corridor and gave her what she hoped was a telling look.

"Think about what I said, Lexi. I mean it. Love you."

"Love you, too." Lexi smiled back, and she closed the door.

Visiting Lexi and seeing the photos in her room had made Rainey realise that she did not want the house to be empty of her Uncle Jason anymore. When they returned home from the hospital, Rainey retrieved the boxes full of the remaining photos and memorabilia, and over the next few days she began to scatter them around the house. It took Aimee all of one hour to notice one of her photo frames housed a different picture. Rainey walked into the room to find her mother frozen in front of the frame. Rainey watched her carefully, waiting for her to move again, but she couldn't. She just stood there, staring at Jason for almost fifteen minutes before Rainey started to think that maybe she had made a mistake in trying to bring Jason back into their lives. Maybe she should have checked with her mother first, or at least asked for her father's opinion on the matter. It was her father in the end who distracted Aimee by standing between her and the photo, after his attempts to speak to her had been unsuccessful. When he finally managed to break her stare and snap her out of the trance she was in, she suddenly became aware that she was not alone. She swallowed loudly like she was trying to swallow the grief she had kept hidden for so long, before taking one last look at Jason, the only true friend she had ever really had, and running from the room.

After spending hours locked in her bedroom, Aimee eventually materialised and asked for the picture to be left where it was. From them on, her reactions to finding Jason's belongings around the house grew less dramatic with every item. After a few weeks of acknowledging every one of the little pieces of his life that Rainey had managed to retrieve, she began to smile at the fond memories the items brought her. By the time Lily had turned six months old, every one of Jason's items had been returned to their original places in their home.

Rainey's routine visits to Lexi had returned to their normal daily schedule. Lily visited with her most days, and she managed to light up the sitting room with her beautiful blue eyes and gleeful giggles. Her dark hair had grown thick and long, and Rainey tried to tie it up into little bunches as often as she could, but Lily loved to pull them out at any given opportunity.

William regularly tried to detect any sign of power Lily might begin to display, but her gift had not declared itself yet, and though William had tried countless times with not a single hint or clue to guide him, he was adamant that she would be strong. Although she had shown no powers herself, Lily loved nothing more than to watch the others use their own. Rainey would play with the water during Lily's bath times, moving it around, shaping it, making miniature waves and whirlpools, and Lily would giggle hysterically. Joe made tiny balls of light for Lily to look at, but she grew frustrated when she could not grasp them in her little fingers. Lily's favourite game was to watch her mother sketch patterns on to her own skin. When Lily tried to catch them under her fingers, they would disappear, reappearing on another part of her body. And when Lily touched Rainey, she could sketch on to her skin too.

Lily would giggle for hours when they played, stopping only to be fed or to nap. And when she did sleep, she would be in the arms of her parents or her grandparents. Sometimes she would be placed in her cot, where Rainey enjoyed to watch her sleep. She could sit for hours and gently run the tips of her fingers along the soft pink skin of Lily's cheeks. She would smile to herself every time Lily raised her eyebrows as she dreamt or suckled or smiled, or when her fingers and toes twitched as though she was trying to catch something. She wished that she could see into Lily's dreams. Whatever Lily dreamt of was bound to be better than the recurring nightmares haunting Rainey's sleep. As much as Rainey loved to see her Uncle Jason in her dreams, she could not bear to relive that moment of devastation when she awoke to find that it was not real. Jason was still gone.

The dream that visited her most frequently was Jason's death, when Rainey had run to his home to find nothing but ash and smoke in its place. Every time she woke from the dream, she could feel her joints aching from the run, her lungs gasping for air and the smell of smoke burning her nose and throat. But the last few dreams had been different. Rainey had noticed something, something that she had never seen before, despite having the same dream almost every night for the past few months. What looked like a small wooden box, singed around the edges, had appeared, lying a few feet from the rubble of the house in a patch of scorched grass. But every time she moved closer and tried to approach it, it began to fade, and eventually disappear. Then there were the strange markings on the ground. They looked like burn marks, which would not have been so strange considering the house had just burned to the ground, but the marks were nowhere near the house. They stretched out around the remains of the smoking rubble, not touching anything or each other. At first, they looked like sooty footprints, smudged into the grass. The next night they appeared, Rainey realised they had been burned into the ground. But what terrified Rainey the most was the time she had woken in the night after Aimee had slapped her hard in the face. Joe had tried to wake Rainey by shaking her and had even resorted to throwing a glass of water over her when she had started to scream, but it had not worked. Aimee heard the screams and rushed into their bedroom.

The dream had been mostly the same. It was her birthday. They were heading back to the car when Aimee's phone rang. Rainey ran to the house, she screamed and cried for Jason, she lost control for a fraction of a second, making purple clouds roll across the sky, and then the lightening began. That was normally when she woke. But this time, she did not. She stopped screaming and concentrated on regaining her control. Turning away from the remains of Jason's house, she squeezed her eyes tightly shut and tried to steady her breathing. When she had calmed herself down a little, she opened her eyes, expecting to see the tall Leylandii bushes towering over the lawn. But instead, her eyes settled on a figure standing to the side of the bushes. Rainey took in a startled gasp when she realised the figure was watching her with a sickening smile spread across his face. He was short and balding with pale skin. His eyes shone an electric blue, just like hers, and she understood then that he was a Gifted. He wore a black suit and a crisp white shirt, and his red tie seemed to be the only stab of colour standing out sharply in the monochrome dream.

When he realised Rainey no longer had her eyes closed, his own eyes widened. Spinning on the spot, he took one last look at Rainey before bolting from the garden. Rainey tried to spring forward, but it was just a dream, and she could not move, her legs felt disconnected from the rest of her body. She willed herself to move, but by the time she reached the edge of the Leylandiis, the man was gone. He hadn't been particularly fast and there was nowhere for him to hide in the open fields outside of Jason's garden. He had simply disappeared. It was his smile that had frightened Rainey the most. It was not a kind smile, or a sympathetic smile. It was a cruel and spiteful grin that sent shivers through her body.

Rainey could not understand why her mind was adding these details to her memories. She scanned through what had happened that day but found there was little she could remember after years of repressing the memory of that day. If he had really been there, why would he be smiling at her? And if he had not been there, why was he appearing now?

She hadn't bothered to tell anybody about the new developments in her dreams. Joe, Aimee and William all shared worried glances every time the word 'dream' was mentioned, like they all thought she was one more sleep away from needing a permanent room next to Lexi's.

Rainey pulled the curtains closed in the nursery to block out the sunlight pouring through the window. She tip-toed over to Lily, sleeping in her cot. Rainey tucked the blanket around her tiny body and gently brushed her fingers over Lily's cheek. Then she crept from the room, careful not to make any noise.

Aimee had decided to spend most of the day in the garden, cutting down the flowers which had begun to wilt in time for autumn. Joe and William had spent almost every day of the last two months up in the office. The restaurants had been busy, and an opportunity for a new project had arisen to keep Aimee entertained. William saw it as a perfect time to throw Joe in at the deep end, under his watchful eye. This left Rainey to her own devices, but since she had already visited Lexi earlier in the day and cleaned anything she could find which Aimee hadn't already cleaned herself, there was nothing left for Rainey to do but try to have a lie down while Lily slept.

Flopping down on the edge of the bed, she opened the drawer on her bedside table and pulled out the notebook she kept in there. Lately, Rainey had been keeping notes of any changes making an appearance in her dreams. She was not stupid enough to write down the details of each dream, just in case anyone came across it and thought she was going mad. But she had written a date for each dream, and next to it a few words to remind her of what had happened. She scanned across the last few entries with her index finger.

12th August – Wooden box
13th August – Man
15th August – Wooden box again
19th August – Marks in grass
20th August – Marks in grass, burned
28th August – Wooden box, closer
29th August – Man
30th August – Man
1st September – Man

She flipped through the blank pages, stopping on the last page. Staring down at the clean, white paper, she pictured the stranger from her dream, standing in the middle of the page. Rainey reached back into the drawer and pulled out a sharpened pencil. She began to draw the man. Drawing was something Rainey had always been good at but not something she really enjoyed. She liked everything to be perfect, a quality she assumed had inherited from her mother, and drawing was an activity that she could criticise herself on for hours. Roughly, she sketched the image of the man and shaded in his dark suit. When she had finished, she tilted her head to one side and examined her work. She pulled a sky-blue pencil from her drawer and coloured his eyes. It was almost exactly how he had looked in her dream. But seeing his face drawn on to the paper did not help her to place him, she was still just as confused as she had been that first night.

"What's that?" Aimee said, appearing behind Rainey at the other side of the bed.

"Jesus! You scared the crap out of me!"

"Hey, language young lady,"

"Knock next time, yeah?" Rainey snapped the notebook closed and threw it back into her drawer with the pencils. "It's just a doodle, I was bored."

Aimee looked at her suspiciously.

"Hmm, well, if you're so bored, do you think you could put dinner on for me? The garden is taking me a little longer that I had planned, and I don't really want to stop until it's finished."

Rainey looked her mother up and down and laughed. Aimee was covered from head to toe in dirt from the garden. She had taken her shoes off before coming into the house and her socks were the only item to have survived the soil. It was even smudged across her face.

"You look so hot right now, Mum."

"Ah, sarcasm. The lowest form of wit."

"And the highest form of intelligence." Rainey added.

"When did you get such a smart mouth?" Aimee frowned.

"I learnt from the best." Rainey stuck her tongue out at her mother.

"You sure did." Aimee smiled, letting her off for snapping at her.

Jumping up from the bed, she made her way out of her bedroom and down to the kitchen to start dinner, with Aimee following close behind. When they reached the kitchen, Aimee began taking ingredients from the fridge and giving Rainey detailed instructions on how to make lasagne. Rainey had made lasagne a hundred times before, but Aimee liked things to be done her way. By the time it was ready to be put in the oven, Rainey could hear Lily babbling away to herself and banging on the bars of her cot from upstairs. She placed the lasagne dish on the worktop by the oven and decided it would have wait there for a few minutes while saw to Lily. She crossed William and Joe on the stairs who were finally coming down from the office for the first time that day.

"Hey Dad, can you go and put the lasagne in, it's just next to the oven. I'll be back in a sec." Rainey called out as she passed them.

She took the stairs two at a time as she rushed to Lily's nursery. She edged her head around the door to find Lily sitting up in her cot and happily chewing on one of her many rattle toys. When she saw Rainey, she grinned and banged the toy playfully against the bars again. Rainey smiled from the doorway and held her hands out to her as she walked toward the cot. She carefully lifted her out and gave her a kiss on one of her round cheeks. Then she headed back down the stairs to make sure William had done as she had asked. As she approached the kitchen, she could hear hushed voices. Holding Lily tight in her arms, Rainey leant towards the edge of the wall. She could see Aimee and William standing around the table, looking at something lying flat on its surface. She recognised it as her notebook. Why would they have her notebook? What was so interesting about it to make them steal it from her drawer and have secret discussions over the kitchen table?

"What do you think this means?" William asked Aimee.

"You know what it means, Will. If this is what she's seeing now, then who's to say he wasn't there all along? He's responsible for this. First Lexi's family and now this."

Aimee's hands were balled into fists at her sides, and she spoke so fiercely that Rainey couldn't tell if she was very angry or very scared.

"But what good could it possibly have done for them?" William replied.

"He was training her. He taught her things that they didn't want her to know. This isn't fair! She can't help what she is, what she does." Aimee looked up into William's eyes. "We're not safe here anymore. I think it's time we moved on."

Rainey listened intently while Lily kicked her legs in Rainey's arms and began to gurgle.

"Shhh, Lily." Rainey whispered softly, and she bounced Lily on her hip until she stopped.

She ran through Aimee's words in her head. Were they talking about her? *She couldn't help what she was or what she did?* What had she done? She leaned back against the wall while Lily started to chew on the sleeve of her top.

"Aimee, we can't just up and leave. They will always find where we are. It doesn't matter where we go." William said gently.

"But we can't stay here either. If they come, they could hurt her. We can't take that risk. Especially not now."

"Who is to say she hasn't been dreaming about him all along? We don't know for sure that this has only just started. Aimee, be reasonable. If she has been dreaming about him for months, years even, and he hasn't come for her yet, then maybe he's not coming at all."

Aimee's head snapped up from the notebook on the table. Her face distorted with anger.

"Is this something you are willing to risk? If he comes here and sees Lily, then he will not stop until he gets what he wants. You know that as well as I do. Need I remind you what happened the last time he got his dirty little hands on a child he wanted."

William stumbled back a step as though Aimee's words had punched him in the gut.

"We don't have time to make up theories. We need to leave, and we need to do it as soon as possible. I won't let him get his hands on my daughter. Not like he did with me."

"Our daughter." William said, holding his wife's gaze for a long second before looking back to the notebook on the table.

He ran his fingers across the page. Aimee nodded her head.

"You're right. I'm sorry." She said, taking his hand in hers.

"You're sure that it has to be now?" William asked.

Aimee looked at him pleadingly.

"Look at what she's drawn, Will. That's him. That's Smith. I would recognise him anywhere, even in a sketch." Aimee looked down at the picture in disgust as she spoke. "It definitely has to be now."

Smith? Who the hell was Smith? Rainey was struggling to take it all in. She had never heard of anyone called Smith before. And surely if he was a big enough threat that they would have to leave their home the moment his name was mentioned, then her parents would have warned her about him. Her mother's words repeated in her head.

If he comes here and sees Lily, then he will not stop until he gets what he wants. I won't let him get his hands on my daughter. Not like he did with me.

What was happening?

"She won't leave without an explanation. And what about Lexi?" William said, looking at Aimee with sadness pulling at the corners of his eyes.

"Lexi will do as she is told as long as she knows she is protecting

Rainey. We'll just have to figure out a story for the both of them. We don't have any other choice. If we tell her the truth, she'll take it into her own hands and who knows what she could end up doing. We just need to play it safe, like we always have." Aimee looked around the room and ran her hand slowly over the kitchen worktops. "I am really going to miss this place."

Rainey heard footsteps coming from the stairs and she ducked behind one of the sofas, cradling Lily against her. She knew it could only be Joe, but she didn't want him to know she had been listening in on her parents' conversation. He walked straight past her and around the corner into the kitchen. Rainey jumped up again and tiptoed back to the wall, leaning around it carefully, just in time to see Joe inhale deeply and nod at both of her parents, who both nodded back with morbid expressions. Then he picked up the notebook from the table and headed back towards Rainey. She just managed to catch a glimpse of the drawing she had made earlier, before rushing out of the room as quickly and as quietly as she could. She headed straight for Lily's nursery, hoping she would not be spotted sneaking away. Then she lowered herself down on to the floor, resting Lily in her lap, still chewing happily on her sleeve. She began to rock them both forwards and back, while the scene she had just overheard repeated itself in her head.

12

Rainey

Rainey wasn't sure how long she stayed on the nursery floor. Lily remained patient as ever on her lap as she rocked them both. The conversation she had eavesdropped on didn't make any sense to her. She played it over and over in her head. She could not remember ever hearing of anyone named Smith before, and she had definitely never met anyone who looked like the man in her dream, or at least, nobody she could remember. But their reaction to her drawing confirmed that he was real.

Why were her parents so worried? Why did Joe appear to be in on their secret?

Rainey startled as Joe stepped into the room.

"What are you doing in here?"

He looked at Rainey on the floor with a quizzical expression.

"Lily woke up. We were just playing and I must have lost track of time."

"Ok. Dinners ready. Are you coming?"

"Actually, would you mind taking Lily for a while? I'm not feeling too well."

She felt perfectly well, but she needed some time to think before facing her parents. She was finding it a little difficult just looking at Joe while knowing he was keeping some sort of secret from her.

"Yeah, sure. What's wrong?" Joe asked as he lifted Lily from Rainey's lap.

"I don't know. I just feel kind of tired. I think I'll go get some fresh air."

She smiled up at Joe, but he wasn't buying it.

"Is everything ok?"

"Yes, fine. Like I said, I'm just tired."

Joe looked down at her for a moment as he tried to read her face. Whatever he saw there must have convinced him because he leant down again, this time to kiss Rainey on the forehead, before turning and leaving the room.

"Take as long as you need." He smiled at her from the doorway.

Rainey listened to him talking nonsense to Lily all the way down the stairs. As soon as she thought it was safe to do so, she pushed herself up from the floor. She grabbed a pair of sandals from her room as she passed and quietly, she crept down the stairs and through the front door. The heat of the afternoon hit her as she stepped outside, and the summer breeze caused her long, colourful dress to wrap around her legs and fan out behind her. Rainey wandered down the driveway and out into the meadow, picking a shaded spot under a tree to sit down. She ran her hands through her hair as she inhaled a deep breath of warm air to help clear her head.

It hurt her to know that her family were lying to her, but she knew there must be a reason for it. She closed her eyes and listened to the wind, rustling the leaves in the tree above her. Rainey played back the conversation she had overheard in her head. Starting at the beginning, she tried to think of an explanation for each of the things her parents had said.

Firstly, she had no idea why the dream she had had almost every night had suddenly begun to change and now housed a man who she had never seen before. And the fact that her family seemed to know who this man was, confused her even more.

Secondly, she could not imagine what Lexi's family would have to do with any of it. Rainey's parents rarely spoke of Lexi's mother and father after they had died. How could they make the assumption that they were involved in whatever this was?

He was training her. He taught her things that they didn't want her to know. That could only be Jason, he was the only one who had ever tried to train her properly, besides her mother. Nobody else had stayed with them for long enough to teach her everything they knew. Her Uncle Jason was obviously a big part of this. But what had they meant when they had said, *'He's responsible for this?'* Responsible for what? Did they mean Jason's death? It was no secret to her parents that she dreamt about it almost every night now, but how could they know that the man from her drawing had appeared during that particular dream? What else was there to be responsible for?

A cold shiver spread through Rainey's body. She had so many

questions and not a single answer to any of them. She pushed the heels of her hands into her temples and squeezed her eyes shut tightly. Her head hurt with the strain of trying to figure out what was going on. She fell back into the tall grass and tried to relax her body as she searched her mind for any hints or clues which might help her to understand.

And the next thing she knew, she was opening her eyes, back in her own bed. Pulling herself upright, she blinked until her eyes focussed. Joe was lying in bed next to her, watching her with a smile on his face, with Lily fast asleep on his bare chest.

"What time is it?" She asked, rubbing her eyes.

"Ten thirty. You slept right through the night. I knew you were tired, but not *fall asleep in the middle of a field* tired." He laughed.

Rainey smirked back at him, trying to hide her embarrassment.

"Me neither," she said.

The morning sped by in a blur. Rainey couldn't think about anything else but the secret conversation between her parents, and it bothered her that not Aimee, William nor Joe were acting any differently today. Rainey had kept an eye open for any more suspicious whispering, secretive eye contact or even the occasional look of guilt on their faces, but they had not done anything of the sort. By the time it reached Lexi's visiting hours, Rainey felt so mentally drained she thought it might be best if she went for a lie down. This time in her bed and not in the middle of a field.

"You're really not coming?" Joe said, when she told him.

It would be the first time in months Rainey had missed a visit to see her best friend.

"Honestly, I'm fine. I just feel tired again. Maybe I'm coming down with something."

"Ok. I won't be long. Your mum asked if she could take Lily into the garden for a while this afternoon anyway, so I'll make it a quick visit. I hope that creepy nurse, Anya, isn't there today. She gets weirder every time we go."

He pulled Rainey into his arms and kissed her along her jawline.

"Hmm, maybe you should hurry back," she smiled.

He gave her one last cheeky grin before leaving through the front door. Rainey made her way through the house, gave her mother a quick explanation as to why she had not gone with Joe to see Lexi, and kissed Lily a few times while she giggled, before heading up to her bed.

It was mid-afternoon and her room was bright with the last of the summer sunlight streaming through the window, but she didn't mind. She opened the window wide, and the light summer breeze swept across her face. She could smell the few remaining lilies and roses from the garden, the smell helped to sooth her. Lying down on top of the quilt, she slipped her shoes off the side of the bed and wrapped her cardigan tightly around herself.

Her eyes began to droop immediately, and as she fell into unconsciousness, she hoped she would have a dreamless sleep.

The first thought to hit Rainey when she woke was how comfortable and content she felt. She smiled to herself as she realised she had not had to suffer through any dreams. Keeping her eyes closed, she stretched out her arms and groaned as she moved for what felt like the first time in a while. Her eyes fluttered open and she looked at the alarm clock on her bedside table, she had slept for less than two hours, but she felt fully refreshed and much more relaxed. She pulled herself upright and started to swing her legs over the edge of the bed when a rush of panic froze her body in place as a chilling scream sounded from somewhere within the house. Rainey strained her ears and listened. Everything was silent. So silent that her ears began to ring irritably. It had been Aimee's scream; Rainey knew it had been Aimee's. But Rainey had never heard her scream like that before. It wasn't playful, like she did when her and William pretended to fight, or over dramatic, like she had found a spider in the bathtub. It wasn't the same scream that repeated night after night in her dreams.

She listened for any indication of what could have made her mother produce such a noise. And then she heard her talk. Not talk, plead.

"No, please. He will be good, we both will. Please, just don't hurt him. Please! No!"

Rainey's body tensed as she heard a muffled thud, closely followed by a gurgling, choking sound. Her mind reeled and panic gripped her insides as she tried to grasp what was happening downstairs. She could hear somebody gasping for air. Aimee cried out again, an agonising shriek, which cut into Rainey like a knife to her heart. As quietly as she could, Rainey placed both of her feet on the floor and began to tiptoe across the room. There was no need to find a weapon, her powers were greater than any weapon. She moved as quickly as she could towards the door, careful not to make a sound as a hundred thoughts rushed through her mind at once. It had to be a Gifted. The only way anyone would be able to inflict pain on her family would be if that pain came from a Gifted. It couldn't be a normal human. They had always been so careful to remain as normal as possible around others, with the odd exception of Jerry. Nobody but the Gifted knew what they were. There was no reason for anyone to come for them. If it was a normal human, Aimee and William would have knocked them down before they were even on the driveway. It had to be a Gifted, or more than one of them.

From inside Rainey's head a voice screamed to her. *Lily, Lily, Lily.* Rainey's fear rushed away from her and was replaced immediately with anger. Pure, heated anger as the thought of anyone trying to bring harm to her baby occurred to her.

The bedroom door was ajar, just as she had left it, and she peered through the gap. She couldn't see anything unusual on the landing, so she silently crept out of her bedroom. The carpet on the landing cushioned her footsteps, helping her to move quicker towards the stairs, stopping a few feet away from the first step. She could see two patches on the carpet halfway down the stairs. They looked as though they had been flattened down by something heavy, like a piece of furniture had recently been moved. She watched, bewildered, as the flattened carpet moved up a step, and then another. Rainey took a step back, realising too late that the flattened carpet was two boot prints, moving closer to her. She turned to run but she was thrown backwards by a force so hard it knocked the wind straight from her lungs. Her body flew through the air and slammed into the wall, a large crack forming in the plaster. Gasping for breath, she struggled to find her feet as she tried to push herself upright. Her head whirled and her eyes could not seem to find anything to focus on as she searched the empty space in front of her for her attacker. She spotted the two flattened patches on the carpet again. But they were no longer at the stairs. They lingered a few feet in front of her, and she watched as they edged closer still. Rainey held one hand out in front of her and a blue-white bolt flew from the palm of her hand. It hit with an ear-splitting crack followed by wail. She watched as the electricity coated the shape of a man, standing directly in front of her. She could see him now as his invisibility flickered. He was tall and muscular, wearing dark jeans and a black leather jacket. An angry, red scar ran down the length of his cheek, over his jaw and down his neck, disappearing under the collar of his black t-shirt. He looked down at Rainey and smirked. A shiver ran down her spine. The man stepped closer again as Rainey fired bolts from both hands. Each bolt only made his smirk grow larger. Rainey didn't understand. The bolts should have been enough to kill him, but here he stood, glaring down at her.

He took one final step towards her, and wrapped his fingers around her throat.

13

Rainey

Rainey had no choice but to grasp hold of the fingers clinging to her throat. Her legs flailed as she tried to shake herself free of his grip, but he was too strong. She tried desperately to gasp some air into her lungs, but each time she did, the man's hold tightened. It felt as though her neck might snap at any moment and black spots began to cloud her vision.

Abruptly, the man let go, dropping Rainey to the floor. Her head hit the ground with a crunch and pain flashed through the left side of her face. She opened her mouth to scream but instead she gasped and spluttered, filling her aching lungs with oxygen.

"Well, well. If it isn't the girl herself."

He crouched down next to Rainey and pulled her chin up roughly, taking a better look at her face.

"I'd heard you were a good looking one. Even with all this blood, I wouldn't say no. Just like your mother."

He laughed to himself as Rainey looked beneath her to where her face had landed on the floor. Fresh blood was smeared into it, strikingly dark on the white fabric. She could feel it running down her face and falling from her chin in droplets.

"Hmm, maybe I'll just take you home for myself. Wouldn't want a pretty little thing like you to go to waste."

He licked his lips as his eyes looked greedily up and down Rainey's body. He leaned in closer to her face. Rainey tensed, waiting for him to make his next move. He squeezed her chin between his thumb and index finger and leant further forward until Rainey could feel his breath against her skin.

"Get the fuck off me." She said, her voice calm and even despite her heart racing in her chest.

She jerked her head away at the exact same moment she swung her arm back and slammed her fist forward with as much strength as she could muster. Her fist connected with the man's eyebrow. She tried to scramble backwards while he was momentarily distracted, but she could not move fast enough. She did not have time to react to his next blow, she could only watch as the man's hand appeared out of nowhere and slapped her hard across the face. It had not been any normal slap. Rainey's body was thrown across the landing floor, her head snapping sideways. She blinked rapidly to clear her vision, but everything looker blurred. The whole side of her face felt as though it had been dipped in hot oil. She tried to lift her head, only to find a puddle of red forming beneath her.

"Enough," said a new voice from the stairs. "Take the girl to the others. And try not to make any more mess."

Rainey opened her eyes to see a woman's figure standing at the top of the stairs. She couldn't make out a face but there was something about the way she stood which seemed familiar to her. Before she had time to process what she was seeing, the woman turned and walked back down the stairs.

"And we were having so much fun." He moaned. "I like it when they have a bit of fight in them."

He placed a hand on the back of Rainey's head. Taking a handful of her hair, he yanked her to her feet and Rainey yelped in pain. He didn't let go of her hair as he pushed her ahead of him and guided her roughly towards the stairs. Rainey was careful to make sure she didn't slip, she knew if she did, he would pull the hair from her scalp. Her face throbbed, and she could feel the skin around her cheekbone tightening as it swelled.

The attacker led Rainey through the hallway and into the living room, where a group of people were gathered in the centre of the room. They all wore black, some in suits and others in jeans and shirts. Rainey's eyes darted around the room, searching each person's face for one that she recognised. The group turned in unison to face her, before they began to spread out, revealing Aimee standing behind them and William kneeling on the floor. Aimee's eyes widened in horror as she saw her bloodied and bruised daughter being dragged into the room by her hair.

"You bastards!" She screamed.

The people around her all sniggered at her outburst. Rainey looked into her mother's eyes and bit down hard on the inside of her cheek to stop herself from crying. She would not cry for them. She would not let these people humiliate her in that way. She couldn't bring herself to look at her father, kneeling at Aimee's feet. There was something so demeaning about his posture. But even without looking at him, she could tell that he was staring at her, his mouth hanging open.

Rainey was quick to realise that Joe was not with the group, and she prayed that he hadn't come home from visiting Lexi yet. Whoever these people were, this was not a social visit. And whatever they planned to do next probably was not going to be pleasant. She could not bear to think of Joe being harmed by these people. But where was Lily?

As she searched the room again, her eyes landed on a woman standing at the back of the group. She wore a black skirt suit with pointed shoes, her hair pulled back tightly into a bun on the top of her head. It was the woman from the stairs. She turned her head slowly to face Rainey, keeping her back to the group, and Rainey's heart dropped into her stomach when she saw the woman's face for the first time.

"Anya," Rainey said, recognising the nurse from Lexi's hospital.

"I am so sorry, Rainey. But this is something that I just have to do."

She didn't look at Rainey as she spoke. Slowly, she turned herself around, revealing the sleeping baby in her arms.

"No. Get away from her!" Rainey shouted across the room.

"I'm afraid I can't do that, Rainey." Anya's voice sounded almost mechanical, she spoke in a calm, eery way that terrified Rainey.

"Get away from her, now!" Rainey screamed.

"Or what, pretty girl?" The man from behind her laughed as he let go of her hair and she fell to her knees on the floor.

Rainey could feel the anger building up inside of her. If she wasn't careful, anything she did to Anya would also harm Lily. Instead, she focused on the group in front of her. She tried to lift one of her hands, hanging limply at her side, but she could not move it. Not just her arm, she could not move at all. Her entire body was frozen to the spot. She strained against the invisible force, but still, she could not move any part of her body. Realising that there was nothing she could do physically, she attempted to control the air around her, conjure up a bolt, anything. But nothing she tried would work.

What was wrong with her? Was she paralysed? Or was somebody doing this to her? Her eyes darted from one face to the next and she screamed in frustration. A woman from the very centre of the group laughed in return.

"Annoying, isn't it?" She said.

Rainey glared at her. She could not have been taller than five feet, with mousy blonde hair and a permanent sneer on her lips. She held one hand out in Rainey's direction and the other towards Rainey's parents.

"Go fuck yourself," Rainey seethed.

"Don't fight them, Rainey." Aimee said, defeated.

Rainey's eyes flickered towards her parents. Only now, did she realise the awkward positions they were in. William was not kneeling on the floor, he was hunched forward, with both of his hands held behind his lower back. Aimee stood with her legs slightly apart and her arms held a few inches out from her sides. Her hands were balled into fists with her wrists pointing outwards towards where Rainey knelt, a few feet in front of her. They were paralysed too. Only William's eyes moved as he tried to look up at his wife with a stare that said *don't let her see you quit*.

"What is this, Anya?" Rainey called out.

Anya smiled and moved a few careful steps closer before she answered.

"Your parents have tried to protect you from a lot of things in your life, Rainey. As have your friends. Not that you would know anything of what they have done for you. What they have sacrificed."

The corner of Anya's mouth turned up into a smile, as though she had shared a private joke. She continued to speak in a quiet voice as she moved gradually closer to Rainey, and Rainey had to strain her ears to hear what she was saying.

"But there are some things that you cannot be protected from. Things you have to face for yourself. Like giving birth for example." She brushed the tips of her fingers across Lily's cheek.

Rainey tried to thrash against her restraints, but it was no use.

"What are you talking about?"

"Oh, Rainey. You were never allowed to have a child," Anya laughed, cruelly. "Your mother was never allowed to have a child. There was too much fear over what could be created. And though at first you seemed not to hold any powers of your own, you developed into, well, this." She waved a hand over Rainey. "Heaven only knows what you have created, and we must make rules in order to protect ourselves, as well as others. Especially, when it comes to a situation such as this."

"We both know the real reason you're here." Aimee spat.

"Oh, do we? Well, please enlighten your dear daughter and tell her the real reason we are all here then, will you?" Anya snapped sarcastically.

"Is that a hint of jealousy?" Aimee smirked. "Smith never did move on, did he?"

Anya pursed her lips angrily.

"I'll take that as a yes, then." Aimee said.

"What business is it of yours, Aimee?" Anya said, slowly pacing the floor. "I had no idea you were so interested in Smith's current love life. He will be pleased to hear."

Aimee's eyes landed on William for a split second before she looked away again. But it was enough for Anya to see.

"I wonder if your new lover here lives up to his predecessor?"

Rainey looked at her father's face. She saw him grinding his teeth tightly together.

"What's wrong William? Don't you have anything to say about your wife's past?" Anya teased.

William's eyes flickered up to Rainey and Anya's head snapped back in her direction.

"Oh." She laughed cruelly. "She doesn't know."

Anya took another step closer to Rainey. She crouched down by her side, close enough to whisper into her ear.

"You better keep that mouth shut." Aimee warned.

"Did you ever wonder where your mother and father met, Rainey? Or how she seems to know so much about delivering Gifted babies?"

Rainey could see Lily's sleeping face from the corner of her eye, just inches from reach. But she was still paralysed, she could not even turn her head towards her baby. A tear ran down her face and dropped to the floor.

"I swear, Anya. If you don't stop this right now, I'll make sure you regret it!" Aimee growled.

"Your perfect mother started out as nothing more than a mistress, Rainey. A common whore. She betrayed the one man who cared for her more than anything and ran away with him," Anya pointed a manicured finger at William. "She ran away and proved how much of a little tramp she really was."

Rainey fixed her eyes on a drop of blood on her mother's white rug and bit down on her cheek again. How dare Anya speak of her mother like that? A wave of red-hot anger flashed through her and she began to tremble. Anya looked anxious and she turned to look at the smallest member of the group.

"You are supposed to have control of her. Why is she moving?" She said in a sharp tone.

"I didn't realise how strong she is," the woman replied. "I've got her."

She appeared to be struggling with the effort of keeping Rainey's body still.

"So, I'm right then?" Aimee shouted up, distracting Anya. "That is the real reason you're here. I bet it tears you up inside, knowing that you'll never be as good as the teenager he once owned."

Anya's eyes flashed dangerously.

"I am here because you can't follow the rules, Aimee. You knew what the consequences were when it came to children. Not only did you create your own piece in a war, but you allowed her to do the same." Anya replied, as calmly as she could manage.

Rainey was trying to piece together what she was hearing, but none of it was making any sense. She couldn't concentrate on what Anya was telling her while all of her concentration was focused on how to get Lily out of her arms and into her own.

"Lily doesn't have any powers," Rainey tried.

"Oh? So, the birth went well, did it? No complications? I am sure your suite on the delivery ward was just lovely with all that spare money that your parents seem to have. And was your midwife just a delight?" Anya's voice oozed with sarcasm and a few of the strangers in the group looked to Aimee and laughed at the mention of a midwife.

"There were no complications." Rainey replied.

"Liar! I stuck around in that dump of a hospital for months to keep an eye on you, and you think I didn't notice how you just stopped visiting? I was there the night your little boyfriend showed up covered in your blood. Do not try feeding that crap to me."

Anya began to walk around the outside of the group, the heels of her shoes tapping loudly on the wooden floor. She laughed to herself, thoroughly enjoying what she was putting Rainey and her family through.

"Rules are rules though, sweetheart. And I'm afraid there's nothing any of us can do about that. Poor Lily here will be the one who suffers for your mistakes. But your parents can suffer for their own."

Anya gave one solid nod of her head to the group gathered around

Aimee and William. Two of the larger men moved towards Rainey's parents and took their positions behind each of them. Aimee's hands were pulled back behind her, and the man held them tightly with his own. William was pulled to his feet and forced into the same position as Aimee. They looked to each other, and Rainey saw words pass silently between them as they spoke to each other through their eyes.

"We will go with you," William said quietly as he continued to stare into Aimee's eyes.

Rainey opened her mouth to argue but she didn't know what to say. What did he mean they would go with them? Go with them where? Where they not here to kill them all?

"You say that like it's optional," Anya said.

"We will go with you, now. We won't fight. We will do everything you wish," William continued.

"Damn right you will." Someone from the group called, laughing.

"On the condition that our daughter goes unharmed."

William still hadn't looked away from Aimee as he spoke. Their eyes remaining fixed on one another. Rainey watched the pain work its way into every detail of their faces as they agreed to be taken away from their daughter.

"I can't promise that." The brute behind Rainey said.

Anya held a hand up to silence him, and he grunted in return. She considered William's words for a moment as she continued to circle the group.

"If you come with us, in return for the safety of your daughter, of course, then you cannot contact her again. Is that clear?"

Aimee nodded her head.

"You will be signing yourselves over to us, to do with as we see fit."

"Well, at least Smith will be happy to see his long-lost girlfriend again." The brute spat.

William's head jolted up at his words, no longer under the power of the small woman's invisible force. He yanked his hands free and spun around so quickly that the man who had been holding on to him could not get out of his way in time. William swung back his arm and punched the man under his chin. There was a loud snap as the man's jaw slammed shut and he fell backwards into the small woman behind him, distracting her long enough to free Rainey. Two more men raced forward and jumped on top of William, trying to grab his flailing arms. Aimee struggled against the man who held her arms tightly behind her back, but she could not fight her way free. Rainey leapt forward, throwing her hands out in front of her. Two large bolts arched their way out of her palms, striking both of the men now wrestling with her father. The bolts hit them with a loud crack, and they shook with the electricity surging through their bodies as William scrambled away from them. Rainey withdrew the bolts, knowing they had been successful as she watched both men crumple to the ground, their eyes in the back of their heads. William wasted no time. He turned to the nearest person and began throwing punches again. But Rainey had not been fast enough to pull herself away. She felt a familiar hand take hold of her long hair and yank her back to him. She knew her bolts had little effect on him, so she focused instead on using her energy to push herself away from him. She could not risk using any of her other powers with Lily so close to her. But it was no use, the man was too strong. He had his hand back around her throat within seconds. He pulled her body against his own so that her back was pushed against his chest, and with his free hand he pulled a knife from his belt. He pushed it painfully into the flesh on Rainey's throat, and she could feel the sharp edge begin to slice into her skin.

"Stop. Right now. Or she's dead." He bellowed across the room.

William and Aimee froze instantly, and two more men grabbed William as the tiny woman recovered enough to place her hold on them again. Both of her parents watched, wide eyed, as the knife sank slowly into Rainey's flesh and a single drop of blood ran down the blade and over the man's fingers.

"Honestly, you should know better." Anya said quietly, as she passed Lily to another woman who stood at the back of the group.

Lily didn't even stir in her sleep. Anya moved to stand in front of Aimee. She lifted her hand into the air and swung it forward, slapping Aimee hard around the face. Rainey could not move, with the knife pressing further into her skin. She watched as her mother's head snapped to the side and remained there for a moment. She showed no emotion as she slowly turned her head back to look at Anya's smirking face, just inches from her own, and she spat a mouthful of blood and saliva directly into it. Anya didn't so much as flinch, she simply took a tissue from her pocket, wiped her face and tensed her jaw.

"You are going to regret that."

"I highly doubt it." Aimee said.

Rainey had to admire her mother's bravery and pride. She had never witnessed Aimee under true threat before, but she had the feeling that this was not the first time Aimee had had to experience it.

She wondered again what her mother had dealt with in her youth.

"I think it's time to leave. If either of you try anything again, then she dies." Anya looked from William and back to Aimee as she pointed at their daughter as another drop of blood spilled over the blade and down her chest.

Anya nodded to the group, and they began to move towards the hallway, taking Aimee and William with them. The men Rainey had managed to take down were dragged along behind, and Rainey couldn't tell if they were dead or unconscious. She looked to her parents and a flash of panic ran through her body. She could not just let them leave. Would she ever see them again? Would they still be the same if she did? She couldn't bring herself to think about what these people might do to them.

Rainey felt the knife being pulled from her throat and the grip around her neck released. She stumbled forward and felt the invisible force of the woman bind her where she stood.

Anya took a now stirring Lily from the other woman's arms and stepped towards Rainey. Rainey couldn't breathe, the panic of what was about to happen gripped her whole body. She tried to fight against the invisible force holding her, but she could not move any part of her body except for her eyes.

Anya stood in front of her and tucked a loose strand of matted hair behind Rainey's ear. Rainey glared back at her, sheer fury pouring from her every fibre.

"Rainey, this is your last chance to say goodbye to your daughter. Are you going to waste it looking at me?"

She looked down at the perfectly round cheeks of her daughter's face, her long eye lashes brushing against them. Rainey's heart ached to hold her, to protect her from the monsters who were about to take her away. Her eyes flicked back up to Anya's.

"Can I at least hold her?" She pleaded.

"I think you already know the answer to that. But I will give you your hand back." Anya nodded to the woman. "It's Ok, she won't hurt me while I have hold of the baby."

Rainey felt the restraint on her arm loosen. She flexed her hand before running the tips of her fingers across Lily's cheek. Tears ran freely down her face. In one last effort to give Lily something of herself, Rainey pressed her finger gently to the inside of Lily's wrist, where a minuscule grey heart appeared, identical to Joe's and Rainey's. Lily's tiny fingers wrapped around Rainey's thumb for just a moment, before Rainey felt her arm stiffen again.

"No. Please, Anya." Rainey cried, as Anya took a step back. "You were our friend. Why are you doing this?"

Rainey couldn't hold back her tears. She sobbed as she pleaded with Anya, begging her not to take Lily away. Anya looked back at her, watching her intently. She did not look angry anymore, she looked upset and full of regret, as though she did not want to do what she was about to do. And yet, she was doing it anyway. And Rainey felt the anger rise up in her again.

How dare she? How dare she come into my home and hurt my family? How dare she lay her hands on my daughter?

"I will kill you, Anya." She managed through clenched teeth.

Rainey's whole body began to shake as she tried to push the invisible barrier away again. Anya looked nervously from Rainey to the small woman.

"What's happening?" Anya questioned the woman.

"She's too strong. I can't hold her as well as I do the others."

"They've never been too strong. How is this possible?"

"They've never been as strong as her! Hurry!" She shouted back.

Anya turned away from the woman, obviously annoyed. She faced Rainey again and took a few small steps backwards.

"You won't find us, Rainey. It doesn't matter how hard you try. And it would be better for your parents and for your daughter if you were a good girl from now on and followed the rules."

Rainey didn't answer her. She closed her eyes briefly and tried to calm herself down, so that she could take one last look at her daughter. When she opened them again, she looked over to where Aimee and William watched her from the hallway.

"I love you." Aimee mouthed to her through her tears.

Rainey took a deep breath in to steady herself. William nodded once at her as tears began to fall from the corners of his eyes and Rainey had to look away. When she looked to Lily, she had opened her eyes, and the bright grey-blue pierced through Rainey's heart as she looked back at her.

"I love you, Lily."

Anya looked down to the heart on Lily's wrist and then back to Rainey. She held up her spare hand and waved her fingers. The group began to move again, and Rainey could not tear her eyes away from Lily to see her parents leave their house and her life for good. The last to leave were Anya, with Lily cradled against her, and the woman whose power continued to hold Rainey in place.

"Hold her for as long as you can when we leave," Anya instructed, before waving her out of the building too.

Now only Anya remained, staring back at Rainey. And as she took a step closer to the door her face transformed into a mixture of guilt and sympathy.

"Please, Anya. Please, don't do this. I can't live without her. You don't understand." Rainey pleaded, her tears making tracks in her blood-stained face.

"I am sorry, Rainey. Really, I am." Anya's voice was soft now and rang with her sincerity, as though she had not just broken into her house, had her parents beaten by her gang and was now kidnapping her baby.

She looked down at Lily and then held her closer to her chest as she turned and walked out of the room. Rainey heard the front door close behind her. She sucked in uneven, panicked breaths and attempted to move her limbs, but she was still frozen in place. She fought as hard as she could against the invisible shield as she listened to their vehicles screech down the driveway and on to the main road. An agonised scream burst through her lips and her body shook with the effort of breaking through the hold. Every part of her ached, but she could not stop, she had to keep trying, or it would be like she had given up. Given up on her baby. On her Lily. And suddenly, she could move again. She ran to the door and yanked it open. The tyre tracks were visible on the drive. She sprinted along the gravel, the stones digging into her bare feet, but she did not feel them. When she reached the road, she searched with her eyes, but they were gone. Rainey screamed, a long heartbroken cry which bounced back to her from the surrounding trees. Lightening streaked through the sky in great forks, closely followed by a deep roll of thunder as thick black clouds drained the sun from the sky, and then the heavens opened, sending vast sheets of rain plummeting towards the earth.

She ran back to the house and searched frantically for her car keys, her clothes dripping a mixture of rainwater and blood on to the floor. She hunted through every inch of the house, but her keys were not there. She gave up and began searching for her phone, if she could get hold of Joe then maybe he would know what to do. There had to be something they could do. She could not just allow those people to take Lily away, innocent and defenceless Lily. She didn't stand a chance against the savages who had broken into her house and attacked her family. Rainey's tears made it impossible for her to see what she was doing, but she kept on searching, refusing to give up. The only room she had not checked was the nursery.

She walked up to the door and slowly pushed it open. The only sounds to echo through the house came from the lightening, which continued to slice through the sky, and the thunder sending tremors through the walls. She edged her way into the room and ran her hand along the length of the cot. Her eyes scanned over the lines of soft toys on the bookshelf and the pile of freshly laundered clothes sitting in a neat pile on top of the changing unit. Rainey reached into the cot and pulled out Lily's soft, white blanket. Raising it to her face, she inhaled. Lily's smell flooded her nostrils. A heavy sob rolled up Rainey's throat and she squeezed the blanket tightly in her arms. Her legs shook and collapsed beneath her, leaving Rainey crumpled on the floor, clutching at the blanket and heaving deep, desperate sobs into the silence of the empty house.

14

Joe

Lexi had not been too happy when Joe broke the news to her that Rainey would not be joining them. She spent the first fifteen minutes sulking before she finally allowed her usual bubbly self to make an appearance. The minutes turned into hours as Joe and Lexi talked about Aimee's obsession with preparing her garden for the autumn, William's obsession with teaching Joe everything there was to know about running a business, and Rainey's obsession with waking the entire house with her screams every time she tried to sleep. They theorised about what Lily's power might be and how they would get through the terrible twos if she turned out to be stronger than her mother. Joe had made his way through three cups of tea by the time Mrs. Noland distracted him by requesting to take his measurements for a lime green jumper she was knitting.

"It looks beautiful," he said to her politely. "But I have just realised the time. I should really get home."

They suppressed a giggle as she scowled at him and returned to her armchair.

"Nicely avoided. Although, I really do think that that colour would work great on you." Lexi grinned.

"I'm sure it would," he replied sarcastically. "But I honestly did not realise what time it is. I need to get back and see how Rainey's doing."

He stood up to leave and pulled his jacket over his shoulders, pushing his arms into the sleeves as Lexi collected their used teacups.

"Can you at least give Rainey a huge hug from me? I hope she's not coming down with something. It might sound super selfish, but if I have to go without seeing her again tomorrow then I swear I'll kill myself," Lexi said, rather over dramatically, gaining her a few concerned looks from anyone within earshot.

Joe couldn't help but laugh.

"Probably not the best place to joke about suicide, Lex?"

"Oh, right. Oops." She grinned back, glancing around the room to make sure the nurses hadn't overheard. Luckily none of them had. "See you tomorrow, then?"

"Yeah. See y…"

But the sound of thunder crashing through the sky and shaking the pictures on the walls cut Joe off mid-sentence. The lights flickered, creating chaos throughout the visiting lounge as the other patients dashed for their rooms or began to scream. Joe looked at Lexi, who stared back at him with wide eyes. They understood instantly that the thunder was not the beginning of some freak storm. Yes, it rained a lot in the North of England, but thunder came rarely and was usually very tame. It was almost unheard of to experience the kind of thunder that rattled through the inside of your bones.

The lights flickered again before plunging the room into complete darkness. Joe glanced down at his watch, but he already knew that it was not late enough to be dark out. He rushed to the nearest window with Lexi right behind him, just in time to see a fork of lightning reach through the clouds and strike the earth a few miles away. Deep purple clouds rolled across the sky, and they could see a sheet of rain making its way towards them, about to engulf the hospital.

"Something's wrong," Joe whispered.

He turned and sprinted for the door, straight through the chaos of the sitting room, where the other patients were still screaming and clambering over one another in the darkness as the nurses tried frantically to calm them. Lexi did not hesitate to follow him, and she did not stop when they reached the doors to the staircase. They hurtled down the stairs until they made it to the ground floor and the front entrance. Luckily, Jerry was on duty and actually awake for once. He saw them coming and pressed the buzzer immediately, unlocking the front door before they even had a chance to explain. He stood from his chair and leaned across the desk to watch them as they sped past. Jerry knew only a fraction of what Rainey could do, but he was not stupid. Seeing a freak storm with such intensity, magically appear out of a sky that had, just moments before, been clear blue, Jerry had put two and two together. He didn't ask questions; he simply sprang into action. Joe slammed into the door without slowing and it burst open, allowing them both out and into the howling gusts of wind. Lexi glanced back over her shoulder to see Jerry battling against the wind to pull the door closed again.

The rain hit them as they reached the car. Great sheets of water fell from the sky, soaking their clothes and hair in seconds. Joe unlocked the doors and they both threw themselves inside.

"Are you sure you want to come?" Joe shouted above the noise of the rain pelting down on to the car's windshield with so much force it was difficult for Lexi to hear.

"Yes!" She shouted in reply.

"I won't think any less of you if you get out now, Lexi. I swear."

He forced the keys into the ignition and started the car. It made a low rumble as he revved the engine. Lexi grabbed a hold of Joe's free hand and gave it a squeeze.

"I'm sure. Now let's go, before we get struck by lightning."

Lexi glanced out of the window nervously, but she could not see anything past the rain. Joe threw the car into reverse and swung it out of the parking space, narrowly avoiding the cars on either side of them. He put his foot to the floor and sped out of the car park. They didn't talk as the car slid dangerously around corners and skidded through puddles on the country roads. Joe needed to concentrate on driving, but he could not stop his mind from racing through the possibilities of what had happened to Rainey. He wrapped his fingers tightly around the steering wheel until his knuckles turned white and looked as though they might break through his skin.

"Please be ok. Please be ok. If anything's happened to her then I swear to God," Joe murmured to himself.

"Joe, stop it! She's fine. Do you really think this storm would be possible if she wasn't? It's not Rainey we need to be worrying about." Lexi said, as she squeezed her hands together nervously.

"What if it's them? What if it has finally happened? They won't exercise restraint, you know that."

"I know." Lexi said, looking away from him.

Joe could see Lexi's face from the corner of his eye. He knew that he was scaring her even more with the fear and panic he could feel displayed across his own features. Of course, Lexi knew they would not exercise restraint. She knew more than most what could happen, and if it did, then it would not be the first time for her.

"It might not even be them, Joe. Maybe we're over reacting."

"We better hope it's not them."

Skidding to a stop on the gravel outside the house, they threw themselves out of the car and rushed to the front door. It was wide open and the doormat that lay just inside was covered with a puddle of water which had found its way in through the open door. As soon as Joe was inside, he began searching the rooms for Rainey, Aimee, anyone. He didn't dare to think of Lily, he couldn't bring himself to think that something might have happened to her.

"Joe, look at this place." Lexi said, pointing to the blood and broken furniture in the sitting room.

"Rainey!" He yelled, and he hurled himself up the stairs, taking them three at a time, with Lexi close behind him.

He threw each door open with such force that it slammed back against the wall on the other side. When he finally made it to the nursery, he froze in the doorway. Rainey was curled into a tight ball on the floor where she clutched at one of Lily's blankets. Her clothes were covered in blood and soaked through, and she shook as she cried. Small gasping sounds came from her as she tried to breath in. Joe could not bring his feet to move forward as the realisation of what had happened crashed down on him. He didn't need to ask to know that Lily was gone.

Slowly, Rainey lifted her head to look up at him and he stumbled back when he saw her. Rainey's face was smeared with blood, and she had cried tracks through the blood which coated her cheeks. Her left eye was swollen shut and her cheek was so distended that her cheekbone didn't shape her face anymore. Her lips were cut and swollen. As she straightened up, Joe eyes fell on to the bruises which had begun to form around her neck. Deep purple and red blotches curved around her throat like fingers and seemed to darken more as each second passed. A deep cut displayed itself across the bruises and fresh drops of blood oozed from the cut.

"They took her." She whispered through her sobs.

Joe fell to his knees beside Rainey and pulled her into his chest as he heard the words he feared would come. A hollow feeling washed through his body as though someone had torn his heart from his chest and the familiar, reassuring thud it was supposed to make seized to exist, leaving a ragged, gaping hole. He pulled Rainey in closer, wrapping his arms around her.

There was a shuffle of footsteps behind them as Lexi appeared in the doorway. When she saw Joe on his knees holding a broken Rainey, her hand flew to her mouth. Lexi had never seen Joe cry before. She knew that he believed that it was his place to support Rainey while she cried and not the other way around. But Lexi looked at his eyes now, as they turned red with the pressure of the tears building behind them. Lexi fell back against the wall and slid down it until she was crouched on the floor with her head in her hands. And her own tears began to fall.

They didn't move for hours. They stayed on the floor of the nursery, Joe holding Rainey as she cried. Until, eventually, no more tears would come. Then they were silent. Rainey stared at the empty space in the cot which should have held her baby, warm and safe.

"I need to heal you." Joe finally croaked, sitting up straighter and gently pushing Rainey away.

"I don't need healing," she whispered back.

"Rainey, you're a mess. I need to fix you."

Joe ran his fingers gently over Rainey's cheek, then trailed them up over her cheekbone and across her swollen eye. He placed his other hand on the back of her head, where a large cut had oozed blood into her hair. Rainey watched the colour drain from Joe's skin as he forced his own health into her wounds. When she felt her swollen eye begin to open again, she held up her hands and pushed him away.

"That's enough," she said.

Joe leaned back to take a look at her. Most of the swelling and the worst of the cuts had gone, but her neck was still badly bruised, and she winced as she tried to move it. The bruises on her face were more obvious now that the swelling had gone down. Lexi shuffled closer and reached for Rainey's hand.

"Rainey, I..." But Rainey silenced her with her hand.

"Don't, Lexi. Don't say that you're sorry."

Lexi looked down at their hands, linked together.

"How did this happen?" Rainey said to no one in particular. "I don't understand. Everything was so perfect."

Joe lightly brushed his fingertips over the bruises on Rainey's neck but stopped abruptly when she cringed away from him.

"Who did this to you?" He said.

Rainey stared at a spot on the floor while she tried to gather the words in her head.

"I woke up and she was screaming," she closed her eyes and pushed her hands against her temples. "I listened to them, hurting my parents. Mum was begging them to stop. I tried to get downstairs but there was a man there. I didn't see him at first but then, there he was. And he tried to-" Rainey ran her fingers across her throat and Joe's hands clenched into fists. "But she told him to stop, and then he took me downstairs. There was a group of them, all standing there around my parents. There were at least ten of them, men and women. My parents, they tried to fight, to get loose, but then he hurt me again, so they stopped." Rainey's voice shook.

Joe got to his feet and began pacing across the floor.

"And then I saw her. Holding, holding Li... she was holding her." Rainey couldn't bring herself to say Lily's name, what was left of her heart tore painfully when she tried. "She said that everyone had sacrificed things for me and that I was never allowed to have a baby. She said that my parents could pay for their own mistakes and that my baby would pay for mine." Rainey looked up and met Joe's eyes. "And then she took them."

There was a long silence in the room while Joe and Lexi tried to process what Rainey had told them.

"It was Anya." She said.

"What was Anya?" Lexi said. "What do you mean?"

"Anya took them."

Rainey closed her eyes again and leaned back against the wall.

"I don't understand. Why was Anya there? What does she have to do with anything?" Lexi said, getting to her feet.

Joe looked to Lexi.

"Anya? From your hospital?" He said, and Lexi nodded her head. "What the hell is she doing with them?" He spat the last word.

Rainey did not miss the recognition. Her head pulled up to look at him and she resisted the urge to cry out in pain as the muscles in her neck strained against her.

"Wait. Who is '*them*'?" She shot at Joe.

Joe looked to Lexi who stared back at him with wide eyes.

"Who are they, Joe?" Rainey pushed, louder this time.

"Rainey, listen. I don't know who they are exactly, but your parents knew that something like this could happen one day."

The confusion on Rainey's face began to transform as her temper began to rise inside of her.

"Just wait a minute, Rainey." He said as he raised his hands in front of himself. "You need to listen to me. This is a very long story which goes way back to before we were even born. You need to give me a chance to explain it."

"Give me the short version." Rainey hissed, and from the corner of her eye she saw Lexi take a step back.

"Your parents have been running from these people for years. I don't know the full story, only parts of it. They didn't know when they would come for us, or if they even knew where we were. Your parents didn't want you to know until it was absolutely necessary. They wanted to protect you from it all. They didn't think that they would come, not yet. But then Aimee recognised that man you drew from your dreams, and she started to panic. We were going to move, all of us, move away for a while. But we didn't get enough time." Joe stumbled over his words as he watched the anger on Rainey's face grow.

He backed away a few steps when Rainey's hands began to glow a faint blue and tiny sparks danced across her skin.

"You kept this a secret from me, for my own protection? So that I wouldn't overreact and demand that we do something? At least then one of us would have been acting rationally! We should have been moving, constantly. We should never have stopped. But you wanted to protect me?" Rainey screamed. "And who was there to protect me when they did come? Nobody was there. Nobody was there to protect me! Because we couldn't even fight back!"

Joe cringed as Rainey's words ripped through him.

"My baby is gone! My daughter has been taken by some crazy bitch and her gang of psychos and all you can say is '*they did it to protect me*'?"

Rainey tried to breathe deeply in an attempt to calm herself down before she electrocuted everything within a fifty-mile radius.

"Rainey. You need to calm down now, before you do something stupid." Lexi warned from the corner of the room.

"Did you know about this?" She turned on Lexi.

Lexi didn't answer right away.

"Yes," she whispered, eventually.

Rainey let out an infuriated scream and an electric blue bolt fired from the palm of her hand, striking the floor beneath her. It lit up the room for a fraction of a second before it retracted back into her hand, leaving a black scorch mark in the wood. Joe flinched back and Lexi shrieked in shock. He locked eyes with Lexi and nodded. She stepped forward and grabbed the top of Rainey's arm tightly. Before Rainey had time to react, she dropped to the floor, and Joe leapt forward just in time to stop her head from hitting the solid wood.

"Give her some time to rest," Lexi whispered. "We can leave in the morning. We'll find them, Joe."

Joe did not reply. He lifted Rainey into his arms and carried her through to their bedroom. He laid Rainey's bruised body on the bed and pulled off her dirty, blood-stained clothes. He pulled the quilt up to her waist, then he disappeared into the bathroom, returning a moment later with a damp flannel. Carefully, he washed away the blood from Rainey's face and dabbed over the deep purple bruises on her neck. His jaw tensed as he fought against the fresh wave of anger which threatened to take control of him.

"I will kill the bastard who did this to you," he whispered. "I don't care how long it takes to find him. He's dead."

He finished bathing her skin and then pulled the covers up over her chest. Then he discarded of the flannel in the bathroom and removed his own clothes before stepping into the shower. He turned the water on and allowed the cold liquid to run over his skin. Gradually, the water began to warm, and when it finally ran hot, he stood under the stream, letting it run over his tight muscles, unknotting them. Tears ran silently down his cheeks, mixing with the water and disappearing down the drain.

After a while, he stepped out of the shower and dried himself off. Then he threw on some underwear and crawled into bed beside Rainey. He could not lie down and go to sleep with the emptiness of the house threatening to crush him, so he propped himself up on his elbow and watched Rainey silently as her chest rose and fell again with each even breath she took. He brushed a stray strand of hair out of her face before lying next to her and taking her hand in his own under the covers.

Joe did not know how long he stared at the ceiling, but eventually his eyes drooped, and he drifted into unconsciousness.

15

Rainey

Rainey's eyes fluttered as she tried to rouse herself, but the heavy feeling in her head threatened to pull her back into unconsciousness and she quickly recognised that this was not the usual feeling of being refreshed that she expected to feel after a long sleep. She knew that it must have been a Lexi induced mini coma, and then the crushing realisation of the previous day dawned on her. Lily was gone. Taken away by a group of strangers. Her mother and father too. And judging by what those strangers had done to Rainey, she knew that they were more than simply dangerous. *Strangers,* she thought to herself. But not all strangers. Anya was not a stranger.

Tenderly, she ran her fingers over her eye, before she remembered that Joe had already healed the worst of it. Careful not to wake Joe, Rainey edged her way to the end of the bed. Every inch was agony as the damaged muscles in her neck tried to support the weight of her head, but Rainey didn't care. She crept over to the chest of drawers and silently pulled out a pair of jeans and a black cami. There wasn't any point in checking her reflection in the mirror, she threw on the clothes and tiptoed out of the bedroom and on to the landing, where her dried blood was smeared into the carpet and across the walls. Rainey managed to make it down the stairs and into the kitchen to collect the keys to Aimee's car without waking anyone. She passed Lexi, curled into an upright ball on the sofa, but she did not stir.

Rainey found the keys where Joe had thrown them on to the worktop in his panic the day before, and headed for the front door and the small pile of shoes next to it. Now that her limbs had woken a little more, she could creep about faster without making too much noise. Or so she thought. After slipping her feet into a pair of laced plimsolls, Rainey stepped back to pull the door open when a voice behind her stopped her in her tracks.

"Where are you going, Rainey?" Lexi said.

She held on to the door handle as she considered not answering at all and walking straight out of the door.

"To find Lily," she finally replied.

"On your own? We need to work out a plan. Think about where to go first and-"

"Seems to me like you two had plenty of time to work out a plan before any of this happened."

"That's not fair. Let us explain what we knew and then you can judge us."

"No thanks."

Rainey pulled on the door handle and it creaked open. Aimee's car sat a few feet away from the door, where Joe and Lexi had left it the night before.

"Joe!" Lexi shouted behind her, in the direction of the stairs. "Joe! Help me out here!"

Rainey could hear his footstep on the floor above them as Joe rushed to the landing. She didn't want to waste any more time, and she could not bring herself to look at Joe right now, knowing what he had kept from her. Knowing that because of that secret, she hadn't been given the chance to save her own daughter. Her Lily.

Rainey ran towards the car. She yanked open the door, climbed into the driver's seat and locked the doors behind her. Joe ran out after her and pulled on one of the handles.

"Rainey open the door. Where are you going?" He shouted through the glass.

Then it dawned on Rainey that if she drove away now, they would just chase her in her own car. The keys might still be missing, but it wasn't difficult to hot-wire a car with the help of the internet. She unlocked the door and pushed it open.

"Move," she ordered Joe, and he stumbled backwards, narrowly avoiding the door as it swung open.

She hopped out of the car and stuffed the keys into her back pocket.

"Rainey, what is going on?" Joe tried again.

Rainey ignored him and stormed towards the garage. When she reached the door, she bent down and dug her fingers underneath it, pulling with all the strength she could manage and ignoring the protest from her injuries. Joe and Lexi were not far behind her.

"Come back in the house." Joe said, but Rainey ignored him.

The door rolled up and Rainey stepped under it before it was all the way open. Holding one hand out in front of her, palm facing outwards, Rainey sent one single blue bolt from her hand into the first tyre of her own car. The metal alloy began to glow red, heating the air in the tyre and melting the rubber until streams of black began to pool on the concrete. The noise of the tyre finally exploding was so loud that Joe and Lexi jumped back in shock, shielding their heads with their arms. Rainey headed for the next tyre.

"What the hell are you doing?" Lexi shrieked.

There was another loud bang as the second tyre popped. Rainey knew she would not need to destroy the other two, but she did them anyway. When all four tyres lay in shreds beneath her car, Rainey turned and strode straight past Joe and Lexi, not looking at either of them as she passed. They exchanged a worried glance before following her to the front of the house.

"Rainey. That's enough!" Joe shouted, finally losing his temper.

She stopped next to Aimee's car, and slowly turned to face him. Rainey wondered if Joe had realised that she had not looked at him yet, and even now, as she stood a few feet before him, she could not look him in the eyes. She fixed her stare in the centre of his chest instead.

"What are you doing?" He asked, his voice level again.

"What does it look like I'm doing?" Rainey spat back.

Joe flinched at her tone.

"I know you're upset, but this-"

"Upset." Rainey said, testing the word on her tongue.

Joe took a step back and held his arm out to his side, forcing Lexi to move back too.

"Upset?" She screamed.

"Look at me." Joe said.

Rainey ignored him.

"Look at me!"

Rainey's eyes flicked up to meet Joe's and she was surprised by the reaction which stirred inside of her, or rather, the lack of reaction. She had expected anger to burn fresh through her veins when she was forced to look at the one man she had trusted more than anyone, who had failed her by keeping a secret which had now destroyed her family. But what she did not expect to feel, was nothing. She looked at Joe, then at Lexi, and back to Joe. Still, nothing stirred inside of her. And Joe could see it, in whatever expression lay upon her face, and devastation washed across his own features. Rainey was surprised that he could feel any more heartbroken than he already had after everything that had happened in the past few hours, but clearly, he could.

Without another word, she turned her back on them and placed a hand of the handle of the car door.

"Rainey, please?" Joe pleaded, and he took a step closer on the gravel with his bare feet, his voice breaking.

Rainey turned to look at them both standing a few feet away from the car, half dressed and pleading with her not to leave.

"Don't follow me." She said, and her hands rose up in front of her.

The ground beneath their feet began to tremble. A crack appeared inches from where Joe stood, and he jumped back, pulling Lexi with him, who stumbled and fell to the ground. They watched, wide-eyed, as the crack in the earth grew longer and wider, swallowing the gravel, and Lexi scrambled back, grazing her hands.

"What are you doing? Stop it!" Lexi yelled over the noise, but Rainey didn't pay her any attention.

She turned and threw herself into the car, leaving Joe and Lexi to gawp at what she had created in the earth. She pulled the keys out of her pocket and thrust them into the ignition. And within a few seconds she had started the car and reversed it into position. She paused for a second, just long enough to see that the crevice in the ground had stopped expanding. It was large enough for the car to fit into. She looked through the window and into Joe's eyes. She could see his pain and she wondered briefly what he could see in her eyes. She pulled her gaze away and pushed her foot down on the pedal, speeding out of the driveway.

The car screeched to a stop in the car park outside the hospital. Rainey didn't bother to turn off the engine. She jumped out of the car and headed for the locked front doors at a brisk walk. As she approached, she raised her left hand and manipulated the air to slam against the doors with such a solid wall of force that both doors buckled on their hinges and crumpled inwards. She lifted her leg and kicked hard on what remained of one of the doors, it fell off completely and slammed loudly against the floor. Rainey stepped over it and continued down the corridor, ignoring the security guard who shouted at her from behind his desk. She knew he would be on the phone to the police in less than a second, but she didn't care. She would be long gone by the time they arrived.

The next set of doors caved easier than the first and within a couple of minutes she was tearing her way through Lexi's floor. Rainey headed straight to the small office joined on to the visiting room. All around her she could hear patients screaming and nurses trying to calm them as they herded them away from the danger.

Let them scream, she thought. *What do I care?*

Rainey yanked each drawer out of the filing cabinet in the corner of the office until she found what she was looking for. Across the top of the file in bold black lettering read: Hall, Anya. After a quick search through the remaining drawers of the filing cabinet and the desk, Rainey snatched up the yellow file with Anya's name and headed back to the car.

As she passed the security guard at the front desk, she could hear him whispering into the phone.

"They're not coming quick enough! Oh god, she's back-"

It did not take a genius to figure out who he was talking to.

16

Joe

Joe heard the gravel on the drive crunch as Rainey slammed her foot on the brake. He had been watching out for her through one of the large windows overlooking Aimee's garden. He saw Rainey's body slam forward in her seat as the car came to an abrupt stop. She winced and rested one hand across her bruised neck and the other across her forehead.

By the time Joe had made it to the front door, Rainey was already pushing past him into the house.

"Where the hell have you been?" Joe fired at her.

"Pack a bag, we're leaving." Rainey said in a steady and demanding tone.

"Leaving? What do you mean leaving?"

"Leaving." Rainey repeated. "You need to pack a bag for us both with some clothes and a few essentials. Tell Lexi to do the same. She can take some of my things."

Joe did not move. He stared at Rainey in complete bewilderment. And then they heard the first of the sirens in the distance. Rainey's head turned towards the noise and her eyes widened a little, just enough for Joe to notice.

"Rainey. What did you do?"

"Just pack the damn bag!"

17

Rainey

Rainey ran up the stairs, across the landing and up the second set of stairs. It was dark in her father's office; the blinds had not been opened from the last time her father had been in there. She turned on the desk lamp and looked around the room. Rainey felt physical pain when she thought of how her father had been in this room just a few short hours ago, shut away, doing his work. None the wiser that soon he would not be in his home anymore, but in a car full of lunatics who would gladly beat up his teenage daughter before snatching him away. There was no time to stand and stare at her father's favourite room in the house, she was there for a reason, and as she heard the sirens growing louder, she knew she was running out of time.

She climbed up on to the desk and grabbed hold of the framed picture hanging on the wall. It was a painting Rainey had made when she was seven years old, of herself holding hands with both of her parents. Her father was so proud of it, he had had it framed. But it wasn't the picture Rainey was interested in. She yanked it off the wall and dropped it to the floor. Behind it was her parents' safe. She pinned in the code and pulled open the door. Inside lay stacks of notes, all tied together with rubber bands. Rainey grabbed as many as she could carry and was about to slam the door shut again when her eyes fell on to a small, round hole hidden behind the money. Carefully, she placed the cash on to the desk before using the end of her little finger to reach into the tiny hole and pull out the board covering the back of the safe. When it came loose Rainey threw it on to the floor, on top of her painting.

At the back of the safe was a pile of passports, a single key ring and a folded piece of lined paper. Rainey pulled a passport from the top of the pile and opened it. She found a picture of herself looking back at her, but it was not her name printed on to the document. The name read Stephanie Whitworth. She checked the next one and there she was again, only this time the name read Rachael Davies.

Lexi came running into the room, banging the door back against the wall and making Rainey jump. In her hand she held an empty pink rucksack.

"What is the deal, Rainey? Why is Joe running around stuffing everything he can grab into bags?"

"The police will be here any minute, and we have to get out before they get here. I'll explain everything when we leave. Pass me that bag."

"The police? What the hell happened?" Lexi yelled as she gripped the bag tighter.

"I went back to the hospital and took Anya's file. I don't know what details are in there but there has to be something. The bag, Lexi." Rainey demanded.

"Oh. Well, that doesn't sound so bad," Lexi said, as she stepped further into the room to help Rainey.

She pulled the sides of the bag open and watched with a frown as she realised what the bag was being used to carry.

"I didn't exactly ring the doorbell and wait for them to answer, Lex." Rainey replied, as she shovelled money into the rucksack.

When it was almost full, Rainey reached up for the passports, and Lexi watched with an open mouth as she threw them in too. Finally, she picked up the note and the key ring, she didn't have time to look at them now, but if they were in the safe, they had to be important. She put them in the bag and pulled on two zippers to close it. Then she jumped down from the table using Lexi's hand to steady herself as she landed, and they rushed down the stairs together.

Joe was in the bedroom, opening drawers and stuffing anything he could lay his hands on into three large weekend bags which lay open on the floor. Lexi helped to fill up the remaining space and then zipped them up before heaving them to the top of the stairs, where she waited for the other two to join her. But there was one last thing Rainey could not leave without. She headed to Lily's bedroom door and Joe followed her. When they entered the room, Rainey swallowed hard, and Joe gave her a light squeeze on the shoulder. Her eyes trailed down the gossamer veil above the cot and over to the bookshelf with the books she herself had loved as a child. She ran her hand along the soft toys all lined up, until she saw the one she was looking for, a small pink bunny, its ears flopped down either side of its face. Lily had fallen asleep next to it the day she was born, and although she had cuddled a different toy almost every day, the bunny was the one she always seemed to go back to. A matching blue bunny sat beside it; Aimee had bought both, just in case Lily had been a boy. Rainey picked up the bunny and turned back to Joe who had already found Lily's white cotton blanket on the floor where Rainey had left it the night before. Without looking back, Rainey strode out of the room with Joe close behind her. The room didn't mean anything anymore. Not without Lily in it. Lily was out there somewhere. And until she came home, this house would not mean anything to Rainey. It was empty, broken. A memory of what had been torn away from her when she had had everything.

The three of them grabbed a bag each, and Rainey threw the pink rucksack on to her back. They carried them down to the car, loaded up the boot and climbed in. Rainey chose the back seat and warned Lexi with a look not to sit next to her, she did not know how long she would be in the car with Joe and Lexi, but she did know she would not be having any friendly conversations with either of them any time soon. She needed her space from them, which would be difficult enough to find while they were cramped into the car together.

Joe drove them down the drive, on to the main road and out into the country. They did not look back at the house. Joe and Lexi looked out at the road ahead as they listened to the sound of police sirens growing louder behind them. Rainey looked only at the title of the yellow file, laying on the seat beside her.

Hall, Anya.

18

Aimee

Aimee's head spun as her consciousness returned. The feeling of vertigo was almost enough to make her vomit. Flashbacks flooded her mind. She kept her eyes firmly closed out of fear that somebody could be close by, and she listened intently for any sound, but all she could hear was the gentle rumble of an engine. Her limbs ached from lying in the same position too long on the solid floor. Her hands were bound behind her back, making her even more uncomfortable. A small lump on her neck stung from where the needle had punctured her skin, pumping her blood full of what Aimee assumed had been the reason for her unconsciousness.

Cautiously, she lifted her left eyelid, hoping that if someone was watching her, they would only be able to see the part of her face which was not pressed to the filthy floor. She did not dare to look around, just a quick glance ahead of her. On the floor, a couple of feet in front of her, she could see William. His eyes and cheekbones looked badly bruised and dried blood covered the stubble around his mouth and chin. Aimee had to fight every instinct in her body to stop the sob from escaping her lips. She looked away from him and attempted to get her bearings. The vehicle she lay in had a large, open space where the seats must have been at some point. Now, it lay empty except for her and William. The windows had been covered over with black film and the ceiling of the vehicle seemed very high up from where Aimee lay on the floor.

Definitely a van, she thought to herself.

Aimee almost flinched when she heard a shuffle of feet behind her. She closed her eye again and fought hard to relax her body as she sensed someone lean over her, heard them suck in gulps of air and then felt the heat of their breath blow across her face. Two stubby fingers pressed against her neck where her pulse indicated that she had not died by steadily beating away.

Breathe! Aimee reminded herself. *People who are unconscious do not hold their breath.*

"All still alive back here," the man called out to someone at the front of the vehicle.

Aimee listened to his footsteps as he made his way back to his seat. She risked opening both eyes this time and was startled to see William staring back at her. He did not move, he understood just as well as she did the importance of playing comatose right now, they needed to get as much information as they could before anyone realised that they were awake.

"Are you ok?" Aimee mouthed silently to William.

He did not reply, but ever so slightly nodded his head. William was lying on his side in front of Aimee, facing towards the two people Aimee already knew were in the van. She watched as William's eyes wandered above her head and to the front seats, then he looked back to her and made five exaggerated blinks.

"Ok." She mouthed.

Five people.

"Lily?" She mouthed again.

William shook his head in response, and they shared a desperate gaze. William and Aimee had been a team for so long, they had survived together through everything that had been thrown their way. But Aimee was not so sure what would happen this time, and she could tell by the apprehension she saw in William's eyes, that he had his doubts too. They had known this would happen sooner or later, but they had hoped for the latter. A few more days and the house would have been empty. Lily would have been safe and sound in Rainey's arms halfway across the world. There would have been nobody home when Anya came looking. Anya. Aimee swore to herself then, that if she ever saw Anya again it would be on the receiving end of one her lightning bolts.

A screech sounded beneath them as the van came to an abrupt stop. Aimee and William were thrown across the floor, and this time Aimee could not stop her instincts, she pulled her knees up to protect her face as best she could while her hands were still firmly tied behind her back. She squeezed her eyes shut, silently praying her reaction had not been noticed.

"Well, look who's decided to join us. And just in time." Came a woman's voice from behind Aimee. "I wouldn't try anything if I were you. Not that you'll be able to anyway."

Aimee recognised her voice as the woman who had paralysed her back at the house, and sure enough, as she tried to wiggle her fingers, they were now frozen in place. Her eyelids held firmly shut by the invisible force that had taken hold of her body.

Heavy footsteps came towards them, and a rough hand grabbed the back of Aimee's hair, yanking her to her feet. A sharp intake of breath from Aimee alerted William to her pain, and he began to groan as he strained against his own invisible barrier.

"Tell your *friend* to shut up," the man holding Aimee barked.

She remained silent.

"Ok then, let's try this your way."

He pulled Aimee's head back further until it was resting on his shoulder, and brought his other hand up to pull back the collar of her shirt. William watched with wide eyes as he traced the tip of his index finger over her bare skin, until it came to rest on the point of her collarbone, beside the hollow of her throat. He looked down at William who continued to groan in protest on the floor, and smirked. Aimee's scream erupted from her mouth before she could stop herself. She tried to squeeze her lips tighter together to prevent herself from crying out, but the pain was so raw and concentrated, she struggled to hold it in. Where the man's finger began to slowly run along the curve of her collarbone, an angry trail of melted flesh followed. Aimee did not want to give him the satisfaction of begging him to stop. She bit down on her tongue until her mouth filled with the metallic tang of blood. She could not be sure of what he was doing to her, but she felt as though the entire side of her chest had been set on fire, like the man's fingers were white-hot pokers sinking into her burning flesh.

William stopped his fight against the invisible force and watched in horror, as his wife's face grew paler with every millimetre the finger edged over her body. He finally stopped when he reached her shoulder and dropped her limp body to the floor next to William, where she fell into a heap and sobbed silently. The man laughed to himself as he stepped over them and opened the doors at the back of the van, jumping out. William listened as the two doors at the front opened and slammed shut too, leaving them alone. He tried to wiggle his fingers and they moved. He shuffled forwards and leant his head against Aimee's as she continued to sob on the floor. Then he kissed her gently on the top of her head. There was nothing he could say to comfort her. They knew what would be waiting for them when they were dragged from the van.

Aimee tried to calm herself, taking in deep and steadying breaths, forcing her sobs to settle and die in her throat. When her body no longer shook with the effort of controlling her tears, they lay silent, listening for any sound of voices from outside the vehicle.

After what felt like a long time, William tilted his head to the side. He could hear the earth crunching under heavy footfalls. He looked into his wife's panicked eyes.

"Aimee, it will be ok. We will be ok."

"I love you," she whispered.

"No, do not give up. You have to fight them, for Lily."

"They've already won, Will." Aimee cried.

William did not need to say anything in return. His eyes spoke for him. The doors of the van opened with a loud creak and three figures stood on the other side, observing them. Two were men, Aimee recognised the first as the man with the burning touch, but she had never seen the other. A woman stood with them, looking down at Aimee with a livid expression burned into her features, the woman who could freeze their bodies. Aimee wished she knew her name, if she ever got the chance, she would kill her too.

The second man grabbed William around the ankle and yanked him out of the doors. Aimee flinched when she heard a crunch as his body hit the ground.

"Jenna, can you handle the woman?" The man with the burning hands said.

"Please." She scoffed. "I could handle all four of you, James. Don't try to act like a big shot with me."

James scowled back at her before turning away. Aimee felt Jenna's hand wrap tightly around her ankle before dragging her too from the van. She hit the back of her head on the bumper as her body slammed to the floor. Her eyes watered with the shock of the impact, but she did not have time to process the pain. She was yanked to her feet and pushed towards a door, nestled into the side of a concrete wall. William walked ahead of her with James keeping a constricting hand clamped tightly on his elbow.

Aimee did not bother to look around her. She had no doubt in her mind where they were being taken. She could sense it in the smells of the desert and how the heat had hit her when the doors of the van had first opened. There was no mistaking the building she had spent the worst years of her life in. The same building she had fled from when she discovered she was pregnant.

This was Smith's building. *The Smith Institution*. Or *TSI*, as he liked to call it. It was known as 'Smith's army', or 'Smith's Institute', to everyone else. To Aimee, it would always be her own personal hell. The place she had been kept as a teenager and trained to help the Gifted. Little did she know at the time that she was helping to build an empire. An army.

Aimee hadn't even realised that her feet had stopped dragging her forward until Jenna placed her hand between Aimee's shoulder blades and pushed her hard, making her stumble.

"I could freeze your body so fast you wouldn't even be able to breathe." Jenna warned, as she pushed Aimee onwards yet again.

Aimee laughed at Jenna's threat.

"You think I can't do it?" She challenged.

"I don't doubt for one minute that you could. But I don't think that you will." She laughed a little more as she observed the rage wash across Jenna's face. "Why bring us all this way if you're just going to kill us as soon as we get here?"

They reached the door and Jenna's face reddened as she struggled to think of something clever to say in return. She growled in frustration and roughly jabbed a code into a pad on top of a metal container on the wall. It beeped loudly when she pressed the enter button and they heard a lock clicking from inside. Jenna pulled the door of the container open and pushed another button on what looked to be an intercom system. After a few short seconds, a woman's voice called to them through a speaker.

"Yes?" She said impatiently.

"It's Jenna, let me in."

"Jenna, who? I'm afraid you'll have to be more specific. I'm sure that there's more than just the one Jenna in the world."

Aimee was delighted to hear that she was not the only one who did not appreciate Jenna's company.

"Let me in!" Jenna yelled back at the speaker.

There was a loud clunk and the heavy metal door slowly swung forward. Aimee and William were pushed through and into a small room with no windows. When Jenna closed the door behind her, the only light came from a small flickering bulb hanging from the centre of the ceiling. Jenna led the way through another door and down a series of corridors which all appeared to be identical. Plain metal doors after more plain metal doors lined each white painted wall. Eventually, they reached an elevator and all seven of the group stepped inside. Jenna pressed a button, and it began to lower them deeper into the ground.

Aimee risked a glance in William's direction, but his eyes stared blankly at the floor. The elevator slowed before coming to a complete stop and the doors edged open. They were led along a short passageway with a double doorway waiting for them at the end, its doors already propped open. As they approached, Aimee looked into the large open space before her. It was lit mostly by a fire, burning in the open fireplace at the back of the room. A few small lamps had been positioned on tables around the outside of the space, but they looked to be merely for decoration purposes. Two large, brown leather sofas lay opposite each other in the centre of the room with a fur rug between the two. And the walls were covered in Honduran Mahogany panels, giving the room what should have been a warm and cosy feel. If it had been anywhere else, Aimee might have liked this room. But this was not her first visit.

Jenna cut the rope binding Aimee's hands and gave her a shove on the shoulder, but Aimee did not move. She winced in pain as Jenna's hand brushed against her burn. From the corner of her eye, she saw William lift his head to look at her. She could not move her feet forward. She tried to, but they would not budge. And it had nothing to do with Jenna. Aimee knew who was in that room, and she knew what would await her when she stepped inside. Years of abuse she had suffered in this building, and it had left her with a scar that no healer could fix. That same scar throbbed inside of her now, bringing with it flashes of her devastating past inside this very room.

Jenna grabbed hold of Aimee's hair and dragged her forward, and William was pushed along behind her. She stumbled forwards and a smirking Jenna watched Aimee's panicked eyes focus on her surroundings. They settled on Jenna's smug expression and a flash of blinding rage washed through her. Aimee launched her fist straight into Jenna's nose. Jenna seemed too shocked to move for a moment, until a gush of blood from her nose snapped her back to reality. She stared hard at Aimee, and her body froze again. Aimee tried to push back against her, but she could not move, she could only watch as Jenna's arm pulled back, her palm held out flat, before it rushed forward through the air to connect with Aimee's face. With her body frozen in place, Aimee's head did not move with the momentum of the slap, the full force of Jenna's hand struck her hard across her cheek and eye. She felt the sting of the blow turn into a burn over one side of her face and she stared with her eyes wide in fury as Jenna rubbed her hand. But when Jenna looked back to Aimee, Aimee knew that Jenna feared her. Aimee's eyes burned into hers with such intensity, she could feel the fear behind Jenna's carefully constructed mask. And she knew that Jenna was silently hoping Aimee's life would be brought to an end before she ever had the chance to get a hold of her.

"Is that any way to treat our guests?" A man's voice called from the corner of the room.

Aimee felt her heart drop into her stomach.

"Release her."

"Yes, sir." Jenna said, obediently.

She took a step back and Aimee felt her limbs loosen, only to be replaced with a crippling fear that tightened and knotted every muscle in her body. Footsteps moved across the room towards the group and Jenna and James took a few steps back away from Aimee and William.

"What's the matter, Aimee? After all of this time apart, will you not even look at me?"

Aimee did not turn around. She stared straight ahead to the spot where Jenna's eyes had held her own just a few seconds before.

"And William," the voice continued calmly. "My loyal old employee. Such a delight to have you both back with me. I cannot tell you how pleased I am to see you again. Well, one of you anyway."

There was a long pause, as neither Aimee nor William would turn to look at him.

"Jenna, James. Escort William here to one of the empty suites. Please ensure that he has a... comfortable stay. I would not wish anything less for such an important guest."

Aimee couldn't breathe. Her stomach contracted even tighter as the cocktail of dread and fear overwhelmed her. If they took William, it could be the last time she ever saw him. She heard him begin to protest, and then the wind gush from his lungs as he received a blow from James. She raised her hand and aimed it towards Jenna as her palm started to spark with the bolt that would kill her instantly, but as she focused the bolt on Jenna's conceited face, her arm pulled back sharply against herself, and the sparks died. Aimee knew what had happened, what had stopped her from giving Jenna the pain that she deserved.

"Thank you, Smith." Jenna said, bowing her head before stepping forward and taking hold of one of William's arms.

Aimee remembered all too clearly the powers that Smith possessed. Jenna might have been able to freeze her body enough to stop it from breathing, but Smith could physically take over her body, *any* body. Control it, as it if were his own personal puppet on strings, manipulate it into doing anything he wanted. Including using its powers as though they were his own.

Jenna and James dragged a frozen William out of the room and back into the lift. Aimee could not look at him, even if she had wanted to. Smith would not allow it. Footsteps approached behind her, and her breathing accelerated with every step until it was nothing more than that of a trapped animal, awaiting its death. Smith stopped behind her and released his hold. He knew that she would not run. He would only stop her if she tried. He pulled her long hair back over her shoulder gently and she could feel his breath against the back of her neck, making her skin crawl.

"Oh, Aimee," Smith moaned. "How I have missed you."

He brushed his lips against her neck and a shiver shook through her whole body.

"It would appear that you have missed me too."

Aimee remained still and silent but closed her eyes as Smith placed a hand on her shoulder and dragged it slowly across her chest as he walked around to face her. She gritted her teeth as his fingers brushed over her burned skin.

"I cannot begin to tell you how much I have dreamed of this moment."

His hand, palm flat against her skin, ran slowly down the middle of her chest and settled on her stomach.

"How I have longed for you to come back to me. You do things to me Aimee, that no other has managed to achieve."

Smith leaned closer and Aimee could feel his face just centimetres from her own, his breath hot on her cheek.

"But you have been disloyal. You have disobeyed me. And that is not something that I can forgive."

His hands grabbed Aimee roughly by the shoulders and spun her around. Again, his fingers pressed painfully against her wound and Aimee bit down harder, refusing to cry out. Smith pulled back her wrists, binding them tightly with his stubby hand, before pushing her against the wall. With his free hand he grabbed a fist full of her hair and pulled her head back until she felt his lips brush against her ear. He moulded his body into her, crushing her between him and the solid wall. Aimee struggled to pull the air into her lungs.

"I will make you wish that you had never left," he whispered into her ear. "And then I will make you beg me. Beg me to save your *precious William*." He spat.

Smith bit down hard on Aimee's ear before kissing her neck hungrily. Still, Aimee did not react. She had taught herself many years ago how to handle Smith's attention, when he had been a regular horror she had had to endure. She switched her mind off and left her body. She didn't focus on anything, she couldn't see anything, hear anything. She drifted into nothingness. But Aimee had spent years of her life healing her soul after Smith's abuse, and the survival skills she had taught herself were almost a distant memory.

"Beg me, Aimee." Smith breathed.

Aimee remained silent.

"Beg me." He said again, his voice rising.

Aimee stared blankly ahead, fixing her eyes on a chip in the wooden panelling.

"How do you dare? After everything I have shown you. You know what I can do, what I am capable of."

He paused to wait for her reply, but when she said nothing, it only infuriated him further.

"Beg me. Beg me not to kill him. Beg me not to tear him limb from limb, for taking what belongs to me!" He screamed. "And if you do not, I will take you to him right now. And you can watch it happen."

Smith would not hesitate to kill William. He would relish in it. Aimee knew now that that was why they hadn't killed him on the way here. Smith would use William as bate, every time she thought of disobeying him. Aimee dropped her shoulders, defeated, and Smith sniggered, knowing he had won.

"Beg me not to kill him, Aimee. That is all you have to do, and William lives." He whispered against her neck.

A sob escaped through her lips, making Smith grin wider, but still Aimee did not talk.

"Beg me!" Smith yelled at her again, and he forced her head forward.

Her nose smashed into the wall and her eyes filled with water from the impact. She blinked rapidly, trying to clear her spinning vision. Her nose throbbed, but she could not be sure if it was broken.

"Please," she whispered, her voice breaking around the word.

"I can't hear you, Aimee."

"Please," she said, louder this time.

Smith tightened his grip on her hair and released her wrists, which she pressed against the wall on either side of her face, her nails digging into the wood.

"Please!" She screamed as loud as she could manage. "Please!"

His hand reached around Aimee, and he fumbled greedily with the button on her jeans. A shudder ran through his body as they fell to the floor.

19

Rainey

Rainey had spent the first twenty minutes of their journey looking through Anya's file, searching for anything that could be considered useful, while Joe and Lexi argued about the best routes to take and how best to avoid the police. Her next twenty minutes had been spent being questioned by Joe and Lexi about any information she had found. Her answers had been short and to the point.

"She came from Nevada, in The States, but she's English."

"It says she's 33."

"Yes."

"No."

"It doesn't say."

"Her surname is Hall."

"How the hell should I know if it's her real name?"

Rainey had remained silent in the back seat as she listened to their theories about Anya and how she could be involved, but she lost interest quickly. The truth was, she couldn't bear to hear the woman's name. When she pictured Anya in her head, she also pictured Lily in her arms, as she was taken away. Rainey squeezed her eyes shut, trying to erase the image that would not go away. She didn't care how Anya had been involved, just as long as she ended up dead.

"How you feeling?" Joe called over his shoulder.

He looked between the road ahead of him and the rear-view mirror, where he could see Rainey in the seat behind him. Rainey did not bother to open her eyes.

"How do you think?" she replied, harshly.

Joe didn't answer. He shared a look with Lexi in the seat next to him before returning his concentration to the road. After a few minutes of silence, Rainey leant over the back seat and reached into the boot of the car. She pulled out Lily's bunny and blanket. Lexi watched as Rainey settled back into her seat and clipped the seat belt back into place. Gently, she ran her fingers over the cuddly toy's face before lifting it to her nose. It smelled of Lily. She knew she should not hold on to them for too long, the less she touched them, the longer they would keep Lily's smell. But as she ran the blanket through her fingers, she couldn't help but lift it to her cheek and lean her face into it. She didn't care that Lexi was watching her from the corner of her eye, Rainey closed her eyes and let the tears fall silently down her face.

After what felt like a long time, she drifted into a dreamless sleep.

Rainey woke to the slam of the car's boot. She looked down to see that she still held both the bunny and the blanket tightly against her body. Neither Joe nor Lexi were in their seats in the front of the car, and Rainey peered out of the window to see Joe standing outside, facing away towards the overgrown fields, with his fingers locked together on the top of his head.

Carefully, Rainey set Lily's possessions down on the empty seat beside her. She unbuckled her seatbelt and climbed out of the car. Her legs were stiff from sitting still for too long and her head throbbed slightly, but as she took a deep breath of the fresh evening air, she began to feel more alert. The car had been pulled into a lay-by which cut into the edge of a field, away from the main road. Joe stood on the edge of the grass, looking out over the countryside. The dried earth crunched beneath Rainey's feet as she stepped closer. Joe's hands fell to his sides at the sound of her approach. Rainey took his hand in hers and looked out across the rolling fields. Her eyes drifted up to the sky, where long thin clouds spread across the sky horizontally and the setting sun shone a bright orange in the gaps but a warm pink beneath the clouds. Joe sighed, as though he was content, but it was empty of emotion.

"I'm sorry." Rainey said.

"What for?" Joe replied.

"For being a bitch."

Joe laughed. Not a real laugh, just a noise which seemed to fit the conversation.

"I just... I know that you're going through exactly what I am. But I have been so wrapped up in my own head that I didn't think about how you must be feeling."

"No, I'm not," Joe said plainly.

"You're not what?"

"I'm not going through exactly what you are," he continued quickly, before she could argue. "Rainey, today you found out that your boyfriend and your best friend have been keeping secrets from you, and your parents and your daughter were kidnapped, possibly as a result of that secret. And we have no idea where they are. I am not going through exactly what you are."

Rainey nodded her head.

"They've been parents to you too since you were fourteen," she replied.

He squeezed her hand and looked up into the clouds.

"Where are we?" She asked Joe, looking around.

"Well, I assumed we would be leaving the country, since you seem to be a wanted criminal these days."

Rainey frowned.

"There's a sentence I never thought I'd hear," she said.

"We're on our way to Dover. I think we can make it there in about half an hour from here, not that I have ever driven to Dover before."

"Half an hour? How long was I asleep?"

"A few hours. You needed the rest. Those bruises are looking a little better." Joe smiled.

Rainey ran a hand across her neck.

"You healed them?"

"Not completely, just enough to take the edge off."

Rainey ran her thumb across Joe's cheek. When she was satisfied that his handiwork had not cost him too dearly, she let her hand fall back by her side.

"So, we catch a ferry to Calais, right? Then what?" Rainey guessed.

"I have no idea. I don't even know if we'll get on the ferry. I have my passport in the car, I never really needed it before, so it's been in the glove box for months. But Lexi doesn't have a passport at all, she said she hasn't needed one for years so the only one she did have isn't even valid anymore." Joe chewed his lip. "Great plan of ours. I don't suppose you have yours on you?" He added, hopefully.

"I have a passport. In fact, I have a few passports. I'm not sure about the names on them though," Rainey said as she turned back to the car.

Joe followed her with a quizzical expression. Rainey pulled on the door for the boot of the car and jumped back as a shocked-looking Lexi greeted her.

"Aaah!" She yelled. "What the hell are you doing in there?"

Lexi laughed. She laughed so hard she had to cling to her sides as her muscles began to ache. Joe joined in, and the corners of Rainey's mouth began to pull up into a grin, but she stopped herself quickly as a wave of guilt washed through her. Her guilt was quickly followed with a fresh batch of self-loathing. How could she possibly want to laugh? Joe and Lexi noticed the change in her, and their laughs died in their throats, their smiles fading as their own guilt began to set in.

"I'm in the boot because we are almost at Dover, and I can't board a ferry. Although, if you two get caught smuggling me out of the country, then none of us will be able to board a ferry."

Rainey reached over Lexi and pulled out the pink rucksack. She dug her hands into the bag and pulled out two handfuls of passports. Joe watched with raised eyebrows.

"Here," Rainey said, passing Joe one of the passports.

He opened it and read out the information.

"Jasmine Thompson. With a picture of Lily."

"I found them in the safe. I don't know why they were there. There are a few here for both of us, all with different names. None for Lexi though. There are some for my parents too."

"I guess I shouldn't be surprised. Aimee has always planned ahead. I just didn't think she would ever be planning for us to be fleeing the country as wanted criminals." Joe said.

"I don't think it was the police she expected you to be running from. What else was in the safe?" Lexi asked.

"Money, mostly. I took as much as I could fit in the bag," Rainey dug her hand into the bag and pulled out the key ring. "This was in there too." She handed it to Lexi.

"I guess we're going to Italy then," Lexi said, matter of fact.

She threw the key ring to Joe who missed it and watched it land in the dirt at his feet.

"Thanks for the warning, Lex," he said, as he bent down to pick it up.

The key ring was a thick, oval shape made from clear acrylic with a miniature model of the Leaning Tower of Pisa inside.

"What's in Italy?" Lexi asked.

"One of the restaurants, but it's nowhere near Pisa." Rainey replied. "Maybe Maria can help?" She added as she turned to Joe.

"Who's Maria?" Lexi asked.

"Maria is the manager of William's restaurant in Turin. I haven't talked to her much yet, but Aimee and William were close with her.

She is also a Gifted. I don't know how much she knows about any of this, but she might be able to help us. We don't have any better ideas. We may as well start somewhere."

Rainey dug her hand into the bag and pulled out the rolled-up scrap of paper. She handed it to Joe and then carefully placed the passports and the key ring back in the bag. Joe unrolled the paper and stared at it for a moment.

"'*Make a new life for yourself*'," he read out loud.

Rainey raised her eyebrows, urging him to read more, but that was all there was, '*Make a new life for yourself*'.

"No." She said simply, snatching the note back from Joe and throwing it into the bag.

From the bonnet of the car, they watched the last embers of light disappear below the horizon while Joe explained the relationship between Maria, Aimee and William to Lexi. Rainey fished her phone out of her pocket and began searching through the web, giving an agitated moan every time a new page took a little too long to load. After a few minutes she interrupted Joe mid-sentence.

"Is anyone hungry?" She questioned.

"Well, yeah. But-" Joe replied, and he was cut off again by Rainey.

"Tired?"

"Oh God, yes!" Lexi shouted, a little too loudly.

"We need a plan. So, for now, I think we should find a hotel for the night. We can rest, eat, and in the morning, head for the ferry. We have passports we can all use but one of us will have to board on foot and the other two in the car. I am pretty sure I could pass for my mother, with a little altering maybe, that means Lexi can use one of my passports." She took a deep breath before continuing. "I'll go on foot and you two can stay in the car, we can meet up on the ferry. When we get to Calais, we're going to have to drive from there to Italy, maybe we should change cars first?"

"Why do we need to change cars? I like this car," Lexi argued.

"Because there is a good chance the police know we are using this car. We should probably get new phones too." Rainey replied.

"Oh, come on. Breaking into a mental hospital is not something the police are going to chase you around the world for. Are new cars and phones and all these bloody passports really necessary?" Lexi said.

"And what if it's not the police who are following us, Lexi?" Rainey was mad now and her voice steadily rose as she questioned Lexi. "I have no idea who these people are, who for some reason have decided to kidnap half of my family, but you knew something about them, didn't you? So maybe you should decide if we need to take extra precautions or not."

That shut Lexi up. She shared a nervous glance with Joe before lowering her head and staring at a spot on the ground as though it suddenly really interested her.

"Ok, we will find a new car, new phones. Whatever you think we need. And for now, we can head to a hotel and get some rest. We'll work out a route to Italy before we head for the ferry in the morning," Joe said, trying to calm to situation.

"We can't board the ferry on foot until 08:25 tomorrow morning, and we need to get there forty-five minutes before, so that gives us a few hours to rest." Rainey said, sharing her research.

Lexi clambered down off the bonnet and climbed into the back seat when Rainey chose to be in the front. Joe climbed back into the driver's seat and put the keys into the ignition.

"Anyone know of any hotels in the area?" Joe called, as he started the engine.

The three of them looked at each other but remained silent.

"I guess not. Let's just drive until we find somewhere."

The car pulled out of the lay-by and back on to the road. They headed in the general direction of the port and stopped at a couple of B&Bs, but both were fully booked. They had started to think they would be sleeping in the car for the night when they spotted a large hotel owned by a well-known chain. Rainey recognised it from the television adverts.

A room big enough for all three of them was available and Rainey counted out the correct amount of money before removing it from the rucksack, careful to keep the contents of her bag hidden. They made their way up to the room with a bag each and the pink rucksack hanging from Rainey's shoulder. The room was small with a double bed and a pull-out sofa. There was a desk with a mirror hanging above it, a TV rested on top of the desk and a small fridge underneath. A large window covered one wall of the room with thick, red curtains hanging at either side from the rails above. A wardrobe with wonky door stood tall in one of the corners. And the bathroom door was ajar, revealing the end of a large, white bathtub.

Rainey dumped her bag on the floor and headed straight for the fridge. Joe and Lexi watched as she pulled out several miniature bottles of spirits. She opened the first, and without reading the label she knocked it back. Then she did the same for the second, and the third. She screwed up her face as the burning sensation in her throat trickled down into her stomach. As she turned to grab another bottle, she caught a glimpse of herself in the mirror and gasped. She was unrecognisable. Her neck was covered in angry purple bruises, even after Joe had healed her for a second time. Some parts were obviously fingerprints, where others merged together to form a trail wrapping around her throat. One of her eyes was badly bruised and what should have been the white surrounding her iris was blood red. She hadn't really thought about how she must look to other people. If her bruises were not enough to scare somebody off then her tangled, matted hair and her wide, crazed eyes would definitely do the trick.

Rainey made a sound in her throat that she had intended to be a laugh, but it came out more like a choked sob. Joe disappeared into the bathroom with a pained look, slamming the door shut behind him, the lock clicking into place.

"I see why they said the other B&Bs were full," Rainey said.

She looked at Lexi, waiting for a reply, but it didn't come. Instead, Lexi joined her at the desk and reached into the mini bar for herself. She pulled out her own handful of little bottles.

"I hope the bar downstairs is fully stocked because this is not going to be enough alcohol," she said, standing the bottles next to one another on the desk.

"Should we go eat? The restaurant's open." Rainey checked her watch as she spoke.

"Yes! I am starving. Mind if I borrow some clothes?"

She didn't wait for an answer before she picked up a bag full of Rainey's things and tipped it out on to the bed. She picked out an outfit and then stripped out of her clothes, creating a pile on the floor. She slipped her feet into the legs of a pair jogging bottoms she had chosen and bent forward to pull them up at the exact moment Joe walked out of the bathroom, earning himself an eyeful of Lexi's backside. Joe swore loudly and spun around.

"Did nobody ever teach you to knock!" Lexi yelled, pulling the trousers up.

"I was in the bathroom! How was I supposed to know you would be half naked?"

"Whatever, Joe. If you wanted to look then all you had to do was ask."

She was trying to lighten the mood and it was working, Joe's cheeks flushed pink, and Rainey finally smiled.

"I'm decent now, by the way, so you can turn around."

Joe turned back towards them to find that Lexi had pulled her trousers up, but that was all. She still wore only a bra to cover her modesty on her top half.

"Oh, come on, Lexi!" He shouted.

She laughed as she pulled a t-shirt over her head. Rainey had begun trying to brush through her hair, but she gave up quickly. She looked at her reflection in the mirror and her tangled strands started to move on their own, forming a messy bunch of hair on the top of her head which she then secured into place with a hair bobble. She pulled out a wet wipe and carefully moved it over her face and neck.

"Joe, I really do not want you to have to do this, but I think I need a little more help healing. We can't walk into the restaurant with me looking like this," she pointed to her black eye. "But only do what is necessary."

"It's all necessary. And you're not going to argue with me this time," he held a finger over her lips to stop her from disagreeing. "We will go eat and then we can come back to the room and rest. I'll be fine."

He placed his hand gently over Rainey's eye and cheek, his palm cupping her face. Then he trailed his hand down her face and around her neck. By the time he had finished, Joe's skin had changed from a beautiful, tanned glow to a grey-white. He stepped back and wobbled on his feet.

"There. Now, let's go," he said, grabbing a handful of money out of the pink bag before throwing the remainder into a small safe hidden in the wardrobe and deciding on a code. He tested it a couple of times while Rainey looked at her now healed neck in the mirror.

"Thank you," she said to Joe, as they headed out for dinner.

She didn't mention the injuries covering rest of her body. Healing her face had been taxing enough.

In the restaurant they ordered a meal each and some drinks. Rainey didn't feel much like eating, but she forced herself to try the fish pie she had ordered while Lexi and Joe pushed their own food around their plates. When she could stomach no more, she ordered a bottle of white wine and Lexi followed suit. When it was time to head back to the room, Rainey struggled to walk unaided. They opened the bedroom door and Lexi ran in, diving on to the bed.

"I should not have done that with a full stomach." Lexi said, as a huge burp rolled up her throat.

Joe flicked on the TV and perched himself on the end of the bed. Rainey grabbed some clean underwear and one of Joe's shirts out of his bag and headed for the bathroom. She flicked on the shower, undressed and stepped under the cold water. Her skin tightened as the freezing water ran down her back, and over her chest, trickling down her stomach and legs. Slowly, the water began to heat, and as it did Rainey felt her muscles unknot and relax. She washed and conditioned her hair using the complimentary hotel bottles and she watched the water turn red with what was left of her blood as it ran off her, before it swirled away down the plug hole.

When she stepped out of the shower, she dried herself with a towel and hung it on the empty rack. Dreading what she might see, Rainey stepped up to the full-length mirror and took note of the bumps and bruises covering her body. There were a few dark marks around her ribs and some smaller bruises spotted down the length of her spine, but other than that, it wasn't too bad. She was about to turn and pick up her clean clothes when she spotted Joe in the mirror, looking through the gap in the door. A look of torment and frustration burned in his eyes as he too made a note of the marks on Rainey's body.

Rainey pulled on her underwear and Joe's white shirt and pushed the bathroom door open the rest of the way, just as the bedroom door slammed shut.

"Where's he going?" Rainey called over to Lexi.

"I don't know." She shrugged.

Rainey grabbed hold of the door handle, ready to run after him, but Lexi stopped her.

"Let him go, Ray. Give him some time to cool off."

Rainey was tempted to ignore her instruction, but then she nodded her head and moved over to the couch. She collapsed on to it, bringing her knees up to her chest and wrapping her arms around them. Lexi sat beside her and pulled Rainey's head on to her shoulder, wrapping one arm around her middle. And there they stayed, not talking, not crying, just silently staring into space. Until Rainey finally fell to sleep.

20

Aimee

The room was silent but for Aimee's unsteady breaths. She lay uncomfortably in a heap on the floor, listening for any noise, any sign that he might be coming back. But there was nothing. Only the sound of her breaths as her tears streamed silently down her face and on to the floor.

So, here she was, back in the prison she had once called home. She felt just like her teenage self again, not like the typical teenager who had arguments with their parents about what time they needed to be home for, or crying over some teen fling and her first heartbreak. No, Aimee's teenage years had not been typical at all. They had been spent much like the last hour of her adult life had. Cowering beneath Smith. She had managed to control herself this time and battle her impulse to fight back, it did no good to fight against Smith, she had learned that the hard way a long time ago.

A noise from the other side of the doors made Aimee startle, and she held her breath, silencing herself. She listened intently as the footsteps grew louder, too many for it to be Smith alone. The doors swung open to reveal three men. Aimee did not lift her head to get a better look at them. What did it matter? Her body was already broken. Smith stepped back into the room first. He ran a hand over his shining head as he looked down at Aimee on the floor.

"Put her in with William." He ordered.

Smith's men approached Aimee. She did not have the strength to move from her spot on the floor. So, they picked her up, hooking one arm under each of hers, and propping her upright. She flinched as they lifted her. Smith had not been gentle.

Slowly, Smith examined her with his eyes, looking her body up and down, enjoying the fear he could sense in her eyes with his every movement. He held out a hand and took hold of Aimee's chin, rubbing his thumb over her bottom lip. He jerked her head roughly, forcing her to meet his eyes.

"Let him see what a cheating little rat she really is." He said to the men, not breaking his gaze with Aimee.

He leaned close to her face, and Aimee held her breath in anticipation, waiting for him to strike her again.

"I hope you're looking forward to seeing me again. I will not be waiting quite as long this time." He whispered.

It took everything Aimee had in her to not react. She knew that if she retaliated, it would hurt her more than it would hurt him. But she could not stop herself from fantasising about how his face might look if she were to give him even a small shock with one of her bolts. She pushed the thought from her mind, knowing that the consequences would strike her tenfold. Aimee would have to settle for a smaller retaliation. She could not let him think that he had won, that he had broken her spirit beyond repair. She had always known she would end up back here, with him. She had always known that he would never rest until he had his way. She had had the last nineteen years to prepare herself for the horrors that lie within Smith's office. And she had vowed never to allow him to break her soul. Her body, sure. What choice did she have? But never her soul.

With her chin still firmly in Smith's grip, she released a mouthful of saliva into his face. Smith did not look surprised. He simply wiped the spit from his face and looked at the mess on his hand. He laughed, before raising his other hand so quickly Aimee did not have time to contemplate what was coming. He slapped her hard across her face. The slap burned her cheek and a rush of pain washed through her, making her dizzy. She gritted her teeth together and fought against her reflex to cry out. She would not give him the satisfaction. He turned away from her, giving the signal for his bodyguards to leave, and they dragged Aimee across the room and towards the doors. She did not fight them. She allowed her body to trail lifelessly across the floor.

Aimee paid little attention to her surroundings as she was dragged for what felt to her like a long few minutes through the winding corridors of Smith's Institute. There was little point in trying to decipher where she was being taken. She would never escape this place. Not again. He would never make the same mistake twice. When they finally stopped at a locked door, the taller of the men tapped a code into a pad. There was a clunk as the lock unlatched and the door swung forward. They moved through, and Aimee heard it swing shut behind them. Then she was pulled down another corridor, passing endless identical plain doors, until finally, they came to a stop. What looked to Aimee to be a light-switch on the wall beside yet another identical door, turned out to be a door release. Again, the taller of the men stepped forward and pushed in the switch, holding it there for a moment. The lock clicked and the other man pushed it open, dragging Aimee through with him.

William stood in the centre of the room with two small metal bed frames on either side of him, each topped with a thin mattress. A pile of folded blankets lay at the end of each bed. The room was barely large enough to house the bed frames, with very little floor space to move around, and no other furniture. The walls and floor looked as though they had been painted white, but the dim yellow light made them appear dirty and un-kept. There were no windows, the only source of light coming from a single lightbulb dangling from the centre of the ceiling. And a camera hung from the corner of the room, a red blinking light indicating it was watching their every move.

Aimee did not look at William as she was dragged into the room, her eyes remained firmly on the ground beneath her, but she could feel his gaze following her as the men deposited her on to the closest bed. Without a single word, they backed out of the room, leaving them in silence. The door clicked again as the lock fell back into place behind them.

William did not speak. He stood frozen, watching Aimee as she tried to hold back her cries. She lay facing the wall, hiding her face in her arms. She could not look at him. She could not tell him what Smith had done to her. Knowing it would destroy him. And yet, she knew that he must already know.

"Aimee?" He tried.

She did not answer.

"Aimee. Please, tell me he didn't."

A sob escaped through her lips, and she squeezed her eyes tightly shut, willing herself to hold it together for him.

William's hands balled into fists at his sides, and he shook uncontrollably with rage. He gasped in a deep steadying breath before he carefully climbed on to the bed behind Aimee and wrapped his arms around her. She clung tightly to his hands and squeezed his arms closer to her body. And then she cried, great tormented sobs, while her tears ran down her face and pooled in the mattress.

William held Aimee for a long time. He did not let go of her until her tears stopped falling and her body stopped shaking. When Aimee was finally ready to talk again, William tried his best to disguise his own grief, but he knew that she could hear it in his voice.

"It's like we're seventeen, all over again," she whispered.

"Are you hurt?"

When Aimee did not reply he pushed himself up and gently pulled Aimee into a sitting position. He looked at her face and saw for the first time the angry red handprint across her cheek. He lifted one arm at a time and carefully scanned them with his eyes for any signs of Smith. He traced his fingers lightly across the angry red lines around her wrists, then, slowly, he began to roll up her shirt, revealing her back. He grimaced as the first few centimetres of her skin were revealed, and he struggled to contain his emotions as he rolled her shirt up higher and higher. Bite marks covered her body. Some had not broken the flesh, but others had, and the blood they had produced had dried and hardened over her skin. The marks continued on to her stomach and chest and down her body as far as William could see. He could not bear to look any further.

He lowered Aimee's shirt and watched as she curled back into a ball on the bed.

"I'll kill him," he whispered.

William climbed off the bed and stood with his head in his hands.

"I'll kill him!" He screamed.

He leapt at the closed door and began to hammer on it with his fists.

"Do you hear me, Smith? I will kill you! You sick son of a bitch!"

William turned to look at the camera in the corner of the room. He climbed on to the end of the empty bed and wrapped a trembling hand around it.

"You are dead!" He bellowed into the camera before ripping it from the wall and launching it at the door, where it shattered and fell into pieces on the floor.

He sank onto the bed.

"He's dead," he said to himself, his voice breaking. "I need him to die. I need to kill him."

Then he leaned his head back against the wall and cried, because William knew just as well as Aimee did, that there was nothing he could do to stop Smith from hurting his wife.

21

Lexi

As soon as she could be certain that Rainey was asleep, Lexi wriggled her way off the sofa, slipped a coat over her pyjamas and a pair of shoes on to her feet, and tiptoed out of the room as quietly as she could. She began her search for Joe, having no doubt in her mind where he had disappeared to. It did not take her long to find him in the bar. The room was empty but for Joe and a young waitress, who was walking around the tables collected the leftover glasses.

Joe was sitting on one of the bar stools, resting his head against his hand, staring down at his half empty glass.

"Hey." Lexi said as she walked up to him.

Joe looked up and nodded in acknowledgement. She took a seat on the stool next to him and gave the woman a hinting glance she was ready for a drink.

"We don't have to talk," Lexi said to Joe. "We can just drink if you'd prefer."

There was a crash behind them as the waitress dropped a tray of glasses on to the floor. She cursed loudly before she stepped over the mess and headed for Joe and Lexi.

"What can I get you?" She asked, looking flustered.

"Whatever he's drinking, please."

The woman looked Lexi up and down. Lexi looked old enough to drink, but whether she looked sane enough in Rainey's pyjamas and coat was a different matter altogether. She placed the drink on a coaster in front of Lexi and took the note Joe had pushed in her direction. She returned a moment later with his change and then busied herself in sweeping up the broken glass.

"I've never seen her drink before," Joe said in a morbid voice. "Not once since we first met, did she feel the need to drink."

They were silent for a moment.

"Why did you bail?" Lexi asked bluntly.

"I couldn't look at her like that."

"It's not like she was drunk-"

"I'm not talking about her having a drink! I'm talking about the bruises. She is covered in them." He rubbed his temples with his knuckles. "Every time I close my eyes all I can see is her skin, covered in those bruises."

Lexi did not know what she could say to make him feel better, there wasn't really anything she could say when she shared Joe's disgusted herself.

"Why would they do this?" Joe said into his hands.

"You know why they're doing it. Lily could be so strong; they're taking an extreme precaution."

"No. There's more to this than just that. If Lily was the threat, then why take Aimee and William too? These people are supposed to be protectors. They are supposed to be the people who help us go unnoticed, stop the humans who try to ruin us and save the Gifted who are under threat. Beating up teenagers and stealing children is not what they are supposed to do!"

The waitress shot a concerned look in their direction.

"Shh! Would you be quiet!" Lexi whispered.

Joe lifted his drink from the bar and watched the clear liquid swirl in the glass for a moment before throwing his head back and swallowing what was left. Lexi raised her drink to her lips too. She took a sip and scowled.

"What the hell are you drinking?" She choked.

Joe shrugged his shoulders.

"It burns, whatever it is."

She emptied the glass into her mouth and swallowed it anyway.

"So, what do you think they are doing then? If Lily isn't the real reason behind this, then what is?" Lexi asked when her throat had stopped burning enough to let her speak.

"I don't know. Aimee and William both have a history with these people."

"But we don't know what happened there. The history they share could be something as simple as leaving their jobs with bad references." Lexi said.

"Lexi, Aimee and Will met while they were working for a man called Smith and they ended up running away together and hiding out for years to get away from him. When Rainey drew a picture of a man she was seeing in her dreams, Aimee freaked out. I mean, really freaked out. Like she was having a panic attack or something."

Lexi was silent for a moment as she considered Joe's words.

"My parents knew Smith. He asked them to work for him," she said.

"Aimee mentioned your parents, along with Jason, when she tried to explain to me who Smith was." Joe's eyebrows knitted together as he tried to piece together the different parts of the jigsaw.

He did not push Lexi to say any more about her parents. Lexi rarely spoke about them, and when she did her face clouded over as she relived her memories of them. The memories she had of her parents were too painful for her, a topic Rainey and Joe had learned to avoid discussing. Joe fished around in his pocket for another note and held it out in front of him between two fingers while he waited for the waitress to come back. She rushed over when she spotted him.

"Another two?" She asked.

Joe nodded as she took the money from his hand. She returned with two drinks and a few coins before Lexi snapped out of her memory. She shook her head to clear it and they each took a drink, knocking it back. Joe swirled his glass in his hand, watching as the ice decorated the surface with beads of water.

"Was she asleep when you left her?" He asked.

Lexi nodded, unable to speak while her throat again tried to clear itself of the burning sensation. They stayed silent for a while. Until, finally, Joe pushed his stool back from the bar and wobbled to his feet. Lexi hopped down next to him and together they headed back to the room.

Rainey had not moved from where Lexi left her on the sofa. Joe stumbled into the room and headed straight for her. He brushed a loose strand of hair from her face and ran his fingers across her forehead and down her cheek. Careful not to wake her, Joe gently rolled up one side of Rainey's shirt and traced his fingers over the angry purple bruises surrounding her ribs. Lexi watched as the marks softened and faded from purple to yellow, and Joe's skin drained of colour, his veins standing out strikingly along the lengths of his arms. His head flopped forward and the effort of standing alone seemed to be painful for him. His fingers pulled away from Rainey's skin, where they hovered for a moment before he dropped his hand to his side.

He searched the room with his eyes until he found a blanket hanging from the end of the bed. He retrieved it and draped it over Rainey's curled up body, before he turned and collapsed on to the bed.

"You should not have gotten drunk," Lexi said in a low voice.

"Excuse me?" Joe replied, too tired to prop himself up and look at her.

"You shouldn't have drunk so much."

"Oh, well. I am sorry, Lexi. We can't all be perfect." He replied, sarcastically.

"I'm serious, Joe! Don't let this happen again. Rainey needs you right now, and we have a lot ahead of us. The last thing we need is to be wasting time getting drunk and being hung-over," she snapped.

Joe's eyes closed and he cringed as images danced across the back of his eyelids. Letting out a sigh, Lexi stalked past him and grabbed a toothbrush and a tube of toothpaste from one of the weekend bags. She headed into the bathroom and locked the door behind her.

The shower took a little while to heat up, and when the water ran hot Lexi jumped in. It stung her skin a little at first, but she soon became accustomed to the temperature. She did not stay in there for a long time. She hopped out of the shower, dried off and pulled her pyjamas back on. Then she brushed her teeth and had a quick tidy around the bathroom before heading to bed. Joe was already asleep in the exact same position she had left him fifteen minutes earlier. She did not bother to wake him so that he could change out of his jeans and t-shirt. Instead, she climbed under the section of covers she could pull loose from underneath him and curled up. Her eyes grew heavy quickly and it did not take her long to drift into a restless sleep.

The sound of the kettle bubbling woke Lexi. She looked around hopefully and smiled when she spotted Rainey fussing over sachets of coffee under a dim light. Rainey spotted her watching her and smiled.

"I'm guessing you want one of these?" She asked.

"Well, yeah. Joe could probably do with one too when he wakes up. What time is it?" Lexi replied.

"We have about an hour and a half before we have to leave. Let him sleep a little longer."

When the kettle finished boiling, Rainey tore open two of the coffee sachets and poured them into mugs, then she filled them up with water from the kettle and added a little carton of milk to each, adding a couple of sachets of sugar to Lexi's mug. She carried Lexi's drink over to her, and Lexi propped herself up in bed. Rainey passed her the cup of coffee before taking her own cup and sitting at the end of the bed with her legs crossed. They inhaled the rich, bitter smell of their steaming mugs.

"I figured we could do with it being a bit on the stronger side today." Rainey said as she took a sip.

Lexi looked over to Joe who still had not moved since he had fallen to sleep the previous night.

"Are you sure he's breathing?" She joked.

They drank their coffees quietly while they waited for the time to pass by and after thirty minutes or so they decided to wake Joe and prepare themselves to leave. After many attempts of calling Joe's name, Lexi ran out of patience and gave him a nudge in the ribs with her foot, causing Joe to startle so dramatically that he fell off the side of the bed. He gave Lexi an angry glare before accepting a cup of coffee from Rainey.

When Joe finished his drink, the three of them began to pack away their belongings and plan for the day ahead. They each took a handful of money to keep in their pockets and picked out a new passport. Luckily, most of the details on their new passports were exactly the same as their originals. They memorised their new names before storing them away safely. Lexi would be Rainey for the day, or Jessica Lewis as her passport claimed. Rainey would be Aimee, or Jane Thomas, and Joe would be himself, Kai Grover.

After loading everything into the car, they had twenty minutes to spare before they needed to set off for the port, so the three of them headed to the restaurant. Their nerves for what the day ahead may hold prevented them from eating, and when Joe finally gave up on pushing his scrambled eggs around the plate, the other two gave up too.

Lexi and Rainey headed to the car while Joe settled the bill, and before long, they were leaving the car park and heading for the ferry port.

The car ride was a quiet one filled with nervous fidgeting and *'what ifs?'*.

What if the passports did not work?
What if they could not make it to Calais?
What if one of them was caught and not the others?
What if...

What if…
What if…

As they approached the turnoff to the port, Joe pulled over into a lay-by and turned off the engine.

"I suppose I should make myself look more like my mother," Rainey said as she pulled the mirror down to look at herself.

Lexi and Joe watched as Rainey's skin transformed, draining a little of her colour, Aimee's skin had always been a fairer shade than her own. Her lips gradually grew darker, giving the illusion of appearing fuller, and hints of dark circles began to appear around her eyes to add an extra few years on to her age. When she was finished altering, Rainey stared at herself in the mirror. She was Aimee. Everything about her was Aimee. Rainey had always looked just like her mother, her eyes a perfect replica of grey-blue, but she had not realised just how similar they were until now. The only real difference was their age. But Aimee's passport photo had been taken a few years back and Rainey hoped that the changes she had made to her features would work perfectly.

She pulled herself up straighter and unbuckled the seat belt before pulling her top up as far as it would go without actually taking it off, revealing her black bra. She ran her thumb along a stretch mark which zigzagged down her stomach and then prodded at one of her yellowing bruises suspiciously.

"What are you doing?" Joe scalded as he tried to yank her top back down.

He glanced at the cars driving by to ensure nobody was watching as they passed.

"I'm making sure my skin colour matches. Is this why you were so tired this morning?" She said, pointing to what remained of her injuries.

Joe hesitated for a moment before answering.

"Yes, I healed you. No, I don't want to hear any more about it."

Rainey opened her mouth to argue, and Lexi chewed on her lip anxiously, she had been hoping for a more settled day, one where they could all agree to work together with no arguments and without an appearance of Rainey's earthquakes, splitting open the ground and threatening to swallow them whole. She was relieved when Rainey seemed to think better of it. Rainey turned to face Lexi and held out her hand.

"I hope this works," she said as she wrapped her fingers around

Lexi's.

Lexi watched with an open mouth as the skin on her hand darkened. The colour spread up her arm like paint seeping through clean water, in swirls and twists. It took a couple of minutes, but eventually all of Lexi's skin was the same tanned shade as Rainey's. Lexi pulled her hair out of her loose ponytail and let it fall around her face. Then she pulled a borrowed baseball cap down over her forehead and looked to Rainey with raised eyebrows.

"Well?" She demanded.

"Close enough," Rainey shrugged.

"Close enough is not good enough. This isn't going to work."

"Always the optimist, Lex." Joe muttered, rolling his eyes. "But, just in case, do we have a plan if this doesn't work?"

Rainey thought about it for a short moment.

"We can only do what we're best at. If anyone gets suspicious then Lexi will have to drain them, just enough for them to pass out. Hopefully, everyone else will be too busy bothering with that to worry about you two. If anything goes wrong on my end, then you'll know about it."

Lexi laughed.

"Lightning? High winds? Heavy rain? Let me know what we're looking out for here."

"All of the above?" Joe added.

"Something like that," Rainey smiled.

Rainey stepped out of the car and Joe followed her. From inside, Lexi watched as they said goodbye and hugged one another tightly. Rainey smiled to Lexi and set off walking. When Joe climbed back into the driver's seat Lexi hopped over the armrest in the middle of the car and fell clumsily into the passenger seat beside him.

They stayed there for a while, waiting long enough for Rainey to get a good head start. Neither spoke, and the silence began to feel painful as their minds ran through the possible outcomes of their attempt to flee the country.

"Radio?" Lexi asked.

Joe pressed some buttons on the radio and music began to play throughout the car, it was not a song they recognised but they tapped their feet nervously as they listened. When the song ended, a news reporter began to give a brief overview of the day's news. The female reporter spoke fast to fit as much into her allotted time as she could. The weather forecast for the day, which, as usual, would be grey and windy. The details of a local event taking place. And something about a spate of break-ins in the area.

"And, finally," her voice lowered dramatically. "Police continue to search for a vehicle in connection with a robbery at a psychiatric hospital in Yorkshire. The car was last seen leaving the scene after the robbery and is thought to be driven by eighteen-year-old Rainey White, who is local to the area. Police believe White was assisted in the robbery by a hospital patient named Alexa Dennon. Neither have been seen since the incident. Police say they are likely to be extremely dangerous and should not be approached. Searches of the family home have given no clues as to where White may be, but neighbours did agree to speak to reporters this morning."

A new voice with a heavy Yorkshire accent spilled from the speakers, filling the car.

"Yes, they're a strange family. Kept t' themselves mostly. A lot of strange goings on when it came t' them. A while back it were rumoured they had them Gifted genes. Never noticed anything me'self like, but I've stayed away just in case. Better t' be safe than sorry."

Joe swore and punched the steering wheel with his fist and Lexi jabbed at the off button on the radio.

"We need to ditch the car," she whispered.

Joe started the engine. He pulled back on to the road and searched for a turn off. Within minutes they were on a quiet country road surrounded by overgrown green fields, bushes and trees. The car pulled sharply to the left and through a gap in the hedges.

"Fit as much stuff into your bag as you can, whatever doesn't fit will have to stay." Joe said as he pushed open the door.

Together, Lexi and Joe emptied out all three bags. They took one bag each and began filling them with the most important items. Money and passports were the first to go in, and they put an equal amount in each. The next items were Lily's blanket and her bunny toy. Then they piled in as many as they could fit and zipped the bags closed. Finally, Lexi pushed the toothbrushes and toothpaste in through a gap on the zipper. Joe pulled his bag up on to his shoulder and Lexi followed his lead, then he pulled a lighter from his pocket. He looked at the car for a moment, Aimee's pride and joy, before picking up one of his left-over t-shirts. He pulled open the petrol cap and stuffed the t-shirt in as far as it would go. When he pulled it back out again, small blotches of fuel covered the material, and he held the lighter under a corner of a sleeve and waited for it to catch a light. When the flame began to climb its way up the fabric, Joe placed the t-shirt on top of the remaining clothes in the boot of the car. Lexi stepped forward with a can of hairspray she had tried, and failed, to fit into her bag. She pulled the cap off and aimed it at the flame, then pressed down on the top. The flame erupted through the boot of the car, singing the leather on the back of the headrests. When the rubber lining covering the floor began to melt, Lexi let go and threw the can into the fire.

Holding their bags tightly to their chests, they set off running. Lexi had not participated in a great deal of running since she had been admitted to the hospital, and it showed. Her chest throbbed painfully, and her throat stung as she gulped in breaths of fresh air. The added weight of the bag was not exactly helping, the strap dug painfully into her shoulder and the added weight made it even harder for her to breath. After a few minutes of running solidly, they had almost made it back to the main road.

We can't be too far behind Rainey now, Lexi thought.

"Joe... I can't... I can't keep running," Lexi gasped.

"We can walk from here. I don't think it's much further."

They slowed to a fast walk and Lexi tried to catch her breath.

"It's a shame... that we couldn't... come here... in better... circumstances," Lexi said between gasps.

"Why?" Joe asked.

Lexi waited until she had caught her breath before answering.

"I always wanted to see the white cliffs of Dover. You know, like in the song?"

Joe thought about it and then laughed.

"Out of everything that has happened in the past forty-eight hours, the thing that you think is a shame is missing out on the white cliffs?"

Lexi laughed too.

"I suppose that does sound silly."

"There'll be blue birds over..." Joe sang.

"The white cliffs of Dover." Lexi joined in.

They sang along as they rushed down the road. They knew how ridiculous they must look, but they didn't care. Singing distracted them from what they had just done, and what they were about to do. The traffic was growing busier, and Lexi could smell the sea air each time the breeze brushed across her face. She followed Joe through the busy roads and eventually through even busier car parks. It seemed to take forever to find the right building, but finally Joe slowed his walk and started searching through his pockets for his chosen passport.

"Hand me your passport," he said, holding out his hand.

Lexi passed him the little booklet and looked up at him.

"Let's hope this works," Joe said, and he squeezed Lexi's hand reassuringly.

Together, they walked through the final car park and up to a large, concrete building. Joe held his arm out in front of Lexi just as she was about to walk in through the glass double doors.

"Lexi, look," he said, pointing behind her.

She spun around and followed Joe's gaze. She could just make out something white in the distance.

"The white cliffs." Lexi said. "Hmm, I pictured them bigger in my head."

Joe rolled his eyes and pushed the doors open. Inside, there were people everywhere, standing in queues, going through luggage, drinking coffee. There were people asleep on benches or leaning on their bags against walls. Joe took hold of Lexi's hand and pulled her through the crowd to an information desk, where a man typed into a computer from behind the desk, a phone pinned between his ear and his shoulder. Each time he laughed and bobbed his head, his perfectly highlighted hair bounced. He had a round face and a fake, orange tan. He did not look up as they approached, and he continued to frantically bob his head in agreement to the conversation. His name tag read Scott.

They waited patiently for Scott to finish on his call, but after a little while Joe began to pointedly check his watch, hinting at their lack of time. Still, Scott paid them no attention. He clearly had no intention of ending his phone call prematurely. Eventually, Joe cleared his throat and a huge sigh sounded from Scott's direction before he continued on with his conversation. Joe cleared his throat again. He knew he needed to be careful, Scott could be their only chance of getting on the ferry, but he was testing his patience. Scott gave another sigh, then leaned the phone away from his mouth.

"Yes?" He said rudely. "Is there something I can help you with?"

Joe gritted his teeth and asked the man where he needed to go to buy two tickets for the ferry to Calais. Scott began to click the mouse on his computer.

"You may as well book them here. Names?"

Joe handed over the passports. Scott took them both and flipped through the pages, then he typed in their borrowed names and set to work booking the tickets.

"Do you need me, or can I go and get us some coffee?" Lexi asked.

Joe opened his mouth to answer when Scott held up a hand with Lexi's passport. He looked at the picture in the passport and then at Lexi. Lexi's heart began to pound in her chest, and she felt too hot all of a sudden. She considered how close she should allow Scott to get in realising she was not who she was supposed to be, before helping him to lose consciousness, when Scott dropped the passport on to the computer keyboard.

"You can book for her," he said to Joe.

Lexi turned, breathing a sigh of relief, and headed to the closest coffee stand, leaving Joe to handle the tickets. She scanned the menu before deciding on two mochas, a drink which Aimee had introduced her to. She gave her order to the girl behind the stall and moved across to allow the next person to place their order.

"What the hell are you two doing here?" A voice whispered behind Lexi.

She startled and spun on the spot. Rainey stood next to the coffee stall with a cardboard cup in her hand.

"Jeez, Rainey. You scared the life out of me," she scalded.

"Why are you not in the car?"

"Have you listened to the radio lately? You're a wanted criminal, Ray Ray. And so is the car, apparently. And potentially me, too. We torched it."

Lexi enjoyed watching Rainey's face transform as she let her news sink in.

"You did what? I love that car!"

"Well, tough. The police are looking for us. We heard a radio report saying that they're looking for the car and a girl who broke into a hospital and performed a robbery. We had no choice but to get rid of it. Sooner or later, they'll find it all burned out and it won't take a genius to figure out we've hopped on the first ferry to France."

Rainey did not know what to say. She ran a hand through her hair.

"Hey, remember when we were normal?" Lexi said.

"No?" Rainey replied, and they smiled.

The girl behind the coffee stand called out her order and handed Lexi two cardboard cups. Lexi gave her some money and told her to keep the change. They headed to an empty table and waited for Joe to join them with the tickets.

"Did Lexi fill you in?" He said to Rainey, after he joined them and kissed her on the forehead.

She nodded and gave a brief smile to show she was not too concerned with the news of how she was now a wanted criminal.

"We are booked on to a ferry for ten-fifteen. Just enough time to finish our drinks before we have to board." Joe said.

"We can't go on together. Our passport pictures look too alike for us to just be friends," Rainey said as she waved her passport in front of them.

"Ok. Rainey can go on first and we'll follow," Joe replied.

Rainey and Lexi nodded in agreement. They sipped at their coffees and waited impatiently for the announcement. When the announcement finally came twenty minutes later, they finished the last few mouthfuls of their drinks and Rainey collected the empty cups to throw into the bin. They allowed a rush of people to go ahead of them and joined on to the queue close to the end, with Rainey squeezing in half-way down the line. Lexi's heart began to beat faster as the line grew shorter.

Finally, Rainey made it to the front of the queue. She handed over her passport and ticket and the man took a quick look at the details, then at the picture on the passport, and finally at Rainey.

He smiled, returning the ticket and passport, and ushered her through the door. Lexi and Joe let out a quiet sigh of relief.

"One down, two to go," Joe whispered.

It took another fifteen minutes before they made it to the front of the queue. Lexi was now so nervous that her hands shook, and she had to squeeze them together tightly to stop them from vibrating. She smiled sweetly at the man as Joe handed over their tickets and passports.

"Ok then, Mr. Grover and Miss. Lewis, if you could just follow the corridor down to the bottom and out on to the dock. Someone will direct you from there."

His eyes fell on to Lexi's hands, wringing together, and he looked at her suspiciously as he noticed the sweat covering her skin. Joe took hold of one of her hands.

"I hope there's plenty of sick bags on board," Joe joked. "She gets terrible sea sickness."

Lexi gave a little nervous laugh and shuffled towards the door as Joe pulled her along by her hand. The man smiled and his glare softened.

"You won't be the only one," he said.

They walked down the corridor quickly and out on to the dock, along the side of the ship. Lexi gasped. She had never seen a ferry up close before. It made her feel minuscule with the hull of the ship towering over her. Ahead, they could see several sets of steps, all leading up to the ship. A woman in a fluorescent orange jacket pointed them towards a set of stairs and they hurried towards them. After another quick passport and ticket check at the bottom of the steps, on they climbed.

They found Rainey waiting inside the doorway with a huge grin on her face as they stepped off the stairs and on to the boat. They had done it. They had made it on to a ferry using fake passports and fake names while harbouring a wanted criminal. They followed the stream of holidaymakers down the corridors and up a few flights of stairs, until they made it to the top deck.

The crisp sea air hit them as they emerged. Rainey took a deep breath in, calming herself as the cocktail of coffee and adrenaline stirred within her. She headed for the stern of the boat, with Lexi and Joe trailing along behind her.

After a little while, a horn sounded, making all three of them jump, and slowly the ship began to inch forwards. As they left the dock, Rainey rested her head on Joe's shoulder, their fingers intertwining. Joe looked down at their linked hands and ran his thumb across their matching sketched hearts.

"We'll find them, Rainey." He said.

"I know," she said back, squeezing his hand.

Lexi pointed behind them.

"Wow! Look at the cliffs. They look amazing from here." She shouted, struggled to contain her excitement.

Joe smiled, and Rainey wrapped her arm around his waist as they watched the cliffs drift into the distance.

22

William

It had been a long night; Aimee had eventually cried herself out and given in to her heavy, burning eyelids. William had watched her sleep. He had not moved for hours. He had not slept. He had not eaten. He had not done anything but watch his wife sleep. One thought ran through his mind, over and over. Smith must die for what he had done. He would suffer under William's hand and pay for every moment he had caused Aimee to cower beneath him. And when that time came, William would make it slow and full of pain. He would only kill him when he finally decided to show Smith mercy.

Mercy, William thought. *Ha! There wouldn't be a whole lot of that.*

A sudden noise from the door made William jump from the bed, his joints aching as he moved them for the first time in hours. Another noise, this time followed with a clunk as the door was unlocked from outside. William rushed back to Aimee.

"Aimee!" He whispered, frantically. "Wake up!"

Aimee's eyes fluttered and the features of her face changed as she began to register where she was.

"There's someone coming." William whispered, gently tugging on her hand.

Aimee clambered from the bed and flinched as fresh pain brought her back to the present. Smith's assault had taken its toll on her body. Her face relaxed a little as the pain began to subside with the help of the adrenalin pulsing through her. The door began to swing open slowly, and William stood in front of Aimee, protecting her from whoever awaited them on the other side. The barrel of a gun inched its way through the gap in the door, held by the guard who followed it into the room.

William had never seen Smith's army use weapons before. What use did a Gifted have for a gun? Smith would only employ the most dangerous or useful of the Gifted. During all of William's time working for Smith, they had never needed guns. It could only mean one thing. His army was weak.

The guard was a man they had not yet seen. He was tall and broad, forcing the black clothing he wore to stretch across his wide shoulders. His face looked hostile and was covered in small scars, causing his top lip to drag out in an odd direction.

"If either of you try anything, I'll shoot a hole in the other one's knee. Got it?" He snarled.

William and Aimee said nothing, they watched as another armed guard stepped into the room.

"Out. Now." He ordered.

They did as they were told. William took hold of Aimee's hand and led the way through the door to where a third guard waited for them in the corridor.

"Let's go," said the first, as he walked out of the room, slamming the door shut behind him.

The locks clicked back into place as soon as the door closed, and they set off walking, with one guard in front of them and two behind. The only sound came from their shoes lightly tapping on the linoleum floor. William could see two more guards walking towards them. Black clothing appeared to be the dress code for all of the guards, making the woman walking between the two of them, stand out strikingly. She looked young, maybe a little older than Rainey, and she was dressed all in white; from her loose-fitting, long-sleeved top, to her linen trousers and slippers. But the most noticeable feature of all was her ballooned stomach. She was very heavily pregnant. As they approached, Aimee shot a nervous glance towards William, who squeezed her hand tightly in return. They had both worked in the Institute a long time ago, and they understood perfectly well what would happen to the pregnant woman when she was not pregnant anymore. If they had not run away all those years ago, Aimee would probably have been the one to work on her.

The guards did not acknowledge each other as they walked by, despite the corridor being just wide enough for them to squeeze through without knocking into one another. But William watched as Aimee's eyes met the young woman's. They turned their heads to watch the three of them pass, and William noticed that the third guard, the only guard who was yet to speak, did not keep his eyes on the corridor ahead as the other two did. He looked right at the woman in white, and a brief moment of agony slipped into his composed expression. He realised his mistake too late, and looked forward again, only to see both Aimee and William watching him closely. His sadness was quickly replaced with anxiety. He intentionally met both of their gazes and gave his head a little shake. Aimee and William exchanged another glance before they faced forward again. The exchange had taken only seconds behind the backs of the other guards, who had not noticed a thing.

After walking through yet more corridors, the group stepped into a lift, which carried them down a further two floors. They stepped out into a large room, with seats lining the walls all the way around, and a large door at the opposite end of the room. The first guard pointed to a section of seating.

"Sit." He ordered.

William pulled Aimee towards the chairs and they both took a seat. The guard walked across to the other side of the room and signalled for the second to follow him, leaving the third on his own to watch over William and Aimee.

"What's going on?" Aimee whispered to William.

"I don't know. Are you ok?"

"I'm fine. The guard with the pregnant girl," Aimee started, and William nodded. "This place has not changed." She said, sadly.

They looked over to the guard who stood alone, looking miserable. His eyes were sunken and tired, and his head hung forward. He seemed to realise that he was being watched and he straightened up a little. William could not help but feel sorry for him. That woman would likely be dead within the next few days, and he was clearly hung up on her. William's mind began to drift into the past, and how it had been when he himself had worked in this very building and loved a woman he was forbidden to see.

The doors at the far end of the room swung forward and a group of people walked through them and into the room. William instantly recognised the small woman at the back, the same woman who had brought them here, the one who could freeze her victims – Jenna. His top lip curled involuntarily as hatred briefly filled his thoughts.

There were a few new people within the gathering who William did not know, but there was no mistaking the two men at the very front of the small crowd. Smith, obviously, was leading the group into the room. But Smith's right-hand man was not someone William had ever expected to see again. He knew that Aimee had spotted him too because her entire body seemed to react. Her hand clamped down hard around William's and he almost cried out in pain. He could feel her arm shaking in her efforts to control herself. At least, that was why William assumed she shook, because Aimee was not afraid of this man. Not anymore.

"Well, look who got himself a nice little promotion." Aimee spat sarcastically across the room.

"Calm down, Aimee." William warned under his breath.

"If it isn't the world's number one father," she said with complete venom.

Hatred and anger oozed from her every pore. Smith laughed loud and clapped his hands together.

"Now, now, Aimee. Let us not ruin a family reunion," he called.

Now it was William's turn to control his anger. Seeing Smith was difficult enough, but hearing him speak Aimee's name was unbearable. Smith looked to William and smirked cruelly. He held William's gaze as he spoke to the entire room.

"*My* beautiful Aimee here, has come back to see us. Isn't that lovely?"

"You do not own her. You never have." William said, his voice strained with the effort of staying calm.

Smith's face changed from his disgusting smirk to an angry snarl.

"I *own* whatever I want to own, William. It would do you well to remember that."

Aimee tugged at his hand.

"It's ok," she whispered. "Don't let him do this to you."

"Now, as much as I would love to waste some more time on our little reunion here, I actually have a far more important issue to deal with first. Aimee, my dear, I have a gift for you." Smith said as he took a few steps closer to them.

William kept a tight hold on Aimee's hand. He would not let her go. He did not care what happened to him, he would never let go of her ever again. Luckily, Smith was not interested in taking her away again just yet. Instead, he motioned for the guards to join them again.

"Follow me, if you will." Smith said to the room.

William pulled Aimee along with him as he followed. His mind was racing through every possibility, but he knew there was no way to escape. Aimee could electrocute as many people as possible with William's help to purify her power, but they would just keep coming.

And if they didn't take Smith and Jenna down first, they would never stand a chance. And that was before taking into consideration the powers of the others too.

They followed the group through the large doors, with the guards closely behind them. William was careful to keep his distance from Smith, who walked a few feet ahead, and Aimee's eyes burned into the back of her father's head. He was grateful that at least Aimee's father had chosen to stay at the front of the group, far away from them. William did not think for one moment that Aimee would be able to resist the temptation to use her power on the man she was supposed to call 'Dad' if he came too close to her. It may have been Smith who inflicted the damage, but it was Aimee's father who had brought her here. It was him who had allowed her to be used so that he could get friendly with the boss. It was his fault Aimee had been abused. And it was his fault that they were back here now. Smith might have found his way to Aimee in the end, whether her father had helped him or not. But they would never know that, because he had handed her over like nothing more than an object at the first opportunity.

Animosity rolled through William's body, and he shook his head to rid himself of the white-hot feeling in his chest.

The group arrived at another door, and they walked slowed as they manoeuvred themselves into single file to step through. On the other side of the door, the light was much dimmer and when the door closed, shutting out the light from the outside, William had to squint to avoid bumping into people. The group formed a line in front of Aimee and William, blocking their view. Smith stepped through the line and motioned for them to follow. He stopped in front of what appeared to be a figure sitting in a large wooden chair, in the very centre of the room. As William moved closer, the people nearest to him stepped aside to allow them through.

"I think you can leave now." Smith said, nodding to a select few members of the group, and the guards William did not already know quickly turned and left the room.

Light shone in momentarily as the door opened, but it revealed very little of what lay in front of them. The room seemed to be empty except for the large chair and the unknown figure, who remained hidden behind Smith.

"I am a little surprised that you were foolish enough to think that you could hide from me forever. Especially you, Aimee. You were always so clever." Smith said.

There was movement in the chair behind him.

"You were both such good employees during your time here, we really did worry when you left. Of course, in time, we replaced you both. Well, we replaced William's role rather quickly actually. Aimee's role in midwifery was a little more difficult, although Anya has tried her best to fill that particular post. Truth be told, you proved to be quite irreplaceable. You have met Anya, yes? She has a way with children, you know. But your... other role, Aimee, was most difficult to fulfil. Indeed, it is easy enough to do what you did in that role, but nobody ever really seemed to fit as well as you did."

He smiled darkly as he spoke, and a shiver ran along the length William's spine as he watched Smith display Aimee to the group. He knew Smith was picturing her body in his twisted head, broken and beaten and naked. He squeezed his eyes shut and reopened them, willing the images to go away.

The body behind Smith became more and more agitated as Smith spoke and William realised that they must be restrained. William trained his eyes on the figure and strained to get a better look, but it was too dark.

"What is this, Smith? Why are we here?" Aimee asked, impatiently.

At Aimee's words the restrained figure began to shout, but the voice was muffled, and William knew then that they had been gagged too.

"Who is that?" William said.

"Oh, I am sorry. Where are my manners? I haven't introduced you. Marcus, could you get the lights please?"

Aimee's father moved across the room and flicked a switch on the wall. Light beamed down on them from separate spotlights in the ceiling, forcing William and Aimee to shield their faces while their eyes adjusted to the sudden change. They lowered their hands to see that the person behind Smith was a man. He wore torn clothes which looked as though they had not been changed for months and were covered in a mixture of blood and dirt. A black sack had been pulled over his head and both of his arms and legs had been bound securely to the frame of the wooden chair. William noticed that they had used chains to tie him rather than rope. He took a step back, fearing whose face could be hidden beneath the head covering, and he pushed Aimee behind him, holding her hands tightly in his own.

"Who is that?" Aimee said, barely louder that a whisper. "Why is he chained up?"

Smith's laugh was so loud that it startled everyone in the room.

"You mean you don't recognise him? Oh, Aimee. I fear that you will be gravely disappointed in yourself."

William eyes widened at the prospect of who the man could be, and his fear of the sack being lifted to reveal Joe's face beneath made his palms begin to sweat. If Smith had taken Joe, he would have Rainey too. Aimee's grip tightened around his hands, and he knew that she feared the same outcome.

Smith took a step behind the wooden chair and placed a hand on the top of the sack covering the man's head, wrapping his grip firmly around the material. The man stopped struggling against his restraints and his entire body tensed, frozen in fear. William risked a quick glance over his shoulder. A spark of realisation began to flicker in his chest when he saw how Aimee's eyes would not settle on one place. They darted back and forth, looking at every inch of the man. His skin, his clothes, the way his body rested when he stopped fighting against his restraints. And then he saw the concoction of recognition, horror, relief and joy begin to spread across Aimee's face, and William understood.

Time seemed to slow down as Smith yanked the covering away from the man's head to reveal a wide-eyed, beaten, gagged and broken shadow. The shadow of a man they had once loved. The shadow of a man they still loved. Aimee rushed past William, who was too stunned to stop her. She fell to her knees in front of the man and a desperate cry burst from her mouth.

"Jason."

23

Rainey

The journey to Calais had taken a little under two hours. They had managed to exchange some of their cash into euros on the ferry, ready for their long trek to Italy. Another panic attack and a passport check later, and they had walked away from the port without raising any suspicion. They took a bus to the closest train station, and after a long and confusing study of the timetables, Joe finally figured out which route they should take to get them where they needed to be. The cost of the train tickets had taken a wedge out of their supply of euros, but Rainey knew they had plenty to keep them going for a while. They switched out their passports for new ones, making sure that they did what they could to leave no trail for anyone to find them, and they tucked the old passports into a side pocket of one of their bags so that they would remember which ones had already been used.

The train carried them through France and Switzerland before it arrived in Milan, where they caught the next train to Turin. Rainey slept for the first part of the journey, until she could not stand to endure any more of the same nightmare repeating itself over and over in her head. She woke herself up and instructed Joe and Lexi to catch up on some sleep while she took her turn to listen out for their stop. She thought about how to explain what had happened to Maria, if they could find her.

When the train finally arrived in Turin, Joe took hold of Rainey's hand and she took hold of Lexi's. They hurried their way through the crowd and made it to a taxi, where they had their pick of the cars sitting outside the station, as they waited for train passengers to fill them. After throwing their bags into the boot, Joe instructed the driver to the name of the hotel they were looking for. Luckily, the driver knew the city well and he set off as soon as the three of them had clipped in their seatbelts. Rainey could not speak Italian, at least, not fluently, and she did not fancy her chances at attempting to give directions. The driver put his foot down as the car made it on to the roads, and it was not long before they reached the centre of Turin.

Rainey began to recognise the buildings and streets she had visited as a child with her parents. Her father had worked for most of their holidays, but Rainey had spent all of her time with Aimee on days trips out, eating ice cream and visiting all of the local monuments and attractions. Rainey bit down on her lip to stop it from trembling and wiped the tears from her eyes before they could spill over.

The car swerved off the busy road and on to a cobbled stretch, which took a large arch back on to the road. They braked suddenly, and the car came to a stop outside the hotel. Lexi complained loudly and rubbed at the mark on her neck from the seat belt, while Joe threw a few notes at the driver. They climbed out and headed to the boot to pull out their bags.

Rainey had not been expecting the rush of emotion she felt as she looked up at the huge building in front of her. Her legs felt unsteady, and she struggled to compress her desire to scream. Looking up at the building did not just make her feel broken and torn up inside, like she had expected. It made her feel angry. More than angry. She should not be back here without her family. It felt wrong to her. She closed her eyes and tried to calm the hot feeling quickly spreading through her chest. Vaguely aware of the car speeding away from behind her, she sensed she was being watched. She breathed deeply before opening her eyes, and sure enough, Joe stood a few feet away, watching carefully while Lexi fussed over how best to carry one of the bags. The look on Joe's face sent a shiver down Rainey's spine. Pity. That was what she saw. Pity and fear, all mixed together with exhaustion, anger and all of the other messed up emotions Rainey had not ever imagined Joe would ever have to experience. It forced her heart to sink, knowing Joe had to handle not just his own pain, but Rainey's too. It made her sick to her stomach that she knew she should care more, she should want to help him, instead of focussing on herself, but there was no space left inside of her to worry about him too. Right now, she didn't really even care what happened to her, all that mattered was Lily, finding her and getting her home safely. Along with her parents.

Rainey looked away from Joe and began walking toward the doors. Joe followed with Lexi closely behind him. A concierge wearing a navy-blue suit stepped out of the hotel to greet them, but when he laid eyes on the three of them, he appeared to change his mind. It had not occurred to Rainey how they must look, which was probably not particularly fresh. They definitely looked as though they had not had a decent night's sleep in weeks. Their hair was uncombed, and their clothes creased. The man quickly closed the doors and took up a stance in front of them.

"Posso aiutarla?" He said as they approached.

Rainey stared at him for a moment while she tried to translate his words in her head.

"Something about help," she said over her shoulder to the others. "Erm... Ciao. Ci Piace... erm... dentro?" She waved her hands towards the doors.

The man took a step closer and Rainey jumped back a little.

"What did you say?" Lexi whispered.

"Hello. We would like to go inside. I think that's what I said, I don't remember any of my Italian."

Joe joined Rainey in front of the concierge.

"Mi scusi," he said.

The man did not move, and he continued to glare at them suspiciously.

"Qualsiasi Inglese?" Joe tried again.

The man nodded.

"This is not the hotel you are looking for," he said in perfect English, with a sultry Italian accent.

Lexi laughed behind them.

"He speaks English and he's been enjoying watching you two say who-knows-what in Italian," she managed between laughs.

A look from Joe silenced her.

"Yes, actually, this is our hotel. So, excuse me." Rainey said, her tone disfigured with her irritation.

"No. You need to wait here while we call a car for you."

"Do you not hear us talking? Move!" Rainey's voice rose.

He stepped forward again, but this time he snatched the front of Rainey's top around the collar. Joe leapt forward and grabbed hold of the man's arm, but he took a step back again when Rainey began to laugh.

"You really, *really*, don't want to do that." Rainey's voice was calm in a terrifying way.

"What will you do, little girl?" He taunted in return.

Rainey smiled dangerously as she raised her hand and held it just above his as it remained clutching the fabric of her collar.

"Rainey, no." Joe stepped back further, before she electrocuted the both of them.

The doors of the hotel burst open just as Rainey's fingers brushed against the man's skin. She held them there, on his hand, and smiled, daring him to push her further.

"Che cosa sta succedendo qui?" Came a woman's voice.

Rainey beamed as the woman came in to view. All five foot of her. With the wildest and darkest curly hair, beautiful olive skin and perfectly voluptuous lips. She yelled at the man in Italian until he let go of Rainey's collar, and only then did she pay any attention to the three visitors. Her eyes widened as she looked at Rainey for the first time.

"Non può essere," she whispered.

"Hello, Maria." Rainey said.

Maria placed a hand on either side of Rainey's face.

"What are you doing here?" She asked.

Rainey had always loved Maria's strong accent when she spoke in English.

"We came to find you," Rainey replied.

Maria looked around at Joe and Lexi and smiled when she recognised at least one of them. She had never officially met Joe in person, but she had spoken to him over the phone and on video-calls while William had been training him.

"Look at you all! You must come in."

Maria turned and strutted through the doors which were now held open for them, and they followed her into the hotel. But Rainey stopped as she passed the concierge.

"He's fired." She said, staring at the man.

"What?" He said.

"What?" Joe said at the same time.

Rainey ignored Joe and looked to Maria.

"He no longer works here."

"Who do you think you are, little girl?" The man laughed.

Rainey turned and closed the gap between them.

"I am the daughter of your boss." She said. "The next thing you'll be *grabbing* is your P45." Rainey smiled at the look of complete shock on his face before turning and striding away.

She could not be sure that they had P45s in Italy, but she had made her point.

"Done." Maria nodded.

"Rainey, you can't just come in here and start firing people," Joe started.

"I can do whatever I want!" She yelled back.

From behind her she heard the man's feet rush forward.

"Spoiled little bitch," he said as he grabbed hold of the top of her arm.

Rainey did not so much as flinch. A mild electric current ran over the entire surface of her skin and the man began to scream, but he could not let go as the muscles all over his body constricted. After a few seconds Rainey relaxed, and he fell to the floor in a crumpled heap. Joe and Lexi did not move. They both stared in horror at Rainey. Maria was the only one who did not seem to be remotely interested in what she had just witnessed. She simply shrugged her shoulders before addressing the now twitching man.

"Antony, you're fired. Collect your things," she said, before walking through the lobby towards a large desk stretching the full length of the room.

Rainey followed her without looking back. Maria stopped at the desk and spoke so quickly in Italian that Rainey could not seem to find one word which sounded familiar to her. The young lady behind the desk frantically typed into the computer, and a moment later, she produced a key card from somewhere beneath the desk. Maria snatched it up, before twirling and striding toward the elevators. Her tiny feet clipped on the marble floor as she hurried across the lobby and Rainey wondered how she managed to move so fast in such high heels. The doors of an elevator opened as Maria approached and she ushered the small group inside. Then she pushed the key card into a slot underneath the buttons and the doors closed.

"I have booked you into a room on the top floor, you won't be bothered there by anyone and you may stay for as long as you wish." Maria's voice was calm and soothing, and her accent made her voice roll and purr, making it impossible for anyone to feel unwelcome in her presence.

"I am assuming you are in some sort of trouble. Why else would you come here without warning?"

Rainey opened her mouth to answer but Maria answered her own question before she had a chance.

"You would not be here if there was not trouble."

The lift slowed to a stop and the doors glided open. Maria stepped out first into a large, bright room, followed by Rainey, Joe and finally Lexi. Both Joe and Lexi had to fight the urge to gawp as they examined the room before them. A hard wood floor stretched out into the room with a step which ran the width. Two large, cream sofas sat opposite one another in the centre of the space with an elaborate rug and a glass coffee table separating them. A grand piano was alone in one corner and a spiral staircase stood on the left side of the room, close to the elevator doors. Glass sliding doors replaced a wall at the far end of the room, revealing a huge balcony equipped with a dining table and eight chairs.

"Have a look around, Tesoro," Maria called to them as she picked up a phone from a side table and pressed a button.

Rainey actually did know that Italian word. Maria had called her *Tesoro* since she was a baby. It meant treasure.

They walked to the closest doorway and Lexi peeked inside.

"I want this room first!" She blurted out.

Rainey edged around the door and first saw the marble floor, then the jacuzzi-sized bathtub in the centre of the room. It had so many different taps and nozzles that Rainey could not imagine what they must all be used for. A walk-in shower covered one wall, with glass doors which offered no privacy.

Joe led the way to the next unexplored room, which was hidden at the top of the staircase. It was a bedroom housing a large four-post bed with white sheets and matching veils hanging from the posts, waving gently in the breeze from the open balcony doors. The remainder of the room was filled with the usual furniture which could be expected in a hotel room, only much more extravagant. Rainey did not dare to touch anything for fear she might break it. After a quick tour of the rest of the apartment, they headed back to the living room and to Maria, who was now surrounded by room service trollies covered in food. Rainey's mouth watered just looking at all the different dishes.

"You must be starving, Tesoro. Help yourself." She held out a stack of plates and they did not hesitate to dig in.

Rainey piled her plate high with various different breads, cheese and continental meats before taking a seat next to Maria on the sofa.

"Now, tell me. Why are you here?" Maria questioned.

Rainey hesitated for a moment. She didn't know how much she should tell her. She could only hope Maria would listen to their story and have some sort of solution as to where they should turn next.

"Smith has Aimee and William." Joe said, wasting no time.

Maria sprang to her feet so suddenly that they all jumped up too, knocking plates of food all over the floor. She ran her fingers through her thick hair a few times before she started to pace floor.

"This is bad. This is very, very bad."

"Can you tell us anything about Smith? Where we can find him maybe?" Joe asked.

Maria stopped her pacing and stared at Joe with wide eyes.

"You do not find him. If you go there, he will kill all three of you, if you are lucky. If he gets his greasy hands on you two then he might keep you. A fate worse than death. You are useful to him if you are powerful." She pointed to Lexi. "What do you do?"

"It's not very nice." Lexi shrugged.

"Can you harm others?"

"Yes."

"Is it strong?"

"Yes."

"Then you cannot go to Smith." Maria said, and she began to pace the room again.

Rainey stepped in front of her and placed her hands on Maria's shoulders.

"Maria, he has my parents. I have no choice. But... they didn't just take Mum and Dad."

She waited for Maria to comprehend what that meant. Her eyes widened.

"He took the bambino?"

Rainey nodded and tried desperately to push down the anger bubbling hot in her stomach.

"Why? Why would he do this? The girl is an innocent, she is defenceless. He has no use for her. I don't understand..." She said to no one in particular.

Rainey noticed something moving from the corner of her eye and she looked down to see what looked like strips of black material growing from Maria's fingers. She jumped back in horror and gaped, as the strips grew longer. They swirled in the air, as though they were made from a mixture of black smoke and ribbon. Lexi and Joe stared too, unable to draw their eyes away while they watched the tips of Maria's fingers extend into the black tendrils. The longer they grew, the more of them there seemed to be. Rained could see that there was more than just one coming from each finger now, maybe three or four, and each of them split as they grew longer, making more and more.

Maria did not seem to notice.

"I need to think. What is the reason for this? Now, after all this time," Maria continued to talk to herself while Rainey, Joe and Lexi edged backwards, avoiding the tendrils.

"Ok." She shouted loudly, clapping her hands together, and the black material instantly shot back into her fingertips. "I think it's time-"

"What the hell was that?" Lexi screeched.

Maria looked confused. She followed Lexi's glare to her hands before shaking them into the air in front of her.

"That is what I do. They help me to fight."

When Lexi did not reply and continued to stare in horror at Maria's hands, she continued.

"Rainey, Tesoro. I think it is time you learned some more about your parents."

Maria pulled Rainey down on to the sofa. She held her hands tightly and Rainey tried her best not to cringe away from her touch after the recent show of her powers. Only now did she notice Maria's fingernails were long and black, filed into perfect points and polished so flawlessly she could just about make out her reflection in them.

"I want you to listen carefully before you ask any questions. I will tell you what I can, Rainey. But there are some parts of your parents' pasts that I cannot tell you."

Rainey nodded slowly. Joe and Lexi positioned themselves on the opposite sofa and listened carefully.

"Aimee did not have a good childhood, and I trust that you already know this. She did not know her mother. Like many of the Gifted, she died during the birth, and her father blamed Aimee since the day she was born. When she met Jason, her life began to change. They helped each other though the unthinkable difficulties they shared as children and Aimee grew happier. Until her father took them to Smith." Maria paused briefly as she studied Rainey's face. "Aimee's father struggled to pay for their home and their food, but Smith offered to take them in and find him a job. He did not care for them; they were just two more soldiers to add to his collection. Aimee was ripped away from Jason and they both suffered greatly. As she grew into a woman, she trained to deliver the babies of the Gifted and it became her passion to help prevent the deaths of the mothers. Of course, it was not long before Smith discovered that Aimee was more than he had hoped for in a soldier, and he was cruel to your mother in ways that I hope you never know."

Rainey opened her mouth, but Maria continued, stopping her from asking any questions.

"After many, many months, Smith finally gave in to Jason's begging and gave him a place in his army, but this time he could not save your mother. When your father first met Aimee, she fascinated him, and Aimee feared that Smith would punish him for it. They could not be together if they stayed, but if they ran, they would be forever running. They decided against it for a long time, until they discovered that Aimee was pregnant. They wanted more for their child than Smith's army. So, they ran away with Jason's help, and Smith hunted them for years. The life they built for themselves would always be temporary, they knew Smith would eventually find them. You lived in many places before you were even born. But as the years passed by, his efforts faded."

Maria paused for a moment while she considered her next words.

"But now, Smith has finally found her. Rainey, I believe that your parents were taken for revenge. As was your daughter. And I believe that you will be his prize."

Rainey gasped in sharp, panicked intakes of breath. Tears ran down her cheeks and on to Maria's hands as they gripped Rainey's tightly on her lap. She looked around the room until she found what she was looking for. Slowly, she stood from the sofa and shook Maria's hands away. She walked steadily towards the bathroom door. Lexi and Maria rushed to follow her, but Rainey did not acknowledge them.

"Rainey." Joe pleaded.

He had not moved from his seat where he remained frozen in place. Rainey ignored him too. She stepped into the bathroom and threw the door back. It slammed shut, the ear-splitting bang echoing around the marble room. Rainey placed her hands on her head, her nails digging into her scalp. She leaned back against the cold, solid wall and slowly sank to the floor. Then she opened her mouth and screamed. She screamed and screamed. Her throat felt as though it were being shredded with glass, and blood began to pool under her fingernails from her scalp, but still she screamed.

Revenge. Her family had been taken from her for revenge. She would never see them again.

Joe

On the other side of the door Joe sat with his head in his hands, listening to Rainey's screams. He rocked back and forth as he tried to absorb Maria's story. Lily had been taken from them to teach Aimee and William a lesson. She had been taken for revenge.

Joe knew that this changed their chance of finding Lily, Aimee and William in no way. But it did change their chance of finding them alive.

25

Rainey

Rainey woke with a cold shiver running through her body. It took her a moment to realise she was curled into a ball on the bathroom floor, the cold marble leaching the heat from her skin. She pushed herself into a sitting position and stretched out her limbs. She did not know how long she had dozed off for, but it could not have been more than an hour. Her head felt foggy and heavy. She examined the blood under her nails which had dried and transformed to a dull brown, before pushing herself up from the floor and stepping closer to the bathroom mirror. Looking at her reflection only made her feel worse, she could see the broken look deep in her eyes and she pushed herself away before she lost herself again. Her eyes landed on the bathtub and she began to undress herself. The taps on the bath were pretty straightforward but the various buttons confused her. Some seemed to control the jets scattered around the inside of the tub, others looked as though they might start adding things to her bath which she was not in the mood for. She decided not to touch any of them and settle for just hot water.

When the bath finally looked deep enough, Rainey stepped in. The heat of the water made her skin tingle. She watched as the blood began to disappear from under her nails before she held her breath and slipped her entire body under the water. She liked it under the water. There was no noise to shatter her thoughts. No bright lights to break through her closed eyelids. Peaceful. She longed to stay under the protection of the water and empty her mind completely, but she could not hold her breath for very long, and already an uncomfortable feeling had begun to climb up her throat as her body longed for more oxygen. She gasped in air as her head broke the surface of the water, and after wiping it from her eyes, she realised she was no longer alone in the bathroom. Joe stood silently by the door, watching her as she studied him with her eyes.

"Are you giving up on me?" He said, barely loud enough to hear over the water as it continued to run from the taps, gradually filling the bath.

It took Rainey a moment to understand what Joe was asking her.

"Of course I'm not giving up." She said.

Joe tensed his jaw and took a steadying breath. Then he rushed forward so quickly that he made Rainey jump, sending splashes of water over the edges of the tub and on to the floor. He pushed his hand through Rainey's wet hair and cradled her head as he kissed her passionately, forcefully. Rainey kissed him back and wrapped her arms around his neck, soaking his shirt. Joe ended the kiss as quickly as he had started it. He watched her carefully as he leant forward and this time lightly brushed his lips against hers. When he pulled away Rainey saw the pained look in his eyes. She pulled him back by his shirt and roughly pressed her mouth to his again. He did not stop her, so she pulled his shirt up over his head and threw it carelessly on to the floor before she fumbled for the button on his jeans. Joe ran his gentle fingers through her hair, over her shoulders, down her back, letting the curves of her body guide his hands. He kicked off his jeans and allowed himself to be pulled into the tub and on top of Rainey without breaking their kiss. Rainey wrapped her body around his, gripping his hips tightly between her legs and digging her nails into the muscles on his shoulders. Water sloshed over the sides of the bath, flooding the floor. Rainey's mind was forced to focus on less complicated matters, like the feel of Joe's skin, the smell of his hair, the heat of his breath against her neck. But all too soon, her brief feeling of freedom escaped her, and she was dragged back into the reality of her life.

They clung to each other as they caught their breath. Rainey's eyes felt heavy, the brightness of the bathroom suddenly painful in her overcrowded head. She allowed her gaze to drift down to the smooth skin on Joe's back as she rested her chin on his shoulder. And then she saw what she had done. She snapped her hands away with a look of disgust. A mixture of guilt and self-loathing began to stir inside her as droplets of blood seeped from the deep gouges in Joe's skin. She thought about the pain she must have caused him and how he had said nothing. He could have stopped her. He could have pushed her away. But instead, he allowed her to hurt him. And Rainey had enjoyed it. She had enjoyed inflicting pain. She lifted her head from Joe's shoulder, afraid that she might throw up if she looked again at what she had done.

Softly, Joe kissed Rainey's cheek before he climbed out of the bath. He dried himself off with a towel and pulled on his jeans, leaving his shirt in a puddle of bathwater on the floor. He did not look at Rainey before he left the room, pulling the door shut behind him.

Images of the deep lines etched into the soft skin of Joe's back ran through Rainey's thoughts. It wasn't like she had never scratched him before during a fit of passion, but that had been different. This time, the marks she left on his back and shoulders were not just scratches, they tore deep into his skin, drawing blood and leaving dark purple lines.

Rainey pulled herself up and shut off the tap which continued to pour steaming water into the bathtub. Luckily, Joe had accidentally removed the plug with his foot, saving the bath from overflowing.

After drying herself with a towel, Rainey pulled on her clothes and headed out of the bathroom and into the main room. Joe was nowhere to be seen, but Maria was waiting for her, sitting patiently on the sofa. Rainey joined her and squeezed her hand apologetically.

"What did you do to the boy's back?" Maria asked.

Rainey looked away, too embarrassed to meet her eyes. She was not ashamed of what they had done in the bathtub, but she could not explain why she had hurt Joe. Her chest tightened uncomfortably.

"There is a darkness inside you, Rainey. You must fight to contain it, just as your mother has. Because if you do not, it will consume you."

Rainey's eyes snapped back to Maria's. She searched for the kindness she was so used to seeing there, but she found only unforgiving certainty.

"There is nothing inside me but my determination to find Lily and my parents and bring them home."

"What do you plan to do?" Maria said.

Rainey did not know what she planned to do. She did not know if there was anything she could do. But before she could answer, Maria spoke again.

"If you think that you can go to Smith, fight him, threaten him, even plead with him, it will not work, Rainey. His army is too big and too strong."

"I can't just leave them." Rainey replied.

"You must." Maria said, harshly.

"I can't!" Rainey shouted. "What if it were your daughter, Maria? What would you do? Just let them have her? Turn her into one of their army or hurt her? Could you sit here every damn minute knowing that somewhere your child is in danger, crying for her parents who are halfway across the world?"

Maria could not answer her.

"It doesn't matter what they have or how strong they are. I have to try. I can't live with myself knowing that I didn't try for her." Rainey said, desperately.

She had been hoping Maria would offer her help, anything that might guide them in the right direction to where Smith had taken her family, but now Rainey doubted that Maria would help at all. They stayed silent for what seemed like a long time, until Rainey finally stood up to leave. She would find Joe and Lexi and arrange a taxi to take them away from here. They would find Smith on their own if they had to. But then Maria cleared her throat.

"He is in Nevada."

Rainey looked at her hopefully.

"I will write down the address for you."

She pulled a pen and a tiny pad of paper from her pocket and began scribbling an address.

"You don't know what they can do. If something were to happen to you because I gave you this address, your parents would never forgive me."

"Why are you so afraid of them?"

"Because I was once one of them. Smith's people control our world. They hunt for us, to find a Gifted who will be bigger, better, stronger. And when they find what they are looking for they take them and use them to find more. If you are too weak or not willing to go with them, they will kill you or torture you. They will use your body to make more Gifted children, or he will use you for his own personal-" Maria stopped herself suddenly.

"Own personal what?" Rainey pushed, but Maria refused to continue.

"What did they do to you to make you so afraid?" Rainey asked.

Maria could not reply right away. After a long, uncomfortable silence, she looked into Rainey's eyes.

"They killed my husband, because I ran from them. I left him and my children, and I ran. And when Smith found out that he was involved with getting my children back to me, he murdered him. I was alone, I had nobody who could help me to hide with the children, so that they wouldn't find us and take us back there. And then I found your parents. They have helped me greatly."

"How can they get away with this? Why doesn't anybody stop them?" Rainey asked, frustrated.

"They have very powerful followers. Smith himself can control your body, only one person at a time, but he can make you do anything he wishes. If the person he chooses to control could start earthquakes for example," she waved a hand in Rainey's direction. "I am sure that you can imagine the repercussions."

If Smith was using her mother as his tool, then he already had a very powerful weapon, but he didn't just have her mother. As temperamental as her father's power could be, if Smith could somehow force him to use it while he controlled Aimee's body, the outcome would be devastating.

Rainey considered Maria's words, but there was something else bothering her, although she could not put her finger on it.

"Is there anyone else we should know about?" Rainey continued, not really wanting to hear Maria's answer.

"His pathfinders change all the time, there are not many left that I know of."

"His pathfinders? What is a pathfinder?"

"It is a glorified job title for the strongest of the Gifted. He uses them to search for more of us."

"Is that what my father did for Smith?" She asked, hoping that 'pathfinder' had not been his glorified title once.

"That is something you will have to ask him yourself."

Rainey understood then that her father must have had a disturbing role in the army.

"You should look out for Jenna, she is a short woman, fat face. She can freeze you as though you are paralysed. If you ever do have the pleasure, please give her an extra little something from me."

Images of her parents, frozen and surrounded by strangers in their own home flickered through her mind.

"I have actually had the pleasure of meeting her already."

Maria placed her hand on Rainey's cheek.

"You have suffered so much already, Tesoro."

Rainey smiled in what she hoped was a reassuring way and Maria withdrew her hand.

"Let's see. James uses a shield. I am not sure how exactly, but it does not work with every power," she continued.

"What does he look like?"

"Tall, big, dark hair. And ugly."

"I've met him too, I think. I tried to shock him but it didn't work."

A noise behind them caught Rainey's attention and she twisted in her seat to see Joe coming to join them in a dry shirt and jeans.

"James, huh? I can't wait to meet that guy," Joe said as he slumped down on to the sofa opposite Rainey and Maria.

Maria gave him a disapproving look.

"James is not only a shield. Sometimes he cannot be seen, and he can burn you with his touch. Do not let him get his hands on you, and do not underestimate him."

"What about Anya?" Rainey asked.

"I don't know of an Anya." Maria replied. "As I said before, many people have died or escaped. There are not many left who I know of."

"How do you know all of this?" Joe said, a little disbelieving.

"Rumours, mostly. Smith's army may be strong, but it is not as well protected as it used to be. People begin to realise what the Institute really is, and secrets escape. Then it is only a matter of time before that particular person mysteriously goes missing. If they are lucky, they will run away in time."

Rainey and Joe exchanged glances.

"So, I guess you will be needing some more supplies if you are planning on a trip to Nevada. Which means shopping, and that is something I *can* help you with."

Maria jumped up from the sofa.

"You two rest and make yourselves at home. If you need anything, room service will get it for you. I will be back later today."

Maria pulled them in one at a time for a kiss on both cheeks, then she briskly walked over to their bags, which lay open by the door, and she began to drag items of clothing out of them. Rainey and Joe watched as Maria seemed to find what she was looking for, before she carried them into the elevator with her. They waited for the doors to close before Rainey turned to Joe.

"So, what now?" She asked.

Joe shrugged his shoulders.

"Let's call room service."

They ordered two large pizzas with fries and shook Lexi awake from her nap while they waited. It did not take long for their food to arrive, and they devoured every last bite, not realising how hungry they had become. When the food was finished, Rainey filled Lexi in on the new information Maria had provided, but she did not have any suggestions on what their next move should be.

The remainder of the afternoon was spent waiting for Maria to return, and after hours of sitting around feeling helpless, they decided it would be best to get some rest while they still could, before their journey to Nevada, and Smith's army, began.

Rainey and Joe headed up to the master bedroom as Lexi had already claimed the other bed for herself. They climbed on top of the covers and collapsed against the soft feather pillows. Within minutes they had both fallen into a deep sleep.

Rainey awoke to the sound of Maria's heels clip-clopping across the wooden floor in the room below. She pushed herself up and gently stroked Joe's forearm to wake him.

"Maria's back," she whispered.

Joe opened his eyes, stretched, rolled over and almost fell to the floor. Rainey smiled and waited patiently for him to find his feet. When he did, they made their way towards the stairs to find Maria waiting at the bottom with a pile of shopping bags around her feet. She picked up a few of the bags and rushed over to the sofas, where she began to unpack the bags as she waited for the others to join her. Rainey and Joe followed Maria's lead and took a seat on the opposite sofa, just as Lexi appeared in one of the doorways with what looked like some form of roadkill strapped to her head. She pointed first to Joe and then to Rainey before she joined them on the sofa.

"Do not you say anything. I am aware that I look like crap," she warned.

"Vision of beauty, Lex. As always," Joe said, sarcastically.

"Yes, yes, you all look beautiful and young. Now, can we concentrate please?" Maria said with a roll of her eyes. "I have some supplies for you which you are going to need on your trip."

"Is that why you stole our clothes before? To find our sizes?" Rainey asked.

Maria nodded and held out the first item of clothing. It was just a plain t-shirt, black with no markings, one for each of them. Then a pair of jeans each, again, black with no markings. And the jackets, which for Rainey and Lexi, looked like black leather biker jackets, but they had a slanted zip across the front. And for Joe, a plain black leather jacket.

"I did not know what your size would be in the shoes, so I bought a few pairs. Go and try them on."

Maria signalled in the direction of the elevator, and sure enough, in a small pile beside the doors lay a dozen pairs of black boots.

They each tried on a pair and picked the ones that seemed to fit them the best.

"I'm not questioning your motives here, Maria, because I am sure there is a very good reason for you sending us into the desert dressed all in black. But I may actually die of heat stroke if I have to wear this outfit." Joe said, examining the material as he ran a pair of jeans through his fingers.

"When you get there, Smith's people will mostly wear black. These outfits may help you to blend in a little. You have a spare outfit each in your bags, along with some basic supplies. I have booked you the correct flights and a cab will be here an hour from now to collect you."

The three of them stared at Maria in disbelief.

"Now, go change. And say goodbye to your belongings, you will not be able to take them with you."

They each took hold of a large paper bag containing their new outfits and headed towards the bathroom at the same time.

Joe reached the door first and he laughed sarcastically as he closed it behind himself.

"You two will take forever trying everything on," he shouted through the closed door. "I'll only be a minute."

"You would think that for the amount we're paying for this place there would be more than one bathroom." Lexi joked.

Forty-five minutes later and the three of them stood facing Maria in their all-black get-ups as she looked them up and down.

"Hmm, you will have to do," she said.

"Ah, that's so sweet of you," Joe gushed, rolling his eyes.

Maria fished around in her pocket until she found a few loose hair bobbles. She handed a couple to Rainey and Lexi and pulled three or four on to her own wrist.

"Come here, Tesoro," she said, and she held her arms out to Rainey.

Rainey turned and bent her knees a little for Maria to reach her hair. Maria expertly pulled her fingers through Rainey's dark strands, securing them into a ponytail at the back of her head, with a few loose strands falling down around her face. Then Maria spun her by her shoulders before taking a step back to look at her.

"You are so beautiful. Just like your parents." She said. "Now, hurry up. The car will be here very soon."

Rainey searched through her old weekend bag one last time and pulled out Lily's blanket and bunny. Her intention had been to leave them with Maria and hope that one day they would make it back to Lily, but as she inhaled the sweet, slightly floral scent of her daughter, Rainey knew she would never have been able to leave them behind. Carefully, she placed them into her backpack and zipped it shut.

"Let's go," she said.

Saying goodbye to Maria had been difficult. They had agreed to keep it short and sweet to avoid anything too emotional. Maria handed them three passports each, six from the stash they had brought with them and another three which had belonged to Maria. Rainey would be Maria under various Italian alter egos for the remainder of their trip, leaving Rainey's passports to be used by Lexi.

The tickets for the flight had been booked using three of the passports, and Rainey now had the taxi drive to the airport to memorise as much information from Maria's passports as she possibly could. Unfortunately, Torino Airport was less than an hour away and Rainey's memory was not very reliable. She could just about remember Maria's birthday and the first passport's full name by the time they arrived.

"At least we can get on together this time." Lexi had stated as they walked into the building.

They crossed their fingers and gritted their teeth as they progressed through the airport procedures. Rainey had time to visit the lady's room and alter her looks to match her passport before they checked themselves in. Darker skin, darker lips, darker hair. The only time any of the airport staff grew suspicious of them was as they declared that they carried only hand luggage for their long-haul flight.

"You seem to be travelling light for a holiday to Vegas," she had said, accusingly.

"Oh, no ma'am. Our luggage is already there. Our family travelled out earlier in the week." Joe replied.

It was not long before they were sitting on the plane, waiting for the twelve-hour flight to begin by speeding along the runway.

Rainey chose to sit between Lexi and Joe, and she gripped both of their hands tightly.

"Almost there," she whispered to herself, as the pilot lined the plane up for the runway. "Not long now. Almost there."

The plane picked up speed, pinning Rainey to the back of her seat as it sped along the tarmac. She gripped Joe's and Lexi's hands tighter and squeezed her eyes shut, muttering to herself as the wheels lifted from the safety of the ground.

"I'm almost there, baby. I'm coming to get you."

26

Aimee

Aimee fought against the guards. She screamed into their clothing as she desperately tried to sink her teeth into them. Nobody froze her, nobody took control of her body. They allowed her to struggle and fight her way to Jason, knowing that she would never reach him.

She was dragged backwards from the room, forcing her to watch helplessly as Smith swung his arm around and slapped Jason across the face with the back of his hand.

"No! Stop it!" She screamed.

They dragged her relentlessly, on and on, through the corridors and up the flights of stairs, until they arrived back at the same tiny room they had been locked in the night before.

"If you keep trying to fight us then we will have to hurt you. But if you go in there quietly, we will leave you alone." The guard tried to reason with her.

Aimee realised then that he was the same man who had helped to escort her earlier. Only now did it dawn on her that the guards should have hurt her already. She had sunk her teeth into them, hit them, kicked them, screamed every disgusting name she could think of at them. But they had not retaliated. She nodded, and the man let go of her. The second guard opened the door and held it open for Aimee to walk through, but she did not expect them to follow her inside. When they closed the door, shutting themselves in the room with her, Aimee automatically raised her arms, ready to electrocute them both.

"Stop, please. We don't want to hurt you." The second guard said, his voice drawled with a hint of his Texan accent. "My name is Chris, this is Jonah. Aimee, we want to help."

Aimee lowered her hands a little and her eyes darted from one face to the other.

"How do I know this isn't some kind of trick? You offer me help and when I take it you give Smith another reason to beat on me." She spat.

"Look, we don't have much time. They are bringing your husband back here any minute," Chris paused while he measured Aimee's reaction. "I know where the baby is, and we want to help, but you will only have one shot at this. If you do not get out, Smith will see that one of you is killed. And both of us." He added, pointing a thumb to Jonah.

"Why, then? Why would you help us?" Aimee said, not believing they could help at all.

Jonah took a small step forward.

"If we help you find the baby and we get you out alive, then we need something in return." He said.

"I have nothing! Everything I had is gone."

"You have something nobody else here does. I need you to let us come with you. And I need you to deliver my child." Jonah continued.

Aimee stared back at him, a mixture of shock and understanding momentarily masking her fear as she realised that desperation was why they wanted to help. In all of the years she had hidden, still nothing had changed. She ran her fingers through her hair and shook her head slowly from side to side as she looked Jonah in his eyes.

"I don't... I don't have any equipment, or anywhere to go. The mothers, they can still die when I try to help them," she stuttered.

"But not all of them," Chris said, speaking up again. "Your girl survived."

Aimee nodded.

"We will take any equipment we can get our hands on. We understand it will be difficult, but if you could just try." He pleaded.

Aimee cringed when she heard the desperation leaking into his tone. The desperation that could get them all killed. She looked down at her hands as she considered her options, but it did not take her long. She knew that this was her only one. And that made her desperate too.

"What do I need to do?" She agreed.

Jonah breathed a sigh of relief and smiled to Chris.

"Thank you. Thank you so much." Chris said.

"I know why he wants in," Aimee said, nodding to Jonah. "I saw the way you looked at that woman out there. But why you?" She added to Chris.

"She's my sister." He replied.

Aimee studied him carefully, searching for any hint of a lie in his voice, unsure if she could trust what he was telling her, or if this whole thing was just another of Smith's cruel tricks.

"Well," he continued. "She's not technically my sister. Jonah here is my brother, so as far as I'm concerned, she's family."

Aimee looked from one brother to the other and noticed now how their eyes both pulled down at the corners in the same way, how their noses turned up slightly at the tip.

"Why do you work for him?" She asked.

"Why did you?" He replied.

"I didn't volunteer to come here, I was forced."

"Nobody volunteers to come here. We had no more of a choice than you did."

Aimee that knew some people had volunteered to come here, William being one of them.

"So, what happens next?" Aimee pushed.

As she waited to be given instructions, she heard footsteps from outside the door, followed by William's voice yelling profanities. Jonah shot a panicked glance at Chris before he began speaking as quickly and as quietly as he could.

"The baby is kept in the nursery, on the seventh floor. It is the same now as it always has been and, given your background, we hoped that you would know your way around. There are normally no guards on that floor, but they have the baby covered by at least one, sometimes two at a time. If you are taken out of this room again, without Smith or Jenna, and you know Chris or myself are nearby, then you need to do everything within your power to get to the seventh floor."

Aimee listened carefully, trying to absorb every fragment of information.

"Do not trust anyone else in this place. Not one of them!" Chris whispered, urgently.

"What about Jason? I won't leave him."

Jonah and Chris exchanged a quick glance and then nodded in agreement.

"We will do what we can, but he is under heavy guard. Our chances of saving him *and* the baby are small. If it comes down to a choice between the two of them, then you will have to make that decision." Jonah said.

The door began to open and the sound of the scuffle outside grew louder.

"Hit me." Aimee ordered.

"What?" Chris and Jonah said together.

Aimee took hold of Jonah's hand and raised it to her face.

"Hit me!" She whispered frantically.

Another guard stumbled into the room holding William tightly around the neck just as Jonah pulled back his hand and brought it hurtling forward to connect with Aimee's cheek. The impact forced her backwards and on to the bed, where she watched as William was thrown into the room. He fell on to the bed beside her and the guards began to retreat, Jonah being the final one to leave the room. He gave Aimee a pained look of apology, before backing out of the room and pulling the door shut behind him. They listened for the click of the lock and waited silently as the footsteps disappeared. William placed his hand gently on the fresh red print across Aimee's cheek.

"It's fine," she said, brushing his hand away. "Listen, those guards are on our side. They want to help us find Lily and get out of here. They said that we can-"

"What?" William said in astonishment, raising his voice a little. "You think you can trust them? We just saw Jason. Jason! Who is supposed to be dead. But instead, he has been locked up here, taking daily beatings and being slowly starved to death. And you want to trust these people?"

"William," Aimee tried, but she was cut off again.

"No, Aimee! Just no. I don't care what they told you, these people are not good. Not one of them."

"But they are just like us, Will!" Aimee pleaded. "Please. Just listen."

William turned away and began pacing what little floor space they had.

"One of them is just like you. And the other is Jason. They need to run away with the pregnant woman they both love, so that they can protect her, just like you did. We have to trust them, it's all we have."

Aimee quickly filled William in with the sparse details she had been provided. It took him a while to calm down and stop pacing the floor, but when he did, he began to understand that this would be their only choice. They could stay put until Smith ran out of ways to torture Aimee through William and Jason, or they could put their trust in two men who could give them up at any moment. Eventually, they both agreed that the latter was the better option.

"So, now what?" William asked.

Aimee put her head in her hands and rested her elbows on her knees. She sighed deeply, trying and failing to expel some of the anxiety building inside her chest. William sighed with her. He took Aimee's hands in his own and gently pulled her up from the bed before he wrapped his arms around her.

"Jason," she whispered into his chest.

"I know," he replied, squeezing her tighter.

"I should have looked for him. I should have done... something."

"No." William insisted. "We are not going to do that. We are not going to start blaming ourselves for what they have done to him. He was dead, Aimee. There was a body, we saw the house for ourselves. There was nothing you could have done to stop this."

"But, we didn't even try-"

"No, Aimee. I mean it. You are not going to blame yourself. You need to focus on what we are about to do."

Aimee squeezed her eyes shut tightly as she tried to push the image of Jason's broken body out of her head, but it would not leave.

"What do we do?" She cried.

"We wait," William replied. "And then we will do whatever we have to, to get Jason back and take him home with us."

"We wait." Aimee repeated.

It was difficult to keep track of time in their tiny room, with no windows and the singular lightbulb which remained switched on throughout every hour of the day. Meals appeared at random times and did not seem to have any pattern to them. Aimee and William drifted in and out of sleep, time and time again, waiting for something to happen, but nothing did. The only visits they received were from various guards who pushed a tray of food through the door or escorted them to a tiny washroom twice a day so that they could use the toilet and occasionally clean themselves. William counted eleven trips to the washroom in total, which led them to believe that they had been locked away for at least five or six days.

Today, their meal consisted of a mushy beef and potato stew with a tough bread roll which hurt their teeth to chew. Aimee had finished her meal and was sitting on the floor, next to her empty tray. She held her fingers out in front of her and watched, bored, as miniature bolts began to dance on the tip of each one. She lowered her hand, just centimetres above the tray, and it began to bubble and melt into a lump of grey plastic on the floor. William knelt down beside her and together they watched as the plastic hardened and solidified. This was their only entertainment. When Aimee slept, she dreamt of Rainey and Joe, Lily and Jason. Images of Rainey, beaten and bloody contaminated her dreams. When she was awake, Aimee had to force herself not to think about her daughter, for fear that it would send her into madness. Instead, she spent a lot of her time thinking about all the things Jason had missed. All the times she had cried believing he would never come back. All the memories of the happy times she had locked away in her head because they were too painful to relive. Before Smith had faked Jason's death, and taken him away from her, they had not simply been close friends, they had been brother and sister. They had spent so much of their lives together that their memories were near identical. Thinking about Jason being alive both angered and calmed her at the same time. She was angry Smith had taken him away and subjected him to things she could only imagine. But it calmed her to know that Jason was right there, in the same building as her, within reach and alive. No matter what they were doing to him now, Aimee knew that soon she would have Jason back, and she was willing to do anything to make sure that that happened.

Footsteps outside told her that someone had arrived to take back the melted food tray. Aimee and William pushed themselves up and perched on the end of one of the beds while they waited. The footsteps grew louder as they approached and it sounded to Aimee as though there was more than just one pair of feet making their way towards their room. Something hit the outside of the door hard, and Aimee and William pulled themselves up straighter, listening carefully. Then the door shook, as though someone had kicked it.

"There's a button, idiot." Aimee said sarcastically under her breath.

The lock clicked and the door slowly swung open, stopping after a few centimetres when it hit the melted tray, which seemed to work reasonably well as a doorstop. Aimee could see two guards she was not familiar with, peering through the gap at her.

"Stand up!" He yelled.

Aimee raised her eyebrows at him.

"Time for a walk."

"A walk where?" William said.

The guard stepped away from the gap and waved his hand to someone Aimee could not see.

"Jonah, get this door open. There's something wrong with it."

She gripped William's hand tightly. They looked at each other briefly, before looking back up at the gap between the door and the frame, which was now occupied by Jonah.

"What's wrong with the door?" He said as he tested how far it would open.

"I melted a tray to the floor." Aimee replied casually, as though melting trays to the floor with only your hands was a normal day-to-day activity.

The corners of Jonah's mouth curved into the smallest of smiles. Then he looked Aimee straight in the eyes, waited for her to look back, and gave her one solid nod.

This was it.

Aimee's stomach did a somersault and Jonah's words repeated themselves in her head.

If it comes down to a choice between the two of them, then you will have to make that decision.

Aimee stood up, pulling William with her. He kissed her on the cheek and squeezed her hand. Jonah took a step back and rammed the door hard with his shoulder. The plastic snapped off the linoleum and the door flew back, slamming into the wall. Jonah stumbled into the room, closely followed by Chris, who stepped aside to allow two more guards to pass. The first headed straight for Aimee and held his hands out to grab her by the shoulders, but before he could reach her, Aimee leapt forward, shaping her fingers into claws as she dug them into the flesh on the man's face. The bolts of electricity hit him before he had a chance to consider how he could stop her. He shook violently as his body arched backwards. When she let go, he crumpled to the floor in a heap of black clothing. Then she aimed for guard number two. Jonah and Chris stood frozen in the corner of the room with their mouths hanging wide open.

"Get her, you idiots!" The guard yelled at them.

William stepped forward and punched him in the nose. The man stumbled back, out of the door, and leant against the wall in the corridor. Aimee wasted no time. She flicked her fingers and a blue-white light jumped from her hand and into his chest. His body slid down the wall, his head making a sickening crack as it hit the floor.

Chris grabbed hold of one leg and William the other and they dragged the body back into the room. The air smelled of singed hair. It had taken a matter of seconds, and two of Smith's men were dead.

"I'm glad we're on your side," Jonah said, looking down at his dead co-workers.

"What happened to the camera?" Chris asked, scanning the room.

"I ripped it off the wall on the first night," William informed him, and Chris nodded his head approvingly.

"You must be William. I'm Chris, this is Jonah." He held out a hand to William, who shook it before turning to Aimee.

"Ready?" He asked her.

Aimee nodded and squeezed his arm as she passed him. The four of them stepped out of the room and pulled the door shut behind them.

"To the seventh floor?" William asked.

Jonah looked at him and nodded.

"To the seventh floor."

27

Jason

The dull feeling of hopelessness that had taunted Jason for years, that had made him wish, day upon day, that he could just die already, had been lifted, with the single flicker of light that came from hearing Aimee's voice. He had endured beating after beating after beating, both mentally and physically. He had been starved and tortured, to show him who was in charge, to show him that he would never win, to make an example out of him for anyone else who might consider running, just like he had. But Jason knew that that was not the only reason he was here. Smith wanted to make an example of him, yes. But what he wanted more than anything, was to hurt Aimee. And he knew that the best way to do that was to hurt her family. And, of course, there was the information Jason has been researching about Smith before his capture. Something that Smith had been so desperate to keep a secret. Someone that he had tried so hard to keep hidden away from their world. But Jason knew. Jason had made it his mission to know.

He had long ago accepted that this would be where he died. Smith would order one beating too many, or his body might just give up, after being starved and sick for too many days, weeks, months. But then Aimee had appeared, screaming and fighting to get close to him. When he first heard her voice, he was so happy. A hundred thoughts all ran through his mind at once. Aimee was alive! She had come to take him home. Everything would be ok if he had Aimee. But then the devastating realisation dawned on him that Smith had finally caught her, and there would be nothing but unimaginable pain and fear for her in this place.

He had tried to shout out, tried to warn her, but he was gagged. And what good would it do anyway? She was already here. It was already too late. The best he could hope for now was for Rainey and William to still be safe. But then the covering blocking his sight had been removed, and he saw William standing speechless behind Aimee, before she had collapsed on to the floor. But Rainey was not there, and Jason grasped at the hope that she had not been harmed.

He had only a few seconds to look at Aimee before the guards swooped in on her. Jason's vision seemed to stutter, and he watched in slow motion as Aimee screamed hysterically, kicking and biting and doing everything she could to get away from them.

"It's okay, Aimee," Jason had tried to say, but his voice croaked in his throat.

He did not know how many days it had been since he last spoke.

"It will be okay."

And then she was gone. Jason knew she could not have heard him over her screaming, and he wished he could have shouted, but his body was too broken.

He hadn't thought that it would be possible to feel worse than he already did, but the days that followed proved him wrong. Jason spent his hours praying to a God that he did not believe in, praying that Aimee and William were not being tortured the way he had. He prayed that Aimee's pain would not be a new way of torturing him further, but he knew that it was already too late for that. And, most of all, he prayed that Aimee had somehow managed to avoid Smith. Aimee had already suffered too much because of Smith and his obsession.

Smith's visits began to shorten and the length of time between each grew more spaced, which contributed to Jason's fear that Smith had found someone more important to torment.

The days and hours passed by in a blur. Jason did not know how many months or years he had spent in his prison. There were no windows and the only light to creep its way into the room came from a metal hole in the door, a letterbox that allowed the guards to push through scraps of food, just enough to keep him alive. A single mattress lay on the cold, concrete floor and the only other piece of furniture was an empty plastic bottle which had once been his only source of fresh water. It had not been filled in days. The guards would collect Jason once each day to use the toilet and sometimes to shower. This worked well considering the little food and water he was given, there was not much need to use the toilet more than once each day when he was provided with barely enough to keep him alive. When his water bottle was not filled, Jason used his time in the shower to consume as much fluid as his body could hold.

Jason was made to shave at least once each week and his hair was kept short, cut down roughly with scissors when it began to brush against the tops of his ears. For a long time, he struggled to see why this was important, until eventually he stumbled upon the idea that maybe Smith did not like other people to have a lot of hair when he lacked the ability to grow his own. But Jason knew that that was ridiculous. It was more than likely to prevent the lice. Still, the thought entertained him.

Jason spent most of his time sleeping, because that was all that his diet would allow for, and when he was not on his daily toilet trip, or being beaten for Smith's amusement, there was nothing more to do.

A shiver ran through Jason's body and he curled up tighter, attempting to cover more of his body with his skinny arms, and failing. The cold was relentless, and with every pound of weight he lost, it would only intensify. Another shiver caused his body to shake momentarily. Jason distracted himself by locating a memory from the place in the back of his mind where he kept them locked away, hidden out of Smith's reach. He closed his eyes and watched as the images replayed across the backs of his eyelids.

It was dark out in the street and the rain was heavy, soaking Jason's clothes through as he rushed along the pavement. An angry red burn lay across the back of his left hand, a fresh scar to add to his collection, and he cupped it to his chest protectively. He was twelve years old and had only one place he could run to. As he neared the tiny house with its overgrown garden and boarded up windows, he slowed to a steady walk. Only two windows remained of this run-down little cottage, the first was a small arch, high up on the front door, it reminded him of a Rainbow with its coloured glass. The second was around the back of the house. Which is where Jason headed. He crept down the far side of the garden and down the side of the house. When he reached the back garden, he froze, hidden in the shadows. Aimee's father stumbled across the uncut grass, half a bottle of cider grasped firmly in his hand. He made his way in a wobbly line to the open back door, catching his foot on a broken paving slab on his way and slamming, chin first, into what used to be a patio but was now a pile of cracked paving slabs, rubble and empty cider bottles. Marcus pushed himself up from the floor, cursed loudly and stumbled forwards. When he finally fell through the door and into the house he began yelling, not bothering to close the door behind him.

"Aimee," he slurred. "Where the hell are you? I'm starving!"

Jason glanced down at the watch around his wrist. 11:43pm. Marcus had obviously been on one of his binges. Biting the inside of his cheek to suppress the rage he felt at hearing Marcus speak to Aimee in the same way he usually did, Jason began moving again. He edged his foot in through the doorway and listened carefully for any sound. Marcus was already snoring loudly from the direction of the living room. He walked quietly and carefully to the living room door and peered around it. Sure enough, Marcus was asleep, the top half of his body draped over an old rotting armchair, the bottom half trailed across the stained carpet. He pulled the door shut and began searching for Aimee. He found her in the kitchen, attempting to open a tin of meatballs and gravy with a blunt knife. Tears stained the smooth skin on her cheeks and her eyes looked swollen and red from crying. She was wearing a jumper which was far too big for her, probably one that had belonged to her mother, before she died. Marcus had kept any of his wife's old belongings that he could not sell. Jason pushed the door open as he stepped through and Aimee jumped, dropping the knife into the sink where it clattered loudly. Her body relaxed as Jason came into view. He held his arms open and Aimee fell into them, squeezing him tightly around the middle. Her long, dark brown hair brushed lightly against the raw and melted skin on Jason's hand and he flinched away from her. Aimee stepped back and examined him with her eyes. When she found the burn on his hand, she did not look shocked. Her hands gently took hold of the healthy skin around his fingers and pulled them up to her face to examine the wound. Aimee had helped Jason countless times over the past two and a half years. It had become part of their weekly, sometimes even daily, routine.

"What happened?" Aimee asked, as she pulled Jason's hand towards the tap above the sink.

"I don't know. One minute Mum and Dad were talking about some TV programme that used to be on every Thursday night, and the next, she was flipping out."

Aimee sighed and slowly turned the tap on. The water sputtered at first and Jason edged one end of his burn into the cold stream. He gritted his teeth together and squeezed his eyes shut tightly.

"Hold it there for a few minutes." Aimee said, and she returned her attention to opening the tin of meatballs.

It was slow work, but after a few minutes she had managed to stab a hole into the top. She sawed her way around half of the can. Then carefully edged the tip of her middle finger down the side of the lid and pulled. When the lid had been pulled back as far as it would go, Aimee set the tin on to the hob and turned on the gas. She knew it was not safe to heat food inside the tin, but she had little choice, there were no pans or plates. After a little while the mixture began to bubble, and Aimee lifted the can with the sleeve of her jumper and placed it on to the kitchen worktop.

"He's asleep, isn't he?" She asked Jason.

Jason nodded.

"My fingers are numb," he informed her.

Aimee stretched out a hand to turn off the tap. She wrapped her hands around Jason's and gently dabbed at his unharmed skin with her baggy jumper to dry it off. Leaving the can of unappetising, dog-food-looking meatballs open on the side, Aimee and Jason headed to her bedroom.

Aimee's room was very small and not at all like a twelve-year-old girl's bedroom should be. The walls were bare, with patches of grey and black where the cold had given way to the damp. The floorboards had been left uncovered and most of them were loose, creaking when they were stepped on. The furniture was minimal and old. Aimee did not have many possessions, but anything she did own would not be left out in plain view for her father to steal and sell on to fund his alcohol addiction.

Aimee made her way over to the corner of the room, furthest from the door. She knelt down and pulled at the edge of one of the loose floorboards. Her hand disappeared through the hole in the floor, into the space underneath, and reappeared holding a bright green plastic box with a white cross on the front. Her first aid kit. Aimee and Jason had stolen it earlier in the year from a nearby pharmacy, on a day when Jason's parents had become particularly annoyed by their son's filthy habit of existing. He had received one of the worst beatings he had ever had that day, and their need for a first aid kit of some description had been desperate. If ever they needed more first aid supplies, they would steal them from any place they could. Aimee had even resorted to falling over on purpose outside the library once so that the librarian would offer her a plaster for her grazes. When the first aid box had made an appearance, she had grabbed as much as she could and made a dash for it.

Aimee clicked open the box and fished around inside. When she found what she was looking for she closed the lid and placed it safely back in the secret space, hidden by the floorboard. Holding his hand out, Jason watched as Aimee examined the burn. He noticed that her eyes sparkled with un-spilled tears, making her blue-grey eyes luminous, and her cheeks were flushed a deep pink, highlighting the striking paleness of her skin tone in comparison. Jason realised with a jolt that Aimee was beautiful. He had always known she was pretty, but it was not something he had really thought about. They had always been friends, friends who both desperately needed the company of one another. It was not until now that Aimee appeared to Jason as somebody who could be more than a friend. A fluttering erupted in his stomach, and he wriggled uncomfortably.

Aimee covered the burn with a rectangular patch of cling film, taping the outside edges to Jason's hand using medical tape. Cling film was another item they would regularly take when wandering through a shop, as burns were a frequent occurrence for Jason, whose parents insisted on beating him for the smallest of reasons, and also for Aimee, who had been cooking for herself using the food she could find around her house, or steal from the local shop, for as long as she could remember.

Hours passed by as they waited for Aimee's father to wake. They talked right through the night, watching the sunrise through the remaining window at the back of the house, despite how dirty it was and covered in condensation from the cold night air. They would listen intently for any noise between each conversation, ready for Jason to make a run for the exit.

When Marcus finally did begin to stir, Jason hugged Aimee goodbye. He would be back the next night anyway. Neither of them could go to school anymore. Their parents had not bothered to enrol them anywhere when they had finished primary school, and nobody had pushed for them to be enrolled either, not after they had discovered what they really were. So, they spent most of their days either at home or out running their parents' errands. There was always plenty of sleep to be had during the day, leaving long and empty nights which would regularly be filled with each other's company.

Jason crept through the bedroom door and tiptoed his way down the hall. The back door creaked as he carefully pulled it open, but if it was lifted just right then it could barely be heard from the other end of the hall. Once outside, Jason risked a quick glance through the dirt ridden window which led into Aimee's bedroom. He pulled a face at her through the glass, making her giggle. He held out his injured hand, pressing it against the window and Aimee did the same. Their fingers matching perfectly. The uncomfortable fluttering sensation returned in the pit of his stomach. They shared one last lingering moment, saddened smiles hanging heavily on their lips, before Jason turned and strode away.

The sound of footsteps disturbed Jason from his sleep. He had drifted off, but his memory of Aimee had continued into his dreams. He pulled himself into a sitting position as the footsteps came to a stop outside his door. More than anything, he hoped it would be one of the less inhumane guards, one who might offer him a little more food than his usual daily rations. But he wished for the same thing every time a guard came to his room, and his wishes rarely came true.

The door swung open slowly and two guards stepped into the little space available in Jason's room. Just outside the door, Jason could see a young woman dressed in light green overalls with a thick brown belt around her middle, holding a bucket full of cleaning supplies. He smiled inwardly. Cleaning day meant that returning to his cell would take longer than the average toilet and shower trip. But his momentary high quickly diminished at the thought of how sad his existence had become, excited about spending an extra few minutes inside a toilet cubicle, because it was somewhere different to his meagre living space. He remembered hearing a word once: *Eleutheromania – the intense and irresistible desire for freedom*. It was not that Jason's desire for freedom was disintegrating, more his belief that such a thing existed. He was not sure if that was something he had actually heard before, or something he had just imagined. Maybe it had come from one of the books he had shared with Rainey all those years ago.

The first guard gestured with his hand for Jason to exit through the door. He tried to pull himself up, but a wave of nausea washed over him and he slumped back down on to the hard mattress. The guard pulled a disgusted face and turned to look at his ally, but the second man did not return his obvious animosity. He stepped past the guard and held out his hand, offering it to Jason. Jason eyed him suspiciously, but the man's face showed no hostility, only kindness. He lifted his hand and placed it in the guard's, who slowly pulled him to his feet.

"Thank you," Jason tried through his dry throat.

The guard nodded in reply and pointed to the door with his hand. Once outside, the young girl rushed into the room and set to work.

"If you want to stay and watch the cleaning then I can handle it from here," the nicer of the guards said to the other.

"Good, because I am not spending all day waiting for her finish up in here before we can bring him back." He replied, hinting for the cleaner to hurry.

"This way," the man directed Jason.

Jason's eyebrows pulled together. This had never happened before. He had never been escorted by only one guard. It didn't matter, of course. There was no way that he could escape. But still, it seemed significant in some way. As they neared the end of the corridor and stepped through a set of doors, Jason could hear the guard who had stayed behind shouting for the cleaner to get a move on.

The familiar linoleum floor in the washroom was already wet, and the steamy air clung to Jason's skin as he entered. The washroom consisted of a large changing area, one long bench running the length of the wall, and a few hooks to hang clothing on. Jason had barely stepped into the room when the guard began to rifle through his own pockets.

"Here," he said. "Eat these. It's not much but it's a damn sight better than what you normally get."

In his hands were various sized packets of food. Jason looked at him in disbelief.

"What? I... I don't understand." He stammered.

"We don't have long. Please, just take it."

Jason plucked the items from his hands and began tearing them open. The first contained three sandwich crackers with processed cheese running through the middle. The second was a square of plain chocolate which had been wrapped tightly in foil, and some form of savoury pastry had been knotted into a small sandwich bag. Jason's eyes rolled back as he tasted the chocolate. His taste buds seemed to awaken at the long forgotten creamy texture. It melted on his tongue, and Jason resisted the urge to swallow for as long as he could.

"Bit of a change from your daily portion of brown rice," the guard laughed, handing over a bottle of water.

Jason gulped down the first few mouthfuls, greedily.

"Listen," the man said. "I need to speak to you about a situation which may be taking place shortly. My name is Elliot. I had to do a lot of persuading to be here today, I don't normally guard the more important prisoners, mostly just the younger offenders, sometimes the elderly, if there are any."

Jason watched Elliot carefully as he ate.

"I understand that some close friends of yours were recently captured. Aimee and William?"

Jason stopped chewing the pastry he had stuffed into his mouth.

"There have been plans to help them escape in exchange for Aimee's help-"

Elliot was cut off mid-sentence by a mouthful of Jason's food as it was spat across the floor. He choked loudly and took a gulp of the water before he could speak.

"They're going to escape?" He asked, incredulously.

"There are plans for them to escape, yes. In exchange for Aimee's help to deliver a Gifted child."

"But how can that be possible? They would need help to even break free of the holding rooms." Jason croaked.

"They will have the help of two guards and-" Elliot tried, but Jason cut him off again.

"Two guards? That's it? Surely, Aimee must know that this won't work. She knows how strong the unit is. The best she could possibly hope for is to escape the holding room. And when they catch her, she'll be punished. Smith won't hesitate to kill William. She knows that. She should know that."

"Stop. Just listen to what I know. There isn't much time to explain," he waited for Jason to speak again but he had closed his mouth firmly as he fidgeted uncomfortably with one of the food wrappers. "There are two guards in Aimee's wing who need her help, one of them is the lover of a young pregnant woman and the other is his brother. Their relationship is secret, and the baby she carries is his. There is no hope for her or her child here. They made a deal with Aimee. If they help her to escape, in exchange, she would help to deliver the child. Aimee agreed to these conditions, but she made some conditions of her own."

Jason listened intently, his mind reeling. He thought of Aimee, strong, confident Aimee, who he had protected since the age of ten. He thought of how she would try to run, try to save William. And then he thought of her failing and William being murdered as part of her punishment.

"One of the conditions was that you be helped to escape too," Elliot continued.

Jason predicted hearing those very words as soon as Elliot had told him that Aimee had her own conditions. There was no way Aimee would attempt to leave without him.

"No. No, this won't work. It's too dangerous. You have to stop them."

"The other condition is that she also be allowed to take the baby."

"Take the baby of the pregnant woman? Why would she want to do that?" Jason questioned.

Elliot looked at him, his eyebrows knotting together in confusion.

"The baby was brought in with her."

"She has a baby?" Jason felt lightheaded, and he leaned back on the bench, pressing his shoulders against the wall.

"They brought her in just before they arrived back with Aimee and

William. Aimee refuses to leave without her."

Nodding his head, Jason pulled himself up straighter. If the baby was Aimee's, then he knew she would attempt to escape regardless of any help she might receive. She had succeeded on her first attempt, all those years ago, but things had been different then. They had not all been locked away and heavily guarded for starters. Smith had never suspected that they might run. He did now.

"I would like to suggest that you make the most of the next few minutes and use the facilities, Mr. Cinder. When the alarm sounds, you must be ready to leave." Elliot instructed, calmly.

Jason flinched a little at Elliot's use of his surname. It had been a long time since anyone had called him 'Mr. Cinder'.

"Now? They're going today?"

Elliot nodded.

"What about you? Why are you helping them?"

Elliot thought about it for a moment, before deciding that sharing his story with Jason was the right thing to do.

"Aimee ran away before, yes?" He did not wait for an answer. "And now, more try to escape with their pregnant loved ones. Some people can't afford that option. My Sophia, she was only one of the many women who could not afford to run. So many rumours are heard of workers falling in love and being torn apart, but nobody believes them, not until it happens to you. My Sophia was so pure, so gentle, and they used her for the child who grew inside her. Neither one of them made it through the birth. They say that if Aimee had not fled, there would have been a chance. If it was my Sophia, and she were still here, still carrying my unborn child, then I too would take the risk of helping Aimee."

Jason watched, speechless as Elliot's features slowly began to wipe clean of the pain he had suffered for his lost ones.

"I'm so sorry that you-"

Elliot cut him off with a nod of his head. He held his hand up to the shower cubicle.

"Please, use the facilities, while there is still time."

The shower ran hot over Jason's yellowed skin. He clenched his fists and pushed them into his temples as the water washed over his roughly cut hair, causing small streams of water to drip lazily down his face and over his chest. His stomach had begun to churn uneasily, and Jason wondered if eating food much richer than he had been accustomed to had been a good idea before an attempted escape. Not that he would regret eating it, regardless.

A clean set of clothes lay folded on top of the bench when Jason stepped out of the shower. He quickly used the toilet before dressing himself. Elliot entered the room, holding a pair of black boots in his hands. Jason pulled them on, they were a little too big for his feet but comfortable, and he tied them as tightly as he could to prevent them from falling off. He looked down at his clothing, realising for the first time that he was dressed in black from head to toe.

"You may be less noticeable wearing the colours of the guards." Elliot told him.

Jason stepped forward, placing a hand on his shoulder.

"Thank you, Elliot. I will forever be-"

But Elliot could not hear Jason's words over the siren that had begun to blare loudly through the speakers hanging from the ceiling. Jason shot a nervous glance at Elliot before he felt the pressure of Elliot's hand on the top of his arm. He allowed himself to be dragged through the door, and he thanked his lucky stars that Elliot could be so persuasive. Today could have been just another day, if it weren't for Elliot.

28

Rainey

"This heat is just ridiculous! How can anybody live here?" Lexi complained, loudly.

"Air con, Lexi. That's how," Joe replied.

"Oh, wow. Thanks, Joe. How would we possibly cope without you? Who would answer our rhetorical questions with such wise ass remarks?" Lexi's voice oozed with sarcasm.

Rainey ignored them as she studied a paper road map closely. On the map were the rough directions Maria had provided for them, inked on in thick red pen, but what they really needed to find was a shop where they could get some basic supplies. Maria had arranged for a rental car to meet them at the airport and Joe had driven them for two hours before they had even considered the need for water or food. Now they were lost, at the side of the road, in the middle of the desert, with a paper map which had definitely seen better days.

"This map is useless. I don't have a clue where we are."

Rainey folded the worn paper in half and passed it to Joe, before climbing back into the front passenger seat.

"Let's just keep driving until we find something. We still have quarter of a tank of fuel," Joe said as he climbed into the driver's seat.

He started the car and waited for Lexi to join them.

As they sped through the desert, Rainey focussed on the cliffs and rocks casting dark shadows across the red sand. The only vegetation for miles around was the cacti, making strange shaped silhouettes in the distance, like eerie figures, watching them as they passed.

After two hours of driving, the sun began to sink behind the horizon, cooling the air and setting deep red and orange tones across the sky. Rainey watched the colours in fascination as they transformed and made way for the stars. A warning beeped from the dashboard, pulling her from her brief equanimity. She turned to Joe, who looked back at her with a grim expression.

"We're running on empty. If we don't find a garage in the next few minutes then it looks like we'll be camping out in the desert," he said.

Rainey looked out of the window again, seeing for the first time the dangers that could be hiding out in the shadows, and shuddered at the thought.

"Yeah, that's what I was thinking," he added, reading Rainey's expression.

Joe kept the car at a steady pace in a final attempt to make the fuel last longer, but within moments it began to slow. Rainey squeezed her hands together nervously.

"Why did we not plan for this? We should have brought food and water and a petrol can. Now we're going to be stuck out here with God only knows what kind of poisonous snakes and spiders."

"And scorpions," Lexi added, helpfully.

"Maria didn't tell us what it's like out here," Joe tried, but Rainey stopped him.

"It's not Maria's fault. It's our fault. How can we have been so stupid? We are driving through a desert. Our number-one-rule should have been to bring water at the very least."

The car stuttered and lurched forward in its last dying effort. Rainey put her feet up on the dashboard with her knees in front of her chest and leaned her head against them. She stayed there for a few moments, ignoring the bickering which had broken out between Joe and Lexi. She groaned as she considered for the first time that maybe she wouldn't reach Smith. She had come so far, only to make a stupid mistake that would set them back hours, and that was only if somebody somehow managed to find them out in the middle of nowhere. What if nobody found them? What if they died of starvation or dehydration? What would happen to Lily and her parents?

"Rainey."

What if one of them was bitten by a snake while they searched for help, and their arm or leg swelled up like she had seen on the survival programs on the TV?

"Rainey."

Or if they fell down a hidden drop somewhere and got stuck, just like in that film she had seen once.

"RAINEY!" Lexi screamed down her ear.

"What?" She shouted back, annoyed at being disrupted from her thoughts of impending doom.

"Look, down there. There's a building."

Lexi pointed down the road ahead of them, to where a few pinpricks of yellow light shone through the darkness.

"How far away is that?" Rainey said, not wanting to set her hopes on a building that could still be miles away.

"It doesn't look too far. I think maybe we could make it if we push the car." Joe said.

"You want us to push the car? Look, when I agreed to run halfway across the world with you two, I did not expect to be pushing a car across an infested desert!" Lexi complained.

They ignored her as they unclipped their seat belts.

"We're actually going to do this?" She continued.

Rainey and Joe swung open their doors and slammed them shut behind them. Lexi looked at them in disbelief before she climbed out too.

"I can't believe this! One of us is going to end up getting bitten by one of those camel things and then the vultures will eat us."

"Camel things?" Joe questioned, placing both of his hands on the back of the car.

"You know what I mean, those giant spider camel things." Lexi said, her voice rising.

Joe rolled his eyes.

"You're not even taking it seriously! They're a real thing!" She yelled.

Rainey tried her hardest to bite her tongue and not snap at Lexi, she knew that every now and again her childish side would make an appearance, giving way to the selfish brat Rainey knew she could be at times, it was one of the reasons she loved her so much. Lexi was never afraid to show who she really was.

"If either of you think I will be sucking the poison out of your bites then you can think again. Push the car... I'm not even strong enough! And that's before adding in the hours of hunger and dehydration-"

"Shut up, Lexi!" Rainey screamed.

Joe dropped his hands and stared in shock as Rainey continued to shout at Lexi.

"Just shut up! Who cares if there are spiders out here? Who cares if we have to push the car for a few minutes? All you seem to care about is yourself!"

She regretted her words the moment they tumbled from her mouth, but once she had started, she could not stop.

"Rainey, I'm worried about walking in the night through the desert. I'm just scared, that's all." Lexi replied, quietly.

"Well, we're all scared, Lex. But you don't have to listen to us rattling on about it. Nobody asked you to come with us, nobody forced you. You wanted to come." Rainey said, harshly.

Lexi did not know what to say. She stood very still, holding Rainey's gaze.

"I didn't ask for someone to come and take Lily from me, or my parents. And now I have no choice but to march my way through half of Nevada to find them. You have every choice, Lexi. You can either come with us and keep your opinions to yourself, or you can stay here and wait for help. That's your choice." Rainey turned away from her, and pressed her hands against the car, ready to begin pushing.

"I had just as much choice to come here as you did," she replied in a small voice.

"What?" Rainey snapped, spinning to face her again.

"I had to come with you. That was my only option."

Rainey gave one short, sharp laugh. A sound which Lexi and Joe knew to associate with danger.

"You had no other option? If this is all such a burden on your life then why are you here?"

Lexi stayed silent.

"Why are you here, Lexi?" Rainey yelled, her voice carrying across the deserted sand.

"Because this is all I have!" Lexi screamed back at her. "You broke me out of the only place I was welcome. The only people I care about are either here, missing or dead. I have nothing. I don't even have my own clothes."

Rainey opened her mouth to argue but was hit with an unexpected wave of guilt. She had always felt terrible for what had happened to Lexi when her parents died, but she had never thought of her as having nothing. Now, as Lexi screamed the dejected details of her life in a single breath of air, Rainey felt disgusted in herself for not considering what Lexi was going through too. She felt her next words roll off her tongue before she had a chance to consider what they meant.

"I don't care, Lexi."

A small exhale of breath escaped from Joe, as the horror of what Rainey had said hit him. Lexi lurched forward and slapped Rainey hard across the face. She stumbled back against the boot of the car but made no attempt to retaliate. She closed her eyes momentarily, and when she opened them again, she looked directly into Lexi's hurt glare with an empty and hollow stare. Lexi and Joe watched her as she turned towards the car and raised a hand into the air in front of her. A whistling noise filled the desert around them, and the car began to roll slowly forwards, as Rainey summoned the air to push it away. She moved along at the same pace, leaving them to stare, speechless, at the space she had filled a moment before.

"I'll do it myself." Rainey said, as she moved further and further into the darkness.

"She's not Rainey anymore." Joe said quietly.

His voice travelled through the quiet air as though he had shouted it, and Rainey felt every word like a dagger to her heart.

It took almost an hour to reach the garage. When they finally made it, the lights had been turned off and a sign hanging on the door read: *Sorry, we're closed*. Rainey did not want to waste her time discussing their next steps. She climbed into the front seat of the car, dropped the seat as far back as it would go, and closed her eyes. She had expected Joe and Lexi to join her, but they stayed outside the car, sitting on the dusty desert floor. Rainey ran her tongue over her dry, cracked lips. Her mouth was so parched that it felt as though her tongue had been wrapped in fur. If she had been tired and thirsty before, it was nothing compared to how she felt now, after pushing an SUV halfway across the desert, single handedly.

After an hour of lying awake with her eyes closed, Rainey rolled on to her side, positioning herself so that she faced away from the others, as she tried to eavesdrop on their conversation. It was difficult at first, with the thick glass of the car's windows blocking out most of their words, but as her ears began to adjust, she could make out more and more of their discussion.

"I don't know who she is anymore. The Rainey I fell in love with didn't speak to people the way she does. She would have done anything to keep you happy before, but now, it's like she doesn't care." Joe half whispered, his voice croaking with dehydration.

"She didn't even react when I hit her. I didn't mean to do it. I didn't even think about it. This white light just flashed in front of me and then my hand was moving." Lexi said.

"Her eyes were just... empty. It's like she's running out of fight." Joe said. "We have to get Lily back. If not for Lily, or for myself, then for Rainey. Before we lose her."

Rainey's eyes fluttered open. She lifted a hand to her face to shield her eyes from the brightness. The skin on her arm stung as it peeled away from the leather seat. Every part of her was covered in sweat as the unbearable heat inside the car leached the remaining fluids from her body. The sun blared down on to the SUV, making the still air in the vehicle swelteringly hot. Rainey's skin itched and her clothes clung to her. She pushed herself upright only for her head to throb painfully, as though something were trying to break its way out from the inside of her skull. Rainey had known thirst before, but nothing came close to the desiccation she felt now. She looked at her watch sticking uncomfortably to the skin on her wrist. It had been more than twenty-four hours since their last drink and her body yearned for water.

With trembling hands, she pulled on the lever of the door. It popped open and Rainey spun her legs out, laying her feet flat on the floor. She placed one hand on the inner handle of the door and the other on the doorframe. As she heaved herself up from the seat, the tips of her fingers brushed against the metal roof of the car and she snatched them away as quickly as she could, but her reaction was delayed, her brain sluggish. Her skin clung to the fiery heat of the metal, leaving shining red blisters in its wake. She yelped and clambered from the car, stumbling as she made her way to the doors of the garage.

Cool air washed over her as she stepped into the small air-conditioned store. She inhaled a deep refreshing breath before she rushed to the closest fridge, desperate to find a bottle of water, but it was full of plastic-wrapped packets of bacon. She moved along to the next fridge, every step causing her head to throb painfully. The second fridge contained various canned and bottled drinks. She did not pay any attention to what they were as she yanked open the door and snatched at the closest bottle. She struggled with the top and winced as her fresh burns scraped against the serrated plastic. The first gulp was invigorating. It washed over her parched tongue and down her throat, leaving a freezing trail behind that Rainey could feel deep into her stomach. She gulped more and more mouthfuls, finishing the bottle and reaching for another before a voice sounded behind her.

"I hope you'll be paying for those," the deep, heavily accented voice said.

Rainey turned to see a large man with a deep brown tan that made his skin look worn and wrinkled. He wore great round sunglasses, covering the top half of his face, and a horseshoe moustache covered the bottom.

"Yes, I'll pay," she gasped, pulling the ice-cold drink from her lips.

Behind the man, she could see through the glass in the doors, to where Joe and Lexi continued to bake in the car as they slept. Her eyes travelled down the door to where a stack of baskets had been piled on one side of the entrance. She edged past him and lifted two baskets, taking one in each hand, before heading back to the fridge. She placed one of the baskets on the floor between her feet and held the other up to where the bottled water rested on one of the shelves. Then, with her spare hand, she squeezed her fingers behind the bottles and knocked them off the shelf one at a time. They landed heavily in the basket. When one basket was filled with bottles, she switched the baskets and carefully began to select flavoured beverages, placing them into the empty basket one at a time. Cola, fresh juice, iced tea. Her mouth felt dry again, despite demolishing almost a litre of water just a moment before.

She placed the full baskets on the counter, where the man began to ring them through on the till. As he scanned each of the bottles and placed them into a large brown bag sitting open beside Rainey's baskets, a telephone began to ring. He picked up the handset and pinned it between his shoulder and his ear as he continued his work. While he spoke into the receiver, Rainey began pacing the little shop, picking out packets of food and throwing them into the quickly receding baskets as she listened to snippets of the shopkeeper's conversation.

"That's the one. It's the only gas stop in the area. Right this minute, yes. Maybe, if you're quick." He spoke quickly, stumbling over his words, as though he was nervous speaking to the voice on the other end of the phone.

Rainey fished around in her pockets for the wad of folded dollars Maria had provided for her.

"Road trip?" The man asked, placing the handset back on its base and packing the last few items into a second bag.

"Something like that, yeah."

"Can't have been very well prepared if you're in here buying all these supplies."

Rainey shrugged her shoulders.

"We need fuel too. However much it takes to fill it up." She picked out three one-hundred-dollar bills and placed them down on the counter.

He raised his eyebrows before pushing the bulging bags to the edge of the worktop. Then he picked up the money, examined it quickly and placed it in his back pocket.

"Yes, Ma'am," he said, and edged his way around the back of the counter and towards the doors.

Rainey lifted one of the bags and glanced up at the posters on the wall. The bag slipped through her arms and thudded on to the ground, tearing in half and sending its contents rolling in every direction across the floor. There on the wall, pinned to a cork notice board, hung a poster with large block capitals across the top. WANTED. A number had been added to the bottom, beneath the reward amount, which was more than she cared to think about. And there, right in the centre of the poster, was a picture of Rainey.

Rainey grabbed a pen sitting on the counter top and scribbled the number roughly on to the back of her hand. She bent to retrieve the items she had dropped, scooping them up into the torn bag and cradling them against her chest as she hurried out of the door.

She yanked open the boot of the car, careful not to touch the metal this time, and dropped the bottles and packets in, keeping two bottles of water to one side, which she threw on to the back seat where Joe and Lexi had finally roused from their sleep.

"Start the car." She ordered.

Rainey headed back into the shop to retrieve the second bag. She pulled it under her arm and hesitated for a moment at the counter. If she left the poster pinned on the wall, then surely as soon as the shop owner came back inside, he would recognise her and call the number. Maybe he already had. She placed the bag back on the counter and climbed over, ripping the poster from the wall, before clambering back and collecting her shopping. As she rushed through the doors, her elbow brushed against the handle, snagging the sleeve of her top, and she dropped the bag. Bottles scattered across the dusty ground and she cursed to herself loudly. She grabbed what she could and ran to the boot of the car, throwing everything in and slamming it shut.

"She's all filled up for you." The man yelled over the sound of the engine.

"Who did you speak to on the phone?" Rainey questioned.

He looked back at her with what Rainey assumed was his best attempt at confusion.

"You told them I was here, didn't you?"

"I... I don't know what you mean."

Joe turned off the engine and climbed out of the driver's seat.

"You called the number on that poster. Didn't you?" Rainey shouted.

He glanced down at the poster, scrunched in Rainey's fist.

"What are we waiting for?" Joe said, making his way around the car.

Rainey snatched the key from his hand and pushed the crumpled poster to Joe's chest. He grabbed at it before it could fall to the floor and stretched it out in his hands as Rainey climbed into the SUV. Joe's eyes scanned over the picture before he looked up at her in horror through the windshield.

"Get in the car!" She screamed, and she revved the engine impatiently.

Joe took one last look at the shopkeeper before he clambered into the back seat. Rainey slammed her foot to the floor before Joe could pull the door closed, and the car shot forward and hurtled back on to the road, leaving a cloud of dust behind them.

"What the hell was that all about?" Lexi shouted from the back seat, an empty water bottle sitting in her lap.

Joe handed the torn poster to Lexi and she gasped as Rainey glared back at her from the picture.

"What is this?" Lexi said to no one in particular. "Wanted by who?"

"I would be willing to put all of our money on it not being the police. It must be Smith. He knows we're here." Joe said as Rainey continued to throttle the car along the sandy road.

"The guy who filled the car, he was on the phone before. He said that the garage is the only one out here, and something about being quick. He sounded weird, like he was scared or something." Rainey recalled.

"Shit." Joe said.

He banged his fist against the plastic panelling on the door, causing it to crack. They were silent for a moment, listening to the tyres race over the grit in the road as their minds predicted what could be waiting ahead.

"What is going on with your fingers?" Lexi gasped.

Rainey's eyes flicked down to her hands, wrapped tightly around the steering wheel. The blisters on the tips of her fingers had burst, leaving flaps of white skin hanging from the red sores underneath.

"Funny thing happens when you leave a huge chunk of metal out in the sun for too long." Rainey said.

Lexi looked at her in disbelief. Joe shuffled forward in his seat, stretching his arm out and gently running his fingers over Rainey's cheek. She felt a tightening in the skin surrounding her burns and glanced down to see that the dead skin had dried up and flaked off completely, leaving the raw, burned flesh underneath a light shade of pink as it healed. She brushed Joe's hand away with her own.

"I don't need you to heal it. We have bigger things to worry about right now."

With a sigh, Joe leaned back in his seat and stared out of the window, watching the desert as they sped through it.

"We're pretty far away from the garage now. Do you think it would be safe to stop? At least for a few minutes so that we can get the food out of the back." Lexi asked, after an insufferable hour of silence.

Rainey thought for a moment. She had not taken her foot off the gas since they left the garage. She had been checking her mirrors constantly to make sure they were not being followed. The land behind them stretched out, far and flat, allowing them to see for miles, but the garage had not been visible for a long time now. In front of them the road rose up a large gradual hill, blocking their view.

"Fine. But not for long, we're making good time," she decided.

The car slowed as Rainey pressed her foot down on the brake. There was no real point of pulling on to the side of the road. They climbed out and opened the boot. Rummaging through the bags, they each found a sandwich, more water and a large bag of beef jerky. Rainey cautiously tested the temperature of the bonnet with the back of her hand before she climbed onto it and crossed her legs in front of her.

"I always wanted to try this stuff!" Lexi announced, sounding excited as she waved the bag of shrivelled beef in front of Rainey. "And salt water taffy too."

"I don't think they had any taffy. Fifty thousand packets of raw bacon but no chocolate or sweets. What kind of a shop doesn't sell chocolate?" Rainey said as she took a mouthful of her rapidly warming and unappealing sandwich.

"I could so go for some chocolate cake right now. No, chocolate fudge cake, hot, with ice cream." Lexi closed her eyes while she envisioned it. When she opened her eyes again, Joe and Rainey were watching her with their eyebrows raised.

"Could that be the most ironic moment ever? Dreaming about red-hot cake, in the middle of the most red-hot place you have ever been, while eating a warm cheese sandwich?" Joe smirked.

"Oh, come on. Don't act like there isn't some sort of food you would not kill for right now." Lexi said, matter-of-factly.

Rainey shook her head but smiled.

"Sunday lunch!" Joe shouted. "Pork, vegetables, mashed potatoes. And Yorkshire puddings. God, I love Yorkshire puddings."

Lexi laughed.

"What about you, Rainey?" She asked.

Rainey shrugged her shoulders.

"I can't think of anything right now. But I think I'd take anything over this fake cheese sandwich."

Joe frowned when he noticed Rainey's sandwich had been returned to its box with only one tiny bite missing.

"You've hardly eaten anything in the last few days. The last time you ate properly was in Italy," he nudged the box in her hands. "Try to have some more, your body needs it out here."

"I'm not hungry, I can eat it later."

"I think you should at least try to have a little more now." He continued, but Rainey was not listening, her eyes were glued to a spot just above Joe's shoulder.

"What?" He said, panicking at the thought of a scorpion or one of Lexi's camel spiders climbing over his shoulder.

Joe and Lexi spun on the spot, following Rainey's glare. In the distance, tearing down the hill, drove three shining black Chevrolet Suburbans. Their blacked-out windows reflected the sun back at them, forcing them to shield their eyes as they drove closer, with one leading the way and the others flanking either side.

"Get in the car, now." Joe demanded, striding to the driver's side door and wrenching it open.

Lexi hurled herself into the back seat as Rainey pulled open the front passenger door.

"What do we do?" Lexi panicked.

"We can't turn back. They'll only chase us. Maybe they won't know it's us if we just keep driving. They might go right past us." Joe tried.

"It might not even be them. They could just be locals or police or something." Lexi offered.

The cars were gaining speed, hurtling towards them in a sickening rush.

"It's them." Rainey said.

She took hold of the handle and pushed the door back open.

"What are you doing?" Joe shouted, stunned.

Rainey did not answer him. She slammed the door shut behind her and walked in a steady pace away from the car, stopping fifty feet in front of it in the middle of the road. The vehicles sped towards her.

"Rainey, what are you doing? Get out of the way!" Joe yelled through the window as he tried desperately to open the door.

The handle clicked back into place as his fingers clumsily fumbled with it, holding the door firmly shut.

"They're not going to stop!"

Lexi watched in mute horror as the vehicles careered forward.

A hundred feet away.

Rainey planted her feet firmly on the dusty road. Her eyes fixed determinedly on the trucks.

Seventy feet away.

Fifty feet.

She raised her hands in front of her as if to stop them.

Thirty feet.

Twenty feet.

Ten feet.

There was a deafening slam as the first Chevrolet collided, and Lexi's scream tore through the desert.

29

Rainey

The point of impact in front of Rainey shook so violently that it threatened to throw her into the dusty road. The shining black metal of the Chevrolet crumpled in front of her eyes as it hit the solid wall she had created from the clear, hot air. Both the driver and the passenger lurched forward, crushing their bodies against the glass, killing them instantly as the force compacted their skulls. Rainey watched as the truck was thrown into the air on the impact, raining pieces of metal to the ground. It sailed over her head and landed behind her with a vociferous crash, its solid frame screaming in protest. On either side of her, Rainey saw the two remaining vehicles speed past in a blur of black metal and red sand. The breaks screeched as they were slammed on, spinning the vehicles on the spot to face her again.

Rainey could see the faces of the two men in the truck closest to her, both wore all black clothing, including what looked to be balaclavas, pulled down over their faces, hiding their identity. Their eyes were trained on Rainey, and she watched as their mouths pulled up into snarls. They advanced towards her and she stumbled back. Her hands shook as she aimed them to the ground beneath her feet. A deep rumbling erupted from the earth and the muscles in Rainey's legs worked hard to keep her from stumbling as the ground rolled beneath her feet. The Chevrolets stopped, their drivers yelling panicked profanities as the earthquake shook them to the core of their bodies. Huge cracks began to appear in the sand around them. The drivers wasted no time, the rear wheels began to spin in the sand as they tried to speed forwards. One flew past Rainey, missing her by inches, the wind forcing her hair to whip around her face. The second had not been so lucky. Its wheels continued to spin as they sank deeper and deeper into a fissure in the earth. Rainey watched as it stretched wider, swallowing the front of the vehicle and the men inside. She stared into one of the men's eyes as he disappeared over the edge and into the ground. Her eyes remained transfixed, two electric-blue glows shining through the dust, as another deep rumble shook the ground beneath her feet, closing the fissure and crushing the vehicle with the two men still inside. What remained of the truck lay dismembered in the road, broken and unmoving. A puddle of petrol and blood pooling between the metal and the baked sand.

Rainey looked down at her hands. They shook. Her entire body shook. She was panting and sweating and resisting the urge to retch at the realisation of what she had done. But she was not finished yet. A great gust of wind rose from the ground, spinning faster and faster, gathering up the dust from the desert floor. And with it rose what remained of the first vehicle. She turned on the spot and with every ounce of power she had left, she hurled the truck forwards and through the air. It flew a hundred metres along the road and landed with an almighty crash in front of the retreating third Chevrolet. It swerved dangerously, its rear wheels losing control as it narrowly avoided collision. It did not stop. It did not turn back.

Rainey's legs buckled beneath her. Her eyes darted to her own car where Joe and Lexi both looked on in horror. Lexi's eyes were wide. Her face a mask of complete shock. But it was Joe who caused Rainey's heart to sink. Disgust, loathing, revulsion and fear.

What had she done?

She pushed herself up from the ground and walked steadily towards the car. She pulled open the door and collapsed into the seat. Nobody spoke. They listening to the sound of Rainey's panting breaths. As the minutes passed, Rainey's breathing slowed to a steady rhythm.

"Rainey," Joe started.

"Shut up!" Rainey screamed. "Just shut up! Whatever it is you have to say about me, I do not want to hear it."

Joe turned the key in the ignition and the engine growled to life. The silence was deafening as they continued through the desert. As the minutes turned to an hour, Lexi struggled to endure the glacial atmosphere inside the car. She opened her mouth to speak only to be silenced with a look from Joe. Until, eventually, it became more than she could bear.

"Those men - stop looking at me like that! We can't sit in silence forever!" She added, before Joe could stop her. "Those men must have come from somewhere close. If that guy in the shop called them and it took them, like, an hour I think, to get to us back there, then in theory, they should only be about a two-hour drive from the garage."

Rainey scanned the horizon. There was nothing to see but sand, rocks and cacti.

"That's if they weren't sitting around waiting for that call, or maybe they didn't take the same route as us." Joe said in a stiff voice.

"How would they have known we would be at that garage today, or even in the country? It's too big of a coincidence for them to be sitting there, waiting, on exactly the same day we arrive at that garage. And there are no other routes, they either drove this way or they drove across the sand." Lexi answered.

"Well, then, I guess we keep driving and look out for some sort of sign or a building." Joe said, tightening his fists around the steering wheel and fixing his eyes on the road ahead.

"Can we at least listen to the radio if you two are so intent on not speaking?"

"No signal," was all Rainey would say, half of her attention on the road and the other half picturing the faces of the men she had crushed in the ground, seeing the fear in their eyes as the car rolled forward and they disappeared.

Her stomach tightened uneasily, and bile rose in her throat.

"Stop the car." She managed, clapping a hand over her mouth.

Joe slammed his foot on the brake and Rainey made a grab for the door handle. She threw it open before the car had fully stopped and fell out of the door and on to her hands and knees. Her stomach heaved, forcing the minuscule amount of food she had consumed into a puddle on the ground. Joe pulled on the handbrake and put his head in his hands, rubbing his eyes with his thumbs. As she retched into the sand, Rainey heard another door open, and footsteps approaching behind her. A bottle of water appeared on the ground beside her, and Joe's fingers gently pulled back her long strands of dark hair, holding it bunched together at the back of her head as she continued to retch. Water was all that came out now, with no food left in her stomach. She reached for the bottle of water, unscrewed the top and poured some into her mouth, sloshing it around and gurgling it to the back of her throat before spitting it on to the ground. Then she pushed herself back on to the dirt and pulled her knees up to her chest, leaning her elbows on to them and resting her head in her hands. A sob rolled up her throat and escaped through her lips.

"I killed four people," she said.

Joe remained silent but he knelt down beside her and pushed a loose strand of hair from her face, tucking it behind her ear.

"Maybe six, if the two I electrocuted when they took her didn't survive," she continued. "I murdered six people. I don't even know who they were. What if they had families and children? I just... I can't-" Rainey struggled for words as she cried. "Who am I?"

Still, Joe remained silent. He stood up straight and held out a hand to Rainey. She took it and he pulled her up too.

"You need to eat something before we go," he finally said, pulling her towards the car.

He opened the back door and held out his hand to help her climb in next to Lexi, who wrapped her arm around Rainey's shoulders. They leaned their heads together and Rainey closed her eyes, but she opened them again when images of the day's disturbing events replayed inside her head. Joe passed two bottles of iced tea through the door, followed by a packet of crackers and some beef jerky, before he pushed the door closed and climbed back into his seat.

"If what Lexi said is right, then we should eat and drink everything we can now. We are in no fit state to go storming into Smith's place." He said, as he bit into a piece of jerky.

Rainey tried to eat and drink. She managed to finish her bottle of water, followed by some iced tea, but when it came to eating, she surrendered after just two crackers and a piece of jerky.

The car revved as Joe turned the key in the ignition and set it rolling forwards again. The sun had begun to set, cooling the air to a more manageable temperature and the quickly dimming sunlight helped to settle Rainey enough to quiet her hiccups. Her body and mind were exhausted. She looked down at her hands, resting in her lap. Slowly, she ran her thumb over the grey heart on her left hand and a tear rolled silently down her cheek.

What had happened to the girl who had been so happy only days before? Where had she gone? Would there be anything left of her when she found Lily and took her home? Or would Lily's life be stained forever because her mother was cold and dark on the inside? Maria had warned her that there was a darkness inside of her. She hadn't believed it at the time, but maybe she was right.

She rested her head against Lexi's shoulder and closed her eyes, watching again and again as she crushed the life out of two men she had not known. And though she regretted what she had done, and desperately feared what she might have become, Rainey remembered how it had felt as her power surged through her body and burst out of her, ending four lives. She had liked it.

Rainey's eyes snapped open as Lexi burst out an excited scream.

"There! Over there!" She yelled, pointing towards the horizon. "Look. There's a building."

Rainey bolted upright and leaned forward through the gap in the front seats and on to Joe's shoulder. Sure enough, in the distance, she could see the silhouette of what looked to be a small building. Joe drove a little faster in anticipation until they could see what Rainey had first thought to be a small building, grow bigger and bigger as they approached. The dark outline became clearer as the concrete walls came into view. It was striking and unmistakable against the barren landscape.

"This is it. This has to be it." Lexi whispered.

This was Smith's Institute.

30

Aimee

Jonah and Chris led the way down the winding corridors, through countless doors with locks and code pads, all of which required a different sequence of elaborate combinations. Aimee knew now how unlikely their escape would have been without the help of someone from inside the army. She knew that it had been a long time since she herself had worked for Smith, but the building had developed in more than she was prepared to give Smith credit for. She wondered if her escape had pushed him to install so many additional security measures and hoped that she had not further prevented others escaping after her. Aimee realised that she would always owe her life to Jonah and Chris, whether she made it out alive or not.

When the alarms began to sound, they were not surprised. Smith might have updated his security system, but still he underestimated the lengths his people would go to for their freedom. As they travelled further into the building, sparks of recognition began to ignite within Aimee and before long Jonah and Chris were no longer able to lead the way, leaving Aimee to take the lead. Fortunately, Chris had researched the codes, allowing them access to the nursery.

In all the years Aimee had been away, the doors had not changed, solid wood with thick glass panels. Although the code pad had not existed back then. Chris pulled open the panel covering the pad and jabbed in the seven-digit code. The door sounded three long beeps before clicking open and swinging forward for them to enter. Aimee took two cautious steps, edging her way through the door. The long corridor was lined with plain-white metal doors, each with a small glass panel displaying what lay inside. She peered through the first two doors on either side of the corridor, but the rooms appeared to be empty.

The corridors leading to the nursery felt oddly homely to Aimee. She had spent most of her time at the institute surrounded by the same blank walls when she had lived and worked there. And though she had suffered greatly during that time, Aimee had performed miracles while she was there, bringing new life into the world which, without her, would not have endured.

Aimee edged further along the corridor and nudged open the door leading to the first of the suites, she peered around the room from the doorway to make sure it was safe, before turning and ushering the others forward. As she heard their feet rushing closer, Aimee turned just in time to see the metal door hurtle towards her, smashing into her head and pinning her arm between the door and its frame. She stumbled as the impact ran the length of her spine, and she cried out in pain. The door had been slammed shut, but Aimee could not see who had been responsible. Her vision blurred and her eyes struggled to focus as the outline of a woman came into view. She felt the door release her arm and a hand wrap firmly around her throat, pulling her forwards and through the doorway. The door slammed shut behind her, the lock clicking into place, and Aimee found herself panicking that William had followed her into the room. She could see the others through the corners of her blurred vision, watching through the glass panel in the door, but they made no effort to reach her. The hand around her throat pinned her against the wall, and Aimee tried to focus her eyes. She blinked heavily as she tried to pinpoint her attacker, but she could see multiple versions of the woman in front of her, the figures all falling into one another. She blinked hard again and finally began to make sense of what she was seeing. Not multiple people, just one. A short woman, with dark hair and a round face. Aimee saw her reflection in the woman's dark eyes, as recognition stole her features. She understood then. William had not followed because he could not. He had been frozen, trapped inside his own paralysed body.

"Jenna." Aimee gasped, through what little space Jenna's grip allowed in her throat.

"Welcome back, Aimee." Jenna sneered.

Aimee struggled under her grip.

"Well, as entertaining as this little breakout attempt was, it looks like this is the end of the line for you. It will definitely be the end of the line for those three," she nodded her head to the door, where William, Jonah and Chris stood frozen, staring in horror at the scene before them. "You see, the thing about Smith is that he only keeps what is useful to him, and they are no longer useful. They are disposable. Now, you. Well, you're different. You, he has a use for. Although, I'm not sure what he sees in you myself."

Aimee raised her hand to pull at Jenna's fingers where they dug into the flesh around her throat, but Jenna was quicker. She pulled a pistol from her belt and rested it against Aimee's temple.

"I wouldn't," she said to Aimee. "All of the powers we possess as Gifted, and yet nobody ever thought to use a weapon."

Aimee's glare flicked to William through the glass, his eyes spread wide with fear.

"There is something so satisfying about your pray being utterly defenceless as you shoot a hole in its head."

Aimee heard Jenna's finger tense around the trigger. Jenna leaned in closer, so close Aimee could feel the brush of her lips against her ear lobe as she whispered to her, over emphasising each word.

"Do you know who else is disposable, Aimee? There is a car pulling into the building as we speak. Can you guess who might be in that car?"

Aimee tensed.

"Come on Aimee, everybody loves a good guessing game. Can you take a wild guess at who else Smith would love to get his hands on? Someone else he can torture and torment, the same way your pathetic little friend was. How about I give you three guesses? Does that sound fair? A guess for each of the Gifted who sit in that car."

Aimee squeezed her eyes shut. Her heart pounded in her ears, making it difficult to hear Jenna's whispered words.

"Here's a clue. One begins with an L."

Aimee's eyes squeezed tighter shut.

"Then one with a J."

Her fingers tingled with static energy.

"And the most important one. Well, her name begins with an R."

Aimee's eyes flew open. Her hand moved so fast that Jenna did not have time to block the punch that hit her in the side of her head. Her cheekbone made a satisfying crunch. Stunned, she dropped the pistol and it clattered across the floor. She released her hold on the others, and Aimee dropped to the floor as Jonah raised his gun to the glass and fired. Glass exploded through the room. Slicing into their skin as Aimee pinned Jenna to the floor beneath her. She rained blow after blow down on Jenna's face, blood splattering her clenched fists.

"Stop!" Jenna screamed, but Aimee had pinned each of her arms under her knees, she could not move, only scream.

Her legs flailed desperately as Aimee's blows connected with her face. Blood dribbled down her cheeks and through her hair, pooling under her head. The crunching of her bones breaking muffled only by her screams.

"Just shock me. Kill me!" She shrieked.

Aimee paused with her fist drawn back behind her, looking down at Jenna's crippled face.

"You don't deserve such a kindness," she spat.

Aimee forced her fist down hard into Jenna's face, her head crunched against the floor as it connected. For a second, Aimee thought it had been her fingers breaking with the impact, but Jenna's struggles seized, and her legs collapsed in a tangle beneath Aimee. Aimee looked at her fists, covered in both of their blood. She breathed in a shaky breath and wiped her trembling hands on her trousers. She felt William's hands hook under her arms and pull her up, away from Jenna in one swift movement. He locked her in his arms before taking her face in his hands.

"Are you ok?" He said, examining her face and wiping spots of Jenna's blood away with his thumbs.

"Bitch finally got what was coming to her."

Aimee's hands throbbed, her knuckles bleeding and swollen. She was vaguely aware of Jonah and Chris dragging Jenna's limp body into the corner of the room, a trail of blood smearing across the floor in her wake.

"She's dead." Jonah said, as he checked for a pulse.

Aimee pulled away from William and gripped his hand tightly. She pulled him to a door across the room, and Jonah and Chris followed, leaving Jenna's body hidden behind a row of chairs. The lock had been disabled, leaving them free to enter. Chris stepped forward, wrapping a hand around the handle.

"This is the nursery," Aimee said, before they entered.

Chris stepped through first, but the corridor on the other side was deserted. Doors lined both sides of the walkway, each labelled with a list of names. Aimee rushed forward and ran a finger along the first list, scanning the names, before moving on to the next.

"We find your Lily and then we head to the maternity ward." Jonah said.

"Yes, yes." Aimee replied, impatiently. "Help me look for her."

They each rushed ahead, murmuring the names to themselves as they read from the lists.

"I have a Lily over here. Lily Stephens." Chris called from a few doors ahead of Aimee.

"No, that's not her. Her full name is Lily Rose Emily Denyer." Aimee called back.

They continued to search as the alarm continued to blare from hidden speakers around them.

"I found her!" William yelled over the noise.

Aimee sprinted across the corridor and read Lily's name out loud, running her finger across it. She placed a shaking hand on the door handle and pushed. On the other side of the door was a small room filled with more doors and on each door was a sign with a name displayed in bold lettering. Aimee stepped towards Lily's door. She gripped the handle tightly and gently pushed it open.

A plain white cot greeted Aimee as she stepped through the door, and inside the cot lay a child. A baby. Lily. Her perfect round cheeks were flushed, and her long lashes fluttered with her eyelids as she dreamt. A relieved sob escaped Aimee's lips as her eyes scanned over the heart shaped mark Rainey had sketched on to Lily's wrist. Rainey was still alive.

Aimee reached her hands into the cot and carefully lifted her out, pulling her into her chest, inhaling her scent. She brushed the soft, warm skin on Lily's cheek with a swollen finger.

"We have to hurry," Jonah pushed, peering through the door.

William stroked Lily's dark hair and trailed his fingers over her forehead before pulling gently at Aimee's elbow. Keeping Lily held closely to her chest, Aimee followed Jonah and Chris out of the room, with William close by her side. They headed back in the direction they had come, and when they reached the main corridor of the nursery, they turned, walking deeper into building.

"The maternity ward used to be this way," she said, pointing further down the hall. "There was a cut through you could take in emergencies."

Chris nodded for them to move forward and they set off cautiously, listening out for the sound of distant footsteps. They could hear the alarm in the distance, ringing shrilly through the air, and as they neared the ward it grew louder again. Lily stirred in her sleep. She opened her eyes and rubbed them with her chubby balled up hands. When her eyes settled on Aimee, a smile lit up her tiny face, and Aimee hugged her tighter.

"Hello, gorgeous girl." Aimee said. "We're going home, back to Mummy and Daddy."

William leaned over Aimee's shoulder and waited for Lily's eyes to rest on him.

"Hello, sweetheart. We've missed you," he said, but then his face crinkled as he pulled his eyebrows together with a look of both confusion and curiosity.

He met Aimee's eyes and she tried to read him in the way she normally could, but this time she could not grasp what she saw. The alarm came to a sudden loud shriek in their ears, and her time to ponder had passed. Chris had pulled open the final door between them and the maternity ward and the racket from the alarm was almost painful in their ears. He turned to look at Aimee and she nodded, urging him to continue. They followed Chris through the doors and into the barely lit walkway on the other side. Lily had begun to cry in protest to the noise, and Aimee bounced her against her chest, trying to calm her. Aimee looked around at what little she could see in the dim light, and a lump formed in her throat. The lives she had seen wasted in the maternity ward were incalculable, mother after mother forced into giving up their children to build Smith's Army and then dying for their troubles. The ones who died during the birth had probably been the lucky ones. To this day, Aimee had no idea what happened to the ones who survived, rendered useless.

William wrapped an arm around Aimee's shoulders and guided her onward to where Jonah and Chris had stopped at the end of the walkway. A large metal trolley piled high with various surgical tools still in their sterile wrappers lay before them, and Jonah had begun to grab handfuls and throw them into an open bag.

"I don't know what you need. I don't even know what any of this stuff is." Jonah said.

"The more the better." Aimee replied, offering a reassuring smile.

"Fill the bag, try to get a few of everything." Chris said, and he and William started picking through the supplies too.

Aimee noticed some of the equipment she would need if she were to help with the delivery of Jonah's child, but there were still some items missing. They needed to find more.

"We need to get to the store cupboard," she told them, and she began moving further into the ward.

Holding Lily close to her chest with one hand, she ran the fingers of the other along the wall as she walked, letting them trail across the doors and their frames. The door to one room had been propped open and Aimee glanced inside. Although most of its contents were hidden in shadow, a bed with leg restraints could be seen clearly in the centre of the room. Images flashed through Aimee's mind and she pulled her gaze away. She breathed deeply and continued towards the store cupboard. After walking halfway through the badly lit ward, she stopped in front of an unmarked door, wrapping her fingers around the silver handle. The others stopped behind her and watched as she pushed open the door, revealing boxes and boxes of medical equipment stacked up to the ceiling on metal shelves. Each box had blue writing printed on to the side indicating what it held. Aimee stepped into the cupboard and began pulling the supplies she needed from the boxes. She passed them to William who placed them into Jonah's holdall.

"What about medicine? Pain killers or something like that?" Chris asked, laying his hand on the top of a small box with '*Anaesthetic*' printed on the side.

"Is she a human or a Gifted?" Aimee replied, not drawing her attention away from the box she was tearing open.

"Gifted."

"Then she doesn't need the anaesthetic. It rarely has the desired effect on a Gifted, we burn it off too quickly. For humans, it works fine, but for us, there really is no point." Aimee said, as she pulled out a small plastic case.

"Oh," Chris said. "I didn't know that."

"Why would you, if you've never needed nor administered it yourself? There were always so many healers here. I'm surprised you've even heard of-"

Aimee froze. Above the noise of the alarm she could hear heavy footfalls. People running. Muffled voices growing clearer and louder as the footsteps advanced towards them. She pulled Lily in closer to her chest and wrapped both arms around her, one hand cupping the back of her head protectively. The others stood between Aimee and the open door and braced themselves for the arrival. Fingers appeared around the edge of the door as a hand gripped it, pulling it back. They watched with held breath as the door pulled further and further back, revealing a large, round stomach. Jonah breathed a sigh of relief as the young woman came into view. Her long dirty-blonde pigtails hung loosely on either side of her tired face and her hand rested on the round mound under her bed gown. Her face lit up as her eyes found Jonah.

"Jonah!" She cried, stumbling forward.

Jonah gathered her up in his arms and held her so tightly Aimee feared they had forgotten the baby growing inside her bulging stomach. But when Aimee's eyes flicked back up to the doorway, any fears she had for the young woman's baby vanished from her mind. She let out a disbelieving breath of air and William barely had time to snatch Lily from her arms before she sprang forward and collided with Jason's body.

31

Aimee

"You're alive!" Aimee gasped. "You're here. You're alive."

She took his face in her hands and kissed him. Tears ran down both of their faces.

"You're a mess. We need to get you out of here."

"Thanks, Aimee." He said, a relieved laugh bursting through his tears.

Jason reached out and ran his fingers over Aimee's cheek.

"I can't believe it's you. After all this time, I can't believe you are finally here. I hoped he would never find you, but I knew it would only be a matter of time until he brought you here." Jason's words flew from his mouth in a blur.

"Slow down, Jason. It's ok. We're getting out of here," Aimee said, leaning her face into his hand.

Two more figures stepped around the door and Aimee grabbed hold of Jason's collar, yanking him away from the door and pushing him behind her. She held out her hands and tiny blue bolts danced across her palms.

"Aimee, stop." Jason yelled. "They're with us."

Neither of the men jumped back to protect themselves, they simply stood and watched as Aimee slowly lowered her hands.

"Are you sure?" Aimee said, eyeing the men suspiciously.

"They're safe," Jonah said, wrapping his arm around the young woman.

Aimee took a step back. She let out a relieved sigh before looking around the group, scanning their faces.

"There are eight of us, now. Nine with Lily. That gives us a better chance of fighting our way out if we have to."

She looked to the three strangers of the group and offered them her hand one at a time, but after seeing her electricity spark across them, nobody accepted her greeting. She shrugged her shoulders.

"My name is Aimee, this is William. And this is Lily."

Jason's eyes fell on to the bright-eyed baby cradled in William's arms. Lily was looking around the group curiously and chewing on her fingers, dribble running down the length of her arm.

"She looks just like Rainey," Jason said, looking from William to Aimee. "She has your eyes, Aimee."

"As she should, this is Rainey's daughter." William said, with a smile pulling at the corners of his mouth.

"No," Jason said. "Rainey? She has a daughter? Is she, I mean, did she-"

"She survived, yes. It was close, but she survived. Now, as long as everyone is happy with the brief introductions, can we please, *please* get a move on?" Aimee pleaded.

She linked her arm under Jason's to support him, as did one of the guards, and they edged their way out of the store cupboard and back into the dark corridor.

As they manoeuvred their way through the maze of the building, Aimee grew more and more thankful that their party had doubled in size. Although the majority of them knew their way around the building, some places still seemed alien to them, and what one person felt confident with, the others did not. Chris knew most of the codes to the doors, although not all of them. Jonah knew his way around more than the others, and his girlfriend, who's name Aimee did not know, knew the best places to hide in the maternity ward when two searching guards passed them.

"I've been on this ward for about four months," she said, after the second guard passed them and they started to move again. "I tried to cover up the pregnancy for as long as I could but as soon as the bump started to show they dumped me in here. They gave me a scan the minute they dragged me through the doors. There was no hiding it after that."

Aimee decided that she liked the new girl. She was the kind of girl Rainey and Lexi would like and she hoped that they would get to meet one day soon. Just not too soon.

The thought of Rainey triggered Jenna's voice in her mind, before Aimee had hit her so hard that the front of her skull had caved inwards.

Guess who else Smith would love to get his hands on. Their names begin with L... J... And R.

Aimee stopped dead in her tracks. Chris slammed into the back of her, banging his nose on the back of her head.

"Ow! What the hell?" He started.

"Rainey's here!" She blurted out.

"What?" William said.

"Jenna. That's why I couldn't stop hitting her. She said there was someone else here who Smith wanted. She didn't say their names, but she told me to guess who they were, and their names began with L, J and R."

"Why didn't you tell us this before?" William shouted.

"There was... there was so much going on..." Aimee stammered, her cheeks flushing as a fresh wave a panic rushed through her.

"We can't leave if she's here, not without her. If Smith has her-" a shiver ran through William's body.

Aimee looked at the faces around her, watching her carefully, waiting for her command. She was always in charge.

"We need to find Smith. If Rainey's here, then he has her. Nobody else is strong enough to catch her."

"Wait a minute. We're not leaving? We did not agree to this, Aimee. If we go looking for Smith, he will keep us all here, and I can promise you, that is where we will stay. Whether that be buried six feet under or as his personal playthings." Chris argued. "Who is this girl? Why is she so important to you?"

"That girl is our daughter." William snapped back. "And she is more powerful than all of us put together. If Smith gets his hands on her then *I* can promise *you* that he will use her to kill every single one of us. He wouldn't need to know where we are. Rainey is capable of destroying cities."

"But if he already has her, what is there to stop him from killing all of us now?" He fired back.

"I'm not leaving without her. I'm sorry. I know you need my help, and I will be eternally indebted to you, but I will not leave my daughter here, no more than you could leave your brother's unborn child." Aimee pointed to the unborn baby in the woman's swollen stomach.

Chris and Jonah exchanged looks, but it was Jonah's girlfriend who finally spoke up.

"We will go wherever you go, Aimee."

Aimee nodded gratefully and held out her hand. She took it in her own and Aimee squeezed it gently.

"What do they call you?" Aimee asked.

"Oh, it's Isobel." She offered.

"Thank you, Isobel."

And they began walking again, weaving their way through the deserted corridors as they followed Chris and Jonah to the place Aimee feared more than any other; Smith's office.

32

William

Smith's office was exactly as it had been when William had last seen it, on the day he and Aimee had been brought back. A wave of nausea washed through him, followed by the familiar fire of fury he felt when he thought of the horrors Aimee had had to endure that day. She would not speak of what had happened, and William did not know if that was a blessing or a curse. It allowed his mind to imagine it for himself, creating images of the vile acts Smith could have performed to satiate his sick appetite. William's mind was relentless, forcing him to watch the images over and over. *What had happened in this room after that visit, when he had been dragged from the room, leaving Aimee alone with the monster who was Smith*? His beautiful Aimee, who he would turn heaven and earth to protect, who usually would not require the protection he could offer because she was the strongest, most dangerous person he had ever laid eyes on. That was, of course, until he met his own daughter. But Aimee's strength had a weakness, and her weakness was Smith. After years of fear and abuse, and years of hiding and hoping she would never be found, Smith's presence could crush Aimee's courage like a child crushing a bug. He could transform her into somebody she was not. Somebody who cowered at his feet and flinched if he so much as looked at her. It was what William despised the most about Smith. His ability to break her.

He wrapped his arms tighter around Lily, letting her weight and warmth reassure him. He pushed the images of Smith and Aimee from his mind. Aimee seemed to read his thoughts and she rested her head against his shoulder. He kissed the top of her head and squeezed his eyes shut tightly.

"Now what?" Isobel asked, when they had determined Smith was nowhere to be seen.

"Now, we wait," Aimee replied.

"And if he doesn't come?" Chris added.

"He will. I know him better than anyone. This office is his sanctuary. He brings all of his best prizes here, and Rainey is one hell of a prize." Aimee said, repressing the shudder threatening to run down the length of her spine.

"This is an office?" Isobel gasped, spinning around to get a better look. "You could fit an entire house in here!"

"Probably over compensating." Elliot shrugged.

Aimee took a seat on the floor and Jason settled himself beside her, whispering questions about how they had been captured and discussing how Rainey might have found them. William listened as Aimee recounted every detail of the previous weeks, starting with the dreams Rainey had secretly recorded, down to the food that had been provided for them since their arrival. When she told him how they had been taken to Smith's office before they were separated, Jason caught William's eye for a fraction of a second, and William knew that he knew.

When the distant alarms eventually seized, the group fell into silence, waiting for the footsteps that they knew would come. William looked down at Lily in his arms and allowed himself to imagine how Rainey and Joe would react when they were reunited with their daughter. He looked around the room at the faces he barely knew and the ones he had known for all of his adult life. Jonah and Isobel huddled together on the floor with Chris close by, nodding elaborately whenever Isobel spoke. She smiled reassuringly when she caught William watching. The guards who had assisted Jason's and Isobel's escapes stood together, listening to snippets of conversations and nodding in agreement. Jason had told him one was called Elliot, and he shared what little information he knew of Elliot's story, but all he knew of the second guard was his name. Damian. And then there was Aimee and Jason. They were silent after Jason had briefly shared his experiences of the past four and a half years with Aimee, their hands clasped tightly together throughout. William understood why Jason had kept his story short, sharing only a few key details of his journey. Sitting in a room full of people he barely knew as they waited for a monster and his army to find them was not the ideal time to have a heartfelt conversation with your long-lost best friend, even less so when that room happened to be owned by the biggest dickhead this side of the solar system.

William's knew he should not be surprised by how little the circumstances had changed in Smith's dictatorship. Isobel was a present-day version of Aimee. Aimee had been little over twenty-one years old when she had fallen pregnant and escaped. William prayed that Isobel had not been so unlucky as to have the full burden of Aimee's past. Smith's obsession with Aimee had multiplied the complexity of their escape tenfold, and he could only hope that Isobel's first few months on the run would be easier for her than it had been for him. What happened from today onwards was unknown, and the concept of being able to help the three of them if they did manage to find a way out, and deliver Isobel's baby safely, forced the corners of William's mouth to turn up into a soft smile. He had not had help all those years ago. It had been just the three of them against the world. But William was not an idiot, and the possibility that all nine of them would escape, alive and unharmed, was an unlikely outcome as it was, without the added responsibility of delivering a Gifted baby and keeping the mother alive too. His smile faded and vanished completely. He knelt down beside Aimee and Jason, resting Lily's weight on his thigh where she kicked her legs happily.

"We should pass Lily to Isobel." He suggested. "When it comes down to it, we can't let Isobel fight and we will all need to be ready when he comes."

"*If* it comes to a fight." Jason amended.

"*When* it comes to a fight." William corrected, sadly.

Aimee nodded, running a hand through Lily's hair.

The minutes ticked by, and with every prolonged second that passed, so did their patience. Aimee grew fidgety, her anxiety seeping its way into every movement. Her eyes danced from face to face, searching for an answer that nobody could give her. Where was Rainey? Why wasn't she here yet? The room gradually fell into silence again, and they waited.

"How long has it been?" Aimee eventually whispered.

"Twenty, maybe thirty minutes?" Elliot suggested.

Aimee started to rock forwards and back where she was sitting cross-legged on the floor. Lily grew more and more unsettled as the minutes turned into an hour, and despite William's best efforts of transforming any ordinary object he could get his hands on into a toy, she began to push herself away from him, moaning impatiently. William helped her on to the floor where she knelt on her knees with her chubby hands and arms supporting her weight. Her head swung in different directions as she looked around, trying to decide what to do next, when her eyes settled on Aimee. She crawled forward, wobbling dangerously as she did, and when she reached Aimee's folded legs, she stretched out a hand. Lily's fingers brushed against Aimee's knee at the exact moment a noise sounded from the corridor, cutting though the silence.

They were on their feet within a fraction of a second. Aimee snatched Lily up from the floor and placed her in Isobel's arms, shielding the pair of them behind the group. Aimee's eyes widened as they watched the door handle slowly turn. Then the door swung open, and there he stood. Smith. And behind him, an army of guards.

"Well, well," Smith said, slow and deliberate as he stepped further into the room. "Look at this. Is this a private party or can anyone join?"

His trademark smirk, plastered permanently on his face, caused William's stomach to churn with loathing. He scanned the faces of Smith's men, counting each one in his head. Almost forty, against the eight of them. They didn't stand a chance. Unless of course, their powers as Gifted soldiers were lacking. The presence of their weapons suggested as much.

"I am sure that you know just how much I love to see my loyal employees," his eyes settled momentarily on Jonah and Chris before focusing on Elliot and Damian. "But I feel that this situation may require a more grievous aura than that of a celebration."

Smith looked between the group to find Lily in Isobel's arms and a knot formed in William's stomach. That knot tightened as Smith looked to Aimee next and a sickening smile spread across his face. But Aimee did not cower the way she usually did. Slowly, a smile spread across her own face, and a dangerous light burned deep in her eyes.

"You talk like you expected this to happen because you can't bear the thought of your puppets seeing you lose control. Next, you'll say you set the whole thing up so that we would come to you." Aimee said, her voice rising.

Smith opened his mouth in reply, but Aimee would not allow it.

"Do the people who stand behind you know who you really are? You know, it always interested me, even all these years after we abandoned you and your sick beliefs, just how you manage to force so many people into following you."

"My followers are forced into nothing. They follow me because they see the only way forward is with me. They follow because they know, without an army, we will never be able to fight the scum who rule this world and force the Gifted into hiding." Smith called back.

"And do they know that when you speak of fighting, you do not mean to fight just the 'scum'? You mean to fight everyone. You would cause death and destruction to every innocent man, woman and child, in order for you to gain some deceitful perception of power over the world."

Smith narrowed his eyes but did not break his glare.

"Do the people who stand behind you know why we ran from you? Will they feel the same about your army when their wives and girlfriends have to fill the position I fled from?" Aimee's voice grew louder and stronger as her anger flared.

Smith's face reddened and he curled his top lip in a display of complete disgust. Aimee smiled.

"What's wrong, Smith? Worried I'll tell them why I really left? You never did find the right woman to replace me, did you?"

"You can try to convince them, Aimee, but they will not listen. Your lies will not break their confidence in me." Smith growled.

Aimee looked to the faces hovering behind Smith.

"You believe he will fight for the Gifted? Fight for them to walk freely amongst the people who fill the streets, and not be judged for what they are? But there will be no people left if Smith has his way. He will kill every last one of them. And not only them, he'll kill any Gifted who stands in his way. Any child who does not offer a power strong enough to please him, just as he murders the humans."

"Be quiet, Aimee." Smith said, trying his best to sound bored.

"Or, what?" Aimee yelled back. "You'll have your army beat us and prove to them that what I say is true? You are pathetic."

Smith's eyes widened dangerously.

"Look at yourself. You have nothing. You think these people follow you because they believe in you? They follow you because they are scared of you. They follow you because they know that if they don't, you'll have them hunted down, so that you can take over their bodies and assault their loved ones."

Behind Smith, William could see Aimee's words breaking through the steely facade of his guards. He watched as they began to glance at one another from the corners of their eyes and a ripple of uncomfortable shuffles worked its way through the group.

"You threaten us and torture us. You hunt us and kidnap us. You murder our families and force us to bear children. You rape us." Aimee snarled.

William's and Jason's eyes snapped to Aimee as she spat the only word she had ever refused to use. And then William's body stepped forward unwillingly. He watched helplessly as the colour in Smith's eyes brightened into an electric glow. He felt his muscles tighten as he tried to fight against them, but he no longer controlled his own limbs. The muscles in his neck contracted painfully, forcing his head back. His spine arched and his legs collapsed from underneath him. He dropped to the floor, and then came the pain. Sharp jolts shot up his libs and into his torso like boiling metal rushing through his veins. William fought the urge to cry out, and he bit down viciously on the inside of his cheek, but the pain was too strong and he could not repress it. A desperate moan escaped his lips before the snap of electricity drowned out the sound and Aimee took a deliberate step in front of him. One of Smith's men dropped to the floor in a smoking heap, his charred skin filling the air with the sickening smell of burning flesh. William's pain stopped abruptly as his muscles became limp and his body relaxed.

"Try that again and I'll kill another one," Aimee warned, her hand pushed out in front of her.

William heard Jason cry out in pain and a loud thud as his body hit the ground. He watched as Aimee took another step forward, holding her arm out steadily towards Smith. Jason's body relaxed as a blue-white bolt of electricity shot from Aimee's palm, striking a guard in the hollow of his throat. His body jerked and shook on the spot before he crumpled to the ground at Smith's feet.

"Do you not see how he sacrifices you for his enjoyment?" Aimee screamed, scanning the eyes of every guard in the crowd. "He would rather control your bodies to use you all as his Gifted shields, than be a man and face what he has brought upon himself!"

"But you are the one killing them, Aimee." Smith said and Aimee stared at him in disbelief. "They are here simply to protect me. It is you who came here, and it is you who attacks us."

"Because you threaten my family! You broke into my house, you took my granddaughter, you had my daughter beaten, and *you* brought us here. All because you refuse to get over the fact that the girl you abused for years in this very room, finally grew the courage to run away." Aimee yelled.

Her body shook with the effort of restraining herself and sparks danced dangerously across her skin. Lily began to cry as she clung to Isobel's hip and Smith's eyes snapped to her. William could see the apprehension edging its way further into the faces of Smith's men, and a soft murmur fuelled from the back of the crowd. Smith took a step towards Aimee, holding up a hand to silence the crowd behind him.

"Your daughter?" Smith said, a smirk pulling at the corner of his lips. "Now, there is an interesting topic for discussion."

William knew exactly what Smith would say next, something Aimee could not bare to hear, something that she, William and Jason had sworn never to speak of again in order to protect Rainey.

"She's not just *your* daughter though, is she? She is as much mine as she is yours. Although, it would appear somebody forgot to tell her who her real father is. Instead, you replaced me with this fool." Smith waved a hand in William's direction.

Now it was Aimee's turn to smile.

"Actually, Smith, it would appear somebody forgot to tell you who her real father is." Aimee played his words back to him.

"When you disappeared all those years ago, you carried my child. That girl belongs to me as much as she does you." Smith's voice grew louder and he took another step closer to Aimee.

Every face in the room stared silently as Aimee revealed the truth.

"The child I carried never lived. He died long before he was born. Rainey does not belong to anyone. And she certainly is not your daughter, she is William's daughter."

Smith stared at Aimee for a long moment.

"He doesn't have her." William whispered from the corner of his mouth, and Aimee nodded in agreement.

"Don't lie to me! Her eye's glow, I've seen it. A trait she can only inherit."

"As did my mother's," Aimee fired back. "Your son died a long time ago. Your genes are weak, Smith. You are weak."

"A son." He said.

"His name was Alfie." Aimee said quietly, watching Smith's reaction carefully.

William watched too. He found it difficult to believe that Smith had any human emotion left inside his cruel and disgusting mind, but something was stirring within him. Smith shook his head and looked back to Aimee.

"So, that's it? I don't get so much as a 'sorry, your son is dead' or 'sorry, I didn't tell you'?" His face cleared of all emotion and settled back into the hard and ugly mask he usually displayed.

"You don't deserve an apology." Jason spat, moving through the crowd.

Smith looked at him, thoughtfully.

"No matter," he said. "I already have a son. If I remember correctly, then I do believe he is about the same age as your Rainey. We could have created something amazing, Aimee. There is still time."

William narrowed his eyes. Smith's smile had returned, and he looked back at them with a smug look in his eyes. He clapped his hands together and turned to his guards.

"I want that baby back in the nursery immediately. And I expect her to be mostly unharmed," he ordered.

Aimee instinctively took a step closer to Isobel. William stepped closer too. Isobel wrapped her arms tighter around Lily as Jonah and Chris shielded them from view from Smith's army. Elliot and Damian avoided the gazes of their fellow co-workers, but they crossed the room to stand beside Aimee. And together they formed a protective semi-circle around Isobel and Lily.

"I expected better of you two at least," Smith said as he looked icily at the two men.

"We were brought here by your lies. I used to think you would fight to protect the Gifted. All of the Gifted. But you only care for power, and you are prepared to see us all burn to get it." Damian said.

"You think so badly of me, yet you are willing to let your family and your friends stay here. Do you not have a sister here?"

"She has chosen her side, as have I." He placed a steady hand on Aimee's shoulder before letting it fall back by his side.

"Very well. I will be checking to make sure that your sister has made the correct decision. I can't say that I-" Smith's words stopped abruptly as an over exaggerated clearing of somebody's throat arose from behind him.

Smith turned and raised an eyebrow questioningly as one of his guards pushed his way to the front of the crowd. He took a very deliberate and long look into Smith's eyes before walking across the room and joining the smaller of the groups. Aimee's eyes lit up as another guard followed, and another. A wide and dangerous grin spread across her face and she watched as more and more of Smith's army abandoned him and stood firm in front of Aimee's growing crowd.

When it became certain that the remaining guards were not prepared to switch sides, Smith looked over the faces in front of him and made a loud outburst which William could only decipher as a mixture of a growl and a scream of anger. The two groups had become even in size and Smith's chance of keeping Aimee and Lily had greatly decreased. Without warning the two groups surged towards each other and Smith was lost in the crowd. Aimee and Isobel stayed close to one another, protecting Lily between the pair of them as Jason rushed forward and into the action.

"I'll protect her," Aimee shouted to Jonah. "Go and help them. I promise I'll keep her safe."

Jonah looked at Isobel, then at Chris who was already throwing punches into the mass of guards, then back at Isobel again, before nodding his head and disappearing into the crowd. William pushed his way through two fighting guards to get closer to Aimee and Isobel.

"Stay together. I'll try to round everyone up as soon as I can and we'll use this as our distraction to get out." He yelled over the noise.

He turned and ran into the crowd in search of Jason, but he knew that he would not look for Jason first. First, he would look for Smith. He weaved in and out of men and women fighting with their fists and men and women fighting with their powers. He watched as one guard clumsily grabbed at the air around his throat, the colour draining from his face. He knew it had to be James, invisible, like a coward. William's feet froze. James. James who had beaten his daughter, and burned his wife before he dragged them from the back of a van. James deserved to die the way Jenna had. He spotted Jason a few feet away, his opponent at his feet, but Jason looked worn and exhausted.

"Jason!" He called, and he thrust a hand in James's direction.

Jason's head snapped up. His eyes locked on to the seemingly empty space before William and he poised his hands, ready. William had not used his own powers in a long time, but he could feel the familiar sensation building inside him. He focussed on Jason and felt a rush of power burst from his body. Jason's eyes lit up and wind gathered from the ground, circling the room as it gathered speed. William could not stay to watch. He had to find Smith.

Ducking under a fast-moving fist, William caught sight of the back of a bald and shining head. He rushed forward, throwing people out of his way until he could reach out his hand and wrap his fingers around the back of Smith's shirt. With all the force he could muster he yanked hard on the fabric and Smith stumbled backwards, tripping over his own feet. He landed on his back at William's feet and had just enough time to look him in the eye before William's fist connected with his jaw. William knew he had mere seconds before Smith would retaliate, locking his body in his hold and sacrificing him to one of his guards.

He showered blow after blow on to Smith's face, and when he could hit him no longer, he pushed himself on to his feet.

"You will never touch her again." He spat.

He looked down at Smith, lying almost unconscious at his feet, his face covered in blood and shredded flesh.

"That was the most satisfying thing I have ever had the pleasure of doing."

He took one last look at Smith lying on the ground, swung his leg back and brought it down into Smith's ribcage. The breath rushed from his lungs and he wrapped his arms around his torso as he gasped for air.

"Except for that."

William felt a thick forearm wrap tightly around his neck. He gripped it with both of his hands and threw himself forward, hurling the guard over his shoulders and on to the ground beside Smith. He spun on the spot just in time to see the butt of an assault rifle flying towards his face and he ducked, narrowly avoiding a broken nose as the rifle and his assailant rushed past him. Chaos surrounded him, everywhere he turned. He risked one final glance down at Smith as he cowered on the floor beneath him, then he turned and disappeared back into the crowd.

33

Aimee

Aimee took Lily from Isobel's arms. She balanced her against her hip with her arm wrapped around her tiny body, holding her securely in place, while her free hand was squeezed tightly in Isobel's. But that did not stop her hands from shaking as she watched the madness unfold in front of her. Her eyes searched desperately for William and Jason in the mass of frenzied bodies. She locked eyes with one of Smith's men in the crowd. Blood oozed from a hidden wound under his hair, dripping down his head and over his eye. She couldn't be sure who was on who's side anymore. Did he fight with her? Or did he fight for Smith? The path between them cleared and the man took two large strides forward before Aimee shook her hand free from Isobel's and aimed it at him. He froze, looking from Aimee's open palm to her daring glare.

"Don't," she warned.

He risked another quick glance at her hand before he made up his mind and took another step closer. He was dead before he hit the floor.

"You're terrifying." Isobel gasped.

"Come on," Aimee ordered, pulling on Isobel's arm.

She guided her behind Smith's desk and crouched down, pulling Isobel down with her.

Aimee was not an idiot. She knew that when William had told her he would 'round up the others', what he had really meant was that he would round up the others *after* he had gotten his hands on Smith. She could not stop him while she protected Lily and Isobel. She loved William with all her heart, but she knew that he was no match for Smith. Nobody was.

They tried their best to stay hidden from the chaos with only a desk to shield them. Aimee watched every move, ready to run her bolts through anyone who stepped too close. Finally, William stumbled from the crowd, closely followed by Jason, Jonah, Chris and Elliot. Aimee scanned her eyes over every inch of William's body. Splatters of blood covered his skin and his clothes were torn, revealing more gore. She could not tell if it was his own or somebody else's.

"Where's Damian?" Isobel said, gripping Aimee's hand again.

Jonah shook his head. Aimee dropped Isobel's hand and rushed forward, edging her way around the outside of the room, stepping carefully over the bodies sprawled across the floor. She looked away quickly when she caught a glimpse of a man whose face looked to have been melted away from his skull.

Focusing her eyes on the doors at the opposite end of the room, she moved forward as quickly as she could. Jason ran ahead, and she could tell that he was struggling, his body so weak that she was surprised he had made it this far. Heavily pregnant Isobel moved as quickly as she could, but she flagged behind as she struggled to keep up, the weight of her unborn child weighing her down. Chris and Jonah positioned themselves on either side of her, and they half carried, half pushed her closer to their only way out.

Jason reached the doors first. He pushed them open and held on to one until everybody had made it through. Aimee hurled herself out, with Lily clinging on to her, closely followed by William and Elliot. Jonah pulled Isobel through the door and the last to make it through was Chris. Jason let go of the door and it swung back on its hinges. It grazed the edge of the second door, the handle about to click back into place, when a sudden force slammed it open again. Jason leapt away as it collided with the wall, crumbling the concrete where the handle lodged into the solid material. A guard glared out at them from the empty doorway. He took one look at Aimee, clinging on to Lily protectively, and his hand was in the air.

"No!" Isobel screamed.

Elliot threw himself into the air and in front of Aimee. Their eyes locked for a fraction of a second before his body dropped to the ground at her feet. Jason sprang forward, holding both hands out in front of him. The air tightened around them, making it difficult to breath, and Lily started to squirm uncomfortably, opening her mouth to let out a cry that her lungs would not allow. The man in the doorway looked at Jason, his features twisting as Jason compressed the air around him, squeezing the breath from his lungs. The horrific sight did not last long. By the time Lily's cry had left her throat, the man was dead. Aimee had witnessed Jason crush a body only once before. It was an image she could not forget.

"It's OK, Elliot. Look at me. We're here. It will be OK." Isobel's words pulled Aimee's focus from the mangled body in the doorway.

Isobel knelt on the floor and pulled Elliot's head on to her lap. She ran har hands over his torso in a panicked flurry. His eyes were unfocused and he fought to keep them open as red spots of blood filled the whites. It was clear to Aimee, Elliot was not going to be OK. Isobel stroked his forehead and gently pushed back his dark hair as his breaths became shorter and quieter. And then they stopped. She closed his eyes with a shaking hand and carefully set his head back down on the ground.

"We have to go." Chris said, offering his hand to Isobel.

She accepted it and he heaved her back on to her feet. As soon as she had balanced herself, they set off again, along the long corridor, leaving Elliot's body and the roar of chaos behind them. They moved as quickly as Isobel could manage, following Jonah and Chris through the maze of crossed corridors and locked doors, until, finally, they reached a solid steel door sitting slightly ajar.

"This door should not be open." Chris said, edging his fingers around the frame.

"It's not the strangest thing that has happened to us today," Aimee said, rushing them through.

When they entered the room, Aimee first thought that they were in a warehouse. A large metal frame held the building sturdy around them, and corrugated steel roof echoed their footsteps back at them. But as she stepped further into the space, she could see a number of vehicles parked along the length of one side. Every one of them a shining, immaculate black. Chevrolet Suburbans, BMW X5s, GMC Sierras. Every vehicle another claim of Smith's dominance. Most were stationary, with their doors firmly locked and their lights off. But Aimee could see at least two vehicles and a handful of vans that had been abandoned, their engines running, doors wide open and the headlights shining bright circles on to the walls. The drivers had abandoned their posts in a hurry.

"Somebody check for supplies in those vans. I'll see how much fuel we have. If there's enough to get us out of here then we'll need food and water supplies. I'm not making that mistake again. Quickly! We need to keep moving!" Aimee ordered, already making her way to the first vehicle.

A speedy inspection of the fuel dials revealed that they both had over half a tank. But the vans held few food or water resources. They found mostly cleaning equipment and toilet paper from a long-forgotten delivery in the midst of the chaos. They filled the boot of each SUV with anything they considered useful.

"We split into groups of three, right?" Isobel asked, as she threw a loose roll of toilet paper into the boot and pulled the door shut.

Aimee nodded.

"Look, not that I don't trust you guys or anything, but if you three go together in one car, and I take Isobel and Jonah in the other car, what's to stop you from taking off and not helping us at all?" Chris asked, not meeting their gazes.

"Are you serious?" Jason laughed.

"He has a point." Jonah added.

Aimee glanced over their faces quickly before stepping forward and opening the door to the first car.

"I'll go with Jonah and Isobel," she said.

"No, you won't." William replied. "You think that we'll run as soon as we're out of here? After everything that we have been through so far, have we not proved ourselves? I am not leaving Lily, Aimee or Jason."

"I'll go with them and Chris can go with you," Jason offered, wrapping his arms around Aimee and Lily. He kissed Aimee on the forehead and made his way towards the second car, shaking William's hand as he passed. Aimee looked at Jason, biting back the urge to tell Chris where he could stick his demands. Letting Jason go for any stretch of time would be forever difficult for her now. She would never be able to take her eyes off him again; she would be too scared to lose him again. She gave an exasperated growl and threw her head back.

"Fine!" She snapped, knowing that they had wasted too much time already.

She wrapped her fingers around the edge of the SUV's door and bent her knees to lower Lily on to the back seat, when she froze. Through the tinted glass window, Aimee could see a figure lurking behind one of the abandoned vans. Her eyes widened as she examined the shine of his head, the curve of his cruel lop-sided grin, the blood dripping from his nose and on to his ripped shirt. And the bright blue glow of his eyes. Aimee spun on the spot and scanned every face as she tried to decipher who Smith had taken control of. Her eyes landed on Jason.

"He's here!" She screamed. "He has Jason!"

Every pair of eyes flew in Jason's direction as Smith stepped out from the shelter of the van.

"You're not staying?" He called over the low hum of the engines.

Nobody spoke. They watched in mute horror as Smith neared Jason and the second SUV.

"Give me the child, Aimee." He said, simply.

Aimee stared back at him.

"Give me the baby!" He roared.

William tried to move closer to Aimee, but he stopped mid-step as Jason's arm reached out into the air, his hand directed at William.

"If you so much as speak another word, I will make him burn you where you stand." Smith said with so much venom in his voice that a shiver ran down Aimee's spine. "Now, I am going to ask you one last time, Aimee. Give me that baby."

"Why?" Aimee said at last.

"Because she is my grandchild." Smith replied, frustrated.

"She is not your grandchild! Rainey is not your daughter."

"I didn't say anything about Rainey."

Aimee's eyes flickered over to William's who shared the same bewildered expression.

"Joseph, however." Smith smiled.

"You just can't stop, can you? Every word that comes out of your disgusting mouth is a lie to gain more control. You have no relation to Lily; you have no relation to Rainey and you have no relation to Joe. Now, we are going to get in to this car and we are going to leave, and you are not going to stop us. Let Jason go. You've lost Smith. It's over." Aimee said, fighting the desperation that threatened to contaminate her tone.

Smith considered Aimee for a short moment.

"This is not a lie, Aimee. You see, Joe really is my son."

"I don't believe you. Let Jason go."

Smith's smile stretched out over his bloodied face.

"I can't do that."

"Let him go or I'll kill you myself. You can control only one of us at a time, you're on your own now. You cannot possibly believe you are going to win this." She said, flexing her fingers.

"The moment I see that hand move, William dies. Then, I'll kill Jason, just for the fun of it. And then I may just move on to your new friends over there," he nodded at Isobel as he spoke. "Is that a risk you are willing to take?"

She was out of options. But so was Smith. They were at a stalemate. Smith could not control or hurt her without giving Jason his freedom. And the moment he did, Jason would kill him. Smith could have killed every one of them instantly the moment he took control of Jason's body. And yet, he hadn't. He couldn't risk it. He could not kill Aimee. He could not give her the sweet satisfaction of death when he needed her to satiate his obsession. Aimee knew the reason he needed her. But why Lily?

"Isobel, Jonah, get in the car." Aimee said after a moment of silence.

Isobel glanced nervously at Smith before she fixed her eyes on the SUV as walked steadily towards. She climbed into the back seat and Jonah followed.

"Chris." Aimee commanded.

Chris made his way around to the front of the car and climbed into the driver's seat. Smith could do nothing but watch with wide eyes.

"What do you think you're doing?" He spat at Aimee.

"The second you let go of him, you'll be dead. You're not quick enough to take control of anybody else."

William stared hard at Aimee, trying desperately to communicate with her through her eyes. She could feel his words in her head, 'Just electrocute him. If something happens and we get hurt, then so be it. Just do it. I'll give you power.'

But she could not take that risk. This was their only chance. Lily had to come first. Aimee had to get Lily out, for Rainey. And she knew that her decision would ruin her. She lifted Lily from the back of the car and turned to face her fate. She looked from Jason's frozen face, his eyes panicked as they looked back at her, to William's intense glare. Tearing her eyes away from the both of them, she began to walk backwards, pausing when she reached Chris, Jonah, Isobel and her only way out.

"There's something more about Lily that you're not telling us." She said, barely loud enough for Smith to hear her.

"If you get into that car, I'll crush him!" Smith screamed, and William cried out in pain.

Jason groaned in protest, but there was nothing he could do to fight it.

"I am so sorry," she said to William. "I have to take Lily away from here. I have to."

William looked back at her and she knew that he understood.

"Aimee, so help me, if you force me to-" Smith stopped abruptly.

An eruption of noise vibrated through the steel frame of the garage as the ground beneath their feet began to shake and roll. The alarms of the stationary SUVs began to blare, and a window high above them shattered, sending splinters of glass crashing to the ground. A sheet of corrugated steel shook free of its holds and tumbled to the ground, thundering as it hit the concrete. Aimee and William looked at one another.

"Rainey." Aimee whispered.

"Did you not know that she's here? I left an old friend of yours looking after her." Smith pointed a stubby finger to the angry pink burn cutting along Aimee's collarbone.

Aimee ran her fingers gently over the scar.

"No, James is dead. I saw it," William yelled over the noise.

Smith shook his head.

"Isn't it ironic? Dear little Rainey is a similar age as you were, when you first came here. Oh, the fun we had when you first arrived." He looked deliberately to William.

"Aimee, get out of here," William growled through clenched teeth.

"And leave not only your husband and your best friend, but your own daughter too? That's not really your style, Aimee." Smith teased.

"Don't listen to him. Go. Now. Take Lily and go!" William shouted.

"Aimee," Smith warned.

"I'll come back for you," she promised, tears gathering in her eyes.

"I know you will." William reassured her.

"I love you."

"And I you," he replied, as a tear rolled down his cheek and dripped from his chin.

"Aimee," Smith tried again.

Tears streamed down her face, covering her lips as she spoke.

"I'm so sorry, Jason. You deserved so much better."

Aimee climbed into the empty seat beside Isobel and rested Lily on to her lap.

"The moment that car drives out of this garage, William will die. You will never make it back to him, you will be too late. It will be your fault that he died!" Smith's face turned red with rage, and it shook grotesquely as he roared.

Aimee could not tear her eyes from William's as she pulled the door closed.

"Go," she whispered.

Chris pressed his foot on to the pedal and the car rolled forward. He pressed a button on the dash, releasing the huge motorised doors of the garage and Isobel gripped Aimee's hand tightly in her own. The car sped forward, until Aimee could no longer hold William's defeated eyes. The doors closed behind them as they charged into the desert. Leaving William's screams behind them.

Rainey

"How do we get in?" Lexi said, looking up at the huge building looming over her as they stood in its shadow.

Smith's Institute was a perfect cube of solid concrete. It rose high into the sky and stretched out for what looked like miles. Rainey had suggested they run along the side of the building to find a way in, but after a few minutes of trying, the heat exhausted them. There were no doors or windows for as far as they could see. No stairs to the roof, or hatches into the ground. It was an impenetrable rock in the middle of the desert. Rainey looked back at the fence in the distance, its barbed wire only just visible.

"This can't be it." Rainey said, running a hand through her hair.

"Looks like a prison to me. This has to be it." Joe answered.

"We came all this way, from home to France, from France to Italy. We flew here, almost died of thirst in the desert, killed some guys we didn't know and dug our way under that stupid fence, just to get stuck outside some ridiculous looking building. I mean, seriously, who owns a building like this anyway? It's bigger than our entire city. I think Smith has little dick syndrome." Lexi shouted in frustration.

Rainey looked down at her clothes, covered in dust and sand from wriggling her way under the fence. They had dug with their hands until the sand felt cool and a small gap had eventually materialised. When they squeezed themselves under the sharp woven metal, it had scratched at their skin and torn rips into their clothes. Rainey's nails were filled with sand and she pushed the tip of each one under another in an attempt to clear them.

"We'll break our way in," she finally said.

Joe and Lexi exchanged a look.

"Break our way in, how?" Joe questioned.

Rainey did not answer. She looked up again at the building and then turned away from it and set off walking back towards the fence. Joe and Lexi rushed to catch her up.

"If this is going to be like what happened before with the cars then maybe we should slow down and think about this for a second." Joe suggested.

"I am not wasting any more time, Joe. These people don't care about us, maybe it's time we stopped acting like we care about them and start acting just as ruthlessly as they do."

Rainey looked over her shoulder as she paced. She decided that they were still too close, and she continued to stride away.

"You know you don't believe that," Joe tried. "Not everyone in there is bad. Your parents started out in there. They could be in there now. What if you hurt them by accident? What if you hurt Lily?" He knew as soon as the words had left his mouth that he should not have said them.

Rainey stopped abruptly and turned on him.

"You don't think I know that already? We don't have any other option but to force our way in there. And yes, somebody is probably going to get hurt, but every minute they have Lily and my parents, something awful could be happening to them. Every minute we are out here scratching our heads like idiots, they could be hurting Lily. We are too close to start hesitating now. I am going to get into that building, one way or another, and I am going to pray that Lily and my parents will be fine and that we will find them and take them home. And if any of Smith's disgusting worshipers die in the crossfire, then let it be on his head. He took my baby away from me and now his people will suffer, because of him." Rainey stormed.

She turned to face the building, planted her feet firmly on the ground and glared at a spot at the base of Smith's Institute. Joe rubbed at his eyes with his thumb and middle finger. From the corner of her eye Rainey saw Lexi nudge Joe with her elbow, and before Joe had time to look up at her, Rainey pounced on Lexi.

"If you have something to say, Lexi, then just say it."

Lexi looked from Joe to Rainey, rolled her eyes and called Joe something crude under her breath.

"How exactly are you going to do this, Rainey? Just so that I know what to expect. Are we talking more holes in the ground? Tornados ripping through the roof? Or, what…?" Lexi trailed off and waited for Rainey to consider her options.

"Well, what do you guys think?" She said.

"You actually want our opinion?" Lexi asked, a little shocked Rainey had not just leapt in with some dangerous manoeuvre and hoped for the best.

"Yeah. Why wouldn't I?"

"Before all of this happened, you used to be the sensible one. Now, I'd say that you are way more irrational than I have ever been." Lexi stated.

"Before all of this happened, I had everything I had ever wanted. People do crazy things when they're cornered." Rainey said.

"Look, I don't-"

"Stop stalling, Lexi." Rainey cut her off. "We have a couple of options. The easiest is to start an earthquake. If I can make some damage to that wall, we might be able to get through. Fire is more difficult to control, and I don't know if it would do any good anyway. And the same goes for wind. The air isn't difficult to control, until it gets strong, and we would need one hell of a tornado to break through solid concrete. And water is not an option, there isn't enough of it out here for it to do any real damage."

"What about using a bolt to start a fire? Would it make it any easier to control?" Lexi inquired.

"It doesn't make any difference how the fire is started."

Rainey watched Lexi's eyebrows furrow as she thought about the options Rainey had offered them.

"So, there's only actually one option then." Lexi said.

Joe was no longer facing her, he stood with his back to Rainey, looking out into the desert, so she could not judge how he felt about their limited options,. After a while of listening to Lexi argue with herself over the best route to take, Joe finally spoke up.

"Just move the ground," he said quietly.

Rainey nodded at the back of his head and caught a quick glimpse of the look on Lexi's face, before she faced the building again. She struggled to contain the feeling of dread pulling at her stomach when she pictured Lexi's expression, and she shook the image from her head before she focussed her attention on what she needed to do next. Her eyes fixed on a point on the ground at the very base of the building, twenty metres from where she stood. Rainey felt the familiar build up of power surge through her body. Beneath her the earth began to shake, and she parted her feet further to prevent herself from falling. She could see Joe and Lexi at either side of her as they stepped back a little to give her some space. She blocked them out, focusing only on the earth beneath her as she battled with her strength and the temptation to tear the entire state apart. She blocked out the sounds of the desert around her, the rumbling of the ground beneath her feet, the groaning of Smith's Institute as its foundations trembled and began to tear apart. The ground shook more and more, sending violent rolls through the earth, and Rainey had to fight to stay on her feet. The corners of her mouth pulled up into a smile as the building began to show the first signs of its weakness. Cracks crawled their way up the wall and Rainey stumbled back as an enormous section of concrete crumbled and crashed to the ground. She focussed harder on the point at the base of the building, and cracks began to form in the dirt around it. Finally, a fissure opened up and Rainey saw that the walls of the building ran deep into the ground. Lexi started to shout behind her, but Rainey could not afford to lose focus now. She closed her eyes and let her head fall back, her arms falling loosely by her sides with her palms facing outwards. She heard it happen before she had time to open her eyes again and watch, a loud crumbling of brick and concrete, followed by ear splitting thuds as the steel girders collapsed from the floors above. She did not need to open her eyes to know it had worked.

Lexi let out a high-pitched scream of exhilaration and Rainey turned to her, opening her eyes and laughing at the sight of Lexi on the floor.

"You did it!" She screeched, as the rolling under Rainey's feet slowed.

Rainey turned then to look at the destruction she had caused. She was almost disappointed and she reminded herself that it was not her goal to destroy the Institute altogether, only to make an entrance for them to sneak through. Mostly, the building looked untouched. A crumbling gap had formed in the wall, running deep into the ground, and the ends of two steel girders were visible, poking out through the rubble.

"Let's go," she pushed, looking from Lexi's beaming face, to Joe, who would not meet her eyes.

Rainey moved on, searching carefully for any fractures in the ground that she had not yet spotted. When she reached the wall, she kicked the crumbling concrete with her boot, and it fell away under her touch. She placed a foot on to the tip of a steel girder and heaved herself up. She let out a sigh of relief when it held her weight. Through the gap in the wall, Rainey could see that they had broken through just under the ceiling in a small, dark room filled with hundreds of variously sized boxes, all now covered in dust and rubble. A few of the boxes lay crushed under the weight of the girders, and ceiling tiles lay strewn across the floor. Carefully, Rainey climbed through the gap and balanced her way down the girder. Once at the bottom, she called up for the other two to follow her. Lexi came first holding tightly to Joe's hand until she could reach out and grab hold of Rainey's outstretched fingers. Then Joe slid down quickly, his feet hitting the floor with a thump.

"This is insane!" Lexi whispered.

"Why are you whispering?" Joe asked. "If they didn't notice that an earthquake just left a hole in the side of this place, then we don't need to be whispering."

Rainey looked at the only door out of the room. She stepped forward and tried the handle but it did not budge.

"We're locked in," she said, stating the obvious.

Joe squared his shoulders and took a few steps back. Rainey jumped out of the way just in time for Joe to sail past her, his shoulder colliding with the door. It flew from its hinges, hitting the wall on the other side and bouncing back into Joe's outstretched arm. Joe righted himself and Rainey rushed forward to join him on the other side of the doorway. She stopped when she saw his body stiffen. She heard raised voices from outside the room and a rush of feet heading in their direction. Rainey sprang forward, through the empty doorway and directly into the path of two people. They were dressed all in black, and they froze in front of her as they looked her up and down with wide eyes. One, a woman with long dark hair tied tightly at the back of her head and cutting features, pointed to Rainey with a bony finger. She looked to the man standing next to her.

"That's her, right?" She said in a disbelieving whisper. "Go and get Anya."

Rainey laughed out loud and she felt Joe tense beside her. Lexi emerged from the doorway, scanning the new arrivals with her eyes, before planting her feet firmly beside Rainey.

"Yes, run along and get Anya. You'll be saving me a whole lot of time." Rainey's arrogance shocked the couple.

"Come with us. Now." It was the man who spoke this time. His voice was so deep Rainey struggled to understand him.

"No." Joe said simply.

"It would appear that you are not in a situation of negotiation. You can come with us or I can show you what I do." He offered.

"What do you do?" Lexi dared, stepping forward and wiggling her fingers playfully at the couple.

They stared back at her in disbelief.

"You're awfully confident for a bunch of kids," the woman said. "Your gifts won't help you here. The people in this building are trained soldiers."

"I like my chances," Rainey smirked.

The woman's eyes shifted from the three of them to a small plastic box hanging open on the wall with a large green button visible inside. She took a few careful steps back and pushed the button.

"Damn alarm has been going off for an hour already, they won't hear it." The man said, earning him a fierce look from his colleague.

"Trouble in paradise?" Joe asked.

The woman gave him an irritated stare, but Rainey was not paying her any attention. Her mind lingered on the man's words. The alarm had been going off for an hour. What had set it off before their arrival? Joe gripped Rainey by the elbow, snapping her out of her reverie. She looked up to see two more figures approaching in the distance, one looked to be considerably taller than the other. His large frame looked muscular and his scarred face was one that Rainey would never forget. Her body tensed as she locked eyes with him, fighting the urge to run. Joe tightened his grip on Rainey's elbow, and she forced her eyes away to focus on the second person, understanding immediately why Joe was gripping her arm so tightly. Joe had never seen the man who had beaten Rainey on the night Lily had been taken, he had not been there to see it, but he did know Anya. The woman who had played nurse in Lexi's hospital in order to grow closer to Rainey and her family, only to betray them. It was because of her that they were here now, and Rainey would make her pay for what she had done.

Sensing her next move, Joe stepped behind Rainey and wrapped his hands around the tops of her arms. Still, she lunged forward, but Joe held her in place, squeezing her so tightly that her arms throbbed under his fingers. Anya came to a stop just inches in front of her, and Rainey stopped struggling and looked into her eyes. If she reached out, she could grab a hold of her. She could wrap her fingers around Anya's weak neck and throttle the life out of her. She could watch as the warmth left her eyes, and listen as her heart stopped beating.

"You bitch." She growled. "You stupid bitch. You betrayed us. You took my family."

Anya did not speak, she simply stared back at Rainey with no emotion, no indication that she even knew who she was.

"I swear, when I get my hands on you, you'll regret everything you've done." Rainey said through gritted teeth.

Anya raised her eyebrows and Rainey released a mouth full of saliva in her direction.

"How lady like," Anya said, watching as Rainey's spit flew over her shoulder, missing her by millimetres. "You won't hurt me, Rainey."

"I wouldn't bet on it." Rainey said.

"You won't hurt me because I can take you to Smith."

"I don't care about Smith!"

"Smith has Lily." Anya announced, and she smiled when her words had the desired effect on Rainey.

Joe's hands dropped from her arms, but Rainey did not move. She pulled her gaze from Anya's and looked down at her feet. When she finally looked back up, her urge to punch the smirk off Anya's face had not disappeared, but a more powerful emotion controlled her now. Longing. Her heart ached at the thought of Lily being so close, yet still so far away.

"Then move. Take us there."

Anya looked her over and Rainey looked back at her as though she were the most disgusting excuse for a Gifted she had ever had the misfortune of meeting, which was almost true. Her eyes swept across the brute who had beaten her to within an inch of her life. Anya turned and began to walk back the way she had come, along the long walkway.

"Come," she instructed. "Oh, and just so you know, James here can do extraordinary things as a Gifted. He can burn your skin with a touch of his fingers, he can shield himself against the powers of others. He is a force to be reckoned with. I suggest you do not challenge him. Instead, simply do as you are asked."

"What about invisibility?" Rainey said, images fresh in her mind of the carpet outside her bedroom as James's invisible boots had weighted it down.

Joe looked at Rainey from the corner of his eye, but Rainey ignored him.

"*My* power is to make others invisible. At some point or another I have probably used this on James." Anya answered over her shoulder.

Ignoring every natural instinct, Rainey followed Anya, stepping past James. He grinned menacingly as she passed him, and he set off walking behind her. She fixed her eyes on Anya a few steps ahead. Rainey heard Joe and Lexi fall into step behind James, and the two guards behind them, but they did not speak, they simply followed. They walked in silence through the building. Some of the corridors and halls they passed through were completely untouched, the light bouncing from the immaculate white walls and linoleum floors. But Rainey's gift had left its mark, and twice they had to change course as the ceilings had collapsed. Anya led them deeper and deeper into Smith's Institute and the further they walked, the more nervous Rainey became. She felt very aware of how close James was to her and she chewed on her lip as they continued through yet another room. This room was almost empty except for a row of plastic chairs against one wall. It reminded her of a doctor's waiting room, everything so sterile and bland. She thought about what all of the different rooms might be used for. She did not know anything about Smith or the people who followed him. The only people she had met were either her parents or complete lunatics who had tried to hurt her. She considered the lives her parents must have had when they had lived here, and whether they were anything like the people who lived here now. She had known little about her parents' lives until Maria had told her how terrible her mother's time here had been, how she was forced to live in Smith's Institute. The thought of Smith holding her mother here against her will made her feel sick, Rainey did not know what Aimee had suffered under Smith's hand, but it was not something she wanted to speculate on. Rainey's father had wound up working for Smith through choice, and she could not bear to think of the kind of person he must have been to come to such a disturbing place.

"Something wrong, darling?" James said from behind her.

Anya cocked her head to one side but continued on. Rainey gritted her teeth and looked at the linoleum.

"Not talking today? Couldn't shut you up last time."

"James!" Anya scalded. "Enough."

Rainey risked a glance behind her to see that James had fixed his eyes on the floor in front of him. Anya clearly overruled his authority. As she was about to turn her head back, Rainey caught Joe's expression and she saw the mixture of emotions that burned inside of him, confusion, frustration, hatred. Joe's mind was running at a million miles a minute and Rainey knew he would figure out who James was soon enough. Anxious that Anya would not take them to Lily if they did not cooperate, Rainey tore her gaze away from Joe and moved a little faster to catch up to Anya.

Finally, Anya reached a set of thick metal doors with no windows, and a keypad hanging on the wall beside them. She turned to face the small group before tapping a code into the pad and waiting for a long, loud beep. She placed a hand on the door, but before she pushed it open, she looked pointedly at Rainey.

"I understand that you… what I mean to say is, I…" Anya stumbled over her words.

She rested a hand on Rainey's shoulder, giving it a light squeeze. Rainey shook it away and looked back at her, outraged that Anya felt she still had the right to engage in friendly gestures.

"I am sorry for what happened to you." Anya finally said.

"No, you're not." Rainey spat. "You have destroyed me."

Rainey registered the hurt on Anya's face, but she disguised it quickly. With her hand still pressed against the door, she pushed lightly, but stopped again as James spoke up.

"Now there's the Rainey we all know and love," he sneered.

Anya glared dangerously at him and Rainey turned to face him this time, challenging him.

"Them bruises healed up real nice on that pretty little face of yours, didn't they?" James teased.

Rainey's eyes flashed to Joe as the realisation lit up in his eyes, but before she could react Joe was already moving. He slammed into James, sending them both flying through the doors. Rainey rushed forward, desperately trying to reach Joe before James could hurt him, but Anya held out her arms and caught Rainey around the waist, holding her back. Horrified, Rainey watched as Joe punched James in the side of his head. He pulled his arm back, preparing for another punch, when James drew forward his hand and jabbed his fingertips into the bare skin on Joe's chest, just above his collar. Joe roared. His head fell back, his knees buckling beneath him, but James held him up with his free hand as he continued to burn into his flesh. Rainey pulled her elbow up and forced it back into Anya's face, she was rewarded with a satisfying crack. She hurtled forward, blue-white bolts already crackling across the palms of her hands.

"Enough!" A voice erupted from across the room.

Joe's body dropped to the floor and James's body stiffened, pulling up straight as though he had strings attached to his shoulders. Rainey fell to her knees beside Joe, who gasped air into his lungs from where he lay, curled on to his side on the floor. Her fingers ran shakily over his face, brushing back his hair. Bile rose in her throat as her eyes fell to his chest and she swallowed hard. Where James had pushed his fingers into Joe's perfect skin, deep wells of red and melted flesh remained. The wounds did not bleed, and Rainey suspected his skin had been sealed with the heat James had punctured him with.

"What have you done to him?" Rainey screamed at James, not taking her eyes away from Joe.

James did not answer her.

"What have you done? Fix him!"

Rainey screamed profanities, but still he did not answer.

"It's ok, Rainey." Joe whispered between gasps.

She looked up to find James frozen in place. Her eyes followed his gaze and landed on a figure at the far end of the room.

"No need to fret, I hear he's a healer." The man said with a smile.

Rainey had never seen this man before, at least, not face to face. But she had seen him in her dreams. She remembered his sickening smirk, his short rounding figure and shining head. Smith.

She scanned the enormous room they had burst into, its walls curved around them forming a perfect circle, the same dull colour of concrete she had come to expect. It reminded her of a theatre, only without the stalls and the stage. Her eyes stopped on another figure, slumped against the wall where his chains bound him to the concrete. He watched Rainey silently between barely open and bruised eyes. His skin was pale in places and in others covered in blood, and he wore what looked like burned clothing. Rainey cringed when she realised that what she had thought was charred fabric was actually burned patches of flash.

"Dad?" She breathed, the word catching in her throat.

The corner of his mouth moved but he made no sound. His eyes flicked from Rainey's face to the space ahead of him. Rainey turned her head slowly, following his gaze. She could see the shape of an emaciated body as it leaned uncomfortably against the curving wall directly opposite her father. His wrists and ankles were bound tightly with metal chains that flowed deep into the concrete wall. He looked weak and sick and almost unrecognisable. Almost, but not quite. Because Rainey would have recognised him no matter how he looked, she had dreamt of him almost every night since her fourteenth birthday. Her chest tightened painfully and her fingers flexed around Joe's arm.

"Rainey. Do you see him?" Lexi whispered, not trusting her own eyes.

Rainey let out a shaking breath and felt her eyes begin to fill with tears.

"Rainey. It's Jason."

35

Rainey

The room was silent but for Smith's low and dangerous laughter. Rainey stared, too stunned to move, at the man who had disappeared from her life four years ago, the man who had burned to death in his home on her fourteenth birthday. And yet there he was, slouched and bound against the wall, just metres away from her. He was alive.

Rainey's father lay at the other side of the room, his eyes barely open, life slipping from his grasp as every silent moment passed by.

"You must be the famous Rainey." Smith called to her.

She could not draw her eyes from Jason's as Smith spoke.

"I have to admit, I am a little disappointed. I expected more of an entrance from someone as talented as yourself. Although, I am pleased to see you brought your friends."

Rainey finally tore her eyes from Jason's and looked at Smith.

"Welcome, Joseph and Alexa." Smith held his arms out wide in a welcoming gesture.

"Her name is Lexi," Rainey said.

"Ah, she speaks at last. I understand this must be quite a shock for you, Rainey. A man you thought to be dead for years appearing right in front of your very eyes, alive and breathing, and your dear old father here has definitely seen better days. But don't let that frighten you. Here, we abide by the rules. It is only when the rules are broken that these things have to happen." Smith's voice echoed across the empty hall, and though he worked his voice to sound welcoming and friendly, Rainey knew that poison lay just beneath the surface.

"Where is Lily?" Rainey said.

"All in good time, my girl. You see, I have a proposition for you. But not just for you. Should you accept my offer, then your friends could also benefit from this deal." He paused, allowing his words to sink in before continuing. "I would like to offer you a place among us here. You will be a very well-respected member of our army, and with the powers you possess as a Gifted, I can guarantee you will not be starting at the bottom."

"And what is it that your army fight for?" Rainey called across the space between them, her voice echoing back to her.

"We fight to protect the Gifted, of course." He answered easily.

"Protect them from what, exactly?"

Smith smiled. He had been asked the same question hundreds of times and his answer was well rehearsed.

"The humans who wish them harm. You may not have seen it in your quiet little village in England, but those of us who have travelled the world will understand more than others what acts a jealous human is capable of committing on someone of our kind. If you choose to follow me, you will be placed into an experienced team of Gifted. We can make a stand. We can rule above the others. No longer will they be able to refuse our existence and force us to live in exile. When we rule, it shall be them who hide in their houses."

"I have nothing to fear from humans. Why would I ever want to join some deplorable cult in the middle of the desert?" She laughed, disbelieving.

Smith's face reddened before he could prevent his anger from making an appearance.

"I think that you must not understand the benefits of what I offer." Smith said, trying to regain his composure.

"I don't care about the so-called benefits. If you honestly thought I would accept an offer of employment from a power-mad lunatic who has tried to destroy my family, then you are delusional. Here's a word of advice for the next time you're hiring staff. Don't kidnap their baby." She shouted sarcastically.

"Just like her mother." Smith said to himself quietly.

He smiled again, but this time it was not the friendly mask he had tried so hard to compose, it was dangerous and daring. Rainey looked down to Joe, his wounds healing rapidly. He pushed himself upright and Smith eyed him thoughtfully.

"I have a little confession to make," Smith admitted, and all eyes in the room reverted back to him. "As you seem to know so much about my past already, Rainey, maybe I should fill you in on some of the more undisclosed details. You see, a long time ago now, I met a girl named Aimee, who fascinated me more than any other Gifted I had ever met. Her father, a disgusting drunk of a man, begged me for help and I gave it to him by moving him and his daughter here, to work alongside me. I helped that man to clean himself up, and he became a fine employee over time. I gave Aimee the possibilities that her previous life could never have offered her. Without me, they both would have rotted in their bleak excuse of an existence. And I asked for nothing in return."

"Make sure you're listening, Rainey. The psycho's about to teach us a life lesson." Lexi mumbled impatiently.

Smith ignored her and continued with his story, but Rainey could have sworn she saw Jason smile from the corner of her eye.

"As Aimee grew into an adult, she asked to be put into training to become a midwife, one of the more difficult tasks that a Gifted could undertake, which I am sure that you of all people can understand. Of course, I allowed her to do this and I provided her with anything she wished. But Aimee betrayed me when she met William," he waved a hand in Rainey's father's direction.

Rainey's eyes shifted to her father and she bit down on her lip as his eyes drooped lower, threatening to close altogether.

"When she met William, she grew cold towards me and refused the relationship we had built-"

"What relationship?" Jason called out suddenly.

Smith's head snapped around to glare at him. A warmth rushed through Rainey at the sound of Jason's voice. His voice was weak and it croaked with every word, but he still sounded like the same Jason she had grown up with, the same Jason who had taught her how to fight and control the elements.

"There was never a relationship between you and Aimee." Jason continued.

"From the moment that girl was of age our relationship blossomed," Smith said, a smirk lingering on his lips.

"From the moment that girl was of age, you raped her." Jason yelled back.

Rainey's stomach felt as though it had dropped through the floor. She heard Joe's shocked intake of breath and Lexi took an involuntary step forward before she thought better of it and stopped herself.

"In fact, she was even of age in this country? You stole what remained of her childhood." Jason spat.

"I did not do anything to her that she did not ask for." Smith sneered.

Jason pulled against his chains, but Smith just smiled.

"As I was saying, William appeared and suddenly Aimee rejected what I had to offer. When she discovered that she was pregnant she ran away, taking these two with her. They all betrayed me, but not only me. they betrayed what we stand for. So, I searched for her."

Movement from the side of the room interrupted Smith's rehearsed story and he turned his gaze to the slumped figure that was William. Rainey followed his eyes to see that William had pushed himself a little more upright and he held the weight of his head without it falling back against the concrete wall. Smith looked to Joe suspiciously, but whatever he saw there did not satisfy him, and his eyes fell back to William, who stared back at him defiantly.

"Rainey, don't listen to him." William's voice sounded, strained and quiet.

Rainey struggled to hear him across the space, but a wave of relief washed through her as she saw her father's fight return. Smith laughed, and a sickening shiver rolled down Rainey's spine at the sound. Lexi rested her hand on Rainey's shoulder, giving it a reassuring squeeze.

"Now, Joseph, this is where you might like to listen carefully," Smith continued, and he looked to Joe, who pulled his eyes from William to meet his glare.

"Jason's mother, Di was her name, she was a lovely woman, very helpful. She contacted me regarding Aimee's whereabouts, and she asked me to meet her in a café, close to where she suspected Aimee to be. And so, I went, and she gave me the information I required. When she left, I felt rather... hungry, shall we say. I had shared in great detail with Di, why Aimee's return was so important to me, and I found myself craving the relief that she offered."

Rainey's skin crawled at his words.

"I did something unforgivable. I waited in the café and closely observed the staff there. Obviously, they were all human women and I was highly disappointed that I would have to lower myself to such a shameful act. But one woman caught my eye in particular. She was very short and slim, with beautifully tanned skin and eyes the colour of chocolate. She was beautiful, for a human. I waited in my car until the café closed and when I saw her walking home on her own, I could not resist my urge to take her. I relieved the frustrations I felt for Aimee on that human woman, and I left her for dead in an alleyway, presuming, of course, that she would not survive. It was a long time before I discovered the woman had survived long enough to carry a child. The child was born, and the mother died, as is to be expected when it comes to humans with Gifted children. The child was a boy. I believe his name was Joseph. The son of Emily Denyer."

Rainey had been so horrified as she listened to every word of Smith's story, that she had paid little attention to Joe as she knelt beside him. He had not moved from where he rested his healing body on the cold floor, but his head had dropped forward, supported only by his shaking hands. Rainey moved her hand to run over his shoulders, but she stopped herself, knowing that he would not want her comfort. Not yet.

"You can imagine my shock when all those years later, as I studied Aimee's every move, I discovered that my son had managed to find no other than Aimee's daughter, and a relationship began to develop between the two. The irony of it did not escape me. It fascinated me even more so, that when Aimee ran away, she also carried a child, and poor old William here was never granted the opportunity to impregnate Aimee before she left me."

Joe's head lifted from his hands and he finally met Smith's eyes.

"Which would mean that Joseph, as my son, was building a relationship with Rainey, my daughter."

Lexi's hand dropped from Rainey's shoulder and Joe leapt to his feet, leaving Rainey kneeling on the ground, too stunned to move. Smith's words rang through her head, nauseating and suffocating her. Panic rose in her stomach and invaded her chest, forcing her heart to beat harder and her chest to tighten painfully.

"He's lying." Joe said, hysteria edging into his tone. "Please, tell me he's lying!"

Rainey found her feet and pushed herself up. She stepped forward slowly, heading for Smith, and stopped between her father and Jason in the centre of the room. The space was so immense that they were both still fifty feet away from her on either side. She looked to her father, unmoving, his eyes open, his chest steadily rising and falling. Then she looked to Jason, who shook his head once so imperceptibly that nobody else seemed to have noticed. Finally, she looked at Smith.

"Bullshit." She called out.

"Excuse me?" Smith said, a threat lingering in his tone.

"This whole thing is a lie. Maybe Joe could be your son, but William is my father."

William gave her a proud smile but grimaced when the muscles in his cheeks pulled at a patch of charcoaled skin below his temple.

"This is what you do to manipulate people, isn't it? You make up disgusting lies to confuse them and hope to gain something from it. Or, maybe you find some sort of sadistic pleasure in destroying happiness."

"And what could I possibly gain from this?" He questioned, not expecting Rainey to have an answer.

But Rainey had already worked it all out.

"So that you could get your hands on Lily. You want her because you know that one day, she will be strong. You're threatened by her. You're threatened by a baby."

The deep smile-lines around Smith's eyes smoothed as his grin transformed into a snarl of malice. Rainey could not help but laugh.

"Or, could it be that you think my mother belongs to you? And you think you can hang out the bait and she will come running back to you."

Rainey was not threatened by his rapidly changing emotions and she continued, unperturbed by his reddening face. "If you somehow manage to convince the Gifted that your own children have had a child together, then maybe you'll be supported when you try to take her away and destroy her, right?"

As the words poured from Rainey's mouth, they made more and more sense to her.

"I do not lie to those who are loyal to me." Smith spat.

"If any of them believe a word that you say, then they're just as demented as you are."

Smith looked from Rainey's face to the other faces in the room, all of them watching Rainey. His eyes eventually landed on James, as though he had forgotten he existed, and James's frame sagged as the invisible force holding him was dropped. Smith's eyes darkened to a dull brown as the glow died disappeared. James did not move, he fixed his eyes on the ground in front of him.

Rainey sensed what Smith was doing. Releasing James was his way of readying himself for what would surely come. She knew neither side would back down, and it was only a matter of time until one of them acted. She scanned the room again, weighing her options, as Smith tried to communicate something with Anya in the way he pierced her with his dead eyes. There was nothing to help her in this room, she decided. Both her father and Jason were bound to the solid walls by chains snaking around their wrists and ankles. They could move, but very little, and what use would her father be if it came to a fight? Rainey just hoped that he would survive long enough to reap the rewards of a won battle. She shook the thought away and replaced it with the hope that Jason may still be able to use his powers. Jason was strong, at least, he used to be. Then there was Joe and Lexi, and though Joe could fight, his powers would offer them little help. Lexi was more than capable of killing every person in the room, if she could get close enough, but she could only hurt them one at a time, and the chances of her making it to Anya, James, Smith and the two guards one at a time before they had a chance to stop her was extremely unlikely.

She took a deep breath and fixed her eyes back on Smith. Joe walked forward and wrapped his hand around Rainey's, squeezing reassuringly. Smith looked at their intertwined fingers as though they were something he had peeled from the bottom of his shoe.

"I don't believe any of it." Joe said.

"I don't care. If I had ever planned to let you live, maybe you could have researched your useless human mother and found meaning in your pathetic existence as an orphan." Smith snapped.

Rainey made an amused sound, which infuriated Smith even further.

"Just be thankful that you obviously have your mother's looks," Rainey said to Joe, loud enough for it to echo around the room.

One side of Smith's mouth pulled up into a snarl and he called out across the room in a last attempt to pull Rainey in.

"Do you refuse my offer?"

"Where's Lily?"

"She's already gone." Was all Smith said.

Rainey refused to even consider what those words could mean.

"Gone where?" She said, through gritted teeth.

"They left."

A deep breath pulled into Rainey's lungs and her hands shook with the anger she felt coursing through her. But it was Lexi who could not contain her irritation any longer.

"Oh, for the love of… Could you be any more vague please?" She shouted, sarcastically.

"She left with Aimee. They ran off into the desert. I wouldn't worry too much though, I sent a few of the guards out to follow them. Just to make sure that they don't get too far." Smith spoke as though he was bored with the conversation, but he was trying too hard.

"Now, I will ask you one more time. Do you accept or refuse my offer?"

In her head Rainey played back Smith's words, *"If I had ever planned to let you live"*. Even if Smith had offered her the deal of a lifetime, he did not plan to let Joe live past today. He didn't want Joe, he wanted Rainey, and Aimee, and Lily.

"I refuse your offer, Smith." Rainey said, planting her feet firmly on the ground, prepared.

"So be it." Smith said softly.

Rainey heard the doors behind her open and slam closed again.

"Two down, three to go." Joe said helpfully.

But which two, Rainey did not know. Because she could not pull her eyes from Smith's as the dull brown of his iris's began to glow an electric blue again and a strangled cry escaped through Jason's clenched jaw. Rainey winced as Jason's body tensed and she understood at once that Smith that was controlling him now. But it wasn't what she had expected to happen. Did Smith consider Jason the most powerful? Did he not know what she could do?

"Lexi, get James!" Rainey barked over her shoulder.

If James's powers relied on skin to skin contact, then Lexi would win the fight. Rainey only hoped that his shield was no match for her. And Anya was no real threat. Rainey advanced on Smith, and Joe released her hand but moved along with her.

"Let him go." Rainey commanded.

Smith did not reply and he stared blankly through her as though she was not really there.

"Let him go, now." She tried again, raising her hands into the empty space before of her.

Smith looked down at Rainey's hands when she came to a stop with only a few metres standing between them.

"Ah, ah, ah." He said, shaking his head slowly from side to side.

A deep growl sounded from behind Rainey, followed by a loud thud. She did not dare to risk taking her eyes away from Smith's for even a second, but she knew that it had been James's body hitting the floor, and she hoped that it had hurt like hell.

Smith's eyes flicked away from Rainey's face and over her shoulder quickly, before settling back on her again. Anger flared in his eyes. A smug smile filled Rainey's lips and Smith shook with rage. Rainey edged one final step closer and blue sparks crackled on her palms. She was so close. She could not reach him from where she stood, but she did not need to. She felt the familiar surge of power building within her and a dangerous glint flashed in her eyes. And then she froze as a scream echoed around the room. It pierced through her skull, forcing the hairs on the back of her neck to stand on end. She turned without thinking and watched in horror as Lexi writhed in agony on the floor beside James's dead body. Flames danced across Lexi's clothes, melting the fabric to her skin. She rolled across the ground, attempting to smother the flames, but they continued to burn a path across her flesh. Joe sprinted for her and Rainey spun on the spot to face Smith once more. The horror of what Smith was doing fuelled her hatred and she knew that Jason would despise himself for what his powers were allowing Smith to do.

A flash of white electricity leapt free of Rainey's hand and hit Smith in his abdomen. He stumbled back but it did not distract him, and Lexi continued to scream from behind her.

How was Smith still standing?

She fired another bolt, and another. But nothing happened. Rainey bit down hard on the inside of her cheek and the unmistakable coppery taste of blood covered her tongue. She knew what she had to do, and the thought of it made her hate herself, but what choice did she have? She turned to Jason, and an identical bolt flew from her body and hit him on his forearm. She cringed as Jason's face crumpled and Smith finally cried out in pain. He released Jason's body. It had worked, but at what cost? Lexi's screams stopped and Rainey heard Joe offering comforting words as he no-doubt tried to heal her.

When Rainey looked into Jason's eyes, her heart felt as though it might stop beating.

"Keep going." He urged Rainey, giving her permission to torture him further.

Tears filled her eyes and she blinked them away, angrily.

"You little bitch!" Smith screamed through gritted teeth.

Rainey had hurt him just enough to make him pause. If she had tried to do more, she could have killed Jason. She fixed her eyes on Smith again, but it was too late, his eyes already shone with the tell tale blue of a Gifted, and Rainey clenched her fists, as this time, her father began to groan.

Maybe this was why no Gifted had ever tried to kill Smith, Rainey thought. *Maybe this was how he forced people into following him. By taking over their loved ones, knowing that they would not be able to bear hurting them, even if it meant hurting him too.*

She looked at her father's beaten form and tears spilled over her cheeks.

"I'm sorry." She mouthed, before her eyes glowed an electric blue, matching Smith's, and she fired a bolt at him.

Again, Smith halted and stumbled back a step. Rainey's vision was too blurred with tears for her to see her father's face, and she was thankful for that. She wiped her eyes with the back of her hand and aimed at Smith, she felt the surge of power shoot along her arm and dance on her fingertips, but she held it back. Her eyes cleared and she could see Smith clearly again, but Lexi had appeared before him. Lexi leapt forward, her long delicate fingers outstretched, just centimetres from touching his torso, ready to take his life. They barely brushed against the fabric of his shirt when Rainey saw the glint of light reflect from the metal object in Smith's hand. Time slowed down for her as Smith thrust the knife forward and into Lexi's chest.

The scream left Rainey's mouth without her permission. Lexi's hand dropped to her side. She stumbled back and looked down at the knife held in place by her torso, before she looked up at Rainey's desperate eyes.

"I..." she started, but her legs collapsed beneath her.

Rainey leapt forward and caught her in her arms, scraping the skin of her knees through her trousers and softening the blow of Lexi's body on the concrete. The room felt as though it had frozen around her and all that mattered was Lexi. Her fingers clung painfully to the skin on Rainey's arm.

"No, Lexi. No. You're fine. Joe will fix it. He'll make it better." Rainey cried.

"I..." Lexi tried again, and she forced a gasp of air in through her lips.

Her fingers loosened around Rainey's arm and Lexi's body turned limp. Her chest lifted and fell one final time and the light behind her eyes went out. Rainey ran her fingers over Lexi's cheek.

"Lex?" She said, tears running off her chin and on to Lexi's face. "Lexi, please."

But she was already gone. Rainey pulled Lexi's body close to her and held her tightly, rocking her back and forth as she cried. Lexi's blood covered Rainey's hands and clothes. The room was still. And then the silence was broken by the sound of Smith's cold laughter. A scream rose up through Rainey's throat, forcing its way out of her clenched jaw. Her hair whipped back from her face as the still air grew unsettled, and every set of eyes in the room remained fixed on her as a deep rumbling sounded from beneath them. The wind she created grew into a ferocious howl around her and William wrapped the chains binding him further around his wrists, holding them tightly with his burned hands. Jason followed suit and Rainey caught the determined nod William gave her from the corner of her eye. She felt a sudden rush of power swell throughout every cell in her body, a power she had never experienced before.

Joe pushed his way forward, his black clothing flapping wildly in the wind. He reached Jason and wrapped his arm through one of the chains, pushing his back against the wall and gripping Jason tightly with his free hand. Rainey did not care what was happening around her. She could not see anything past Smith's eyes. A crazed fire had begun to burn behind her irises, and for the first time, Rainey saw Smith's fear. He stumbled as he fought to stay upright in the gusts beating against his body. Faster and faster the air spun around the room, collecting dust and twirling around Rainey like a tornado, while she cradled Lexi's body on the floor. Smith's eyes glowed back at her as he tried to gain control of Rainey, but he was not strong enough, and he realised now the mistake he had made in underestimating her power. Rainey could see the panic and confusion spreading across his face. His head snapped to William, clinging to his chains.

"You will die trying to protect her!" Smith screamed at William.

Rainey watched as the wind forced him to his knees, and he clawed at the solid ground in an effort to hold himself down, but there was nothing for him to grasp. In the centre of the chaos Rainey looked down at Lexi's empty eyes. She ran her fingers over her eyelids, closing them.

"You could just be sleeping." She said, and she kissed Lexi's forehead before gently lowering her head to the ground.

Rising to her feet, she looked down at Smith's cowering form. The wind whipped around her body, pulling her clothing back and forcing her dark hair to fray out dramatically behind her. A deafening rumble sounded as a section of concrete tore from the wall above William. It spun dangerously in the funnel of wind, crumbling as it twirled through the room, churning into a mass of rubble. A piece brushed across Rainey flesh as it flew past, leaving a deep scratch across her cheek, but she did not flinch away. Nothing would pull her attention from Smith. His eyes met hers through the dust and Rainey widened the sharp line of her mouth into a sinister grin.

"You will never beat me, Rainey." He shouted through the rush of wind.

Rainey raised her arms and fire erupted from the ground around her, the flames licking at the debris as it spun around the room. Smith scrambled away from her, desperately trying to grasp at the ground. She studied the walls, crumbling into the tornado, until she found what she was looking for. An uneven slab of concrete hung precariously above Jason and Joe. She could see them shouting to her, but the roar of the flames and the rush of the wind were too loud for her to hear them. She lifted the earth beneath her feet in a great roll, shaking the concrete free, and with every ounce of strength she had left in her, she manipulated the crazed air. The wind stopped abruptly, dropping its dust and rubble to the ground. And for a fraction of a second there was silence, before Rainey lifted the great mound of solid concrete with the dominated air and hurled it directly at Smith. It struck Smith's body with the force of a truck hitting a bug, and launched him through the air and into the solid wall. His body slid down the rough surface and slumped to the ground, where is stayed, unmoving.

Rainey dropped to her knees in the deafening silence. Her hair was wild from the wind, her skin covered in dust and Lexi's blood. Her hands trembled as fresh tears rolled down her cheeks, making tracks through the blood that oozed from her scratches. Her arms found Lexi and they wrapped tightly around her delicate body. And she cried out into the silence. Lexi was dead. And Rainey was too late to save her.

36

Rainey

A hand pressed gently on Rainey's shoulder and she recoiled from the touch.

"Rainey." Joe said, softly. "Rainey, we have to go."

She lifted her head from Lexi's chest and looked around. Joe rushed to the other side of the room, where Anya lay curled into a protective ball on the ground. William remained chained to the wall, a great hole in the concrete hovered above his head and his hair was covering in rubble and dust. Jason's chains remained intact too. He had pushed himself on to his knees and he watching Rainey closely.

Rainey looked down at Lexi's peaceful face. She studied her every detail carefully, knowing that she would never see any of them ever again. Her perfect pale skin, the way that her nose pulled up slightly at the end, her full pale lips that had always smiled. Rainey would never see her smile again. She ran her fingers across her cheek.

"I'm so sorry," she whispered.

She pushed herself up and turned to see Joe pulling Anya across the room by her hair. She whimpered as she tried to crawl across the floor at Joe's pace, but her knees pressed painfully against the rubble, and she could not keep up. Joe dragged her to Rainey before he let go of her and she cowered at Rainey's feet.

"Get up." Rainey spat.

Anya placed her palms flat on the floor and pushed herself upright. Her lower lip quivered as she stood before Rainey. She looked down at Lexi's tiny frame on the cold, hard ground and she let out a cry. Rainey sprang forward and slapped her hard around the face.

"Don't you cry for her." She screamed. "You did this. This is your fault."

"No. This wasn't my-" Anya tried but Rainey would not allow it.

"You brought us here. If it wasn't for you Lexi would be safe in her hospital."

Anya's eyes trailed down to Lexi again and Rainey pulled back her arm and slapped her again.

"Don't even look at her," she snarled.

Anya backed away, running her hand over her cheek where Rainey had hit her.

"Untie them." Rainey demanded.

"I can't. I don't have the key." Anya replied.

Frustration gripped at Rainey and she screamed through her teeth. She held her hand out and pointed her palm to Anya's face.

"Untie them, now. Because when I lose interest in you, Anya, you're dead."

"Smith... there is a key... he had it." She stammered.

Rainey stormed towards Smith's body. His chest rose and fell weakly and blood pooled beneath his head from where it dripped out of both ears. His fingernails were raw and bloody where he had tried desperately to cling to the floor, and it satisfied Rainey to see that some were missing altogether. Rainey knelt down beside him and put her hand into his pocket, the first was empty. She leant across his body in search of another and pulled out a small key. She leaned in closer, listening to each rattling breath, until her lips could feel the heat radiating from the skin on his cheek.

"I hope every dying breath is agony, you pig." She breathed.

She rose to her feet and marched across the floor to William. As gently as she could, Rainey twisted one of the metal cuffs that had dug painful, red welts into William's skin. He winced but did not protest. She manoeuvred the cuff until she could see a keyhole, then she edged the key into it and turned it. The lock clicked and the clasp sprang open enough for Rainey to edge the tips of her fingers under the metal and pry it open the rest of the way. A sigh of relief rushed from William as the cuff swung back on its chain and clattered noisily against what remained of the concrete wall. Rainey repeated the technique three more times and watched as William stretched out his sore limbs. But she did not dare to lean forward and wrap her arms around him, as much as she longed to. William was frail and damaged. He lifted a hand to her face and she leaned into it, allowing her eyes to close for just a second as he ran his thumb lightly across a cut in her cheek.

"I am so proud of you," he whispered hoarsely.

Rainey pulled away from him. She did not deserve his pride. Her loss of control could have killed everyone in the room, not just Smith.

"Joe," she said. "Can you heal him?"

Joe appeared at her shoulder. He examined William's wounds closely.

"As much as you can without tiring yourself, we still have to find a way out." Rainey squeezed Joe's hand and turned towards Jason.

As she approached him, she could see his wounds were more superficial than William's. The locks on his cuffs sprang open one by one and again, Rainey pried them open with the tips of her fingers. As the final cuff fell to the floor, Jason locked Rainey in a fierce hug.

"Jesus, you've grown." He said to the top of her head.

Rainey bit down on her lip as she leaned into his chest, squeezing him tightly.

"Jesus is my weekend name. You can call me Rainey." She said weakly, fighting back the never-ending stream of tears leaking from her eyes.

"I am so relieved that you're ok," he said, still clinging tightly to her. "I didn't think I would see any of you ever again."

Rainey could feel the sharp lines of his ribs across his back and she held him. She loosened her grip and took a step back to look at him.

"Where have you been?" She asked.

"Long story," he said, shaking his head. "And right now, we don't have time. We need to get out of here."

Jason separated himself from Rainey and moved across the space dividing him from William. Rainey followed, and when she looked down at her father again, he had noticeably changed. His cuts did not look so deep, his cheeks held a little more colour and his eyes stared back at her, more alert and determined. His burned skin was no longer charred, but red and shiny, more like scars than fresh wounds. William pulled one side of his mouth up in a lopsided smile. With Joe on one side and Jason on the other, William pulled himself up and accepted the support they offered him.

"Can you stand on your own?" Rainey asked.

He let go of their arms and stood as tall as he could manage. Then he nodded, satisfied.

"Where's Anya?" Joe said suddenly.

Rainey spun and looked swiftly around the room. Anya was not there.

"We better get moving before she comes back with more guards." William said.

Rainey bit down on her lip again. Leaving meant leaving Lexi's body.

"We can't take her, Ray Ray." Joe said sadly, reading her face.

"I know." She replied, but she could not meet his eyes.

She did not want to look at Lexi's body again, alone in the middle of a cold and unfamiliar room, surrounded by destruction. Rainey knew that there was no way she could leave her there.

"But we can't leave her here either." She said, her voice breaking as fresh tears spilled from her eyes. "Can we at least move her out of this room to somewhere that isn't filled with rubble and blood?"

Joe nodded grimly. He walked over to Lexi and carefully lifted her petite frame into his arms. He stumbled as he struggled to balance the weight of her body after healing William, and Rainey tried to rush closer to help him, but she saw how Lexi's legs hung over one of his arms and how her head flopped back over the other, and she turned away. She could not look at Lexi dangling from Joe's arms, lifeless. Lexi's life had been stolen from her. She had barely had a chance to experience anything. Her childhood had been taken away from her when her parents died, and now she was dead too. Rainey turned away and headed for the doors, avoiding James's body. She felt every pair of eyes in the room watching her as she fought again to control her tears.

"Wait. What about Smith?" Joe said.

Rainey turned to look at his mangled body, lying in a pool of his own blood. She could no longer see his chest moving.

"He's as good as dead." Rainey said.

Together, they walked through the doors. Jason took the lead, taking them through a series of identical corridors. At the end of each corridor, the doors lay open for them, helping them to navigate a path through. As they progressed through the Institute, Rainey played images of her mother and Lily in her mind and she prayed that they had made it out safely.

Jason stopped abruptly in front of her and she narrowly avoided walking straight into the back of him. She leaned over his shoulder to see what had caused him to stop so suddenly, and there at the end of the walkway, was Anya, positioned between them and the next door.

"I want to help!" She shouted, holding her hands up in the air to reveal a set of car keys wrapped around a long, manicured finger.

Jason raised his eyebrows at Rainey but continued forward. When he reached Anya she handed over the keys with a shaking hand.

"Why?" Jason said, simply.

"Maybe I can make up for some of what I've done. I know it's not enough, but it is a start."

Rainey wanted to argue. She wanted to see Anya dead for what she had done. She wanted to crush her skull into a thousand tiny pieces and pull her limb from limb. But Anya was their ticket out of the Institute.

"You will never be able to make up for what you have done. I will never forgive you, for any of it. But I won't kill you where you stand if you do two things for me." Rainey balled her hands into fists and waited as Anya absorbed her words.

"I'll do what I can," she said quietly.

"You'll have Lexi's body cremated. Properly. She does not deserve to be buried in an unmarked grave, thousand of miles away from where she belongs. And you will send her ashes home."

"I can do that. And the second?" Anya said without hesitation.

"You will take us to the car that those keys belong to, and you will get us out." Rainey finished.

Anya nodded.

"Who did you think left the doors open for you? Come on." She ushered for them to follow her.

She led them into a small room, its door hidden beneath a staircase. Inside was a simple sofa with a television hanging from the wall in front of it. A used coffee cup had been knocked over on to a small coffee table, its remnants staining the wood surface.

"You can leave her in here." Anya told Joe.

Joe knelt down with Lexi still in his arms and rested her body against the sofa cushions. Her hand fell from the cushion and hung lifelessly over the edge. Jason and William waited by the door with Anya, giving Joe and Rainey one last chance to say goodbye. Joe stayed knelt down beside her as he lifted her hands and placed them together on her stomach. He looked at her silently for a long time. The room was so quiet that Rainey could hear every breath, every beat of her own heart. She looked on as Joe said goodbye to their best friend. She could tell that he was speaking to her on the inside of his head, keeping his final words private. When he was done, he kissed Lexi's forehead and squeezed his eyes tightly shut. Then he pushed himself on to his feet and joined the others in the doorway, brushing his fingers across Rainey's arm as he passed.

Rainey leaned over Lexi's body. Joe had placed Lexi's hands so that they covered most of the blood staining her shirt, and Rainey could almost imagine that she was sleeping again, her face peaceful. Almost, but not quite. She brushed her fingers through Lexi's hair, untangling the mess she had created with the wind, and she styled it around her face, just the way Lexi liked it. She used her sleeve to wipe away the dirt on Lexi's face and she straightened the collar on her shirt. Then she stood above her and looked down at Lexi one final time. Then she turned away and closed her eyes. Lexi was not in there anymore. All that remained was her shell. She opened her eyes and strode back to the doorway.

"Let's go." She said, pushing Anya roughly through the door.

Anya stumbled out of the room and waited as the others followed her out. She pulled the door closed and typed a code into the pad on the wall, locking Lexi inside. Then she led them away from the room, leaving Lexi forever.

Cars were not something Rainey had ever had a real interest in. She liked some more than others. And she enjoyed the thrill of pressing her foot to the floor and leaving the dust behind her. But if a car could take her from A to B then she was content. Unlike Aimee and William, who had always wanted bigger and better when it came to cars. Looking around her, Rainey wondered if their love of big cars had come from a time when they planned to run from Smith. They had no money and no plans. Their only hope was to escape and survive. Rainey peered around Smith's garage and knew that this was where her parents' love for cars had begun, because it was filled with them.

A memory of Lexi's words ran through Rainey's head, *"I think Smith has little dick syndrome"*. She almost laughed to herself at the memory, but then her chest tightened painfully again, and she rested a hand on the bonnet of the closest car to stop herself from collapsing under the weight of her grief. Her hand brushed over the badge of the car but Rainey did not recognise the brand. Anya strolled along the various SUVs, weaving in and out as she searched for the one she wanted.

"I have given you the keys to one of Smith's personal vehicles. I thought that you could use the extra protection in the event that you are followed." She told them as she manoeuvred herself through a gap between two of the vehicles.

Jason looked down at the key in his hand.

"Toyota," he read out loud. "What's so good about a Toyota?"

"This particular car has been modified to suit Smith's needs. As you can imagine, there are a lot of people out there, both Gifted and human, who did not see eye to eye with him. He took every possible precaution to protect himself when he left the Institute. This car is heavily armoured, it can withstand bullets, bombs, you name it."

"Can it withstand Rainey?" Jason asked.

Anya ignored his question and continued.

"Inside it has been modified in order to offer maximum comfort during long journeys. It is a large car but there are only four seats, including that of the driver. So, if you do manage to catch up with Aimee, then there will not be enough seats for you all." Anya spoke quickly as she finally approached the Toyota.

It faced towards the large metal door leading out and into the desert. Rainey's eyes scanned over the car almost hungrily. She had never seen anything like it. The black metal curved in all the right places, catching the light and reflecting it back across the vast space. Its windows had been completely blacked out to hide its passengers and the alloys matched the shining black paint of the body. If ever a car could look mean, this was it. Everything about it screamed power, and she was grateful she would not be expected to drive it.

"Pass me the keys." Joe said, extending his hand to Jason.

"I don't think so, kiddo. Leave it to the more experienced drivers." William said, stepping forward and taking the keys for himself.

"Aimee has a couple of hours head start, but there's still a chance you could catch her. Follow the road around the building, it will take you back to the highway. Go South. There's only one route, so if you drive fast enough, you'll find her." Anya advised.

William climbed into the driver's seat and pressed a button behind the steering wheel. The engine roared to life before turning into a gentle purr. Rainey pulled open the back door and climbed inside. The seats were made from a cream coloured leather and various gadgets had been added to the interior, but Rainey paid them little attention. She ushered for Joe to climb in beside her and Jason pulled himself into the front passenger seat. Ahead of them, Anya pushed a button beside the garage doors and they began to slowly pull up and away from the ground. William pressed his foot gently on the accelerator and the car rolled forwards.

Rainey looked past Anya, refusing to meet her eyes. They had not thanked her for her help, but why should they? Anya might have been sorry for what she had done, but Rainey meant what she said, she would never forgive her, no matter how much she tried to make up for what she had done. Anya had betrayed them. After working with Lexi for months and building a relationship with them, she had been the one to take Lily away. If it had not been for Anya, Lexi would be alive. Rainey swore to herself that one day, when Lexi's ashes had been returned home, and her family were safe again, Rainey would find Anya, and she would pay for what she had done.

As they sped on to the highway, Rainey closed her eyes and let her head fall back against the seat. She had tried to be too strong for too long. She was tired of being strong. She was exhausted, both in her body and her mind. The uneven road rocked the car, and when Joe pulled her across the seat, she rested her head on his shoulder and allowed him to wrap his arms around her. They did not speak, they simply held each other as they rushed through the desert.

"What now?" Joe eventually said into her hair.

Rainey looked out of the window and tried to imagine a world without Lexi. She could feel William's eyes watching her through the rear-view mirror, his face pained as he studied her grief. He waited for her to answer, but when it was clear that she could not talk, he answered for her.

"Now we find Aimee and Lily. And we go home."

37

Aimee

The journey had taken what had felt like a very long time. Aimee cried silently as the sound of her husband's screams echoed through her mind. Her thoughts raced between William, Jason and Rainey. She had no idea if they were alive, if they were being tortured, if Rainey had somehow managed to resist Smith's power, or if she had succumbed to him and been used as a puppet to kill her own father. Had Rainey come looking for them on her own? Or had Joe and Lexi followed her?

Aimee did her best to keep Lily content, but she was hungry and tired, and she had cried for a full hour before she had finally fallen to sleep in Aimee's arms. Isobel had been uncomfortable too, the weight of her unborn baby made it impossible for her to sit still for such a long period of time, and she had shuffled uncomfortably, trying her hardest not to wake Lily when she groaned with pain.

When they finally arrived, the car rolled to a stop, and Aimee opened the door and hopped out, stretching her legs. Gently, she lifted Lily from the back seat of the car, where she slept on top of the cardigan Isobel had provided to prevent her soft skin from sticking to the leather.

Aimee fought every urge she had to panic. They had no money and no food, but two grown men, two grown women, and a baby to feed. Aimee knew that until she could get to a telephone and get her hands on some money, they were going to need some help. Chris had offered to stop at the local store and try to steal some food, but all that had led to was an argument between him and Isobel. As it turned out, Isobel actually had a lot of principles.

Aimee pulled Lily into her chest and closed the car door behind her. She turned to look at the building they would call home for their first few nights on the run. The tiny cabin was made from wood with small glass windows. It was surrounded with shrubs and dried-out grass that was slowly dying from its lack of water. No roses and no lilies. This would be the cabin she shared with three complete strangers and her granddaughter before they would have to move on. They had set themselves a limited number of days before they would need to find themselves another safe house.

Aimee hoped desperately that she could find a payphone and some change soon. If she could just reach Maria. Maria would send her some money and Aimee could get a one-way ticket out of Nevada and back to England. But there would be nothing waiting for her there. She couldn't go home, not without her family. And Smith would look for her there. Maybe she could go to Italy instead, where Maria could help her to hide. It didn't really matter where she went, because wherever she ended up, it would not end there. It would never end. Aimee understood that now.

Aimee planned to fulfil her part of the deal and do what she could to deliver Isobel's baby safely. But after that, it would be just her and Lily. She was back to where she had started, all those years ago. Only this time, she would have to do it alone. William was not there to reassure her, and Jason was not there to cheer her up when she feared the future. Aimee didn't know if she could do it on her own. But what choice did she have? She had made a promise that Lily would always come first, and that was what she had to do. She would never be able to go back for them and trust that somebody else would care for Lily the way that she would care for Lily when she inevitably died. Aimee knew that that would be her fate if she returned to the Institute. Smith would not want it, but she would not allow him to capture her again. She would end it herself before he had the chance.

She hugged Lily closer to her and kissed the top of her head lightly. Her heart ached to hold Rainey in her arms, to kiss William and to show Jason the freedom he deserved. But she had left them in the desert, and she knew that she needed to focus on keeping control of her grief, or it would threaten to destroy her. And she could not let that happen. Lily had lived, Lily had her freedom. And Aimee would keep it that way. Her freedom would be limited, and she may never experience the life that Isobel's child could, but she would not grow up locked inside concrete walls, being trained for an army who would eventually try to take over the world. She would be free from pain and torture. Free to love and be loved.

Aimee looked at the cabin again and accepted her circumstances.

This would be her life now. She would do everything within her power to make it work, starting with the cabin and delivering Isobel's child. And then she would go, and she would start a new life with Lily.

And they would always be running. Running from Smith.

GIFTED

Louisa Amy Law

Acknowledgements

This book was roughly around seven years in the making, give or take an extra few years for further editing, because nothing we ever create ourselves can be perfect, right? I have received endless support from many of my friends and family members during this long process, even if some of that support came in the fashion of nagging me to start a new story instead of spending years changing and editing the first one. While I can't mention every single one of the amazing people who have helped me along the way, for fear of the acknowledgement page becoming longer than the actual book itself, I can mention a particular few who have consistently supported me in achieving this little dream of mine.

The best place to start is always at the beginning, with the person who has not only supported me the most, but who also pushed me to continue when I have allowed life to get in the way, my wonderful husband, Jamie. It was Jamie who encouraged me to finally send my story into the big wide world during the lock-down of 2020, and it is Jamie who consistently pushes me to continue, because life does tend to get in the way quite a lot. Both Jamie, and our beautiful daughter, Gracie, have put up with years of stopping mid-conversation so that I can jot down another crazy story idea. I am forever grateful to them both and immensely proud of them too.

The next people I need to thank are my friends, Cal and Becky. When I finished the first draft of this little project, Cal jumped straight into editing it for me. He has been an invaluable help when I have needed to bounce ideas off of someone, and he has pushed for me to keep going from the start. Which is why it was so easy to base one of my favourite characters on him. And Becky, or Becky Boo, who took over from Cal, and has spent hours and hours reading through and editing every word I have ever written. While I am sure that she is bored of my constant messages and emails, she has never told me so. I can't thank either of them enough for their constant support.

I am grateful to all of my family and friends who have never once questioned whether I could successfully complete my first novel, never doubted my commitment, have always celebrated my successes and pushed me back up when I felt at my lowest. But there are three people in particular who deserve the biggest of thank yous, and that is my lovely mum, my mother-in-law and my father-in-law. I can't go into every detail of their encouragement, because I would be writing for days, but I will be forever grateful for everything they have done for me, and every step they have helped me along the way.

You are all angels.

HUNTED

Louisa Amy Law

Anya

The room was silent but for the sharp, rhythmic beeps of the machine. Anya hovered by the door, analysing the space before her. As she advanced further into the room, the deep rattling of an arduous breath interrupted the quiet. Anya waited patiently, but the body of the thickset figure did not stir. It lay, unmoving in its hospital bed, tubes extending from hidden punctures in the skin, connecting it to the machine that had allowed it to escape death. Every minuscule development recorded on the screens as the minutes turned to hours, and the hours turned to days.

Anya's shoes clipped on the linoleum as she approached the end of the bed. She was aware of the two guards standing just beyond the door, watching her every move as she pulled up a chair and perched herself on the very edge.

Slowly, she examined the man with her eyes, studying his every curve and line. Innocent though he seemed as he lay unconscious, his features relaxed into a calm and peaceful mask, Anya knew better. She had once believed that kindness lay somewhere deep within this man. She had hoped that with the guidance of a loving hand, his kindness could be coaxed to the surface and put into practice. But she had been wrong. She understood that now. There was no kindness in the man that she looked down upon. No love or affection deep within his soul. He was incapable of it.

Her eyes followed the tubes leaving his body and settled on the beeping machine next to the bed. She watched as though mesmerised by the strange contraption, forcing the man's chest to rise and fall steadily, and she wondered momentarily if it was uncomfortable being forced to breathe in and out when the machine demanded and not when the lungs naturally longed for the air. She hoped that it was. She hoped that it was excruciatingly painful.

Before she had been permitted to enter, the care team had disclosed the man's condition. They had shared with Anya what she should expect. While his breathing was regulated with machinery, he would begin to breath on his own again when his body was ready. Anya cherished the thought of his body never being ready. A smile lingered on her lips as she contemplated the possibility of him wasting away to nothing, his brain rotting in the prison of his lifeless body as the machine continued its tedious routine throughout.

As her eyes studied the makeshift lung, she considered how long the man might live if she switched off the machine. How long could his body go on without sufficient oxygen pumping through his blood?

Her eyes flicked up to the guards outside the door and back to the machine. As much as she desired it, she could not kill this man. Although she would now fight for the opposing side, her duties lie here, with him. She would have to prove her loyalty all over again in a bid to win back his trust if she wanted to help those who deserved it the most. This man had ice in his heart, and though she had tried, there was no way to thaw it. Anya knew that now.

Lost in her train of thought, Anya did not notice when the fingers of the man began to twitch, his eyelids slowly flicker open, his pupils dilate as they set upon her beautiful, tired face. His hand clenched and then flexed, testing its strength, before it shot up so quickly that Anya did not have time to react. It wrapped around her throat before she could flinch away from his touch. Her fingers fumbled at his clenched hand, but it only caused his grip to tighten.

"Please," she gasped. "Smith… Please!"

A look of confusion and anger washed over Smith's face, and his grip loosened slightly.

"Anya." His voice croaked as he used it for the first time in a fortnight, and he retched at the pressure of the tube lingering in his throat.

Anya gasped as she desperately tried to suck air into her lungs.

"Where is Aimee?"

Anya did not answer. She could not. Instead, she scratched clumsily at Smith's hand. He released it a little more but not altogether.

"Where is she?" He yelled as loud as his neglected voice would allow.

"Gone." Anya choked.

Smith pushed her with the strength of a man who had not just awoken from a two-week coma, and Anya fell sideways from her chair and on to the floor, snagging on the tube of his catheter as she fell. He screamed in pain and anger as a team of caregivers rushed into the room, closely followed by the two guards. They hoisted Anya up from the ground and dragged her backwards out of the room as she stared defiantly into Smith's cold eyes.

As the guards deposited Anya onto the corridor floor, Smith's desperate screams filled the silence. And in that moment, Anya's dreams of watching him rot away to nothing died, just like he should have.

"Where is Aimee? Where the fuck is my Aimee?"

Printed in Great Britain
by Amazon

46275049-ad39-4bfe-9aa9-533164e6f7b4R01